I Choose You

BLUE RIDGE UNIVERSITY SERIES

BOOK 3

KRISTA SWANSON

Dedication

For the girlies who don't want to fall in love with the guy living in the next room who wears those damn grey sweat pants all day long, but you just can't help it...this one's for you

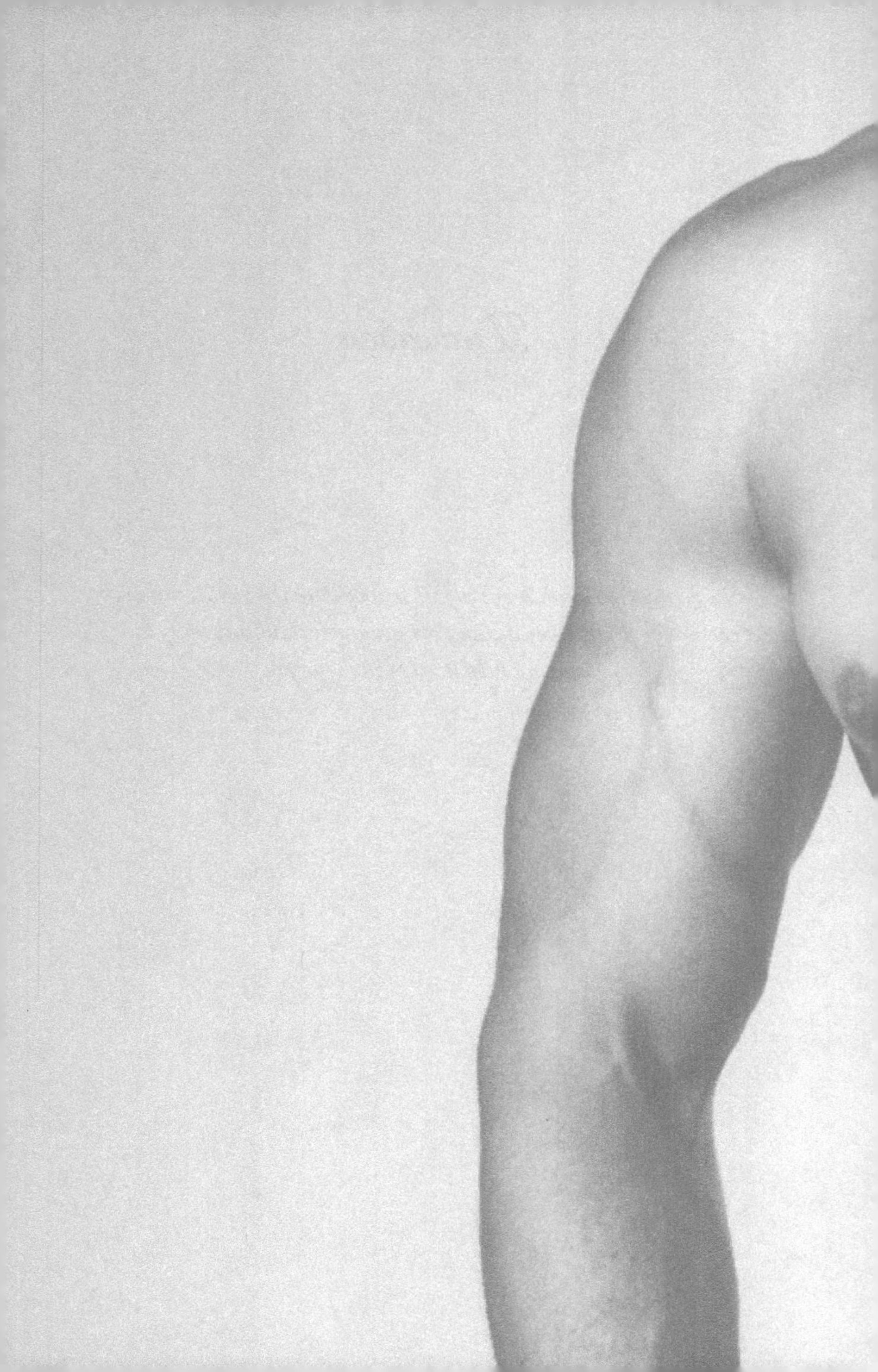

CHAPTER 1

Logan

Why couldn't I get out of my fucking truck? The sweat formed on my temples long before I pulled into the parking lot of the complex. Once I parked, I realized the back of my shirt clung to me under my coat. Ripping off my seatbelt, I tore my coat from my body and threw it behind me on top of the bags and boxes that filled the second row. I gripped the steering wheel tight, the anxiety building the longer I sat there staring at the townhouse ahead of me through my windshield.

Number 1514.

Ty texted me the address last night. I left ahead of my parents by thirty minutes so I'd have time here alone to, well, deal with what I was dealing with at the moment. The chances of me having one of these hitting me at this moment were high, very high, just like my therapist warned. I didn't want to believe her, though, hoping I was in control of my thoughts and emotions enough to ward it off.

But the panic attack was setting in, nonetheless.

My breaths were quick but at the same time hard to come by. As if my lungs were begging my brain to allow me to breathe. My stomach churned at the thought of stepping out of my truck, the knots coiling up tighter and tighter as the minutes passed. Looking around, I confirmed there was no one nearby to witness the almost breakdown that was about to happen in this driver's seat. Throwing my head against the headrest, I forced the air from my chest with a deep groan, the sound bouncing around the cab. My eyes searched for something to focus on, to distract me.

It was a strategy that seemed to help.

There was a small frog statue in the tiny patch of grass in front of the townhouse that my eyes latched onto, its glass eyes seeming to stare back at me. He was cute. There were some lichens growing on him from being outside for so long, but it added to his appeal. It seemed to change his color from the blue tint of the cement he was made of, to a greener shade to make him seem more lifelike.

And he was actually smiling. I don't know why I found that funny, but I did.

My breathing started to level off. As I scrubbed my face with both hands, I felt as though I'd thwarted the worst of it this time.

A success.

Well, I'd like to count it as a success, even though I had a panic attack before getting out of the car. Stopping it as quickly as I did was a success.

Turning my attention back to the townhouse in front of me, it looked empty. There weren't any lights on, and the front door was closed. No one was supposed to be here; that was intentional on my part. Making sure I would be the first to move in at the start of the semester was important to me.

More than important.

It was necessary.

If I had to move back to school before meeting some of my new roommates for the first time...

Well, I had to get here first. I needed to be here and settled long before anyone else was. The sheer fact that I was living with three girls was stressful enough. Throw in that I'd never met two of them and I was completely terrified.

Most guys my age would probably think I was in a pretty good situation, having three female roommates. However, considering my history freshman year here at Blue Ridge University, it was not the perfect setup for me.

Thankfully, Becca was one of the three girls I'd be living with, and I considered her to be one of my best friends. Her boyfriend, Ty, *was* my best friend. Those were two perks I was hanging on to in hopes it would make this whole situation more tolerable.

As I looked back at the building in front of me, so many thoughts raced through my head.

Would I be strong enough to be here and not drink?

Was I ready to be here, surrounded by that temptation?

Could I live with all girls?

Would I be able to continue my sessions with my therapist?

Was I ready to see Lanie? With Xander? After all this time...

The knock on my window caused me to jump so high I hit my head on the ceiling of my truck. "Fuck!" Looking over, I saw my dad, well, my stepdad, Matt, shivering outside, and I rolled down the window.

"You OK, buddy?" I couldn't tell if the shakiness in his voice came more from how cold he was from being outside without a coat or that he was obviously as nervous as I was about my return to school.

The fact that I was still sitting in my truck by the time he and my mom arrived was concerning. The past thirty minutes were gone, and my sweaty shirt and speeding heart were all I had to show for it.

And I think he could tell.

"Yeah, I'm good, Dad."

Even though Matt was my stepdad, he was my dad in every other sense of the word. He earned me calling him "Dad" way back in middle school and I haven't looked back since.

I unbuckled my seat belt to join him outside. Maybe I just needed them here with me, to have their support to do this.

"OK, let's get going, it's cold out here and I want these cars emptied pronto." He walked back to his car as he and my mom started taking bags from their back seat.

Stealing a few more seconds and a couple deep breaths, I finally pushed the door open and stepped out of my truck. The brisk air took me by surprise, and I noticed my breath escaping in white puffs from my mouth.

The drive was only a few hours, but my stiff legs and back definitely felt as though they needed a good stretch. Pulling open the tailgate, I pulled some of the boxes and bags from the bed of my truck and piled them onto the ground.

"Hey sweetie, how ya' doing?" My mom put her hand on my arm as she came up next to me.

"I'm doing OK, Mom." By this point, I was. Turning to look at her, so she could see I was being honest, I continued. "I mean it, I'm good."

She smiled, a warm, real smile. Patting my arm, she started walking away.

"Hey, Mom," I called out, running to catch up with her. "Head inside, it's too cold out here for you." I reached into my pocket. "Here, take the key. Lanie told me my room is on the second floor, on the left. I'll start bringing things up and you can put them away for me."

Her smile turned appreciative as she took the key from my hand and stepped toward the townhouse. I turned to my truck, and the heaviness in my chest lifted slightly with each step.

Maybe it was having my parents here, or maybe it was just finally getting to school that did it. But I was feeling better.

I felt like I could actually breathe.

"LOGAN, IS THERE ANYTHING STILL IN THE CAR?" MATT asked as I came in from outside with a box in my arms.

"Your car's empty, but there are a few things still in the back of my truck. One more trip should do it." As I headed back out, I saw a familiar car pull up. "Better late than never, asshole!" I yelled as he was getting out of his car.

"I'm not late if you're done unpacking your shit. That means I'm right on time." Ty laughed as he walked over.

Our embrace was a big one. We were both excited I was back at BRU, even if we weren't able to live together. I made my decision to return too late with nowhere to live. The fact that Lanie moved in with Xander, although for unfortunate reasons, was my luck and gave me her room here with her old roommates.

"Happy to see ya, man." Ty gripped me tight as he patted my back. "Blue Ridge missed ya." He pulled away, a grin plastered on his face. "I missed you, too."

Ty and I were friends before we came here to college. Freshman year was when our friendship really changed; as roommates, we became closer. But that was also the year I really fucked up.

"Yeah, man, same, but no more sappy shit. Help me get the rest of my crap and come see my mom and Matt."

Ty followed me to the back of my truck, and we grabbed the last of the bags I'd brought from home. Moving into a house was quite different than moving into a dorm. We had furniture we had to bring and put together, which meant tools and shit.

"When will Becca be here?" I asked as we walked through the front door.

"She texted me about two hours ago that she was leaving. Shouldn't be long now." Ty turned toward me. "How do you think it's going to be living with her?"

I had no idea how it was going to be living with my best friend's girlfriend. It felt kind of weird, honestly. We were all friends before they started hooking up last year. However, now that they were together, it was weird that I'd be the one living with her.

"I don't know, but I will say one thing. I'm thankful as shit that you guys worked everything out last semester. It would've fucking sucked if I was coming back to live with her and you guys weren't talking or whatever shit you were going through." I looked at Ty, and he had a small grin on his face telling me he agreed.

We reached the door to my room, and my mom and Matt were trying to figure out where to put my underwear.

"I think I can figure that one out on my own, Mom."

Ty and I barreled into the room, arms full of bags and boxes, and I hoped she would take the hint.

"Ty!" she screamed as she ran to hug him. "Oh, it's so good to see you. How is that baby girl of yours? She must be getting so big already. What is she, seven months by now?"

"That's exactly how old she is, Mrs. Larsen. Great memory." Ty's smile was wide. "And she is getting big. She cut a second tooth over Christmas break, so the house didn't get much sleep. But she's great, thanks."

Ty always had a huge smile on his face when talking about his daughter Savannah. It took some time for him to let himself get to this point, considering the mother of his daughter was *not* Becca, but his ex from high school. Though he and Becca were slowly working through it, considering she only found out about Savannah a couple months ago. I was shocked yet happy to learn she handled it as well as she did; she can be somewhat dramatic.

"That's great to hear, Ty, it has to be...challenging." Her concern was evident in her voice. "And call me Colleen, please. I'm not a fan of the other Mrs. Larsen." Her sideways glance at Matt earned a fake scowl. "Plus, it always confuses Logan's friends."

She took Matt's name, of course, when they got married. But that meant my mom and I no longer shared a last name. I thought about taking Larsen as my last name as well, still might one day.

I decided to come to Ty's rescue with my mom.

"Matt, I think we need to still work on the bedframe, don't we? It's not tightened up all the way yet."

That steered them back to being consumed with getting me moved in.

And Ty gave me a small nod of thanks.

As Ty and I waited for Becca to arrive, I was distracted from my tasks at hand. Instead of unpacking, my brain harped on how the introduction to my other roommates would go. My female roommates. I'd be living with three girls. Me and three girls. I had no real issues living with Becca; we almost lived together last year with how much time she and Ty spent together. But meeting the other girls for the first time once I was already moved in would be tricky. We were supposed to meet up over Christmas, for us to break the ice ahead of time, but it never worked out. They lived too far away and we couldn't meet up. So, we'd be meeting for the first time here.

Now, that happened all the time in college. But not when you're the opposite sex. Becca and Lanie assured me they were both good with me living here. I only hoped that didn't change once we met.

"Becca's here." Ty hustled to the door, a wide smile on his face again.

My parents left over an hour ago, leaving me to finish setting up. Matt realized it was best to get my mom out sooner than later; she was a bit nervous about me coming back to school this quickly. She thought I should have stayed home the entire year and given therapy in the outpatient setting more time. The doctors had assured her, and me, I was more than ready.

But to be honest, I was nervous as well.

I appreciated the safety net of seeing the therapists two days a week in person on a routine schedule. Now I only had a video appointment with my main doctor each week. Having my friends here with me made it seem doable. Ty and Becca would be my support system for sure. I hoped I could depend on Lanie and Xander as well, but there would always be some lingering awkwardness between us.

Because of me. And what I'd done.

My head swiveled to the door that was thrown open and the tornado known as Becca Reynolds flew in, right into the arms of Ty. Her dark hair was longer than I remembered and had these red highlights in it now. The two embraced with a short kiss, but she didn't stay there long. He reluctantly let her go as she pulled away, her eyes on mine from across the room. Her boot-covered feet plodded along the carpet as she came to stand right before me.

Her smile grew wide as her emerald eyes sparkled.

"Logan Somers, in real life," she said as she poked me hard in the gut. "I swear you've gotten even taller. Christ, did I always have to look up this high to see you?" Her curt laugh was loud for a tiny person. "And look at these? Jesus, dude, what did your mom feed you while you were home?"

She squeezed my bicep, which was significantly bigger since she saw me last. There wasn't much to do at home when all your friends were away at school. My online classes were easy and didn't occupy my thoughts enough. Didn't keep me from thinking of the shit I didn't want to think about.

So, I went to the gym. A lot.

It helped in a lot of ways. Plus my therapist agreed it was a good outlet for a lot of things.

Once Becca was done squeezing my arm, I held my hands out wide, hoping she'd give me the hug I really needed.

And she didn't disappoint, falling into my arms, with a warm hug from a friend I'd missed terribly. She might get on my nerves at times, but there was no denying that Becca was one of the good ones. She was there for me last year when most others weren't, and she had only just met me.

"Good to see you, Bec," I said as she held on tight. I pulled back, looking down at the spitfire in front of me. Leaning in again, I got close to her ear. "I'm glad you and Ty are good." As I straightened, she smiled coyly at me. "You look good, kid. What's with the hair?" I tugged on a strand as she pulled away from me.

At first, a shy smile, something very unlike Becca, took over her face as her eyes glanced at Ty. "Oh this?" Her fingers were running through her long strands as she made her way back to Ty and he wrapped her in his arms. "Just an experiment. Trying to see if the guys like me more as a redhead." She laughed out loud while he swung her around.

I knew she was full of shit. She was all his. They had been through enough in the past few months to have proven it to each other. But she was always ready with a comment or two to throw anyone off their game. Ty snuggled into her hair, the two of them getting a bit too inti-mate in front of me for my liking.

"This guy likes it," he said. "Right, Red?" He spun her in his arms as she looped her hands around his neck.

"You guys know I'm still here, right?"

As happy as I was that they were back together, I didn't need them getting busy in front of me. There was enough of dealing with that in the dorm last year. However, seeing it also made me realize it was one thing I knew I was missing most in my life. For whatever reason, I was desperate to have someone special. Sometimes I thought that not having someone was the root of most of my problems. But my therapist continued to remind me I needed to focus on *me* before there could be an *us*.

Becca's loud laugh echoed in the room. She peeled herself from her boyfriend and turned to me, a smile plastered on her face.

"It's good to have you back, Logan." Her demeanor shifted just a bit, and her tone grew serious as her eyes wandered to Ty's. "I really am glad you made it back this semester."

The unspoken conversation they were having in front of me as eyebrows and shoulders rose was a bit annoying.

I knew this was going to happen, yet I wasn't expecting it on day one.

"Guys, I'm fine." My eyes bounced back and forth between the two of them as they stood there, it seemed, waiting for me to say more. "What?" I whined. Turning my back on them, I returned my attention to the box I was unpacking in the kitchen.

"Nothing," Ty responded. "You *are* fine, we know that."

This was going to be more challenging than I anticipated if my two biggest supporters thought I was going to fail miserably. I'd just have to prove them wrong. And I had no problem doing that.

At least I didn't think I did. Before coming back to school, my confidence was intact, strong even. But every minute I was here seemed to drain it a little at a time.

Sitting around waiting to meet the new roommates was definitely a trigger at the moment, so I needed a change of scenery.

And it was as if Ty read my mind.

"Leave that shit," Ty said, pointing to rest of the plates in the box.

"Let's head to campus. You haven't been here in months, let's go see it."

"I do miss the food, the pond, the mountains, all of it. Plus, I need to stop by the bookstore and do some other crap on campus."

They both started getting their coats on before I'd even finished talking. We may not be living on the same floor together like last year, but it felt like old times as the three of us headed out to grab a meal on campus.

"What should we get to eat, guys?" Becca asked, almost giddy, as she made her way to the front door.

Ty and I were right behind her as we all ran for my truck, the three of us piling in the front to get out of the cold.

"I think that should be up to Logan since he's been away the longest," Ty answered as he blew his warm breath into his cold hands. "Whatcha in the mood for, man?"

Pulling on my beanie before putting the truck in gear, I made my way through the windy roads and small parking lots of our complex. It was going to take some getting used to the crazy layout of this place. We only lived about a mile from campus, but it was far enough that it made having your own car convenient.

"I will say that I've been dreaming of a 'Fantastic Frank' sandwich."

"Well, I guess we know what we're having for lunch," Becca announced to no one in particular.

And just like that, I was back at school.

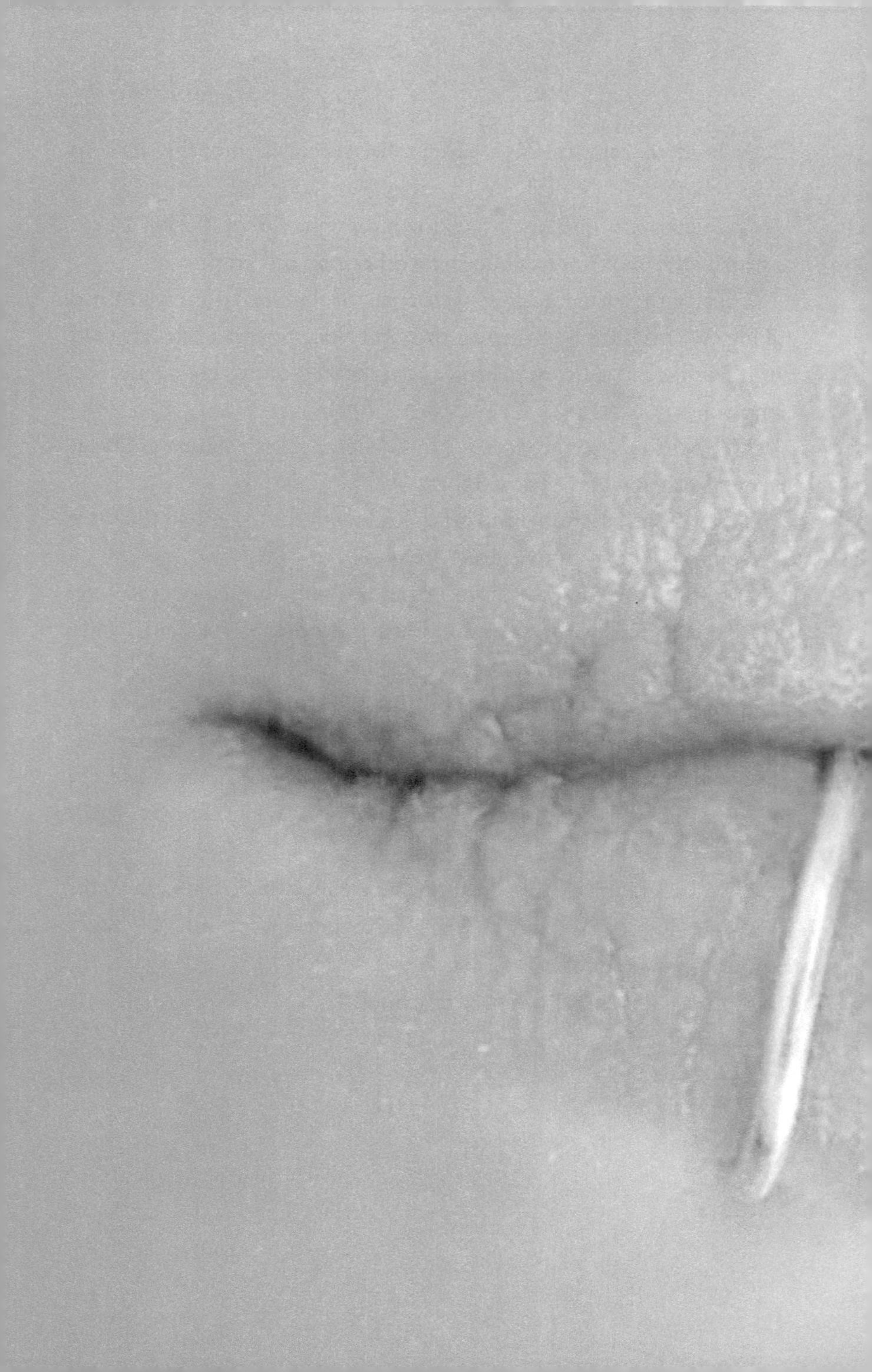

CHAPTER 2

Ava

"OMG, why is it so hard for them to get schedules right?" Macie whined.

We were both waiting our turn in the Registrar's office, along with approximately fifteen other students. I had to agree with my roommate. It was completely frustrating that, time and time again, we needed to have them adjust our schedules we set up perfectly online, which for some reason never seemed to work once the semester was about to start.

"I don't know, but if they don't get more people helping in here soon, I'm going to make a scene." I tried to make my voice as threatening as possible, however, as it carried across the office, I felt it only came across like I was whining. The rational part of my brain knew the men and women who were attempting to help all of us hadn't caused our issues, so I immediately hated how I'd acted. My normal levelheadedness had been railroaded by the temperament of the room, which was escalating. "Ugh, let's go sit down, Mace, this looks like it's going to take a while. At least they're using numbers to keep us organized."

We found the two remaining seats in the back corner of the office. Many of the other students resorted to waiting outside, either at the nearby tables or on a bench, but I didn't want to take the chance of missing our number being called. Plus, it was freezing outside.

"Becca texted, she said Logan got to the townhouse," Macie said as she continued reading on her phone. Her eyes were bright when she looked up from her screen. "I'm excited to meet him, aren't you?"

Was I excited to meet him?

Excited may not have been the word I'd use. Intrigued was more like it. Having a guy move in with us was going to be...interesting, to say the least. Possibly annoying, even. I'd never lived with a guy, never had to worry about what I was wearing while in my own house. Now I'd have to. Not that I walked around naked, but I *would* run to grab stuff from the dryer in my underwear.

Wouldn't be doing that anymore.

Plus, I wasn't completely on board with him becoming our roommate to begin with, yet I'd kept that little tidbit to myself. I would have to live with that secret.

"I remember seeing pictures of Lanie and Becca with him from last year. He's really hot," Macie went on.

Macie was still hung up on finding the perfect guy. I, on the other hand, was convinced the perfect guy didn't exist. They would say exactly what you wanted to hear just to get inside your pants. Once they got what they wanted, chances were you'd never hear from them again. And Macie had fallen victim to that time and time again but hadn't learned from it yet. I'd sat up with her at night, countless times, as she cried on my shoulder about this guy or that ghosting her.

Me, I'd rather be the one taking what I wanted and walking away. I was not looking for a relationship anytime soon. I was the queen of one-night stands, very unlike Macie. I wasn't always like this, I had a boyfriend when I was in high school.

But that didn't end well.

At all.

"Mace, not a good idea." The absolute worst thing either of us could do was fall for our new roommate. The tone in my voice was all she needed to hear; she knew exactly what I was talking about. Her eyes about rolled out of her head as she looked away from me, because telling her that was like talking to a brick wall. Macie would have feelings for whomever Macie wanted to have feelings for.

"Christ, Ava, you have to lighten up!" Her whisper yell started garnering some unwanted attention from people around us. "What good is living with a hot guy if you can't enjoy the scenery of it?"

Macie and I met as freshman roommates and hit it off. She's the yin to my yang, the peanut butter to my jelly, you get the picture. We just got each other. I understood her need for a relationship and continue to help her on her journey to find someone. She understood my lack of need for one and continued to support me on my journey of habitual hookups. And she never judged me.

Ever.

She helped me trust again.

We were the perfect best friends.

But her falling for Logan, or me setting her up with him, would not happen. We'd discussed this and decided together that neither of us would pursue anything with him. I thought she understood how bad it would be for the house.

"Number twelve," the administrator announced from the counter.

We were lucky number thirteen, only one more to go.

Macie still sat with her arms crossed, a bit angry with me for reprimanding her. I knew once she thought more about it and remembered the talk we'd had with Becca before break, she'd get over it. Apparently, she and Jace got together over break, and she's been confused over her decision about seeing him again. He ghosted her for a while last semester, and she'd been mad at herself for allowing him back into her life after doing that. Our entire drive back to school was spent talking about self-worth, self-esteem, and all that shit.

Funny that I seemed to be the one they all come to for that advice. Like, all of them in the house. Every. Single. One.

What kind of wizardry did I use to create the smoke and mirrors there?

Me? The expert on guys and how to handle them and your own self-value?

That's hilarious.

If they only knew.

If I could only take my own advice. I knew eventually, years down the road, I'd like to be in a committed relationship. I hoped one of these days, as I was giving these wonderful tips on love and life to the people in my world, they would rub off on me. Eventually my brain had to realize that if they're working for others, they could work for me. Until then, I'd stick with my hookups and no commitments. Much better for me, for sure.

"Ava." Macie interrupted my self-deprecating thoughts as we sat waiting to be called.

Turning to give her my attention, her sad eyes told me she knew what I'd been thinking about. Most times my thoughts were not obvious or apparent, but I guess I let them slip this time. She reached out and grabbed a hold of my hand, squeezing it tight.

"I won't cause any problems in the house, Ave, I promise, I'm still just pissed at myself about Jace, I guess."

I knew that was what was bothering her. We would have to get her mind off him somehow. Usually that involved another guy, but it couldn't be Logan.

Macie was not what one would call a slut by any means. She was no virgin, but *most* times she didn't give these guys what they wanted. I think that was why Jace ghosted her last semester; she wasn't moving along in the physical department as quickly as he wanted. But I appreciated that about her. She stood her ground when it came to her body. Eventually she would find the right guy who appreciated that about her as well.

"I know you won't, babe. And let it go about Jace, he's not worth it."

She nodded and went back to looking at her phone while we both waited for our number to be called.

"Thirteen," the administrator announced over the intercom.

"That's us," Macie said with a smile.

We both stood and started our advance to the counter, ready to find the worker we were supposed to speak with. As we approached, the main door swung open, a swift wind forcing it to bang against the wall as the person opening it walked through.

All eyes went to him immediately. I wasn't sure if it was because of the grand entrance ensured by the wind or the presence he demanded all on his own.

But in walked what could only be described as a behemoth of a man who took up the entire doorway. Clad in well-worn work boots and equally distressed jeans, he had the appearance of someone who was not a stranger to working with his hands. The thick flannel he wore clung to thick arms as he threw his backpack over his shoulder. I wouldn't have pegged him as a student, not because of his dress but because he had the appearance of being too old.

Once he turned toward us, I could see I was wrong.

His clear blue eyes were shining bright, and they were definitely those of someone our age.

Dark shadows hid in them, like a cloud covering the bright sun on a beautiful day. Like when a moment of darkness takes over, reminding you that everything can be gone in a flash.

His smile seemed a bit forced, too. As if he wasn't sure he wanted to be in this room full of people, but he knew he needed to have a smile on, regardless. His eyes scanned its entirety but didn't really see much of anything, I could tell.

Then his eyes landed on mine, and they stayed there.

They stayed there as he made his advance into the room.

And I couldn't take mine from him.

Macie and I were walking toward the counter, heading to the woman waiting to help us. He was heading to the same counter since it held the dispenser for the numbers being called. We were going to make it there at the same time.

And our eyes were still glued to one another's.

"Who is that?"

The voice at my side startled me out of the trance, and I broke the stare as I looked at Macie. She stared at the giant of a man as well, her curiosity piqued by his appearance. We were only feet from him and the woman was already asking me and Macie some questions. Macie was doing all the talking, taking care of her class concerns. But I was having trouble concentrating on what the woman said since my attention wanted to remain on this man who was standing a couple feet to my right.

He should have moved by now. He had his number already. Yet, he stood in place, stalling, looking around the room, almost pretending to figure out where to go to wait his turn.

He wasn't fooling me, though.

Maybe he wasn't trying to. Because he looked my way again.

Our eyes connected. Again.

Fuck, he was hot.

Like, seriously hot.

There hadn't been a guy I had this much of an immediate physical reaction to since early freshman year.

"Ms. Kennedy?" A voice I'd never heard before saying my name startled me from my dirty thoughts. I turned to see the administrator and Macie both staring at me.

"Uhm, I'm sorry, could you repeat that?"

"Is this the class you need switched?" she said again, a bit annoyed this time. They were busy, and I knew that. She pointed to the class I needed changed on her computer screen, so I nodded enthusiastically.

"Yes, please. I'd like to be in the Monday, Wednesday section, if possible."

The woman turned her back to us, working on her computer. Macie looked at me, her conspiratorial smile making me feel a bit uncomfortable.

"What?" I asked her, looking away. As I did, I realized immediately that my sexy distraction from only minutes before was already gone.

My eyes did a quick scan of the entire room to no avail; he must have gone outside.

Astonished at the disappointment I felt, I turned back toward Macie and the woman helping us. Macie leaned closer before whispering in my ear.

"He was really hot, wasn't he?"

My head snapped to hers as my cheeks heated. Thankfully, our helper turned back around in her wheeled chair just in the nick of time.

"You're in luck, Ms. Kennedy, there's room in that section. Here are your confirmation codes, girls." She handed us the printed forms. "Anything else I can do for you both?"

We looked at each other, happily surprised at how easy this was, and collectively answered, "No thanks, we're good!" With a smile, we were both on our way.

Macie grabbed my arm as we pushed away from the counter and her mouth was as close to my ear as it could get.

"Who *was* that guy?"

"What guy?" I responded with indifference, pulling her by the hand through the mass of students waiting their turn. We made it to the door and through to the alley, the gust of wind blinding us initially as we made our way outside.

With a cursory glance, I didn't see my mystery man out here either. He just up and vanished.

"*What guy?*" Her chuckle told me she wasn't buying my blatant lie. "Ava, you were just about eye fucking him in there. And he was doing the same with you. I mean, I get it, he was hot. Every girl in there was doing the same."

We hustled to the parking lot because of how cold it was, so it gave me the opportunity to avoid responding to her inquiries. Macie hit the fob to unlock her car, and we threw ourselves inside, hoping it was still a bit warm from our drive here. Once we got in, I realized Macie was not about to let the topic die, though.

"I think he looked a lot like our soon-to-be new roommate, don't you? I mean, he doesn't have a lot of pics on his Insta, but it looked a bit like him. Wouldn't that be crazy if that was Logan?"

My heart stopped.

That would be more than crazy, it would be the worst thing possible if it were him.

"I don't think so, Macie, this guy looked so much bigger. Besides, Logan has really blonde hair."

I had myself convinced they weren't the same guy before she pulled the car fully out of its spot. But by the time she exited the parking lot, Macie had me second-guessing myself.

"His beanie covered his hair completely, how could you tell?"

Shit. She was right.

"Whatever, didn't Becca say he's at the townhouse, anyway? Besides, we both know he's a good-looking, off-limits guy who'll be our roommate, so doesn't really matter, does it?"

We were both quiet, and I was thankful because I didn't want to think about Logan anymore.

However, my brain had other ideas.

Last year, when Lanie and Becca came to us with the idea of Logan living with us, I felt a bit backed into a corner. Becca was so excited to have him move in, and Macie was immediately on board.

And Lanie made a strong case. The fact that she needed to *convince* us he would make a good roommate was part of the problem. See, Logan and Lanie had somewhat of an issue last year. He, well, he touched her when she didn't want him to.

But everyone couldn't stop talking about how far he'd come with his sobriety and his mental health recovery. Especially the one he had done the deed to.

He wanted to come back to school. If I said no to him living with us, I was the only one blocking him from doing that.

That was a lot of pressure on me. About a person I'd never even met.

I gave in. I caved.

And now Logan, Becca, Macie, and I would be roommates for the spring semester.

Whether I liked it or not.

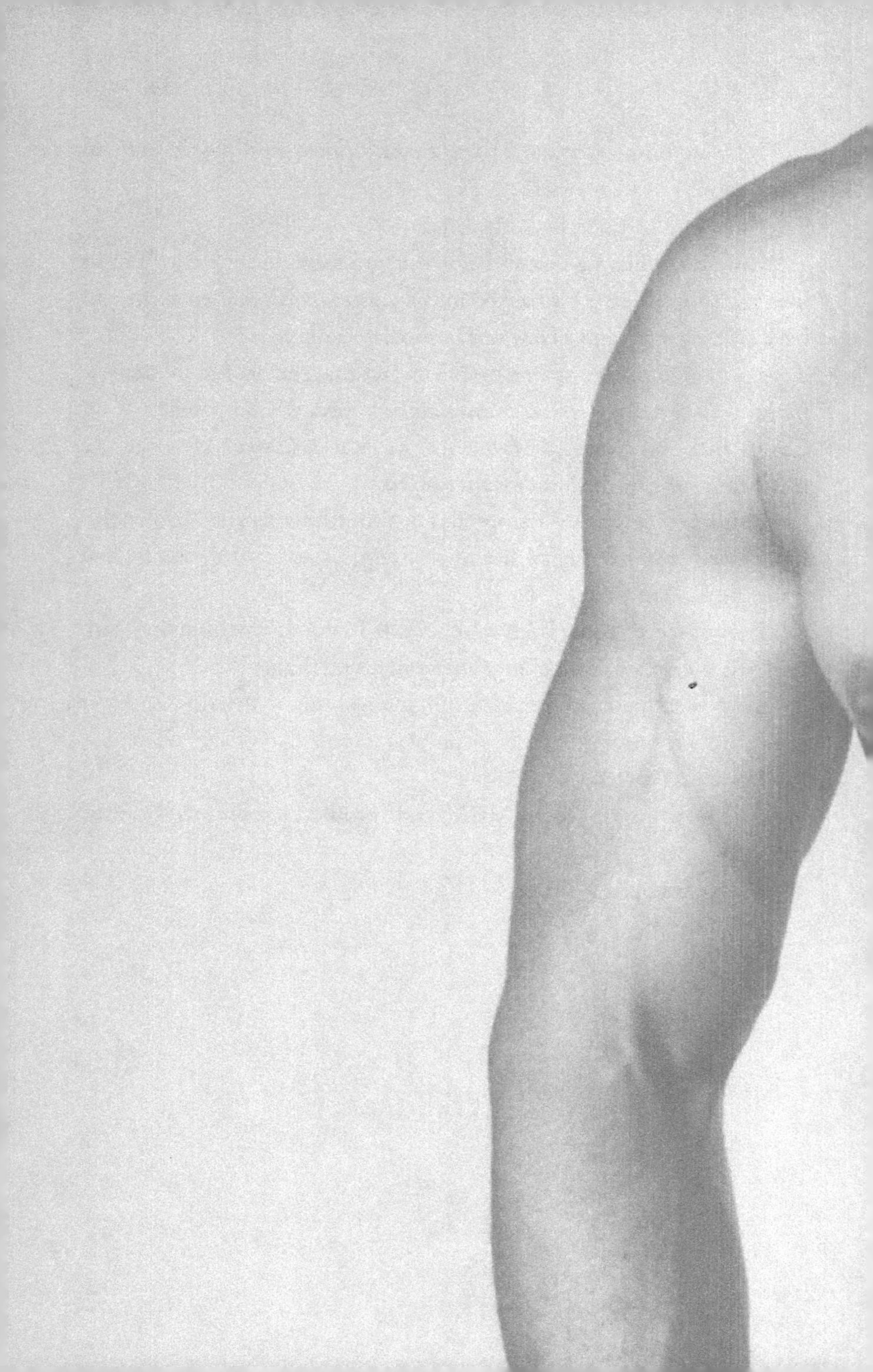

CHAPTER 3

Logan

Fuck. Two *almost* panic attacks on my first day back at school. This was not going well. When I walked into the registrar's office and saw how crowded it was, my breathing hitched immediately and I felt the tightening in my chest. Then, that hot girl started staring at me. It felt as though her green eyes were staring through me, as if she could see into my soul and discover every good and bad thing I'd ever done with one look.

The panic set in. Panic of being in a crowd of strangers, but also the panic of being around someone I felt an attraction to. Living at home made avoiding being in a relationship easier. Being back here, that was another temptation I'd be dealing with.

I had to get out of there.

I bit off more than I could chew on my first day. My therapist warned me of this. She told me I'd feel a level of comfort coming back, that I'd believe I could settle right back into my old ways once back at school.

Boy was she was right.

I hustled right out of there, drove back to the house, and requested a video call with her. Thankfully she was available.

Dr. Jean talked me down from it all. She helped me realize that everything I was feeling was normal for the changes I was going through and that I needed to give myself some grace. At least for the first week or so. Her suggestion was to go a bit slower, maybe stick close to home the next day or two. Classes didn't start for a few days, so I had some time to adjust.

While I was on the call, I heard a lot of commotion downstairs. Becca texted that my other roommates had arrived. Dr. Jean advised me how to handle that as well.

Her suggestion was to approach meeting the girls just as I did when I met others on my floor freshman year. They were my roommates. In her words: "The fact that they're girls shouldn't matter much if you all respect one another as housemates."

My session with Dr. Jean had been over for thirty minutes.

Yet I was still sitting in my room alone.

The knock I was expecting on my door finally came.

"Yeah," I said as the door slowly opened.

Becca peeked her head inside. "Want to come down?"

Standing from my desk chair, I stretched my already tired body as I let out a sigh. Becca's eyebrows went up at the sound and she slid through the door and closed it. With tentative steps, she made her way to my bed and took a seat.

"Or we could stay up here for a while, and avoid the drama downstairs," she said. "You got your room organized pretty quickly. I'm impressed." She looked around my space, which to her had to feel weird. During the fall semester, this had been Lanie, her best friend's room, and now I was in it.

"Yeah, well, when all someone wears are sweats, T-shirts, and on occasion a pair of jeans there isn't too much to unpack. Bit different for us guys."

We both shared a small, awkward laugh, knowing full well we were avoiding the obvious.

Becca leaned back on her elbows as her eyes finally landed on mine.

"So, is my big, brawny new roommate afraid to meet some petite, meek little girls?" she asked. Her satirical grin put me at ease.

"They don't sound meek. Christ, they're loud."

"Yeah, well." Becca stood from my bed. "Apparently Macie saw some hot guy on campus and hasn't shut up about it since getting home. She's on a mission to piss off the guy she was last with and I guess found a new conquest, although Ava doesn't seem on board. So there's been some discussion."

Sitting back at my desk, I still wanted to prolong going downstairs. "What can you tell me about them?"

She sat up, almost eager to answer my question. "Well, they're both amazing. Macie is a sweetheart. She's beautiful and tall, like taller than Lanie. And her skin is amazing, the smoothest, most radiant I've ever seen." She noticed my look. "Ok, you probably don't care about that, but us girls notice. And then there's Ava."

She paused.

"You say that like there's a problem with her."

"Not at all," she continued. "She might be one of my favorite people." She paused again while looking out the window, gathering her thoughts. "She's the complete opposite of Macie. Tiny, short dark hair, and these piercing green eyes, even crazier than mine. She's a special one, but I can't read her completely yet. She's definitely a firecracker."

"Oh christ, if *you're* saying that, I'm in trouble!"

And I meant that as she laughed along with me.

"Shut up, asshole. Nothing wrong with her being like me." Then Becca got quiet again. "She's very insightful, in a good way." She stood from the bed, and as she came toward me at my desk, my heart rate skyrocketed because I knew we were heading downstairs. She stood next to me, her hand gripping my arm. "Come on, I won't let them hurt you, big guy."

We both got the joke as she chuckled under her breath. My smile was small as I moved toward the door, my steps tentative. Turning toward Becca, I made a last-minute plea. "Is Ty down there?"

"Yep, and he needs to be saved from the girls, so let's go." She dragged me out the door.

As I trudged down the stairs, the voices in the living room became more audible. I could make out Ty's as he fake-yelled at one of them to stop whining about something. The tone he used told me he had a good relationship with them, which made me feel better as I rounded the corner of the hallway.

"Finally!" Ty's voice bellowed across the room as he stood from a chair, his wide eyes imploring mine, their message clear. As he stalked toward me, I took note of the others in the room, their backs to me on the couch. But their heads swiveled quickly as they heard my approach.

One by one, they stood and turned toward me.

One by one, our eyes connected.

One by one, the recognition ignited. By all three of us.

First, the one with light brown skin, whom I had to assume was Macie, stood to her full height as she ran to my side, excited. And Becca was right, she was beautiful with smooth skin, gorgeous light bluish-green eyes, a contrast to her skin. It was a stunning combination.

"Oh my god, Logan! It *was* you on campus before!" Her piercing yell had everyone staring at us both. Her gaze bounced back and forth between me and the other girl, who had yet to move away from the couch.

She seemed frozen in her spot as she stared at me.

The same way she did about an hour ago.

Like she was looking into my soul.

But unlike before, the warmth was nowhere to be found in those eyes.

It was a cold stare as her eyes bored into mine, yet I found it impossible to pull mine from hers. The only thing that broke the connection was Becca's voice.

"So, you guys already met?" Her question was directed at me first, then Macie.

"No, we didn't meet, but he was at the registrar's office when we were, and we, well, kinda noticed him." Macie suddenly seemed shy as she reflected on our impromptu meeting earlier. I chanced a look at the other one, but she'd already given up, her attention glued to her phone.

Becca's eyes went wide with realization.

"Logan," Becca said, "this is Macie." She gestured to the girl standing mere inches from me, who had a cute grin on her face. Her skinny braids were tied back into a knot behind her head, and she wore a comfy-looking sweatsuit. A hand with slim fingers and long pink painted nails on the ends extended toward me.

"Hi." A chipper voice went along with the overly spirited person in front of me and I couldn't hold back a smile.

"Hi," I said in return, holding out my hand for her.

She gripped it in hers, squeezing it tight, the other hand coming around and wrapping around the top of our joined hands.

"See, Ava," she said, turning toward our other roommate. "It was him. I told you it was, but you didn't believe me."

We both turned toward her.

But the petite, raven haired "firecracker" had returned to lounging on the couch, leg over the end, her booted foot swaying. She tried to seem engrossed in her phone and completely ignored her friend's comment.

Becca, on the other hand, looked uncomfortable, unsure of how to read the situation. Ty came to her rescue. He was by her side, sensing she needed his support.

"Logan." As he said my name, Becca breathed a sigh of relief. His hand began gesturing toward the silent one across the room. "This is Ava. Ava, this is Logan."

"Hi, Ava, it's nice to meet you." Moving toward the couch, I waited for her to maybe get up, or at least look my way. Long seconds passed before she even responded.

"Hey," she said. But she continued to scroll on her phone without looking up.

And that was it. *Hey*.

What. A. Bitch.

It was totally awkward. I felt bad for Becca and Ty.

Macie tried to diffuse the situation. Looping her arm through mine, she guided me toward the kitchen. "We're so excited to have you living with us. Becca told me you like to cook."

Becca could tell I was thrown off by Ava's reaction to me and took over the conversation with Macie, answering her questions about how I'd started teaching myself to cook over the past six months. While they talked, I found myself continuously glancing at the occupied couch in the living room, wondering what the hell I'd done to receive the lackluster welcome she'd given me.

Lanie, Becca, and I spoke at length over Christmas break about me coming to live here with the three girls. They assured me that both Macie and Ava were more than on board with the situation. That's why this whole scene didn't make any sense.

Unless she was just that, a total bitch. Which was fine. I could live with that. Steering clear of her wouldn't be a problem. The place was big enough for us to live our lives in harmony together and not have to worry about getting in each other's way.

At least I hoped so.

"WHAT THE HELL IS WRONG WITH HER?" AS I FLIPPED burgers on the grill, Ty kept me company. We huddled close to the small flames in an attempt to stay warm as the temperature continued to drop outside. The girls were inside putting together some sides to go with the burgers. Squinting, I tried to look through the sliding doors to see if all three of them were still in the kitchen, but the glare on the glass prevented it. I could only hope the tiny, short-haired bitch decided to go upstairs instead of eating a meal I'd be providing her.

Ty's downturned eyes as he glanced inside the kitchen told me he understood who I was talking about.

"I don't know, man, I have no idea what's gotten into her. I've never seen her like that." Turning toward me, he shrugged. "She's always been kinda cool, especially when me and Becca were going through our shit last semester." He came to stand next to me at the grill, putting his hands up to gain some heat from the flames. "I mean, yeah, she can have a sharp tongue, I always said her and Becca were like sisters that way but try not to read too much into it. Maybe she had a bad day just getting back to school or some shit like that. Who knows, girls can be temperamental, we know that."

Unsure if that was all it was, I piled the burgers on the plate and turned for the door. He slid it open for me and we both entered the lion's den.

Once inside, I immediately saw three girls in the kitchen.

She stuck around.

And I noticed some were drinking.

I stared at the can in Macie's hand. My therapist and I had many talks about how I'd feel being around alcohol, but more importantly, around people actively drinking. As a recovering alcoholic, you feel as though you have your demons conquered on your good days. That nothing will ever get in the way of you accomplishing your goals. On the bad days, well, that's when the doubt creeps back in. When you consider picking up that bottle again. Today wasn't necessarily a bad day, but it wasn't a good one either.

It was what my mom referred to as "meh."

Thankfully, seeing the beer did nothing to me. I had no desire to pick it up at all.

And that made me feel good. Really good.

"Burgers are ready!" I announced to everyone.

Becca and Macie joined us as I placed the meat down. They brought a large bowl of pasta salad to the table as well as buns and condiments. But Ava remained in the kitchen, making herself look busy with some dishes. As we started making our plates, I made my way over to her.

"What's the matter, Tink, you too good to eat my food?"

She froze. Her hand literally stopped midway while putting a glass in the cupboard. Her back was to me and remained that way for long moments as I stood there waiting for a response from her. When it seemed as though I wouldn't get one, I turned to walk away.

"Don't call me that," she said, with venom in her words.

Turning back toward her, her eyes pierced mine with a look ready to kill.

"Why not? I think you've earned it."

Her lips thinned as her eyes glared at me with a ferocity I didn't expect. She said nothing else.

"Whatever, Tink. Food's ready if you want it." Then I spun around and walked away.

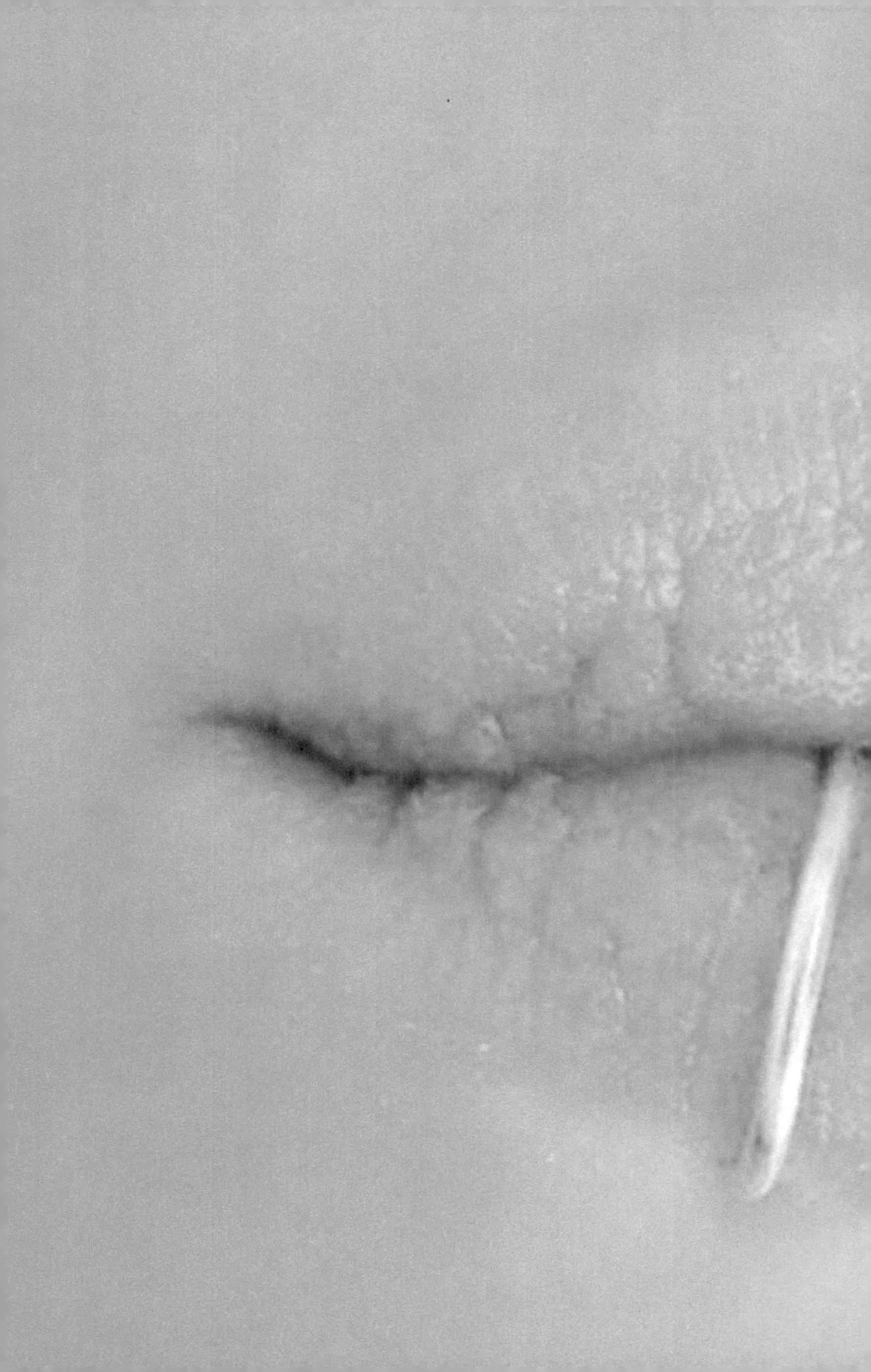

CHAPTER 4
Ava

Who the fuck did he think he was calling me that? He had no right, especially on the first day of us meeting. He was cocky. He was arrogant. And he was egocentric. Did he not realize how mean it was to ridicule someone based on their height? Were we literally living with a guy who was a "mean girl"?

"Hey."

A voice came up behind me as I gripped the counter with white knuckles. As I let go, I turned around to see eyes like mine looking at me with concern.

"Everything OK?" Becca asked. As she said that, we looked at the table. Macie, Ty, and the asshole were deep in conversation, all three laughing about something.

I didn't know why but that pissed me off. So much. Seeing them enjoying each other, having fun, grated on me. But I didn't want anyone to know that, especially him.

"Yeah, just not really hungry right now." I backed away from her. "I'm tired, I'm gonna head upstairs."

She nodded but I knew she didn't believe me. I also knew she wouldn't stop me.

Once in my room, I dialed my mom.

"Hey, baby, what do I owe the honor of a call so soon?"

I loved my mom so much. We had a great relationship. She knew, most times before I did what was wrong in my life and in my head. It was only me, her, and my sister Amelia. She left our dad when we were little and never looked back.

"Just wanted to hear your voice," I told her. Then I went silent, hoping she would fill the silence, which she did. She filled it with stories of her and Amelia's day, and how they went shopping to get her ready for her senior year of high school, what they were having for dinner, how they had snow the day before. And so on and so on.

She always knew what I needed.

"Have you gotten all your books for your classes yet, Ava?" She was making small talk now, to distract me.

"I haven't. A lot of the professors tell us to wait, sometimes we don't need the books. So I'll see what they say once I go to each class over the first week."

Then I remained quiet. We both did.

"Is there anything else you'd like to talk about, sweetie?" she asked.

Should I? Should I tell her what was going through my head?

"No, I'm OK. Just missing you and Amelia. It's always hard when I first come back, you know that."

I heard a small sound of acknowledgment from her over the phone line.

"You know I'm always only a phone call away. But I do need to go. Amelia has practice tonight, and I still need to feed us. Call me later if you want to talk, OK, babe?"

"OK, Mom, love you."

"Love you, too, angel."

I heard the line disconnect.

I threw my head back against my pillow and looked up at the

ceiling as I heard the voices from downstairs carry all the way up to my room. The laughter, I should say. They were having fun. Without me.

It wasn't so much FOMO I was experiencing. Rather, I wanted to return to prove that I wasn't running away from the situation. That I wasn't weak. That the asshole giving me a condescending nickname wasn't going to make me hide in my bedroom.

Even though that was exactly what I was doing.

So up I got and down I went. Strolling into the kitchen, I pulled open the refrigerator and got myself a beer. I don't know what made me do it. I hadn't set out to drink today, and not everyone was. Macie and Becca were drinking earlier, when the guys were out back.

But I grabbed a beer. And made my way to the table, pulled out a chair right next to Logan, sat down, and plopped my bottle on the table in front of me.

It was quite the entrance. So much so that everyone stopped talking. Ty was the first to say something.

"Want anything to eat?"

I didn't answer right away. Instead, I grabbed my beer and took a long chug of the cold liquid. I knew I was being a bitch.

A true bitch.

But I didn't care. He started this feud between us. He just didn't know how well I was at fighting back.

Once I swallowed, I held my beer up against my lips and turned my attention to Ty.

"I'm good, this'll do." I held up the bottle and gestured to my drink. I then looked at Logan, a small smile on my lips.

The table remained awkwardly...quiet.

"Don't let me interrupt the party." I leaned back in my chair, staring boldly at my roommates. It was then I noticed there were only sodas and waters on the table.

Tough shit. I lived here, too.

"Ava," Macie whispered.

"She's right," Logan chimed in. "The more the merrier, and now that Tink has joined us, it's the whole damn family down here, isn't it?"

My eyes stayed glued to the table in front of me, refusing to look at him, as I gripped the glass bottle tighter in my hand. I struggled to not lose my shit at the mention of his ridiculous nickname for me. Two could play at that game.

"Well, *Tank* over here is right," I said, gesturing toward Logan with the bottle. "We are one big happy family now, aren't we? Living all together, eating all together. It can't get any more fucking Norman Rockwell than this, can it?"

Everyone's reaction at the table was the same. They were silent as their eyes went wide and round. All of them except Logan. His look was indifferent. It wasn't the smug smile I expected, rather his eyes probed mine as if trying to discern where my remark had come from. And I didn't like his prying eyes. So I got up from the table, the chair legs screeching along the tiles. It announced my departure a bit louder than I intended.

Becca and Macie shared a look as I walked away from the table and headed toward the stairs. I could hear the whispers between all of them, but I didn't care.

I agreed to live with the guy, but I never agreed to like him. We could live in the same house and not have to see each other much. Maybe our schedules would conflict enough that we would miss each other. Regardless, no one would force me to like him.

No one.

And no sooner had I planted my ass on my bed, there was a knock on my door.

"Go away," I said loud enough for whomever it was to hear.

"I'm not going away," Becca said as she barged in, which didn't surprise me. "And you would do the same for me, so shut up."

She sat at the foot of my bed, pulling a leg up, her knee under her chin. She proceeded to stare at me as if I was going to supply her with information about what was going on in my head. Instead, I picked up my phone and started scrolling through my social media. The sigh she let out made me chuckle.

"Ava, you really think this is funny?"

She stood and came around to the other side of my bed, getting in next to me. We were face to face and I was tempted to turn over, but Becca wasn't who I was mad at. I didn't want to hurt her feelings, but I also didn't want to talk about it. I also knew she wasn't about to leave without that happening.

"No, there's nothing funny about any of this, actually." I maintained eye contact with her to let her know how serious I was. "He's being a dick to me, Bec. And we have to live together."

Her striking green eyes stared back at me as she considered my words.

"How exactly is he being a dick to you, Ava?"

"You don't think calling me 'Tink' is cruel?"

She rolled onto her back, looking at the ceiling. She stayed quiet for so long I thought she might just get up and leave, but then she turned toward me.

"Ava, you know I love ya like a sister. I mean, we're a lot alike, ya know, with our snarky attitude and all that. Some can't handle chicks like us. So you have to know, that if I'm saying this, well..." She kind of trailed off, unsure of how to go on.

"Say what you have to say, Becca."

"OK, I'll say it," she said as she stood from the bed. "You've been a bitch to him today. I mean, when I came downstairs with him before, the very first time you two were meeting, he tried to introduce himself to you, and you completely ignored him. Do you know how hard that was for him to do? I had to almost drag him from his room, he was so nervous, and you acted like that! You wouldn't even get off the couch or look up from your phone. What the hell was that?"

"I looked at him," I countered with a meek voice. "And got up."

Becca's hands went to her hips, the anger flaring more as she tried to gain some control. I needed to be careful; pushing Becca away was not what I wanted to do. Sitting up, I looked her square in the eyes, hoping she would see something in them.

My distress, without having to vocalize it.

But I'm not sure she did. I understood. Logan was her friend first, long before me. She was looking out for him.

I had to look out for myself.

"Yeah," Becca said, "right before you sat your ass back down and completely ignored him. And then at the table just now, why? Listen, we all talked back in the fall, made sure that everyone was OK with Logan moving in, and you were. It wouldn't be fair if you've gone and changed your mind now, Ava, not fair to him at all."

Leaning forward, I wrapped my arms around my legs and laid my forehead against my knees. She wouldn't understand if I told her everything right now. No, she would. I just didn't want to tell her everything right now. Instead, I would lie.

"You're right, I'm sorry. I'll do better."

CHAPTER 5
Logan

"Listen, folks," said Professor Lynch of my marketing class. He seemed like he was an OK guy until the very end of class. "You either know someone in here or you don't. And either scenario makes group work hard. So I'm making the groups for you." He pulled up what I had to assume was the roster on his computer and started rattling off two names at a time. As he did, each person stood and paired off to share their information. Reluctantly.

"Eve Miller and Tommy West."

"Lizzie Singer and Avi Singh."

"Logan Somers and Ava Kennedy."

Wait, what? It couldn't be. What were the chances? We were in a lecture hall, so the class was kind of large. I looked around the room to see if the "Ava" who stood up was a short, green-eyed monster who was going to give me a murderous glare.

And lo and behold, it was my fucking roommate.

My first instinct was to march straight to our professor and demand a new partner. Because I knew full well this was going to be a nightmare. But as she made her way toward me, I wasn't going to be the one who bailed on us.

"Hey, asshole," she said as she fell into the seat next to mine. Ava dropped her backpack at her feet and refused to look at me. "Even our professor has it out for us, it would seem."

I remained standing. We didn't need to trade information, so I was heading out.

"Where ya going?" she yelled.

"Home."

She fell into step behind me as I walked up the stairs and into the hall. As I threw my beanie on my head, she bundled up as well before we made our way outside.

Spring semester was no joke in Virginia. See, it runs from January through May, so even though it's called spring semester, most of it takes place during the winter. And winters at Blue Ridge University, walking across the drillfield, were brutal. Especially on the windy days.

Which, of course, the first day of classes was one.

Wicked wind.

I swear the wind chill was close to zero degrees. The parking lots for students who lived off campus were nowhere near any of the class buildings. The trek to my car felt like it was a trek over the frozen tundra of Alaska.

Once we made it outside, I turned toward her. Her parka was zipped up to her neck, the hood pulled over a hat with one of those pom-pom things on top. She had a scarf wrapped in there somehow and big woolen mittens.

She looked adorable. And I hated that I even noticed that she looked cute. I hid my smile by looking away. She definitely couldn't see that.

"Are you headed home, too? Where ya parked?" It would be rude to not continue walking with her if we were headed in the same direction.

"I don't have a car, I'm heading to the bus stop."

So of course, the question arose within my brain. Do I do what I *want*, and continue walking to my car, alone? Or do I do what *should*? Becca told me that Ava was going to try to make this work between us, so I guess I had to as well.

I stopped walking but kept my head facing forward, refusing to look at her.

"You wanna ride?"

I was sure the delay in her answer was due to her being stunned silent.

"Um, yeah, sure, I guess so. I had to wait for three buses this morning, they were all full on my way to campus. Who knows how long I'll have to wait."

I nodded, and she tried to keep up as I resumed walking, though she struggled.

"Dude, could you slow down? It's like trying to keep up with a giant," she whined.

My steps slowed a bit, but not by much. I glanced back at Ava as her feet worked double time.

"C'mon Tink, speed it up. It's frickin' cold out here, let's get to my truck." I knew the name pissed her off, but I didn't care. Even though we were supposed to be trying with each other, getting under her skin had become my new favorite pastime. Seeing her reaction, a different one each time, was fun. This time it was her mumbling to herself under her breath, but nothing loud enough for me to hear.

We finally made it to the lot, and my truck. Unlocking it, I walked to the passenger side and opened her door.

"Give me your bag, I'll put it in the back seat," I said, reaching for the strap on her shoulder.

"I can do it." She pushed me out of the way and threw it into the second row. But then, as she moved to the open passenger door, she just stared up at the seat. "Christ, this thing was made for behemoth sized humans. How the hell am I supposed to get in it?"

I got a sideways glance as she yanked her mittens off, seeming to look for something to grip. She pressed her lips tight as she pondered what to do.

I pointed to the running board along the bottom of my truck, made specifically for this reason.

"You're not the only one, Tink. Step on that, you'll be able to get in."

She even struggled to step on the running board, so I offered my hand. She stared at it for a moment, unsure if she wanted my help or to even touch me. But she gave in and took it. As she leaned into the cab, my hand went to her back to make sure she didn't fall. Her coat lifted as she stepped up, exposing a small patch of skin on her lower back just as my hand landed on her to guide her.

She froze.

Her skin was warm under my frigid fingers, so I yanked them away quickly.

"Sorry." My hand went to a higher part of her back, making sure to only touch her jacket.

"It's OK, um, thanks."

Her response took me off guard as she settled into her seat and pulled the seat belt across her lap. I was still standing outside the door as she did it, staring at her, dumbfounded.

Did we just have a moment?

"Uh, yeah, sure," I said.

Her glance turned into an eye roll before she turned back to her seatbelt, so I chose not to make much of it. It was a start. I had no idea what I'd done to receive the wrath she'd unleashed on me so far, and I'd like to make amends. But I also wasn't about to let her walk all over me while doing it.

As soon as I started driving, Ava blasted the heat as high as it would go, but the car was still too cold.

"We probably won't even have heat by the time we make it to our house," I told her. As I turned the blower down, I looked her way. She was back to ignoring me, which was fine on our short trip. To fill the silence, I turned on the radio. The country music that came through the speakers calmed me.

Then I saw the red taillights up ahead, and we weren't even off campus yet. What should be a ten-minute drive was going to be a bit longer, and the silence between us was already awkward.

"So, what kind of music do you like, Tink?"

Since we were stopped in traffic, I watched as her head made a slow swivel in my direction.

"Do you even know my real name?"

My laugh filled the truck. I was totally under her skin, and I loved it.

"Of course I do, but you've earned this one."

That landed me a small smile. And as she looked my way, that smile made her green eyes sparkle. It brought me back to when I saw her the other day on campus and first noticed those eyes. I had no idea when I saw her then that she was my roommate. Thank God I didn't act on my emotions in that moment and my anxiety won. Walking out of that office was the best thing I could've done.

"Well, I don't hate this country stuff," she said as she reached for the knob. "But it's not my favorite."

She tuned it to a different station, and suddenly, Nirvana's "Something in the Way" blared through the speakers. The haunting melody was one I was familiar with, but not a song I'd listened to recently. "Now this, this I can listen to all day long."

Leaning back against the headrest, she closed her eyes and her head swayed to the music.

"This is the kind of music I listen to at the gym." I didn't think she heard me due to how loud she had the volume up, and I wasn't even sure why I told her. Maybe I was trying to make small talk, or maybe I was trying to make sure my new roommate didn't hate me. But she reached over and turned it down.

"So you're a gym rat?" My knuckles turned white as I gripped the steering wheel while I stared at the cars in front of us. It wasn't *what* she said, but *how* she said it. The ridicule dripped from her voice. Thankfully, the cars ahead started moving and I made it through the traffic light we'd been stuck at. Driving would have to be my distraction, because talking to her couldn't be. Not anymore.

"Ohh, what's wrong? The big brawny guy doesn't like being called a gym rat?" Her wicked, snide attitude was downright mean.

She really was a total bitch.

We drove the rest of the way home in silence. As I pulled into a spot near our townhouse, I opened my door to get out, but she stopped me when she spoke.

"See, words can hurt, Logan."

THIS TIME, I DIDN'T HELP HER WITH THE DOOR OR GETTING out of the truck. But the frog caught my attention as I passed him. He had what looked like bird shit on him. Using a napkin that had been in my pocket, I did my best to clean it off. He deserved better.

Once inside, I walked straight for the fridge to get some food and was about to head upstairs. That was when I saw both Macie and Becca were in the kitchen as well.

"Hey, Logan," Becca said. "How was it being back on campus?"

My face was still in the fridge, looking for my protein bowl I'd made earlier this morning. Once I grabbed it, I turned toward Becca.

"Fine, until the end of my last class."

I tossed my bowl on the counter and searched for a spoon in the drawer. As I was about to explain to Becca what I meant, my driving companion finally made her way inside. Loudly, as she slammed the front door.

"Thanks for nothing buddy, I almost couldn't get out of that damn truck," she barked.

"Wait, did you two come home together?" Macie asked as she got up from the kitchen table. She and Becca looked like they'd been working on something together. Yet now they both looked...intrigued.

"Yeah," I said. "We have Marketing together."

"And then he stranded me in that monster truck of his, all alone out there!"

Becca leaned against the island, eyeing Ava up and down.

"It was still nice of him to drive you home," Becca said.

Ava threw her backpack toward the couch and then turned her attention back to her friends, me not included in that.

"I had to jump from the seat to the ground. Literally jump. He had time to stop and talk to the cement frog out front, but he couldn't help me."

It took everything in me to not scream "fuck you" at her. I'd never met someone so ungrateful before.

"But did you thank him?" Becca asked. "It was a very nice thing he did as your *roommate*." Her emphasis on the word roommate didn't go unnoticed.

Ava just stared blankly at Becca and then said, without looking at me, "Thank you."

Whatever was going on between them, I wanted to steer clear of it. I picked up my bowl, spoon, and bag, and turned to head upstairs.

"Whatever," I mumbled as I walked away from the girls.

"Did you tell them?" Ava asked, the question directed at me.

I stopped and turned.

"What?" I asked.

Ava let out a bark of a laugh.

"It's ironic really," she said as joined the girls at the table. She had their attention, eyes glued to her. "We have marketing together. And not only are we in the same class, but we're partners for the entire semester. Our grade will depend on it."

Both Macie and Becca's heads turned toward me in unison, their smiles matching.

"Oh my god, are you serious?" Macie asked. "I think that's perfect! You guys have built in study partners right here. I would die for that."

And if it had been Macie or Becca, I think I would share her sentiment. Having someone in the house to do class projects with does make it easier...if it's a person who doesn't want to gouge your eyes out.

Becca looked thoughtful as she scrutinized both Ava and me. I remembered saying how similar she thought the two of them were. Thinking back to when I first met Becca, though, I don't remember her ever being mean. Her snarky comments always came across in the way they were intended to, as a joke.

"Well," Becca said. "I think it could be an opportunity for the two of you to get to know each other a bit better, right, Ava?" She locked eyes on her as they sat across from one another.

"Yeah," Ava said. "Right."

Tink didn't sound very convinced.

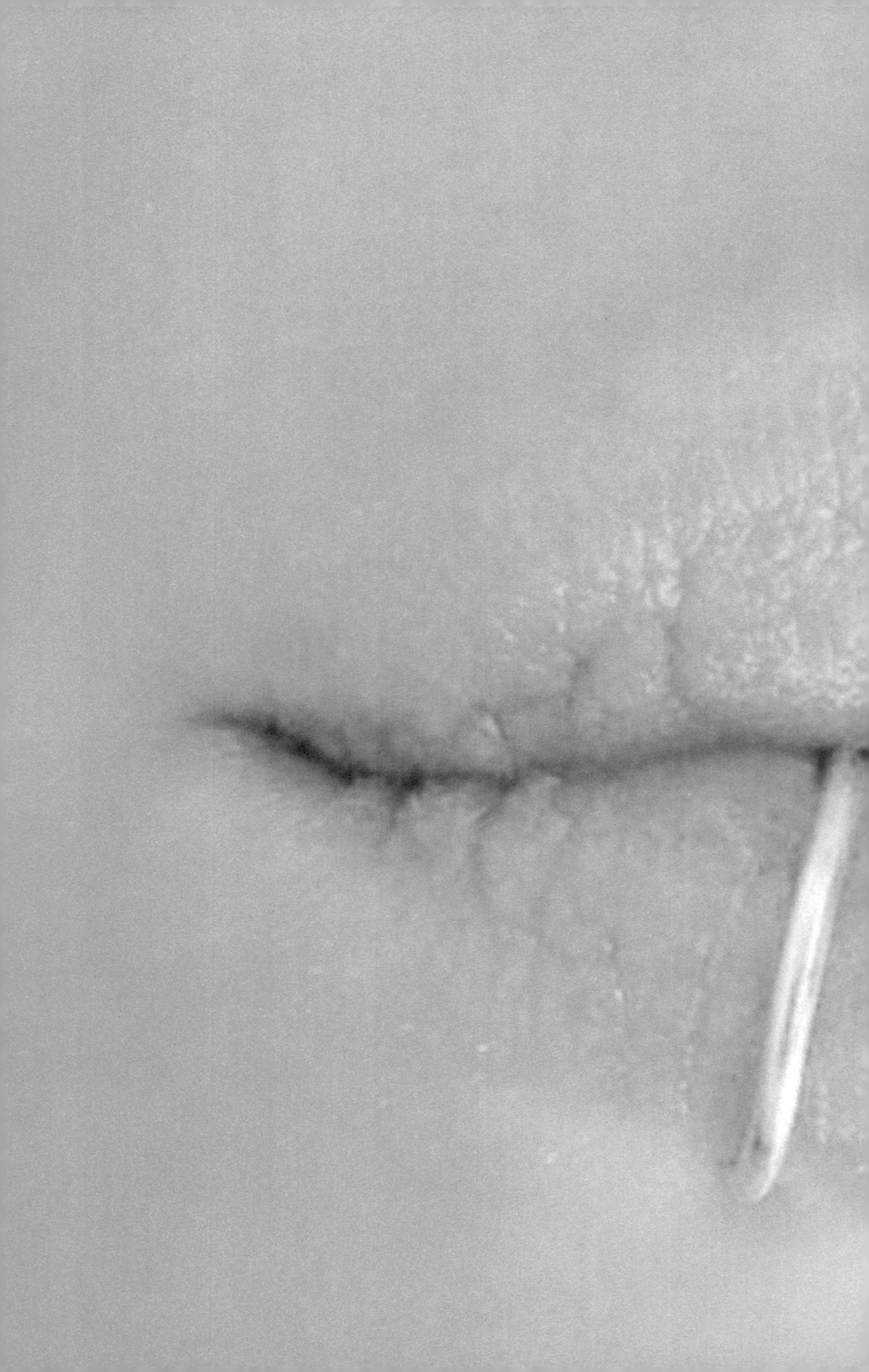

CHAPTER 6
Ava

What in the actual fuck. Not only did I have to live in the same house as him, probably take an occasional ride from him and be in the same class with him...but partners? Are you fucking kidding me? The class was huge. There were so many other possibilities for people to be paired with.

But it was him and me.

For the entire semester.

That sounded like actual hell.

Of course, the thought of going to the professor crossed my mind, but it left just as quick. There was no way I'd give Logan the satisfaction of requesting a different person to work with. He never would've let me live that down.

So I was stuck with him. In so many ways.

"Hey," Macie said as she tapped on my open door. "You almost ready?"

At least today I'd have reinforcements in the truck with me. All four of us were driving together.

"What time is it?" I didn't have my watch on yet, but I thought I still had almost thirty minutes before I needed to be ready. "Why are we leaving now? No one has class for like another hour."

"Don't know, but Becca and Logan wanted to get to campus early."

Would have been nice if someone mentioned that to me, but I wasn't anyone's priority at the moment.

"Yeah, I'll be right down."

As I heard her hustle down the stairs, I hurriedly brushed my teeth. Shit. I wasn't really a makeup girly, but I also didn't like going out with nothing on my face. Throwing mascara on my lashes and gloss on my lips, I rushed to find my boots.

After grabbing my backpack, I made my way to the first floor to find it empty. Great, they were all in the truck waiting for me, that would piss the lumberjack off.

Of course, my lovely roommates left the front seat open for me.

Next to the lumberjack.

As I opened the door, I stared up into the cab of the truck with despair.

"C'mon, Tink, we're gonna be late."

The venom in his words confirmed he was in no better a place with our friendship than I was.

"You know my little legs struggle with your gargantuan of a truck, asshole." I was sure my response didn't help. After throwing my bag into the seat above me, I reached for the armrest on the door to help pull me up.

"And why must you call me that to only ridicule my short stature?" My words were breathy as I finally made it into the cab and settled into my seat. "It's not nice."

He put the truck into reverse as I hurried to buckle my belt. He snickered as he twisted around to look out the back of the truck, his eyes glancing at me as he did.

"Oh, that's not it, Tink. It's really not about your height. It has everything to do with your bitchiness."

I never understood the saying "my chin hit the floor." Yet after his comment, I completely did. My mouth dropped open and I, possibly for the first time ever, was at a loss for words. Spinning in my seat, I checked for the reaction of my two roommates behind me. Macie feigned ignorance as she scrolled on her phone. But Becca stared right back at me, challenging me. She either waited to see how I would respond or actually agreed with him.

Traitor. Why was she now my warden?

Feeling defeated, and alone, I sat back in my seat and kept quiet. Which was not the norm for me. I'd have a talk with Macie about this later, for sure. Regarding Becca, I'd have to decide how to move forward with her. She was his friend before mine. Her allegiance was definitely in Logan's court.

I was left wondering if I'd made a huge mistake agreeing to this arrangement.

"We're meeting up with Lanie and Xander before class," Becca said. Her words were calculated. Selective. Spoken carefully.

Turning to look at her again, her eyes went wide as her chin lifted in Logan's direction. A warning.

My attention turned toward the behemoth next to me. His eyes were now focused on the road, yet there was something about his demeanor. His white knuckles gripped the wheel, and I realized his sarcasm toward me ceased.

"Would you like to come?" Becca asked. "I'm assuming you've got time since you and Logan have the same class to get to. Might be nice for us to see each other, all together. Ty'll be there, too."

That made Logan uncomfortable. His menacing gaze went to the rearview mirror aimed directly at Becca, his laser eyes trying to say the words he didn't want to speak.

I understood. He was going to see the girl he wronged. The girl he apparently used to have feelings for and touched inappropriately. And her boyfriend.

Of course he was nervous. Anyone would be.

But he was doing it. He planned on seeing them.

And that took balls.

And hell yeah, I wanted to see that.

"Sure, got nowhere else to be since we're getting here so early."

OUR STUDENT UNION WAS A VERY BEAUTIFUL BUILDING. IT had multiple levels, but somehow the engineers managed to allow light to flow from the ceiling windows to every floor. On a cold, windy winter day like today, it made it a bit more bearable to see the sun shining even once indoors.

As the four of us traipsed through the first floor, every eye turned to look.

Every female eye, that was.

Every girl stopped what they were doing and stared at Logan as we searched for our friends. It was like a scene from a movie, yet he was completely oblivious. At least it seemed that way.

Macie, on the other hand, was not.

"Quite the phenomenon, huh?" she whispered in my ear. Her eyes scanned the room as the females continued to gawk. "I mean, sometimes I wish he wasn't our roommate. Like, so he would be fair game, ya know?"

Christ, it was like she was inside my head sometimes.

"Yeah, but they don't know him like we do," I retorted. Except my response was not a whisper. Logan turned and looked right at me. But I didn't care.

"Ava," Macie started as we took a group of seats that were empty. "Why are you not giving him a chance? He's really nice once you get to know him."

I snorted. Actually snorted at her comment.

"You'll have to forgive me, Mace, for not wanting to become friends with a guy who is a total douchebag to me. In addition to the fact that he assaulted someone who he supposedly liked, a lot."

Macie pulled me from my seat with a force I didn't think she was capable of.

"Ava!" she yelled once we were away from Logan and Becca. "What is your problem?"

We were up against a wall in a little alcove. She obviously wanted privacy for her next words, which I was sure weren't going to be nice.

"Why would you say that? Especially with him right there?" she reprimanded.

I was known to be a girl who spoke her mind, and I liked that about myself. But I was never known to be a mean person. And that was a mean thing to do, even to him. However, there were things going on in my head, things no one else knew about, that were at play here.

"I don't know, Macie. I don't know why I said it. He's just under my skin, ya know? He's pissing me off on purpose, and I don't know why."

She shook her head at me like a schoolteacher would.

"Ava."

Her hand literally went to her hip. Christ, now I had her and Becca acting like sentries in my life.

"I don't need another mother, Macie. Please, let's not do this, OK? I've already got Becca on my case about Logan, I don't need you, too."

"But you're not seeing that you're the one who started all of this between the two of you. You could put an end to it, too."

I was about to respond. Retort. Retaliate.

Then I realized she was right.

But I didn't care.

"I don't want to do this here or now. Can we talk at home, later?" My eyes scanned the room, refusing to look her in the eye. I lowered my voice as I said my next words to her. "I think it's about time I tell you a little something about me and my past."

The look on her face transformed from schoolmarm to concerned best friend in a millisecond. She reached for my hand and squeezed it before nodding.

"Of course." Her arms went around my shoulders, and she pulled me in for a hug. "Is everything OK?"

I nodded and she accepted that.

I guess I was doing this. I'd be sharing a part of me from my past that no one other than my mom and sister knew.

But I think it was time.

As we walked back toward our group, I noticed that Lanie, Xander and Ty had arrived. We were a large, robust gathering of people in the center of the union. Everyone laughed, hugged, and talked over one another as they caught up.

"Ava!" Lanie yelled. She ran to my side and pulled me into her arms. "It's so good to see you. How was your break?"

I liked Lanie a lot. She was most likely the only reason I agreed to the arrangement of Logan living with us. Lanie had a troubled past, a deeply disturbed ex who hurt her badly. Physically, emotionally, mentally. He'd actually been in jail, but they couldn't keep him in any longer and he was recently released. Xander, her hot boyfriend, insisted she move in with him. That left an open room in our house. Enter Logan, who needed a place to live.

Win-win in everyone's mind.

Everyone's except mine. If I'd spoken up about my concerns of living with him, I'd be the reason he couldn't return to school.

"It was good," I told her. "How was yours?"

"It was OK. Xander spent most of it trying to figure out where Max might be, and plan accordingly if he decided to show up at his house. He's a little obsessed at the moment."

Her distress came through as she threw herself into one of the chairs.

Hearing that made me feel guilty. I hated that her life was filled with this unnecessary drama. She wasn't even twenty years old yet and had to be constantly looking over her shoulder for an abusive ex.

But taking in the people around us, I saw her support system. In that regard, she was truly lucky.

"I'm sorry, Lanie, that sucks. He sounds like such a tool. But you're lucky to have Xander, and these guys, to help you."

A brilliant smile formed on her lips, lighting up her face.

"Becca always told me how good you were at doling out words of wisdom. And you're right, I am lucky, I need to remember that."

I noticed her eyes focus on two people in particular. And they grabbed my attention as well.

Xander and Logan were speaking.

What I saw surprised me. Xander was relaxed, leaning in toward Logan, smiling as they spoke. It was obvious Logan was still nervous as he stood with his hands shoved in his jean pockets. But he seemed better off than when we were in the truck. A bit more relaxed.

His eyes kept darting in our direction, though. Which was crazy that he would be stealing glances at Lanie while talking to her boyfriend. But then it hit me.

He wasn't looking at Lanie.

"Becca told me you and Logan are struggling a little bit," Lanie said, interrupting my revelation.

"Um, yeah, just a little, but we'll be fine. No worries, Lanie."

I wasn't sure if she believed my lie, I didn't think I was good at it. But she let it go. Maybe because Logan was headed in our direction.

"Hey, Lanie. Wish we had more time, we didn't get a chance to talk too much. Xander brought me up to speed about 'the asshole,' though," Logan said.

They shared a look, her eyes serious, as she stood to greet Logan with a hug.

A hug.

"I'm so glad you're back, Logan," she said to him.

As she said it, she held his hands and looked him square in the eyes.

"Me, too," he responded.

His smile for her was genuine. Real. And not a smile one would give to a person they were in love with or anything like that. They had a mutual respect for one another.

"But me and this one have to get going. We've got a class starting soon," he said while gesturing to me with his thumb.

Looking at my watch, I realized we would have to really hustle across campus. Grabbing my bag, I said my goodbyes.

It was a content silence as we walked into the brisk outside air. He seemed to want to be with his own thoughts, and I was fine with that. It meant he wasn't passing any snarky comments my way.

Then his pace picked up. I knew we were possibly going to be late, but I couldn't keep up with him. Instead of complaining, I kept quiet. My pace increased, but Logan was yards ahead of me.

Suddenly, he stopped and turned to find me. Still quiet, he waited for me to catch up. We walked in silence, stride for stride.

CHAPTER 7
Logan

Last night, Becca came to my room to ask about all of us meeting up before classes. She knew I'd wanted to see Lanie and Xander, so she arranged for us to get together. I appreciated her doing it, but then the regret set in. My concern was seeing Lanie and Xander for the first time in front of everyone. Maybe it would have been smarter to do it privately. Sleep was hard to come by since my anxiety made me toss and turn all night. Throw in the issues with Ava, and I was a ball of nerves.

Thankfully, it was mostly for nothing.

Xander was amazing. He spent the time we talked asking me about my recovery, my time home, and how I was adjusting. I didn't have much time to talk to Lanie, but her warm smile and hug told me nothing had changed between us.

The only thing that hadn't improved was Ava. I watched her as she spoke with Lanie, trying to discern if there was anything she said to her that could give me a clue what her problem with me was.

All I got out of it was that I liked how her eyes sparkled in the light coming from the ceiling windows. And I never thought a lip ring would be a turn on.

But it looked like I was wrong.

Whenever Ava listened to someone speaking to her, she pulled the circular ring into her mouth and her tongue played with it.

It was cute.

And hot.

And I fucking hated that anything Ava Kennedy did made me feel that way.

"So, there you have it, folks," Professor Lynch proclaimed. He was pointing to a slide up on the screen. I missed a lot of what he'd said as I thought back on my morning. "Your first group assignment. Due in two weeks. Have a good day."

Fuck. Quickly, I snapped a photo of the slide with my phone so I'd have the assignment guidelines.

"Shit," the kid next to me said, grabbing my attention. "That assignment is a lot for only two weeks. That should almost be a project for the entire semester."

He was half muttering to himself, half talking to anyone that would listen.

It made me stop and take a closer look at the slide up on the screen.

- **20-30 minute presentation**
- **Choose a company and get it approved**
- **Develop a basic social media marketing plan**
- **Create multiple content ideas to market the company**
- **Bonus points if you choose an angle that the company has never used before on their own**
- **DRESS PROFESSIONALLY!**

SHIT. HE WAS RIGHT, THIS ASSIGNMENT WAS NO JOKE. PLUS having to do it with Ava was going to make it even worse.

"Hey, partner." She crept up and startled me. "Looks like fun, doesn't it?"

I couldn't tell if she was being sarcastic or not.

"You know I have another class after this, right? I can't give you a ride home today."

Brushing past her, I made my way up the stairs of the large lecture hall. If I hurried, I'd have just enough time to grab something to eat first. I heard tiny feet working to keep up with me.

"Will you be around tonight? I'd love to get started on this if we could," she said.

She struggled to keep time with my strides. As I was about to exit the building, she gripped my arm. Turning toward her, I wanted to be mad. I wanted to spew harsh words in her direction, because she still hadn't once apologized for how she's treated me since moving in.

But when I looked down, she had the slightest bit of fear in those sparkling green eyes. And I didn't like that. I didn't like that she'd grown to expect the worst of me in the short time we'd known each other. This wasn't who I was.

I came here to prove that I'd changed.

Instead, to this girl, someone who had let me into her home, I'd been a total asshole.

She had to be more than a foot shorter than me. Looking down at her in a coat that engulfed her tiny frame and the pom-pom hat that covered most of her short dark locks, I noticed a few things I hadn't before.

Like the fullness of her strawberry-pink lips. And how, even when she wasn't talking, she kept them open the slightest bit. Sometimes her tongue slid out and licked her bottom lip while she listened to people she talked to.

It was sexier than I wanted it to be, her lip all glistening and shit.

Because she was doing it now as she waited for me to answer her.

"Yeah," I said. "I'll be around. I think it would be good to get a head start, too. Looks like this will be a kickass first project."

I smiled down at her.

"How are you getting home?" I asked.

She looked dumbstruck. As if she couldn't believe I'd strung several sentences together without calling her Tink.

I was stunned, too.

"I, uh..." she stammered. "I'm meeting Macie and we're taking the bus. We decided that last night, once we knew we were all coming to campus together. Her and I are getting lunch first."

Solid plan, neither of them would be alone.

"OK, good. See you at home."

Spinning on my heels, I took off. Because I think both Ava and I knew we wouldn't survive any more niceties.

TODAY WAS A LOT. A LOT OF SCHOOL WAS THROWN AT ME. Aside from the marketing project, there's an exam coming up in my business law class. Christ, an exam in the third week of the semester. And then there's the amount of anxiety I dealt with this morning.

Let's not forget the damn feelings that swarmed my insides about the tiny vixen I'm living with. That took me by surprise.

It warranted a trip to the gym. My workout was intense and long, but it helped. I wasn't one to use the showers there, and I didn't pack a bag, anyway. So I was a sweaty, smelly mess when I finally arrived home, which was hours later than I anticipated. It was nearing eight o'clock already.

Downstairs was quiet, but I heard voices and footsteps from above.

I wasn't alone, which was good. I didn't want to be alone. Torn between eating or showering first, my grumbling stomach won the fight. Regardless of the time, I needed to eat.

Grilled chicken, rosemary potatoes, and roasted carrots.

My diet would not suffer simply because I was away at school. Sliding open the back door, I headed out to light the grill. It took a few attempts, most likely since it was so cold out, but I finally saw the red and orange glow of flames.

Upon returning inside, I was stunned to find a strange guy digging around in our refrigerator.

"Can I help you?" I asked, more than ready to kick this intruder out if needed. I was fairly certain neither Macie nor Ava were seeing anyone, and it most certainly wasn't Ty.

The guy stood back, two bottles of beer in his hands as he turned around.

"Oh, hey man, I didn't know anyone else was here."

"And you are...?" My tone was firm, my stance firmer as I folded my arms across my chest. I wasn't letting this guy think he could rummage through my fridge.

"Oh, yeah, I'm here with Ava." He tilted his head to the ceiling, to upstairs.

And he still hadn't answered my question.

That was when I came to the realization that he was shirtless and sockless. Barefoot in his sweats in my kitchen.

He was *with* Ava.

Why did that fucking piss me off? I wanted to punch the smug look off this guy's face. He was cocky as he stood in my kitchen, almost taunting me with his stare. Soaking wet, he was lucky if he weighed 160. But as I approached him, he didn't back down.

"I could ask you the same question, dude?"

The guy had the audacity to ask me who I was? In my own house?

"Well, I'm Logan, and I *live* here."

"Oh, cool, man. Nice to meet you, I'm Devon." His attitude changed immediately, as if he really thought I was the intruder. He balanced both bottles in the crook of his arm and reached the other hand in my direction.

Of course, I was the asshole if I didn't shake his hand.

"Yeah, nice to meet ya," I said. His handshake was lame, which I expected.

"I better get back upstairs," he said. Then he smiled as he rolled his eyes.

He fucking smiled, like I was in on his little joke. It didn't warrant a response. I went about my business, taking out the pans I needed to continue cooking my meal. He stood in the middle of the kitchen, as if needing permission to be dismissed. When he didn't get it from me, he eventually took off for the stairs.

She told me *we* were working on our project tonight. And I was nice to her when she asked. Because she fucking looked cute, and I thought I was being too much of an asshole.

But now *I* was made to look like the asshole.

And the kicker was...it all bothered me way too fucking much.

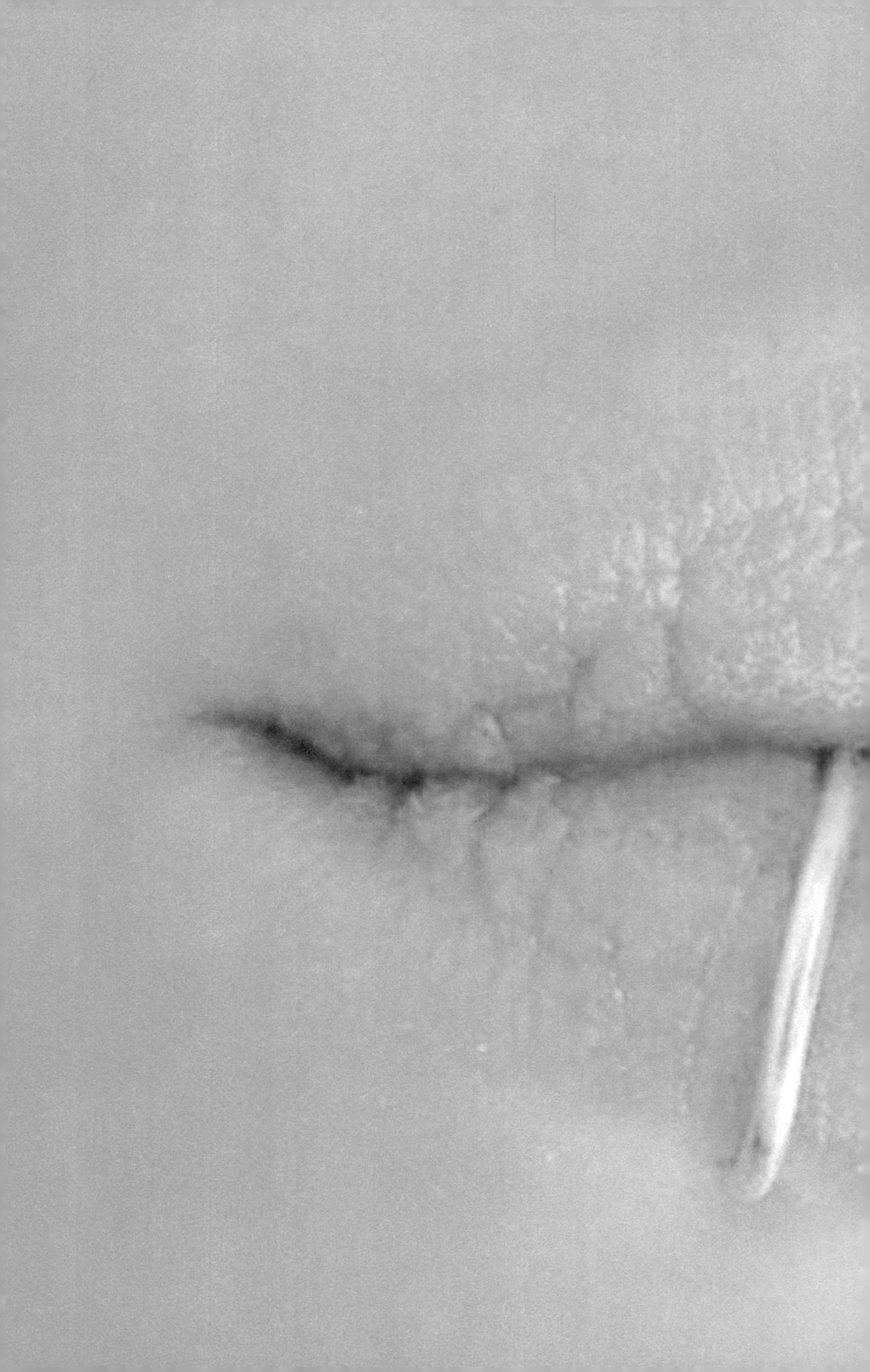

Ava

Today was all kinds of fucked up. First, seeing Logan with Xander and Lanie really confused me. They really did get along. When I got in the truck in the morning and understood where we were headed, Logan's nervous behavior made me curious. He wasn't talking, not even insulting me. I thought I was going to witness him being shunned by those two. But it was the complete opposite.

They welcomed him with open arms.

I didn't know Xander that well, but what I did know was how protective he was of Lanie Montgomery. The sheer fact that he moved her in with him because her ex could *possibly* come back looking for her was proof. So, I guess I was the asshole for thinking Logan didn't deserve their loyalty.

Then, Logan had multiple moments of being normal, even border-line nice, to me. First, he walked with me to class rather than leaving me in the dust. Then, he literally agreed to work on our project tonight.

With a smile.

The coup de grace was he actually asked me how I was getting home. What the fuck? Like, why did he have to do that?

I think I liked him better as an asshole. Because I didn't like how his politeness affected my emotions. It made me think back to the day I first saw him in the registrar's office. The wordless connection he and I had as we stared into each other's eyes was so strong. I left that office with a renewed vigor that maybe, just maybe, I was ready for a relationship. Ready to put myself, and my heart, out there in the hands of someone else. The feelings he stirred up inside me with just a look were overwhelming.

And then the moment of discovery. Lo and behold, Logan, the guy my heart suddenly longed for with a single glance on campus, was indeed my roommate. The roommate that Macie and I agreed neither of us would pursue.

The roommate who put his hands on a friend of mine, unsolicited.

"Here ya go," Devon said as he came bouncing back into my room. He handed me one of the beers while placing his on my nightstand. When he asked if I wanted a beer, I agreed. However, what I really wanted was for him to leave me alone for a few minutes as he went to get them.

I watched him reach for the band of his sweats, ready to take them off.

"Yeah, I think it might be time for you to head out," I said. Most guys were not accustomed to being the one used. They were more familiar with initiating the one-night stand rather than the other way around.

When Devon and I met in the cafeteria earlier today, I knew he was smitten. I knew I needed a release. Something to take my mind off what, or who, it's been focusing on lately. He jumped at the offer to meet me at my place tonight.

His hand froze on the elastic of his pants, and his eyes turned down. He wasn't going to push, no guy would for fear of further embarrassment.

"I've got some homework to get done, and it's getting late," I offered, hoping it would ease whatever it was he was feeling.

He looked pathetic. And sad.

"Yeah, me too, I should get going." He raced to put the rest of his clothes on. "Maybe we can hook up this weekend, my frat is having a party. I'll send you the location."

Sitting up in bed, I offered him a curt nod, but no other reassurances. He started his approach, making a move to come closer.

"See ya, Devon." I dismissed him.

No kiss goodbye, that was my rule. They couldn't think this was more than it was. I stayed on the other side of my bed, facing my window, my back to him.

I made it very clear to him earlier that this was sex and sex only. And he was on board.

He read the room. I heard his steps stop and pivot while he reached for his keys on my desk. He lingered, I guess hoping I'd get up or say something else. But once he realized it wasn't happening, he went for the door.

"Oh, hey man," he said to someone as he pulled it open.

His words made me jump from my bed. It was a knee-jerk reaction, not one I thought through. The door remained open as he greeted the only other guy it could be.

There was no response from Logan, no verbal response anyway. His fixed look moved over the head of Devon directly to me.

"Yeah, um, see ya, Ava," Devon said before sidling past the looming figure in the hallway.

I stood next to my bed in my black lace bra and thong.

With Logan staring at me.

It should have bothered me; I should have rushed for my robe or jumped back into my bed. Instead, I remained where I was, staring back at him.

I saw the slow swallow of his throat, the saliva working hard to pass over his pronounced Adam's apple. His blue eyes grew dark as his gaze lingered.

My nipples hardened under his scrutiny. And I worked hard to not rub my thighs together to tend to the building sensation down there.

Christ, I just had sex. Albeit, it wasn't the best I've had, but he got me off. I shouldn't be this turned on simply by a guy *looking* at me.

Then he turned abruptly and headed for his room

"I'm gonna eat," he said over his shoulder without looking back. "Then I'm showering. Get dressed, we're working when I'm done."

I WAS DOWNSTAIRS FOR AT LEAST THIRTY MINUTES ALONE. There was no one else home, and I didn't know where the others were. Becca was most likely with Ty, but Macie hadn't answered my text. She and I were supposed to have a talk tonight, so she should've been here.

Staring at the front door, I willed her to walk through it. There was no way I wanted to be alone with Logan, not after what happened upstairs.

It wasn't that I was afraid of him. No, I don't think I was. Which took me off guard.

There were other things I was more afraid of at the moment.

"Ready?"

His loud booming voice was a complete contradiction to how quietly he entered the room. I jumped in my seat, not expecting him to be there. Or maybe I was just lost in my own thoughts.

He sat across from me at the dining table and opened his computer.

"It's good we're getting a head start on this, I have an exam in another class next week and that's going to be a time suck for me this weekend," Logan said.

His eyes were trained on the screen in front of him as he worked to pull up the assignment. It lit up his face, fresh from a shower, some droplets of water dripping from his still wet hair. He wore sweat shorts and a T-shirt. I hated I was aware of how formfitting both were on his body.

"Ava," he said.

"Yeah?"

"Are you planning on working tonight?" He gestured to my still closed computer.

Fuck. I hope he didn't catch me checking out the veins on his forearms just then. And why was he acting like nothing had happened before?

"Yeah, sorry, I'm tired, it's been a long day."

And then he snorted. My head snapped up to see him laughing under his breath, the snicker plain on his face.

"What are you laughing at?" My words were sterner than they needed to be, but I didn't need him going back to his old ways after the progress we'd made this morning.

"You're tired, I get it, that's all. You've exerted a lot of energy, I'm sure, in the past hour."

He chuckled again. But as soon as he stopped, his look was serious. As if he regretted bringing *it* up.

"What makes you think it was only an hour?" I challenged.

He tried to hide the incredulous, yet impressed, look that came over him. He settled against the back of his chair, contemplating my words further.

"Nah." He shook his head and went back to looking at his computer. "I saw the guy. He was a fast shooter."

Well, Logan wasn't wrong there. Thankfully the guy took care of me first. But there was no way I was divulging any of that.

"Whatever, dude," I said. "Sounds like you might just be jealous. At least I got some."

Instead of some snarky comeback, Logan remained quiet. Insanely quiet. So quiet it became uncomfortable that those were the last words said between us.

Was I wrong to have said that?

Oh no, did he think I thought he was jealous of Devon? And not that I'd had sex?

As an attempt to change the subject, I opened my laptop to move this back toward our project.

"Put any thought into what company you'd like to use for this?" I asked. Some of my ideas were ones college students frequently used, such as DoorDash, Chipotle, and even Uber. Turning my screen to face him, he saw my list.

He pondered them for a moment but shook his head before responding.

"I understand why you'd think going with one of those would make sense, but I think going with a more obscure company would be better. Then no one really knows too much about it. We have a greater chance at being more original with our ideas."

Well, the blonde stud had a brain after all. I liked his idea, even though he didn't suggest any companies. But the concept he described made sense. So why, when I answered him, did I not say that?

"You had to disagree with me, didn't ya?" Whipping my arms across my chest, I sat back against my chair. There was venom in my voice.

But he didn't bite. Rather, he closed his laptop and stood from the table.

"Where are you goin'?" I screeched.

His laptop went under his arm as he grabbed his water and phone. He proceeded to leave me alone sitting at the table.

"Logan, we're supposed to work on this!"

Turning to face me, his eyes narrowed as he shook his head slightly. He drew in a full breath before talking, clearly working hard to rein in his emotions.

"I think you're right, Tink. I think it's late, and you're tired."

Spinning on his heels, he bound for the stairs without another word.

And left me.

Alone.

But I think I deserved it.

ABOUT AN HOUR LATER, I HEARD VOICES DOWNSTAIRS AND people moving around in the kitchen. I was holed up in my room since Logan ran out on me, too embarrassed to see him around the house. I hoped it was Macie. Since this morning, when I decided to let her in on some of my past, I'd been anxious to do it.

Me: You home? Is that you in the kitchen

Macie: yep, I'll be right up

She came barging into my room, complete with two bowls of ice cream for us. Crawling into my bed, we got comfortable and put on an episode of *New Girl*.

"Thank you for the double chocolate chip ice cream," I told her. "Did you stop for this?"

I caught her with a mouthful of her plain old vanilla with sprinkles as she nodded her answer.

"I thought we might need it. You made it sound pretty serious this morning."

I was glad she remembered. It was easier to start talking about it with her bringing it up. However, now that the time had come, I was nervous and second-guessing telling her anything.

"Where were you tonight? I didn't know you had plans."

My way of deflecting.

"Oh, yeah, I had a meeting with a group from a class. It went hours longer than I expected, mostly because people were talking a lot of the time instead of doing what we needed to."

Hoping we could eat and watch TV in a comfortable silence, I turned my attention back to the wide screen on my wall. Macie obliged and we sat back, bowls in hand, and enjoyed some Jessica, Nick, and the Winstons.

But then the show ended.

And our bowls were empty.

Macie turned her attention to me.

"Do you still want to talk?"

"Yeah, I do," I told her. "There's something about my childhood that might explain why I've been acting the way I am."

She turned herself completely toward me, giving me her undivided attention. It was usually the opposite, me giving her advice or her needing to talk to me. This was an anomaly. But it felt good to have her here, by my side.

"Well," I started. "You know that it's just me, my mom, and my sister at home."

She nodded.

And I blurted out the entire story about why my mom left my dad.

The fact was he started beating her when she was pregnant with me.

And it didn't stop once she gave birth.

Thankfully, he never hit me. According to my mom, he would control her with threats of violence. The acts of violence were few and far between but often enough for her to not forget how they felt.

The problem was, she had no job. She was a stay-at-home mom. He had the upper hand because he controlled the money, and her.

But then the threats, the violence, stopped when I was around one. And she said they seemed to be doing OK. They even had another baby, my younger sister. She would never regret having my sister, she's made that clear. But it was the trigger for the violence to start again.

For whatever reason, the stress of the babies put him over the edge.

And this time, it didn't stop.

It actually got worse. He then started to sexually assault her as well.

Turns out he also had a drug problem, used up all their money. He would get mad at my mom when they ran out of money, all because of him.

Finally, when my sister and I were eight and six, she found the courage to leave him. She moved us in with her parents until she got back on her feet. Her dad, our grandpa, was instrumental in keeping our father away from us that first year. After a while, our dad lost interest and stopped coming around.

Eventually she got him to sign divorce papers.

It took her years, but she made a great life for us.

However, it has definitely formed my opinion about men.

I have trouble trusting them. There's no interest in a relationship because I doubt there is a guy out there worth my time.

Classic psychology study here.

I was quiet for quite a while once I finished my story, allowing it to sink in. It was cathartic finally telling it to someone, though.

Macie's head tilted as her eyes turned down. The wetness in them didn't surprise me. It was a sad story about my mom, I've cried plenty of tears over it.

She reached out, taking my hands in hers.

"I'm so sorry you guys went through that." Sincerity laced her words. "And don't take this the wrong way, babe. But why did you agree to Logan living here?"

That was the million-dollar question, wasn't it?

"Well," I said, "Lanie was quite convincing. But more importantly, if I was the only one who said no, Logan wouldn't have been able to come back to school. That's a lot to put on me, a lot for me to carry."

Pulling my hands from hers, I jumped out of the bed. As I paced across the carpet, my voice increased in volume.

"Don't you see? I couldn't be the one to not give him the chance he worked so hard for. Yet, I feel uncomfortable with all of this."

But I wasn't telling her the whole truth.

I wasn't telling her that I saw how Lanie and Xander were with him this morning. That their trust in him did help me with how I felt about Logan. More than I was willing to admit.

And I wasn't telling her that I was one hundred percent falling for Logan Somers and how that scared the shit out of me.

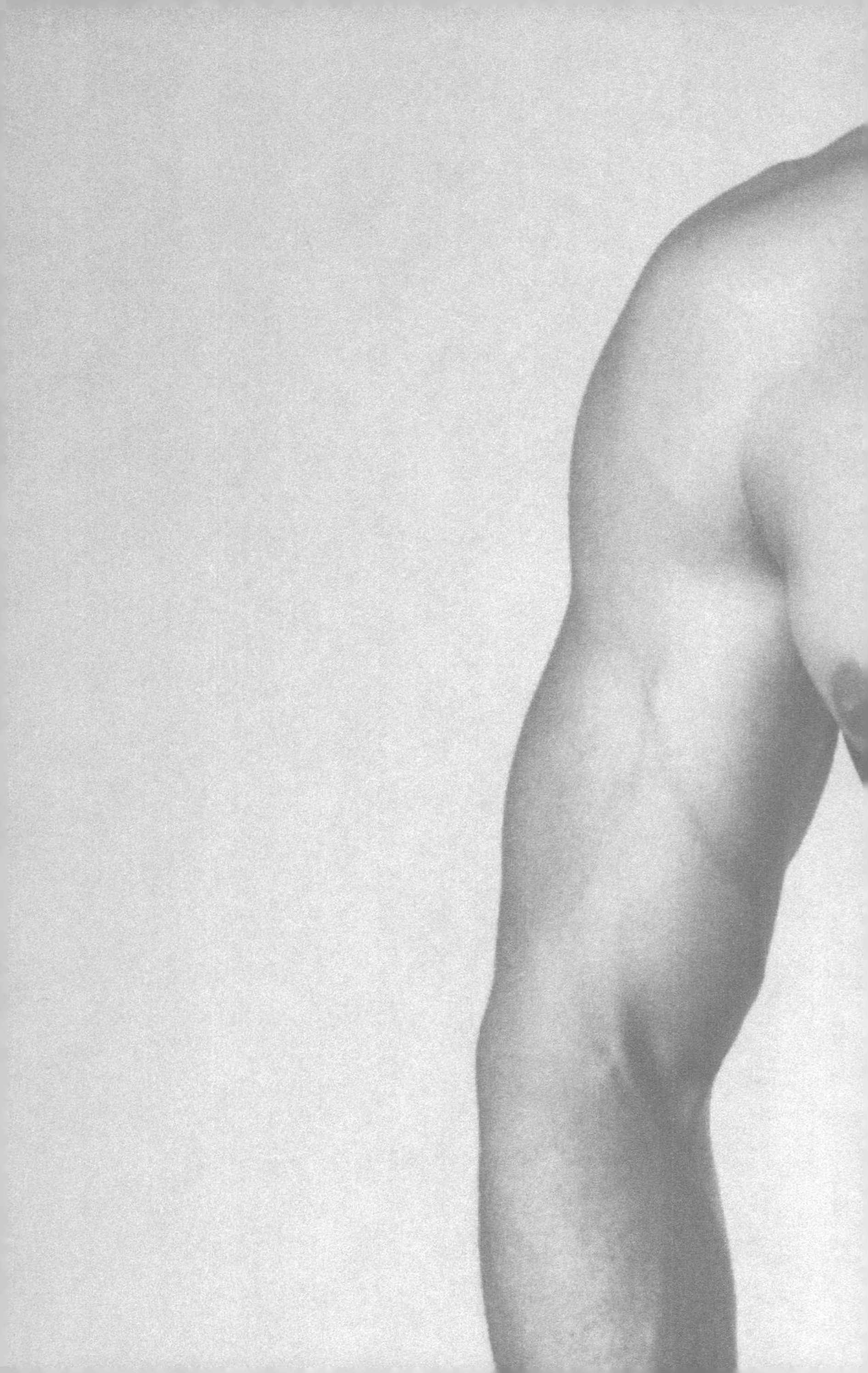

CHAPTER 9

Logan

The gym was my space to zone out. To let my head open up and not think of anything. I could let it all go as I pumped the weights or ran on the treadmill, pushing myself to the limit. The music blasted in my ears and melted all the thoughts muddled in my head.

I asked Ty to join me today. We hadn't seen much of each other since the semester started, which I was afraid of. Since we don't live together, it was more of a challenge. He sure had time for Becca. I got it, they had a rough semester in the fall. I think they were making up for lost time.

But I missed the guy.

"Christ, man, your bench went up a shit ton since last spring," he said as he helped me with the bar.

As I reached for my towel to wipe my brow, Ty took his turn on the bench.

"So, how are things...going...with you and..."

"Ty, stop trying to talk while you're benching."

What I really wanted was for him to not finish his question. I knew where it was headed, and I had no interest in talking about her. But knowing him and his girlfriend, I was sure she put him up to getting some dirt out of me about Ava.

Once he was done with his set, we put the weights back and started for the locker room. It had been a two-hour workout, and we needed to get going. We had plans to go out tonight. His frat was having a party, and I was going to give it a shot.

"As I was saying before, how are things going with Ava? Any changes with you two?" Ty asked. We pulled our bags from the lockers.

Things with Ava were shitty. For reasons I was not about to tell Ty.

I hated seeing her with another guy the other day.

Hated the thought of her fucking him in our house.

Hated pretending to be OK with it.

But fucking loved seeing her in her black lingerie.

"She's still being a bitch most of the time, still acting like Tink," I told him. And that was true. There was a moment when I thought there might be a chance for us to get along, but she ruined it with her mouthy comments.

"Alright, enough about her. What I really want to talk about is tonight," he said. He stopped packing up his bag, giving me his full attention. "Are you sure you want to do this, Logan? I mean, this is a full-on rager tonight. It's the first house party of the semester. It's gonna be exactly what you would imagine a frat party to be, and I'm not sure you're ready for it."

I wasn't sure I was ready for it either, but there was only one way to find out. My therapist and I discussed it during my session yesterday at length. She suggested that I always have a bottle of water in my hand. Plus, to make sure my support system was in place and aware if I needed them. And if I needed to leave, just leave.

"Yeah, I know. I have a plan. And I appreciate it, man, I do. But I can't stop living either. There are plenty of sober people in this world."

"Yeah, but I don't think many of them go to frat parties."

He wasn't wrong. But I knew when to get out, and I was doing too well to screw up now.

"I already decided not to drink tonight," Ty said. He was packing up his bag when he said it, avoiding eye contact.

My gut reaction was to tell him not to do that, but I knew he wouldn't change his mind. And to be honest, I appreciated it and was thankful I'd have him to rely on. As he threw his bag over his shoulder, I gave him a shove.

"Thanks, man."

MY ASS WAS PLANTED ON THE COUCH AS I WAITED. IT WAS already after ten and we had a fifteen-minute drive to the party. All I heard coming from upstairs was girls screaming back and forth asking where this makeup palette was, or where that brush was. I was very happy to be a guy.

The front door burst open, and Ty walked in.

"Still not ready?" he asked.

"Nope."

He joined me on the couch, and I put on the TV. We may as well enjoy ourselves during this torment. As soon as I did, I heard footsteps on the stairs. Long brown hair with red highlights came bounding round the corner into the living room. She made a beeline for Ty, landing on his lap, straddling him.

"Hey, babe," she said, then attacked his mouth with hers.

"I'm right here, ya know," I reminded them.

It did nothing to stop their reunion. They started making loud smacking noises with their exaggerated kisses, and I removed myself from the couch as they both started laughing.

"Jealous much?" Becca asked as she got up from Ty's legs. "And by the way, don't think I've given up on you and Ava making amends." She stalked toward me as if on a mission. "Thought tonight might help, ya know, hanging out, socializing."

"We live together already, Bec. If that's not going to help, going to a party where she's gonna get drunk and look for a hookup isn't going to help the situation."

Right on cue, that was exactly when Macie and Ava decided to show up. Macie bounced into the room, obviously excited about the party. But Ava remained where she stood, staring at me.

"Didn't Becca tell you?" Macie asked.

I looked at her, confused.

"We all decided not to drink tonight," Macie continued. "To help you."

My eyes snapped directly to Ava to gauge her reaction to Macie's words. She continued standing in the same spot, her face neutral as she countered my gaze.

"Why?" I asked. It didn't completely surprise me that Becca and Ty were doing this for me. But Macie and Ava were almost strangers to me. They owed me nothing. Especially Ava.

"Well, silly, that's what friends do for each other," Macie said as she came and sat on a stool next to me. "We didn't want you to feel alone tonight. So, we will be your support system."

She had her hand on my leg, a gentle touch, as if the topic made her uncomfortable.

"Thank you," I said. Then I looked toward Ava to determine if she could handle me thanking her as well. "Thanks."

She gave a curt nod but said nothing.

"OK, let's get going. After tonight, you'll still be our designated driver, right, Logan?" Becca asked. Her laugh as she headed toward the door lightened the mood.

"Yes, Becca, I'll be your Uber driver, for all of you, so your drunk asses can make it home safely."

We piled into my truck, and while I waited for everyone to get seated and buckled, I stole a glance at my frog friend ahead of me. He was like my little guardian. Every time I pulled into this spot, he was smiling back as if to tell me *You've got this.*

"What is it with you and that stupid frog statue?"

Looking in the rearview mirror, I glared at the owner of those words. Even though she was doing a nice thing for me tonight, it appeared she wasn't going to be nice to me while doing it.

"I think he's cute, that's all," I told her as I started backing out of the spot.

"He is cute," Macie agreed. "Look at his adorable smile. I never noticed him before, has he always been there?"

"Yeah, he was there last semester," Becca said. "I remember tripping over him when I was trying to climb onto the balcony when I locked myself out. He helped me get the height I needed to get up there."

That hurt my heart to hear she'd used him as a steppingstone. But at least he helped in a time of need. I knew he had a purpose.

"Oh my god, do you remember that day? You scared the shit out of me, getting stuck up there," Macie said. "And then Gage came to help."

I didn't need to be here last semester to know the mention of that name in this company was going to make it uncomfortable. Looking to my right, he seemed unscathed by it. Macie stopped talking, realizing she shouldn't have brought up that name. Gage was the third party of a love triangle between the three of them last semester. A quick check on Becca and she looked nervously at Ty, as well, but was relieved to see he was fine.

"Alrighty, folks, let's get this night on the right track," I announced. "Thanks for deciding to not drink with me. If you change your mind, I get it. And I won't be mad. This is my life, not yours."

As I drove through downtown, Main Street was busy with students roaming the streets looking for a place to eat or a bar they could get into on a Friday night.

"But I want you to know how much I appreciate the gesture of you choosing to support me, especially my first night out."

OK, got that out of the way. It needed to be said, even to Tink.

"Like I already said," Becca said. "It's going to be amazing having a built in Uber living with us. Your sobriety will be the best thing that happened to our house, dude."

The girls in the back row laughed together at her comment, but Ty was quiet up front with me. He was thoughtful as he looked out his window. Eventually he turned toward me.

"Ya just gotta say the word, and we'll leave. OK?" he said.

I nodded.

He seemed nervous. More nervous than me. It wasn't like I'd never been to a party here at BRU. Last year, Ty and I decided to rush the frat together and were hanging out with the brothers all the time. Before I decided to leave school. The point was, I wasn't naïve. I knew what I was getting into.

And I could handle it.

At least I thought I could.

TURNS OUT, BEING SURROUNDED BY BEER WASN'T MY biggest problem at the party. My biggest issue was being subjected to watching Ava flirt with every guy there. It was as if flirting was her profession. And it was her mission to do it right in front of me.

What made it worse was that she looked amazing. In the month since school started, she'd been letting her short hair grow out. It was down below her ears now, and she wore it all spiky on top of her head.

She surrounded her eyes with dark makeup, but somehow, it made her green eyes almost pop from her head.

And then there was her outfit.

On a regular day she stuck to jeans, flannels, and those big clunky black boots.

She still had her boots on, but instead of jeans she had on a skirt so short I was convinced if she bent over, we'd all know if she had a thong on again. Above the skirt, she wore some kind of tight, black strappy shirt that barely held her tits in place.

I couldn't take my eyes off her tits. They were full and round, and so fucking big. But not so big that they were all over the place, even without wearing a bra. Because that was something she *wasn't* wearing.

I was pretty sure every other guy at the party was also aware.

My challenge was making sure she didn't see me checking her out; that was all I needed.

"How's my beefy, brawny, best guy friend doing?"

Becca startled me as she grasped my arm, showing up out of nowhere.

"Hanging in there?" she asked. Her look was gentle, her smile warm.

"Yeah, I'm good."

We stood against the wall of the basement for a few minutes, watching the drunken fools around us. Then her attention was drawn to our pint-sized roommate in the far corner of the room. Ava was sandwiched between two guys as they pushed their bodies up against hers, dancing to the music.

"Looks like Ava is on the prowl. Par for the course for that one," Becca said. Suddenly, I felt her next to my ear. "Ya know, I really do wish the two of you could at least be friends. She's a good person once you get to know her."

My eyes were trained on Ava and the scene she was making. Ava turned her head my way, our eyes connecting, just as the guy in front reached around and gripped her ass, pulling her closer. Her wicked smile made my blood boil as she taunted me. Then she had the audacity to spread her legs, allowing him to grind against her even more.

Becca followed my eyes to the threesome across the way, then back to me. I wasn't sure what she made of it. But as she watched me grip and destroy the half-empty water bottle, she guided me to the stairs.

"Let's get some air, big guy," she said as we started our ascent.

I didn't argue. We both saw Lanie and Xander on our way to the back door. Lanie made a motion to join us but stopped in her tracks as Becca waved her off. Her lips thinned as she watched us walk by. But I had to agree; I didn't need to be talking to the girl I had feelings for last year about the one I'm pining over now.

Becca threw open the back door, and a gust of frigid air hit our faces.

"Let's make this quick, my tits'll freeze off out here." She turned toward me, an expectant look waiting for an explanation. "Well?"

As I leaned against the metal pole acting as a railing, I didn't know how to answer her, so I didn't. That didn't sit well with her as her hand went to her hip immediately.

"Well what?" I asked.

"Logan, what the fuck did I just watch downstairs? It was as if she was trying to, I don't know, piss you off or make you jealous or something."

I had no response for her. Because she was right on both accounts, I think. Yet I had no idea why. The girl hated me.

"Have you two hooked up?" she asked.

The accusation took me by surprise.

"You're kidding me, right?" I turned to the door, ready to head back inside, but stopped. "She hates me, Bec, you know that. And even if she didn't, she's our roommate."

She grabbed my arm, not letting this go.

"Then why were you so upset? You were working hard to control your emotions down there."

Giving in, I leaned against the cold metal again. The small porch we stood on offered no protection from the elements, and it had to be less than twenty degrees out here. Neither of us had more than a sweater on.

"I don't know. She just gets under my skin with everything she does, you know that." I hoped that would be enough to satisfy her.

Her eyes studied me as we stood there, almost in a standoff, but then they lit up and went wide.

"You like her, don't ya?"

I was not going to answer her. There was no way I was going to answer that question.

Suddenly, the door slid open.

"You guys OK out here? You must be freezing?" Lanie came to my rescue.

"Yeah, let's go inside, Becca, it's cold out here."

Becca didn't protest, but I knew she'd revisit this once we got home.

"I'm going to find Ty," Becca said. "You good, Logan?"

"Yep," I said.

"He's with me, now," Lanie chimed in.

Looking around the first floor, I realized I knew no one but her and Xander up here. It must be all his fraternity brothers hanging on this floor. It was quieter, more like they were hanging out than the party going on in the basement. Xander was deep in conversation with a few guys near the kitchen, so Lanie and I steered toward the living room.

"I think it's awesome how everyone in your house chose to not drink tonight," she said as we took a seat on a couch. "It proves you have some good people in your life."

Nodding in agreement, I knew she was right, but I wasn't feeling that way about one of them.

"Hey, Lanie." A pretty girl sat down next to her. "How's your night going?"

"Hi, Charlotte. I'm good, but you don't sound so good. What's up?"

The two girls spoke quietly, so I decided to get myself another bottle of water. Grabbing two from the cooler along the wall, I was faced with deciding what to do. Should I return to the basement or stay up here? That was when Lanie caught my attention.

"Logan, I want to introduce you to my friend Charlotte. We knew each other a little last year, and now we work together this semester. Charlotte, this is Logan."

Charlotte stood to greet me, and I noticed how pretty she was. Her light brown hair fell in waves past her shoulders. She pushed those waves behind her shoulder as she put a hand forward.

"Hi," she said. Her hazel eyes sparkled when she smiled at me. "It's nice to meet you."

"Apparently, you both have the same major. Finance, right, Logan?" Lanie said. It became all too clear what Lanie was up to.

But then I thought, why the hell not?

As Lanie quietly made her departure, Charlotte and I started talking about some of our classes, discovering we were in one together. We'd found a quiet corner of the room to talk, leaning up against a wall. Quiet was relative; we still had to lean in and almost yell into one another's ears to hear, but it was better than downstairs.

"Lanie said you took last semester off."

Her mouth was so close to my ear her lips rubbed against my lobe.

"Was it hard coming back after being home?" she continued.

We kept talking.

And it was easy.

Even with her asking about me being home, and why. For whatever reason, I had no qualms about telling her all about me. Maybe it was because I thought I'd never see her again, or maybe she had a knack for being a good listener. Regardless, she knew more about me than Ty did in the hour we'd been talking.

The room got more crowded, and our little corner no longer belonged to just us. Our bodies touched as we continued leaning in and whispering our words in each other's ears. She was drinking, some of those seltzer drinks, but it didn't bother me.

"So," she said as her hooded eyes looked up at mine.

I knew what that tone meant.

My dick knew what that tone meant, too.

"Do you have a car?" she asked.

Shit.

Shit. Shit. Shit.

"Yeah, I do, but I brought all my roommates. I'd have to see if they're ready to go home."

Through her disappointment, I saw hope. This girl was not only pretty and had a gorgeous body, but she was nice. Like, a really good person kind of nice. I could use that in my life right about now.

"Take a walk with me, let me see what I can do," I told her.

Taking her by the hand, I took us down to the basement. It had calmed down but was still more party than not. At my height, I was able to look over the top of most of the people and found Becca and Ty immediately.

"I see one of them," I yelled over the music.

She nodded and gripped the back of my shirt as we snaked our way through the tightknit crowd. The partygoers swayed against us as we pushed through, many of them almost losing their footing. Our shoes stuck to the cement floor, which was now sticky with wet beer puddles.

Being sober in a setting like this was nothing short of eye opening.

"Hey, Ty," I screamed over the noise of the crowd. "Can you ask Becca if anyone is ready to go?" I motioned to my companion when I asked him, hoping he'd get the point.

As soon as Ty turned to Becca, I realized that Ava was tucked away behind him. She was so tiny I couldn't see her behind them at first. Her eyes were drawn to Charlotte's hand interlocked with mine. Her brows knitted together when she looked at me, her disapproval clear on her face.

Hypocrite.

She pivoted on her heels and hightailed it upstairs.

"You're in luck, I think everyone is good with heading home." Ty had Becca and Macie with him. He didn't know that Ava took off.

"Let's go," I said as I pulled Charlotte along behind me. Barreling through the crowd, we finally made it outside.

"Where's Ava?" Macie asked as we made our way toward my truck.

I chose not to answer. Instead, I got us to my truck and opened the passenger door, helping Charlotte inside. And I liked the feel of her ass in my hand as I did it.

"Thank you," she said.

"So you're not a total douche," a snarky voice said behind me as I stepped away from the truck door.

Turning, I saw my pint-sized roommate looking up at me with laser eyes as she willed them to shoot me down.

Not taking her seething eyes from mine, she continued. "You have compassion for *some* people who need help getting into this truck."

While making my way around to the driver's side, I barked my comment back. "You reap what you sow, Tink."

Macie, Becca, and Ty all stood motionless outside the truck, watching this debacle unfold as I pulled myself up into my seat.

"Let's go, your ride is leaving!" I yelled to all four of them.

They piled one by one into their seats, completely silent. Charlotte was unaware of what happened, so she started chatting up a storm once the truck was full.

"Hi, everyone!" she exclaimed. "I'm Charlotte, Lanie's friend. So you guys all live together?" Her bright smile was met with solemn stares from the others in the car. All but one.

"Oh christ," Ava mumbled.

I shot her a look in the rearview mirror before taking Charlotte's hand in mine.

"Ty over there on the other side of you doesn't live with us. It's just me with all these fine ladies," I told her.

Charlotte sensed the tension in the truck by this point, squeezing my hand to let me know, and remained quiet the rest of the drive home.

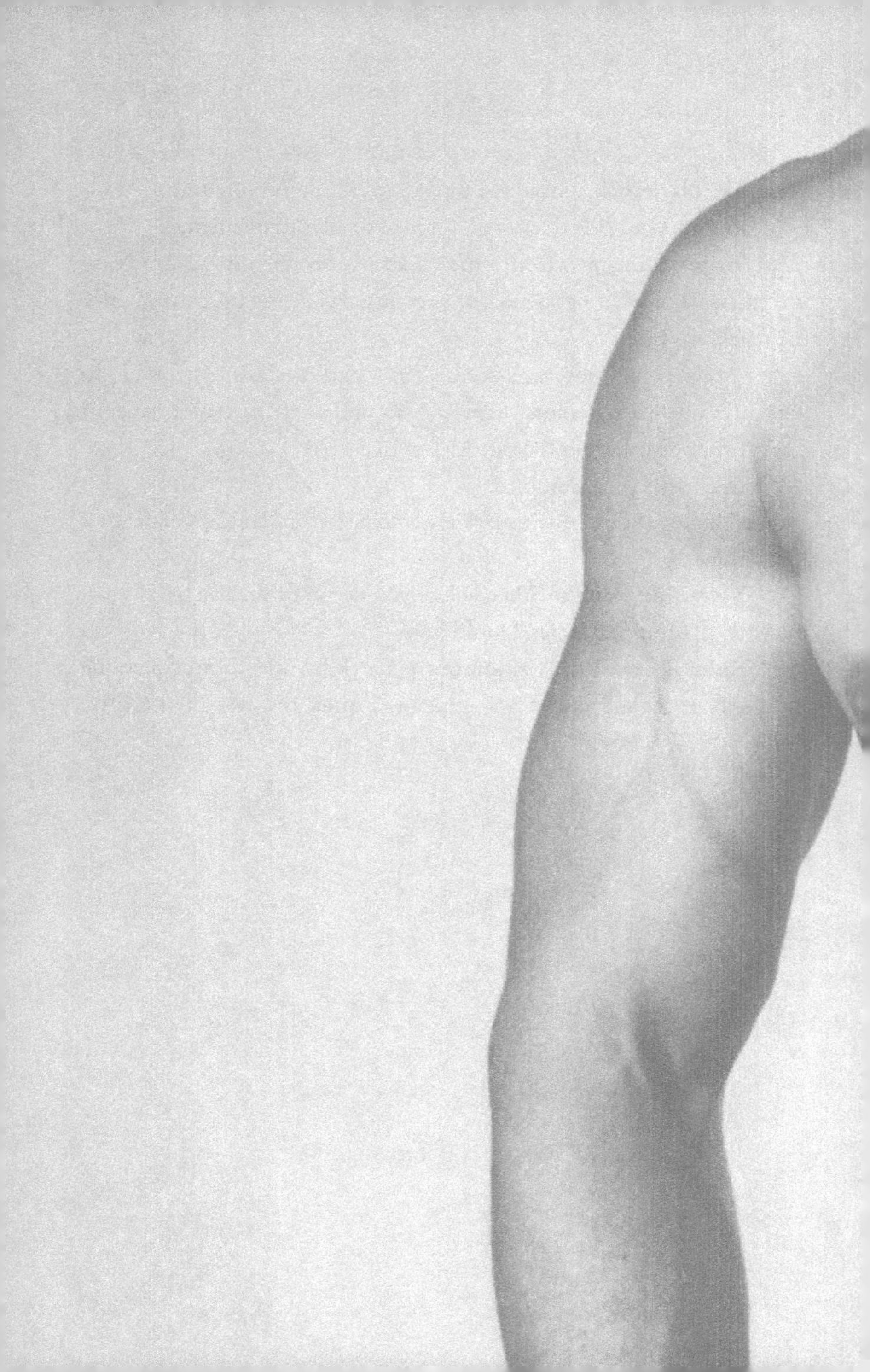

CHAPTER 10
Logan

On the ride home, I'd determined Charlotte was more intoxicated than I first thought. I knew she'd been drinking, but as she slumped against my shoulder during the drive, it became clear how much. She grew as quiet as the rest in the truck, the radio the only sound in the cab.

When I parked, and the doors opened for the others to exit, Charlotte stirred next to me. We waited a few minutes before getting out ourselves. It gave her some time to become more alert. Plus, I hoped it gave my roommates time to get to their own rooms.

"Ready?" she asked.

Nodding, I opened my door and slid out, holding out my hand for her.

"I'm sorry about all of that, if it made you uncomfortable," I told her.

"No worries, roommates can be tricky."

She had no idea how right she was. As we entered the townhouse, I was relieved to find the downstairs empty and quiet. Everyone had gone upstairs. Making my way to the kitchen, I grabbed two bottles of water from the fridge and handed her one.

"Would you like to head up to my room?" I wasn't going to make any assumptions about why she came home with me. "Or do you want to hang out down here? We could watch TV or something."

She came close, her hands landing on my chest as she looked into my eyes. She had pretty eyes, but they were bloodshot from drinking.

"Logan, I didn't come home with you to watch TV." Reaching down, she took my hand. "I'm assuming your room is upstairs?"

I nodded and she started for the stairs, pulling me along.

There was a girl I hung out with at home, Sara, during my break from school. She and I met at the counseling center. It was frowned upon for us to be in a "relationship," especially with someone from the group. But we decided to hang out anyway, we both needed the companionship.

We talked about everything. Our pasts, our problems, our hopes for the future. It was comforting having a friend dealing with similar issues.

Then it became more than friendship.

We had sex.

We had good sex.

There was comfort in her being the one I'd been with. She knew so much about me from our sessions together. And all our late-night talks.

Maybe that was why I felt comfortable with Charlotte, too. She was just as easy to talk to. She didn't judge when I told her why I wasn't drinking. Instead, she found it admirable.

Courageous even.

She reminded me of Sara.

But I wish she was more sober.

"This is my room," I told her, guiding her toward my door.

She walked in ahead of me, looking around, stumbling slightly. I was thankful the room was fairly clean and the bed was made, only a few pieces of laundry on the floor. Grabbing them quickly, I tossed them in my hamper.

Unsure of how to proceed, I turned on my speaker.

"Music?" I asked her.

"Sure." Charlotte sat on the edge of my bed, suddenly looking as uncomfortable as I was. I think that helped because if she were more aggressive right now, I think I'd be chickening out.

"Country or rock?" I asked.

"Let's go country, might fit the mood better." Her smile was infectious, and it made me smile too.

I pulled up "You Make it Easy" by Jason Aldean, and a playlist of songs like that. Setting my phone on my desk, I faced her. She smiled as she patted the bed next to her. I took measured steps as I made my way to her, keeping my eye on her. I needed to make sure she really wanted this. And there was only one way to know.

Kneeling in front of her, I put my hands on her knees and asked.

"I need to make sure this is what you want. That you're good with us getting in my bed."

She reached for the hem of my sweater, pulling it up and over my head as her answer. Her hands went to my chest, rubbing up to my shoulders, down to my waist. But I grabbed her hands, stopping her from progressing.

"That feels amazing, but please tell me it's OK for me to touch you as well."

Her hands went to my face, cradling it.

"What's wrong, Logan?"

How did I answer that? She didn't need that backstory of my life.

"I want your consent. I need it, Charlotte, that's all. I don't want to do this without knowing I have it."

She stroked my face before lowering hers to mine. Her lips were soft as she kissed me. It was a simple kiss, and when she pulled away, she looked me square in the eye.

"Logan, I'd like you to fuck me."

Fuck.

Pulling her to stand with me, I reached down to undo her jeans. First the button, then the zipper. My hands couldn't move fast enough once I knew it was happening. She joined in, undoing mine. We both fumbled with each other's pants, struggling to push them over the hips. Through giggles, we resorted to taking off our own pants and tossing them across the floor.

Her shirt and panties remained, and from the look of it, there was no bra underneath.

Her hard nipples poked through her shirt, begging for me to touch them. I reached for the bottom of the material, lifting it slowly up her torso, my fingers rubbing along the skin of her stomach as I went. When my finger reached the underside of her breast, Charlotte let out a small moan, throwing her head back. Both my hands reached under the thin T-shirt to cup her pert breasts, my thumb and finger squeezing each of her nipples gently as I did.

"Logan," she whispered.

The reverence in how she said my name gave me pause. But then I found myself ripping her shirt over her head. We stood, staring at one another, both in our underwear. Her body was amazing, curves in all the right places. Fit but not so muscular she looked masculine. She took one step toward me, bringing us only inches apart, as she put her hands on my chest.

"Logan." She said my name again as her hands ran across my chest, down my torso. "You're incredibly sexy, do you know that?" Her hand made it to my bulging dick still inside my boxer briefs. "Every part of you is hard, not just your dick, but I love that your dick is hard for me."

Her hand wrapped around me, gripping my cock tight through the material.

Reaching down with both hands, she pushed my boxers to the ground. Her heated look took me in from head to toe. And I liked that. Stepping closer, my finger went to the dip at the base of her neck and trailed down between her breasts. Once there, I circled around her firm skin, cupping a breast in my hand, as her head fell back. Lowering my mouth, I took a pink nipple between my lips, sucking and nipping at it as I did. My hand pulled at her other tit, flicking the taut tip, as she moaned my name under her breath.

"C'mon, Charlotte, let's get in this bed."

As she went to sit on the edge, she missed it, her ass sliding off the mattress and heading for the hard boards of the floor. My hands thrust forward, gripping under her arms, pulling her against me.

"Whoops," she said, with the giggly tone of someone really drunk.

Shit.

Placing her further back on my bed, I laid her head on a pillow and pulled both feet up, covering her body with the blankets. She settled in, almost asleep already.

"Your bed is so comfy," she whispered into the pillow.

Yep, it was a comfy bed.

And now Charlotte would have it all to herself tonight.

There was no way I was moving forward with doing anything with her in this state, so I sat back against my headboard and took out my phone. After playing a few games of solitaire, I heard only soft breathing and an occasional snore come from her. Once I moved my garbage can to the bedside and put the bathroom light on, I grabbed my extra pillow and walked downstairs.

The couch was calling my name.

As I entered the living room, I realized I wasn't alone. The kitchen light was on and the microwave was running. My only hope was that it wasn't *her*.

But of course it was.

I wanted to ignore her. I wanted to keep my eyes on the couch only. However, as I reached for the blanket on the back of the cushions, my eyes betrayed me. They looked right at her, and she was staring right back. Though what I saw surprised me.

There were no daggers, no sneers.

Instead, her look was inquisitive, almost, might I say, tender. But as quick as I saw it, she shielded that shit up.

"What are you doing down here?"

It was not an unexpected question. She wasn't mean, and that's what was unexpected. She stood on the other side of the island, her waist barely visible over it, she was so tiny. My eyes drifted to the tank she wore and how it barely contained her full breasts.

"She, uh..." Suddenly I was embarrassed to tell her what had happened. But I wasn't about to lie. "She had too much to drink, so she's sleeping it off in my bed."

Throwing my pillow on the couch, I made myself as comfortable as I could. Only then did I realize it was far from a normal sized couch, and my feet hung off the end.

Ava worked her way over to me, a bowl of popcorn in her hands. She stood at my feet, a smirk on her lips as she stared down at me.

"You don't fit, Tank." Her laugh was genuine as she kicked at my socked foot. "That's gonna make for a long night. Why not sleep with her in your own bed?"

I was working to get the thin blanket over my body, only to realize it was a tiny throw that only covered me from shoulders to hips. It was gonna be a long night.

Ava left without another word, her steps quiet on the stairs.

Staring at the ceiling, I thought back on my night and decided bringing a girl home wasn't my best decision. The reaction I got from Ava was what I was aiming for, but that wasn't fair to Charlotte.

Then I heard padded footsteps approaching again. Lifting my head from my pillow, it was Ava, headed my way, lugging a huge fluffy blanket in her arms. Not only did she bring it to me, but she placed it over me as well. Again, no words before she left.

But I didn't think any words were needed.

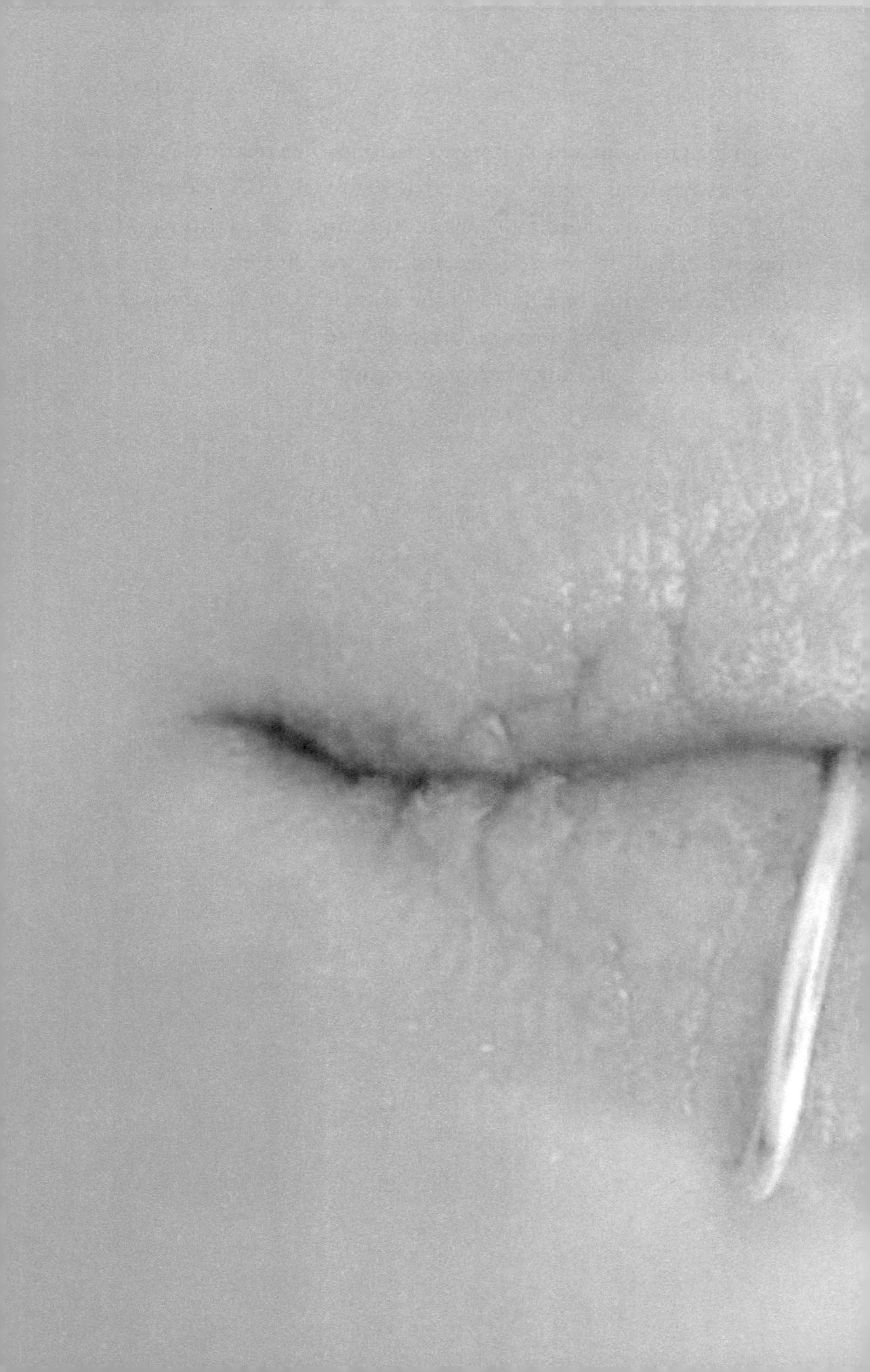

CHAPTER 11
Ava

It was quite refreshing waking up on a Sunday morning...not hungover. When we all talked the other day about supporting Logan on his first night out and not drinking, I wasn't on board at first. My feeling was he had to learn to live in a world full of alcohol and people who drank. The more I thought about it and realized he was depending on us as his support system, I saw the value in that.

But it didn't mean I had to be a total princess while supporting his sobriety.

"Ava?" the voice next to me said.

"Yeah?"

"You've been in la-la land, I've been talking to you," Macie said. More like whined.

We'd gone out for breakfast since we were both up early. Another bonus to not drinking. We sat at a small corner table waiting for our order to be called. It was a small café where you ordered your food yourself and picked it up at the counter, but it was so delicious.

"Last night was fun," Macie said, the exasperation in her voice as if she'd said it a few times. "Wasn't it?"

"Yeah." I nodded. But I wasn't in full agreement.

"You looked like you might hook up with one of those guys you were dancing with," she said, her eyes wagging at me. "They were freaking hot. Why didn't you go home with either of them?"

I laughed. She had no idea, but there was no way she could have.

"What?" she asked.

I couldn't admit what I'd been doing last night with those guys. Yeah, I could've gone home with either. They weren't too happy when I walked away uninterested, but they'd served their purpose. I'd used them simply to make Logan jealous. My guilt was already getting the better of me without her giving me her two cents.

"Macie."

Our food was ready. Thank God.

"I'll get it," I told her.

As I placed our trays on the table, Macie went to fix up her coffee at the coffee bar. While waiting for her return, I desperately tried to think of a way out of talking about last night.

My phone pinged with a text as Macie returned. Looking at it, I was surprised to see who it was from.

> Logan: Where are u we need to work on our project today

"WHO IS THAT?" MACIE ASKED AS SHE STARTED EATING.

"Logan."

Her eyes lit up.

"He wants us to work on our project and he's looking for me." He was right. We did need to get to work on it, time was dwindling. Our first attempt didn't go well.

My attempt at making him green with envy last night backfired on me. Instead, he fell into the arms of another. Although he didn't hook up with her, what he did was even worse.

He didn't take advantage of her. He gave her his bed. He slept on a couch two feet too short for him.

He proved to be a perfect gentleman.

And I wasn't prepared for that.

"Do you need to go?" Macie asked.

"No," I said. "I'm not going to jump when he texts. We'll get there when we get there."

Macie's brows furrowed and her mouth twisted. She obviously didn't like my response. I was back to being a bitch again, but it was my only defense when it came to him.

"Well, I think you should at least text him back, Ava," she said. "You two have to start getting along, don't leave him hanging like that."

I wanted to tell her about my grand gesture last night. About the look on his face as I covered him from head to toe, making sure to tuck him in. And how, as he looked at me like that, it pulled at every muscle in my chest, making it hard to take my next breath. But I couldn't. Because if I did, I think I'd admit to her, and myself, something I didn't want to admit.

"Yeah, OK. You're right."

So I shot him a text.

Me: Out for breakfast, be home later

Yet I also knew we needed to work on this assignment. My incessant desire to annoy Logan contradicted with my need to excel in my classes. Sophomore year was when business students declared their major, and finance was competitive. My GPA needed to be the best it could be.

So instead of enjoying my spinach and feta omelet, I found myself shoveling it in my mouth.

"So we're rushing now, are we?" Macie asked.

"Well, we do need to work on it, I just hate that it has to be with him."

But the look she gave me told me she thought I was full of shit.

When we returned to the house, it was quiet. The dim sunlight shining through the slider and the window over the sink was the only light coming in the rooms. Becca didn't seem to be home, but Logan's truck was parked out front. He must've been upstairs.

"What are you doing today?" I asked Macie.

"I have homework. There's a girl in my one class who actually lives a few buildings away. We planned on meeting up today to work together."

I felt the coldness of the refrigerator as Macie put her leftovers away. As I watched her head upstairs and stood by the island, I was frozen in place, contemplating if I should go to Logan's room or not. It would be just as easy to camp out on the couch, put on a show, and wait for him to come find me.

But then he'd give me shit, and I really didn't want that. To be honest, I was tired of being the bitch I'd been to him. He wasn't a bad guy, from what I'd seen. I didn't give him a chance. Instead, I judged him on one incident from his past.

That one incident had implications with me he didn't understand.

Christ, this was all so complicated.

I turned and trudged up the stairs. Once on the second level, I stopped at his door. It was quiet on the other side, some soft music making its way through. I knocked.

"Yeah."

Opening it, I peeked inside. He was spread out on his bed, making the queen-size mattress look smaller than a twin. He was massive.

Maybe that was part of why he made me nervous. He towered over me by well over a foot. Throw in the thick, corded muscles and he could be scary.

He jumped from his bed when he saw it was me, as if nervous I was in his room.

"Hey." His voice had a tremor in it.

"Hey."

As he stood next to his bed, his hands flexing and twisting at his side with anxiety, I focused on his clear eyes as they looked down at me. His sleeves were pushed up over his forearms, which showed those noticeable veins running across them. It matched a pronounced vein in his thick neck I'd never noticed before.

As immense as he was, he was a dichotomy. His size didn't match his personality one bit. He had the body of a man, but the eyes and look of a sad little boy.

"I'm home," I told him.

"Yeah, OK, I'll meet you downstairs and we can get to work."

My room was dark, but I didn't bother with the light since I only needed my bag. Once downstairs, I set myself up at the kitchen table. It wasn't long before I heard his lumbering footsteps overhead.

There were tiny droplets of sweat on my forehead. I turned to look at the thermostat, convinced someone must have raised it, but it was set at the agreed temperature of sixty-eight.

No reasonable explanation for me to be sweating.

Maybe it was my increased heart rate causing it.

Why was I so nervous? It was me who was usually in control of these situations. I made sure of it. But Logan Somers had me off my game, and I definitely did not feel in control.

"Hey," he said as he took the seat across from me.

I didn't respond. All I did was pull up the document we needed in order to begin working. We had so much to do and only a little over a week to do it. Maybe the little truce I introduced between us last night would do us some good with our project, at least for the week.

Eventually the conversation flowed between us. At least about the work ahead of us. We seemed to be doing fine as project partners, which was a pleasant surprise. He was creative and had a better mind for this advertising crap than I did. We went with a local, college related company, and I liked the ideas he suggested.

We were about two hours in when I suggested we take a break.

"Want anything to eat or drink?" I asked him. Rummaging through the cabinets, I pulled out a bag of chips.

"Chips?"

The condescension in his tone didn't surprise me, he was a gym rat.

"Yeah, chips." As I turned toward him, I munched on one close to his face. He pulled away, his face scrunching in disgust.

"Tink, it's barely after noon."

There was that fucking nickname again. I thought maybe, just maybe, he could call me by my real name for once. Yet even when we were getting along, I guessed I wasn't worth enough for him to do that.

"Whatever," I said. "I'm not a freak about what I eat like you. Not many are."

Logan opened the refrigerator and had his head deep inside. I had to work hard to not stare at his ass bent over in those gray sweatpants.

He turned around quicker than I expected, the ingredients in his hands to make one of those protein bowls he always ate.

"Listen," he said, "I eat chips. But not before I feed my body something it needs first, that's all."

I continued munching loudly on my greasy thins of potato goodness as he prepared his food. He glided through the kitchen like a master chef, like someone who was much more proficient in that room than anyone else our age. He was slicing chicken breast one minute, then spinning around to the sink to rinse some kind of bean in a colander. He danced back to the fridge to pull out lettuce, wielded a knife and chopped it like a professional. He added seasonings and sauces and all kinds of fixings that made my mouth water. Within minutes, he had a bowl I would have paid sixteen dollars for down the road at the local Mexican restaurant.

Once he returned to the table, my wide eyes couldn't leave the bowl in front of him, and he caught me staring.

"Want some?" he asked.

"No." But I did. It looked delicious. "How did you learn to do that?"

His mouth already had more food in it than should fit as he chomped away. He stirred up the contents of the bowl as he chewed, the aroma hitting my nose. It made my stomach growl.

He heard it.

Next thing I knew, he was getting another bowl from the cabinet and scooping some of his deliciousness into it. He plopped it in front of me, fork and all. No words. Then he sat down to his food and resumed eating. Once he finished another mouthful, he spoke.

"I used cooking as part of my therapy while I was home last year. It calmed me. It forced my brain to only think about the task in front of me, and not the other bullshit it wanted to focus on. It helped."

Looking my way, he gestured toward my bowl with the tip of his fork. "Eat it, tell me how it is."

I worked hard to get a little bit of everything on the fork: garbanzo beans, corn, chicken, lettuce, avocado, to name a few. It had to be one of the most mouthwatering dishes I'd ever eaten. I felt some sour cream on the corner of my mouth and reached for a napkin at the center of the table.

Right as Logan did.

Our hands touched.

And just like the time his hand slid across my back when I got into his truck, my skin ignited. From a simple touch of his finger.

I didn't want to pull away.

As it turned out, he didn't either.

Our hands remained on the same napkin, our eyes low, looking at our hands. Neither willing to look at the other. After what felt like forever, Logan gripped my fingers gently, moving them, and lifted a napkin.

He handed it to me.

"Thank you."

With a nod, he resumed eating. As did I.

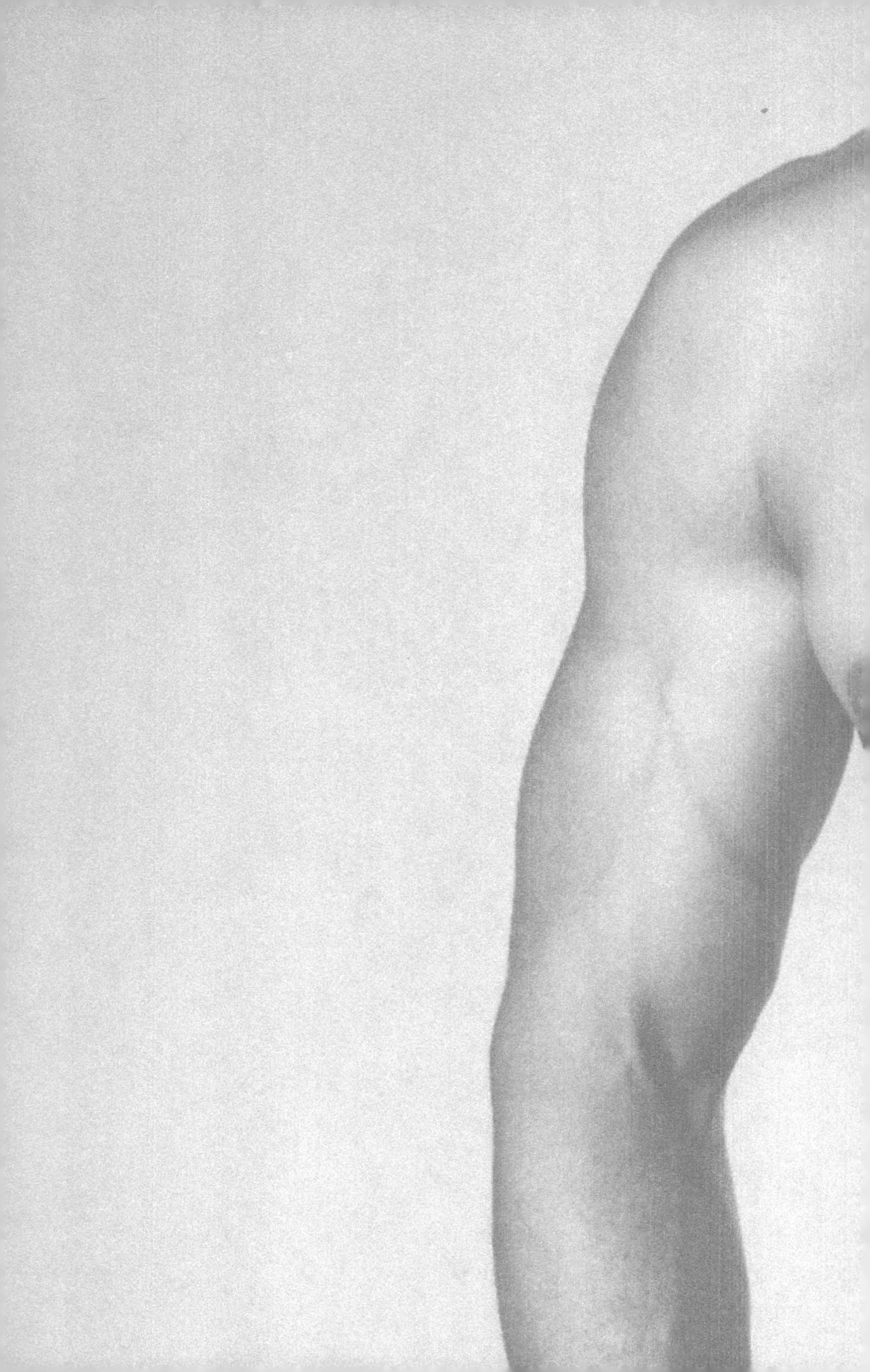

CHAPTER 12

Logan

"So, what you're telling me, Logan, is that you worked on how you were feeling about your roommate, worked on how you were treating her, and it seems to have alleviated the situation between the two of you this week?"

Well, when Dr. Jean put it that way, it sounded like I'd done a good thing this week. And yeah, Tink and I were getting along better. We spent a few nights working well together on our project, which was due next Tuesday, so that had something to do with it. There were still moments she earned her name *Tink* when we weren't study partners, but overall, there was improvement.

But what my doctor didn't know was what I'd been fantasizing about.

My mind had become consumed with thoughts of Ava. The nicer she was to me, the more they increased.

When she smiled at me, I envisioned walking up and pulling her close, wrapping my arms around her tiny waist as her legs wrapped around mine. I'd place her on the kitchen island, stand between those toned legs clad in sleep shorts as her hands landed against my ass. I'd lean in close, my mouth against her neck, feeling her pulse beating faster as her breath hitched. My lips would work their way up her jaw, toward that lip ring that taunted me day and night. Her tongue would play with it as I approached. All signs she wanted this as much as I did.

Like I said, it was a fantasy.

Or when we walked upstairs after a night of working together, and I admired her amazing ass in those tight jeans, my mind dreamt of her taking my hand and leading me to her room. Of course it didn't happen, and I wound up in my own bed. But once I did, that fantasy continued, and my hand wound up on my dick.

It frustrated the hell out of me that I felt this way.

"Um, yeah, I guess you could say that. We've been getting on better," I told her through the screen.

If my therapist knew I was hoping for a relationship, she wouldn't think I was doing as well as she thought. Although, I was hoping for a relationship with someone who only last week still showed signs of hating me, so I was getting ahead of myself.

Was it a relationship I wanted, or was it sex I was after?

"Well, that's excellent, Logan," Dr. Jean said, interrupting my thoughts. "You're doing great. That combined with putting yourself in the setting of the party last week and coming out as well as you did, how does that make you feel?"

How did that make me feel?

Being around the alcohol at the party wasn't the problem, Ava was. So I guess I was doing pretty well.

"I feel...proud. It also feels good to be kinda normal. I mean, I know I'm not partaking while at the parties, but it felt good to be at one. And socialize again."

She nodded at my response, her smile wide.

"Also, I've decided that since I'm not going to be joining a fraternity, I'm joining a team." Her eyes lit up through the screen. "They don't have a club football team, and that was my sport in high school, but they have rugby. That's pretty similar, so I'm heading to a meeting next week and plan on joining."

I'd decided to do it after the party. I couldn't spend all my weekends alone or trying to deal with parties; I needed something just for me. A rough team sport was the perfect outlet for dealing with my own brain.

"Great idea, Logan. And you know how I feel about adding physical activity to your life, so the more the better," she said. But then her face morphed into a look I knew all too well as her lips thinned and her head tilted to the side: the warning was coming. She snickered at my knowing look.

"There is something else I need to bring up. I'm sure you think you're prepared for what I'm going to say," she said. "Usually this is when I tell you to be vigilant with your techniques if you're having any panic attacks, or to call me if you need me more than what's scheduled. But what you need to be prepared for is a relapse, Logan."

I couldn't even swallow my own spit past the lump in my throat. Did she not have faith in me to succeed? Did she see something in me that told her I would fail?

"What are you saying?"

"No one likes to hear it, but statistics show that it's more prevalent than we'd like to admit. Especially in your age bracket. But the positive is you made it well past the ninety-day mark, which is the time frame most relapses occur." She paused. "Of course, the concern now is you have access to your addictive substance." Her smile returned. "Chin up, kiddo. I'm still rooting for you. This in no way means I think you're going to relapse, it's just something we need to talk about because of its prevalence combined with your new circumstances. I'd be remiss to not bring it up."

It was shitty to hear the news, but I was well past the first window. I was nine months into my sobriety already. Reaching a full year was a major milestone. The one thing I hadn't continued with once returning to school were my AA meetings. There just wasn't enough time in the day, in my life, to fit them in. But with her explanation about relapses, maybe I needed to make time.

"Can I ask you one more question?" she asked.

I nodded slowly through the computer screen. My body was going numb at this point, not sure I could take much more of today's session.

"It's been a while since we've spoken about your father, your real father. I know it's a topic you prefer to shy away from, but I'd like to add it to our ticket for next week, if that's OK?"

My father. He wasn't a man I wanted to talk about ever again. Unfortunately, he was a person who still infiltrated my thoughts, my head, more often than he should. And that probably meant I should talk it through.

My eyes looked around my room, bouncing from ceiling to floor, avoiding the screen at all costs. But she gave me the time I needed. Eventually, I found my way back to her.

Her look was calming as she sat in her worn leather office chair. An office I was all too familiar with, and at times longed for. I loved the sound machine she always had on, the sound of soothing ocean waves in the background. Sometimes I felt as though these video sessions weren't quite getting the job done.

"Yeah, we can add it to next week's session," I told her. Though I wouldn't be looking forward to it.

We finished by confirming our day and time for next week and signed off. Every time we did that, I always felt a little down. Like I'd lost a lifeline to one of the people who'd gotten me to where I was. Who dragged me up from my bottom.

But I reminded myself it was me here doing the work, and I was doing a damn good job.

"It's fucking cold out here," Ty said. "Getting across this drillfield is honestly something I've come to dread in the winter."

We walked as fast as we could without breaking into a run. That kind of walk, with your face down, where you could easily ram into someone since you weren't watching where you were going. The wind was whipping, and my beanie almost flew off my head. I'd left my gloves in my truck, so my hands were buried deep in my pockets.

"We're almost there," I told him.

The door to the Student Union was within sight. With it brought guaranteed heat, at least if we moved away from those ridiculous automatic sliding doors that were constantly opening. We barreled through them, continuing our stride to the middle of the open space. Becca and Lanie sat by a small group of upholstered chairs, and we went straight for them.

Ty scooped Becca into his arms, their reunion as if they hadn't only seen each other a couple hours ago.

"They're definitely back together, aren't they?" Lanie said.

I laughed as I peeled off my hat and backpack, taking a seat next to her. "You could say that again," I told her. "Where's Xander?"

"He's back at the apartment packing up. We're heading to see his mom for the weekend."

Nodding in approval, I was happy she had Xander and his family. Lanie's parents no longer lived in the country. They got themselves, and Lanie, mixed up in some fucked-up shit involving her ex-boyfriend and his mafia-related family last year. Instead of sticking around to help her, they took off and left her on her own. They thought giving her some money would be enough to take care of things. Thankfully she found Xander, and his family has taken her in as if she was one of their own already.

"Good," I said. Then I looked at the two who were embarrassingly crawling over each other in one chair. "I hate to bring him up, but any news on the Max front?"

She looked away, a far distant look taking over. I really hated even saying his name. The guy was a fucking bastard and would've killed her most likely if Xander hadn't stepped in last year.

Part of why I had to be happy she had Xander.

He'd already laid down his life for her.

"Nothing lately. Still just that he's out of jail and on house arrest." Her voice was strong as she spoke about him. That was encouraging. "But with him, ya just never know."

I reached over and gave her arm a squeeze. She nodded, and I knew she fully understood I'd always be there for her. Not just emotionally, but physically as well, if it ever came to it again with that guy.

"Wait, aren't Ty and Becca going home this weekend also? To see Savannah?" I asked, putting it all together.

"Yeah, I think so. Unless their plans changed, I think they're leaving soon."

Becca was my buffer in the house with Ava. If things got bad, I could count on Becca putting Ava, or me, in our place to temper the moment. Even though things were going OK this week, Ava was a temperamental little thing and it was never a guarantee. I wasn't looking forward to not having Becca around to help with that.

Or maybe there was more to why I didn't want to be alone with her.

"What's wrong?" Lanie studied me, forcing me to look away.

"Nothing, all good. Looks like I'll have a weekend with Ava and Macie."

Her smile confused me. I couldn't tell what she was thinking about what I'd said, but she definitely had an opinion. Though I wasn't sure I wanted to stick around to find out what it was.

"Gotta go," I told her. "Have a good weekend, Lanie."

Her smile widened as I got up to leave, which made me more self-conscious.

"Ty." I cleared my throat to get his attention since he was still busy with Becca. They both looked my way. "Hey, guys, I'm heading out. Have a good weekend."

Becca jumped from his lap and into me, wrapping her arms around me.

"You too, big guy." She pulled away and looked up at me. "Enjoy the snow, there's supposed to be some coming tonight. That's why we're heading out soon, to miss it."

I'd been so busy with classes and that damn project I felt out of the loop. Not only was I unaware of the impending snow, but I hadn't been to the gym in days. It felt good to be done with classes for the week, so I'd reward myself with a workout.

"I will, thanks for the heads-up. I'm heading to the gym first, though, so you guys drive safe."

Ty came around to shake my hand right before I made my exit.

The gym was empty. Not surprising for a Friday afternoon. Most people weren't thinking about workouts but rather what they were doing that night. It gave me the run of the place, use of any machine I wanted.

I got in a full workout within ninety minutes, which was unheard of at this place.

The campus was equally deserted as I made my way to my truck. The sky had the look of snow on its way. There was always that feel in the air before a storm. A gloomy gray coldness with an edge to it wrapped around quiet solitude. The animals sensed it. They knew it was coming and were in hiding, preparing.

Very different from humans rushing to the market to stock their refrigerators with food for a few days of being indoors. Utter chaos. I was going to stay away from the food store. Thankfully, I didn't need anything.

Pulling up to the townhouse, my frog friend greeted me. As I approached him, I decided to move him further under the bushes. He was close to the edge of the walkway, and I didn't want him getting disturbed by shovels or snow blowers.

Pushing him into the dirt to make him straight, I stood back to take a look.

"What are you doing?"

My head snapped to the sound of the voice behind me. The tiny spitfire was standing with her hand on her hip, looking judgmental as shit.

Standing to my full height, I faced her.

"I'm moving the statue away from the sidewalk. We're supposed to get snow, and I didn't want him to get damaged."

She guffawed. "What is it with you and that thing?" Her key was in the lock, opening the front door before she finished speaking.

"I don't know," I said as I stepped up behind her. "He was the first thing I saw on the day I moved in. It was like his smile welcomed me." The risk of opening up to her suddenly made me stop talking.

And there was good reason.

"A statue *smiled* at you?" The incredulity in her voice was almost vicious.

I was stunned, but I shouldn't have been.

"Oh, I see. Tink is back, and Ava is gone."

She turned to look at me, venom in her eyes.

"Funny, I had no idea you even knew my real name."

That was how our snowy weekend got started.

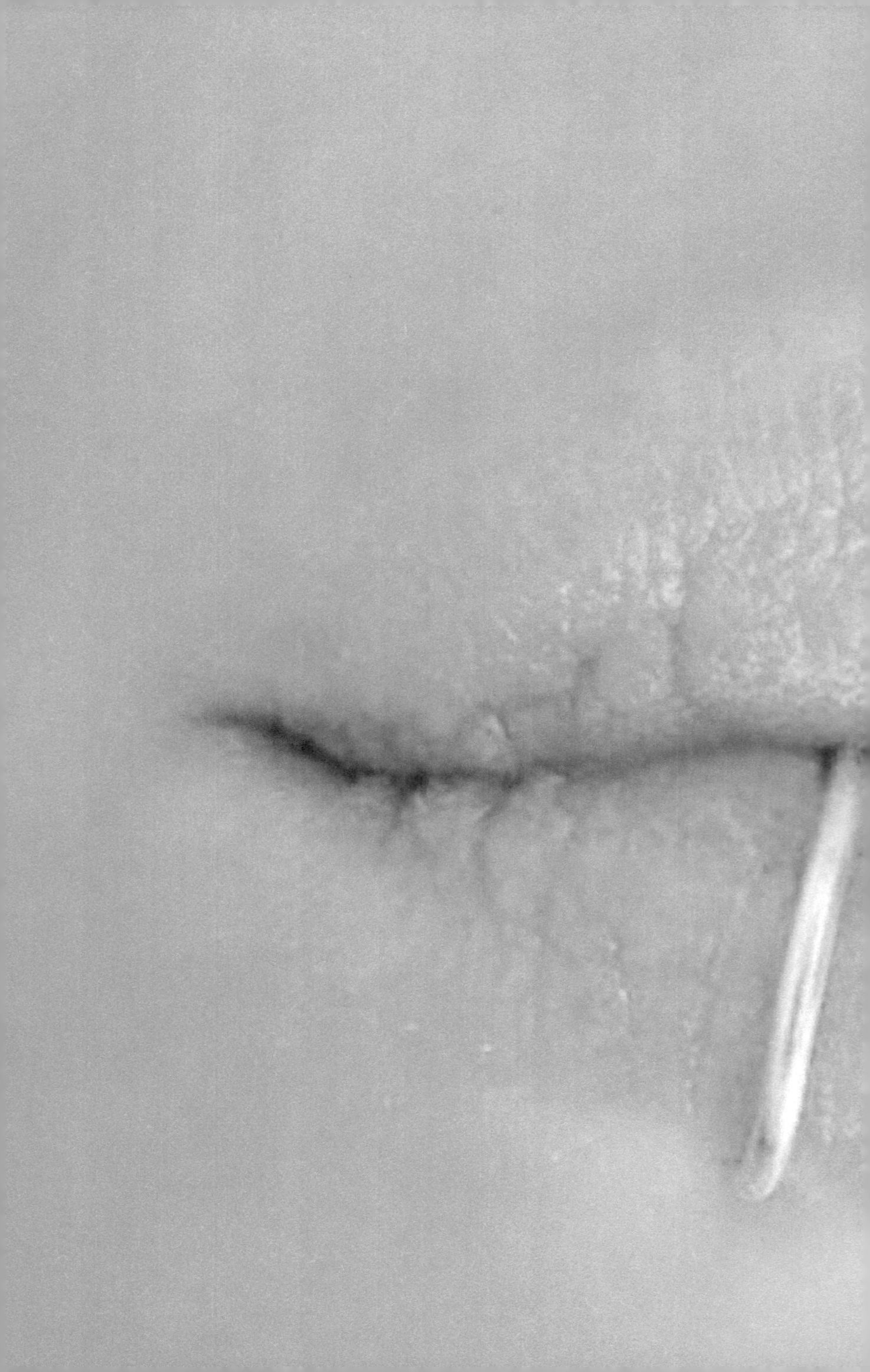

CHAPTER 13

Ava

Fuck. Fuck…fuck…fuck. Why did I always resort to being a bitch with him? He did or said nothing to me that warranted me speaking to him like that. And before I had the chance to say anything, even try to apologize, he'd gone upstairs.

Who was I kidding? I knew full well why I wanted to alienate him. The past few days scared the shit out of me.

We were *getting along*.

And that couldn't happen. Because if we started getting along, then these feelings that were fluttering around in my belly would start making a mess inside my head. I'd start making decisions with the wrong part of my body: my heart instead of my brain.

So, bottom line, we couldn't get along.

"Hey, girl," Macie said as she came bounding into the kitchen. Her smile was bright as she slung an overnight bag across her shoulder.

That could only mean one thing.

"So, I'm guessing Jace called you?"

She froze as if caught with her hand in the cookie jar. Her look of disbelief was quickly veiled by a more neutral face, but it was enough for me to know.

"Macie." My motherly tone was raging.

"I'm fine, Ava. We had a long talk last night, and he seems ready to move on with what I'm looking for. He agreed to us hanging out, spending time together, before taking the *plunge* again." She literally used air quotes.

"You mean to tell me you're packing an overnight bag and you have no plans of having sex tonight?"

She went about packing up a bag of snacks and food items. Enough food to feed her and an army. That was when I knew something was really up.

"Macie..."

She knew I wanted answers.

"OK, fine. I'm going to his place for the weekend. So, yeah, maybe by the end of the weekend it might happen, ya never know."

No amount of warnings would stop her, she'd made up her mind. Maybe Jace would be a man of his word. He wasn't the worst guy she'd been with, and he made her happy when they were together and not fighting.

Gathering her things, she started for the door.

"Be careful," I said.

She stopped and swung back toward me.

"I'm going in smart, Ave, don't worry. This time I won't let things get out of hand with him. If he really seems like he's not on board for a relationship, I'll come back home. I'm good. We really did have a good talk." She seemed more levelheaded than ever. "So, it looks like it's just you and Logan this weekend."

What the fuck?

"What do you mean?" The high pitch of my voice did nothing to hide my panic.

Macie was halfway out the door, grabbing her parka from the hook, as she answered me.

"Becca and Ty went to see Savannah this weekend. You have fun, too."

And she shut the door.

The walls seemed to close in around me.

Suddenly this four-bedroom, three-floor townhouse seemed way too small. How was I going to do this? Logan and I, alone, in the house, all weekend together.

And I had no plans made yet. I'd have to get something going. Call an old hookup and get out of here tonight or tomorrow.

Then I heard his thudding footsteps coming down the stairs. Amazing that in socked feet he could sound like an entire army on these floors. He came bounding into the room, a giddy smile on his face as he ran to the window.

"It's already snowing, Tink. Did you see outside?" As he pulled up the blinds, he seemed oblivious to how I'd just treated him, which made me feel even worse.

I peeked around his large frame, and sure enough, there was already a coating on the grass. Grabbing the remote, Logan turned on the weather station.

"Shit, they're calling for a major storm. At least eighteen inches by tomorrow, maybe two feet by Sunday."

How did I not know about this? Usually my mom would be calling to ask if I was prepared, had enough food, my boots, yada, yada. Sure enough, when I pulled out my phone, I saw two missed calls from her.

"So, I know the last thing you want to do is probably watch a movie with me, but I thought you, me, and Macie could, I don't know, do that tonight. Maybe make some popcorn or hot chocolate? That's what we always did at home when we were stuck inside with a storm."

He didn't know.

He had no idea it was just him and me.

But I didn't feel like being the one to tell him.

"Yeah, maybe." Fiddling with my phone, I started toward my room. "I have to make a phone call."

My mom's number was dialing before I made it to the top of the stairs.

"Hey, honey, busy day? I tried reaching you a few times, wanted to find out if you're ready for the snow coming your way," she asked.

"Busy week." Closing my door, I fell onto my bed fully prepared to come clean with her on the phone.

I needed to tell someone.

"You OK, Ava?"

Such a loaded question.

"Yeah, Mom, I'm OK. I just, ugh, can I ask you a question?"

The silence that followed was unusual. She always responded immediately.

"This sounds serious. Are you in trouble?" she finally responded.

"No!"

Well, not the type she thought, anyway. Though, I had no idea what trouble she was thinking I was in.

"Well, then what's up, my darling? Don't keep a mother on eggshells like this."

"OK, so when you left Dad, you, umm...Christ, this is hard to talk to your mom about."

She chuckled through the line.

"Spit it out, babe. We're both adults, I can take it," she said.

"Did you have any boyfriends after Dad?"

There was no hesitation in her answer, whether I wanted there to be or not.

"Of course I did. I was just really good at keeping it from you and your sister." She let out a belly laugh on the other side of the line. "I went on dates, and there was one guy I got kind of serious with at one point. But I chose not to bring even him around. Unless I thought it was going to end in, well, marriage, I didn't want anyone getting close to you girls and then walking out on us."

That made sense, and I respected that. It probably would've been hard if we'd gotten attached to someone else and then they dipped.

"Why do you ask? Did you think your mom would die a spinster?" She laughed again.

"No...nothing like that."

I sat back on my bed, surrounded by my pillows as my eyes were drawn to the window. The soft flakes drifted through the sky, lazily making their way to the ground. It was beautiful, but it reminded me of what was waiting for me downstairs and the anxiety ratcheted within.

"Mom, how were you able to be with someone else after Dad? Like, how were you not scared that another guy wasn't going to do the same things to you? Hurt you..."

The hum of her contemplation was loud through the silent phone line.

"We try to protect our children the best we can as parents," she said. "But there was no protecting you from what he did, was there?"

The hitch in her voice told me she was crying, and that broke my heart. My intention wasn't to open old wounds for her.

"Mom..." I barely whispered into my phone.

"I'm OK, baby, it just hurts a momma's heart to know you had to witness all of that."

She blew out a loud huff as if to gain strength.

"Life must go on, Ava. All people aren't bad, and you have to trust your instincts and surround yourself with the good ones. Once you do that, you'll feel comfortable opening up and giving yourself over to them." She stopped, the pause giving me time to digest her words. "You obviously have someone in your life you have concerns about. Talk to me."

Moms.

I guessed this was exactly why I called, but the thought of telling her about Logan made me nauseous. For so many reasons.

"Yeah," I said, unsteadily. "It's...my roommate, the guy who moved in this semester. So there's a whole slew of issues."

She remained silent.

"I, um, have some feelings for him, and it's really confusing me because he has a past that bothers me, plus he's my roommate. Macie and I made a pact that neither of us would get involved with him, for obvious reasons. And to top it off, he's an asshole to me most of the time. Do you know what he calls me, Mom? Tink. He calls me Tink!"

All I heard was a muffled giggle on the other end of the line.

"Oh my god, are you laughing? What about this do you find funny?"

She stifled her giggles, finally.

"Most of it. Most except the part about his past. Tell me about that part, babe."

The snow fell heavier outside and the mountain range was no longer visible. The storm Logan spoke about was really happening, and I was going to be stuck here with him, alone.

"Well, last year, he, um, did something to Lanie, the roommate who moved out, that really upset her. He touched her, held her down, and wouldn't let her go until her now boyfriend came and pulled him off her. She freaked out."

I heard my mom's breathing increase slightly as she listened, but she remained quiet. And so did I.

But then I gave in.

"That doesn't concern you?" My exasperation came through. I guess I was looking for her to tell me to run. Run far away from this guy, and I was shocked she hadn't already.

"Of course it does, Ava. Is there anything else you can tell me? I mean, you're living with him now. Plus you're telling me you now have feelings for him, so there has to be something else you see in this Logan guy. Is there more to the story you're not telling me? Or is that it?"

"Well, yeah," I started, then stopped.

"Honey, if you want me to really help you, you need to talk to me, really talk to me. Or, if you already know the answer to your own question, then just move on."

"OK, fine. He was drunk when he did it. Then left school last year to enter a program. He's been sober since and works really hard at it. Turns out he's a really nice guy. So nice that Lanie *and* her boyfriend are literally friends with him now." I threw my hand on my forehead in my own frustration as I stared at the ceiling, somehow thinking the answer to all my issues would be written cryptically up there. "But I've been a bitch to him, and I don't know why, well I guess I do, but I'm not sure I can forget what he did to Lanie. But I want to. And then there's Macie, who would be so pissed at me if I did something with him..."

"Whoa, Ava, slow down, baby. You're going to run out of breath."

And I did. Slow down. And took a few breaths.

"What do I do, Mom?"

"Well, you need to decide one thing. Are you comfortable when he's around? How does he make you feel? Nervous like he's going to hurt you? Or nervous like you've got that feeling in your belly because, well, you know what I mean. He sounds like he's repented for his sin, Lanie and her boyfriend have forgiven him. He's never done anything to you, at least that I'm aware of. And as far as Macie is concerned, I understand the pact you made, and it was probably for good reason. But sometimes you need to take risks in life. If this feels right, this might be one worth taking."

Was she telling me to go for it?

"Ava, listen, I've never met this boy. I can't speak with confidence that you should move forward with something with him. But what I do have confidence in is your intuition about things like this. I trust you. You would never put yourself in harm's way. Trust your gut."

Trust my gut.

"But he calls me Tink, Mom!"

"And your little friend in kindergarten, the one you said you were going to marry, remember him? I think his name was Pete. What did he used to call you? Wasn't it something like 'dragon breath'? Boys make fun of the ones they like."

Trust my gut.

"Thanks Mom."

WHEN I GOT DOWNSTAIRS, LOGAN WAS ON THE COUCH, FEET propped on the table, a blanket covering him from head to toe. My blanket from the other night. I went to the kitchen and took out the popcorn maker, kernels, oil, and butter. He looked over the back of the couch a couple times, acknowledging what I was doing, but left me to it. Once I had two large bowls filled with hot buttery popcorn, I approached him.

"It's just you and me. Macie left for Jace's."

He stared up, an unreadable look across those crystal blue eyes of his. Then he lifted the blanket, inviting me under with him.

And I went.

CHAPTER 14
Logan

When she came to stand next to me, popcorn bowls in hand, my heart expanded. I knew it was her version of an apology for being bitchy earlier. When she then agreed to join me on the couch, under the blanket, my heart did a flip. She was now cozied up next to me, our bodies dangerously close to one another, our bowls balanced on our laps, as we watched *Dune*, the movie. I lied and told her I hadn't seen it yet. It made it easier for me to concentrate on the fact that she was so close to me; I didn't have to focus on the movie.

"I love Timothee Chalamet, don't you?" she asked.

I'd never really thought about it, but I did like him in this movie. And I loved the smile he put on her face.

"He's good at what he does, yeah."

When I learned Macie would be gone for the weekend, so many thoughts ran through my mind. But of course, the most important one of all: we were alone.

That brought me to what I was feeling next.

Nervous as hell. The flip my heart did converted to butterflies in my stomach the size of atlas moths, flopping around, fighting for space. Every time she reached into her bowl, her elbow hit my arm. When she adjusted herself under the blanket, her bare legs aligned with mine, the warmth of them burning through my sweatpants.

It seemed we both were willing to put aside our differences for the time being. I wasn't sure why, maybe to extend an olive branch for the sake of our night alone. Or maybe we were tired of being mean to one another.

As it played on the screen, the only thing we talked about was the movie. We ignored all the big elephants in the room. We ignored *how* we've been treating one another since we've met. We ignored *why* we've been treating one another that way. We ignored all the huge emotions we've both been feeling.

And maybe that was OK. Maybe this wasn't the time for talking.

"I have to pee," she said, peeling the blanket from us. "Can you pause it?"

As I reached for the remote, I caught a glimpse of the tiny sleep shorts she was wearing, that nice curve of the lower part of her ass hanging out from the bottom. My eyes watched her sway across the entire room until the bathroom door closed.

Fuck. I hurried to adjust my swollen dick before she returned.

Our bowls of corn were almost empty, so I dumped mine into hers just as I heard the flush of the toilet. By looking at my phone, I forced myself to not watch her walk back.

She grabbed the remote as she climbed back under the blanket, as if we'd been doing this together every weekend this semester. She made it seem so...normal for us. Meanwhile, every breath was a struggle, and I had no idea where we even were in the movie. All I could focus on was the next time some part of her was going to touch me again.

"Where's my popcorn?" she asked.

"Not much left, thought it made sense to combine them."

She didn't appear to think much of it. But as she reached into the bowl, her hand brushed against mine and her eyes pivoted from the screen. She stared into the bowl, both our hands frozen.

"Sorry," I said.

Our eyes connected. And for the first time since meeting this spitfire, pain in the ass, gorgeous goddess, her eyes held true warmth in them as she looked at me.

"It's OK." But then she yanked her hand out of the bowl as if it ignited from my touch.

She went back to watching the movie, but it was futile for me. All I could think about was *touching her*.

I felt on the brink of my fantasies coming true, but I didn't want to fuck it up. I felt like that could happen so easily with her and her temperamental ways. I never knew if I'd have Tink or Ava.

So far, Ava was sitting next to me.

Suddenly, the lights flickered a few times. As we stared around the house, waiting to see what would happen, the TV went fuzzy.

"Lost the cable," I said.

We both raced to the closest window, pulling up the shade to check outside.

"Holy shit," she cried. "How much is that already?"

Checking for something in the backyard to gauge the amount of snow we'd gotten, I could only use the door of the opposing townhouse.

"I'd say over eight inches already."

The sky glowed bright orange from the moon trying to fight through the snow-filled clouds. In the distance, there was a flash of light that grabbed our attention.

"Was that what I think it was?" Ava asked.

"Lightning, looks like we're in for some thunder snow," I told her.

Her head jerked toward me at my words, disbelief all over her face. She reached out, her hand on my shoulder, turning me to face her.

"Thunder snow? What the hell are you talking about?"

I was speechless as her hand remained on my arm. I wanted to pull her close, wrap my arms around her tiny waist, and bring her mouth to mine.

But the fear of Tink making an appearance, of Ava truly hating me, and completely misreading the little clues I thought I picked up on this past week paralyzed me.

Instead, I went back to examining the impending storm.

"Yeah, you've never heard of thunder snow? It doesn't happen often, but it happens. Could mean we might have a power outage." I started pulling away from the window. "Maybe I should look for some candles, just in case."

Ava held me in place, her brilliant green eyes gazing at me through long dark lashes.

"We can do that in a minute," she said, her voice a bit husky. "Let's keep watching the snow. It's pretty, isn't it?"

She leaned against the windowsill, her chin in her hands, as her breath left a cloud on the glass.

"It is," I said, but only looked at her.

The temptation to touch her was unrelenting, and my hands trembled at my sides. My thoughts were consumed with everything about her: the slope of her neck as her head tilted up to look at the snow; the way wisps of her dark hair fell across her forehead; the tiny freckles across the bridge of her nose; the sparkle of her nose ring; the hole above her eyebrow where a brow ring once was; the pink of her full lips as she licked them.

"I can feel you staring at me," she said.

"Sorry, Ava."

She suddenly turned toward me and smiled, and I couldn't help but smile back.

"I like when you use my name," she said, "and not that awful nickname." Her smile faltered somewhat as her gaze returned to the falling snow.

I knew *Tink* bothered her, and I guess at a point that was the intention.

"I like the nickname I have for you."

Her head slowly swiveled, her cheek laying on her arms folded on the sill. We had resorted to kneeling on the floor below the window for comfort.

"Really?" she asked, the sarcasm thick.

"One of the things I like most about you, and at the same time pisses me off, is your sassy attitude. I don't think you'd be you without it, Ava. You shouldn't change for anyone."

Her drilling look made me self-conscious, and I looked away, staring out the window again.

"You're a strong person, and that's good, that's important, especially for a woman. Yeah, you're exactly the way you should be."

Looking back, I noticed a pink flush dotted her cheeks and found its way down to her chest. She remained quiet and still as she continued to survey the snow, which had increased in its tenacity.

"It's really coming down out there now," I said, gesturing outside. "Since we've been at the window, I'd say another inch fell. What do you think?"

She didn't answer me as she remained unmoving, stoic.

"I'm sorry," she said, out of nowhere.

"What?" I asked. "For what?"

Ava got up from the floor and made her way back to the couch. Her emerald eyes looked up at me once she sat, beckoning me to join her as she patted the cushion next to her. I joined her, attempting to cover us with the blanket. But she pulled back, needing space it seemed, sitting with crossed legs in the corner of the couch.

She sat quietly, and I didn't push her to talk. If I was going to get an apology out of her, I'd give her the time she needed.

"Well," she started, then stopped. Those green eyes looked everywhere but at me. Her teeth fiddled with her lip ring, something I noticed she did when nervous. "I've been kinda mean, wouldn't ya say? So, I'm sorry for how I've been, how I've treated you. It's not who I am to be like that, and it's really been bothering me that I've been doing it."

Once she was done talking, her eyes settled on mine. Hers glistened with the start of unshed tears, that beginning moisture that builds up. It's truly amazing how hearing her say sorry and seeing her almost cry made the past month of me wanting to hate her vanish.

Gone. Instantly.

I wanted to scoop her up in my arms and tell her everything would be OK.

Instead, I chose to encourage more discussion.

"Do you know why? Did I do something?" I asked.

"No," she insisted, her head shaking emphatically. "Well, not exactly..."

Crack.

There was a bolt of lightning and a loud boom of thunder and the room went black.

"Oh shit!" we both yelled.

"Christ, it's dark in here," Ava said.

"Let me get my phone." Once my phone light lit the room, I could see the panic on her face. "You good?"

"Not a fan of no power, to be honest," she said. "I have some candles in my room, I should go get them."

She started to get up, but I held my hand out to stop her.

"You stay, I'll get them. Where are they?"

After putting her phone light on for her, I raced up the stairs to retrieve two candles and a lighter from her desk. I also grabbed some extra blankets from both our rooms, unaware of how long we'd be without power or heat.

"Here we go," I said once I returned. As I lit them, the room took on an ethereal glow combined with the brightness coming from the snow through the windows. "Turn off your phone, conserve its battery."

I covered her with a blanket, then returned to my side of the couch.

"We don't have to keep talking about, ya know, what we were before. I appreciate the apology, Ava, I do. Thank you."

As she pulled the blanket to her chin, she stretched her legs out, her feet landing on my lap. It felt good, but kind of intimate at the same time. I didn't know where to put my hands, so I laid one on the back of the couch, the other to my side.

"I disagree. I think I need to tell you what's been going on with me. You deserve that."

The determination in her words, her voice, took me by surprise yet again. As we sat across from one another, her confidence seemed to drain as her shoulders deflated and her eyes deflected.

She pulled her feet from me, ripped the blanket off as her hands went around her knees, and tucked herself into a ball. A protective ball.

"When Lanie came to us last semester about you, about the living situation, she was quite convincing, regardless of what went on between the two of you."

I felt my fingers twitch with the stress of the topic.

"Becca was, of course, fine with you living here, and I get that, you guys are good friends. Macie wasn't a hard sell, she loves everyone, to a fault." She gave a cynical laugh after that. "That left me. And if I objected, well, you had nowhere to live and wouldn't be able to come back to school. I felt the pressure."

Shit. I had no idea any of this had happened. From the sounds of it, neither had Becca. She told me there were no issues.

"All I knew was you were the guy who touched Lanie inappropriately, got his ass kicked by Xander for it, then left school due to a drinking problem. And I was being asked to have you as my roommate."

"Ava..."

She put up her hand, quieting me.

"Please let me finish." She settled back into her tight little ball. "There's a lot in my past that went into my judgments about you without even meeting you. Where do I even start?"

As she asked herself that question, she threw her arms up over her head, almost in frustration. Her eyes were dark in the glow of the candlelight as it cast odd shadows in the room.

"I guess you start at the beginning." I hoped my words encouraged her, I knew this couldn't be easy.

She sat staring at the flame of the candle flickering, doing its dance, for a minute, gathering her thoughts. That minute stretched into two, and I wondered if our talk wasn't going to happen.

"My father used to hit my mom," she said, barely a whisper. "Apparently it started when she was pregnant with me, the fucking bastard. They didn't know that we knew, my sister and me, but we knew. She could only stifle her screams so much. We were young, but we knew what was going on."

I sat, frozen with her confession, my heart breaking for her.

"Did he..."

She shook her head before I could finish.

"No, he never hit us, thankfully. But I would hear them in the bedroom, I know he forced himself on her as well. Made her do things when she didn't want to. Eventually my mom left him. She was stronger than a lot of women, so who knows if he would have started hitting us too, we won't know. She moved us in with our grandparents. Turns out my dad had a drug problem, and their lack of money had a lot to do with it."

"Ava, I'm sorry."

She pooh-poohed my concern for her, shaking her hand and head as she adjusted herself on the couch. There seemed to be an increase in nervous energy as she couldn't stop moving, now sitting on the arm of the sofa.

"We're good now, the three of us are really good. My grandparents helped us get on our feet, and my mom did a great job, took really good care of us, and we're like the best of friends. But it took its toll. I mean, I have this cloud over me when it comes to trusting guys, I think. Very classic when it comes to all that psychology bullshit."

Well, no shit. And I really fucked this up.

"Ava..."

"I'm not done," she said. Her hands twisted together in a knot as she stared down at her bouncing toes covered in striped socks. "I'm very impressed with what you've accomplished with your recovery over the past, I guess almost, year. I really am, Logan. But at the same time, it scares me. You scare me. And probably not for the reason you think."

She let out a pent-up breath and then jumped from the sofa to her feet. Her frenetic pacing across the room had my head spinning, no clue where this was headed.

"I know you remember when we first saw each other, the first day we met. When we were both in the registrar's office. When you came downstairs back here, I was stunned to realize it was actually you, the guy from campus." She laughed, almost to herself, like I wasn't even there. "Macie knew, though, but I didn't want to believe her. But when you came downstairs, I was...pissed."

She turned and looked right at me. Her moss green eyes, that color after a long rain has saturated the ground, stared deep into me, through me. The dancing light reflected off her irises.

"I was so mad...because I liked you. I was immediately attracted to you, and that never happens to me."

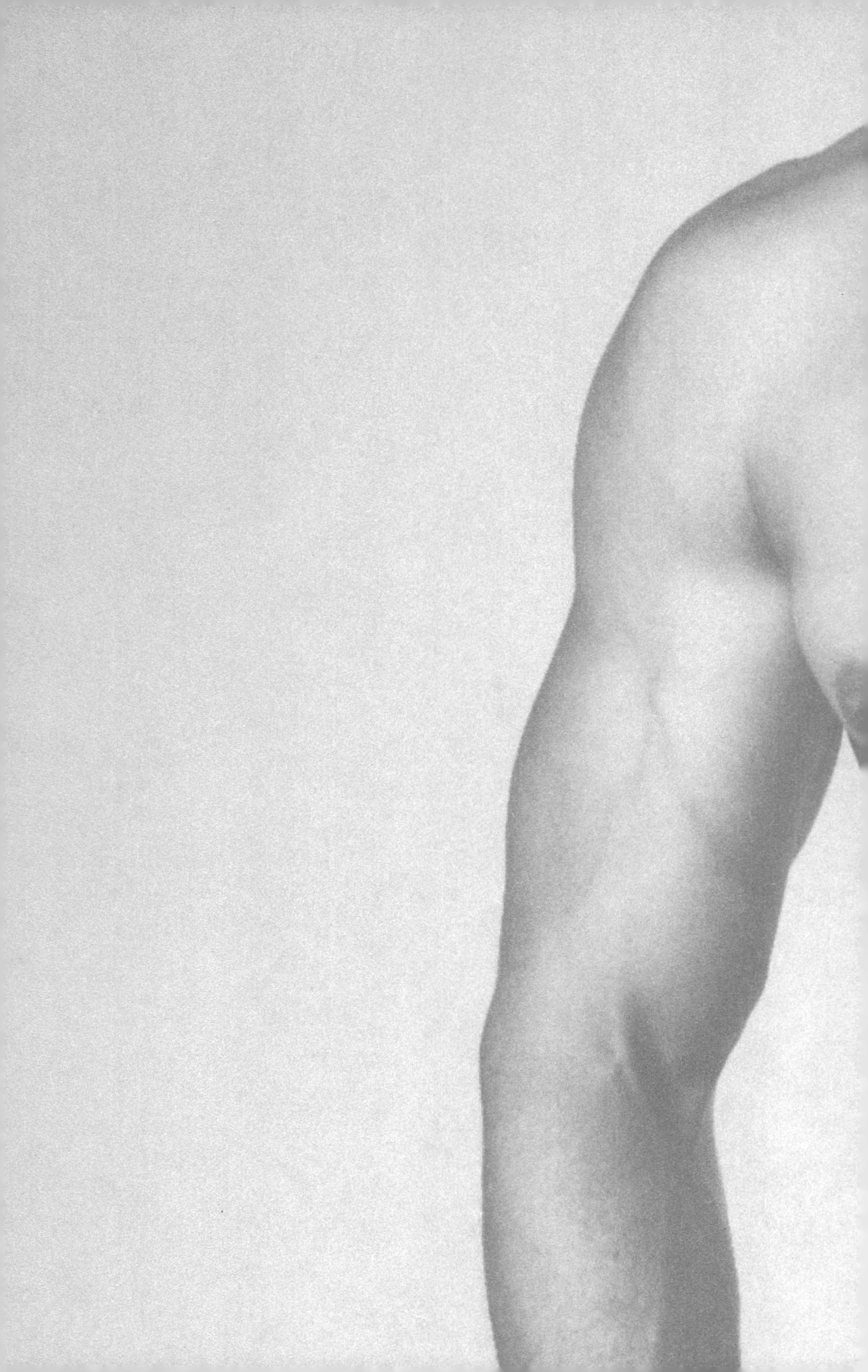

CHAPTER 15

Logan

She liked me. She was attracted to me. Inside my own head, I was reminded of the cartoon "Rudolph" when he finds out that the female reindeer Clarice likes him. *"I'm cute, I'm cute, she said I'm cuuuuute."*

"So, you've been mean to me because you like me?" I asked, a bit of jibe in my voice as a smile took over my face. It might have even been a bit cocky for the moment, but I tried to make it a joke.

It helped to lighten the mood. She smiled back before coming to sit, this time closer.

"Well, when you put it that way, it sounds so fifth grade."

Her laugh was melodic, deep and from the belly. It made her eyes crinkle at the sides as she smiled hard and I noticed, for the first time, a crease-like dimple in her left cheek.

"But I can't like you."

And she was serious.

"Because I'm a recovering alcoholic." My response made her take pause. Her eyebrows shot high on her forehead, the whites of her eyes glowing in the dim room.

"No!" She yelled her answer at me. "Logan, no. I mean it. I'm really proud of you and how well you're doing. In the beginning, I was nervous about your drinking, but getting to know you, it doesn't concern me at all. You're so dedicated to your sobriety and everything about improving yourself."

None of this was making much sense. She'd been paying attention to my actions, how I'm taking care of myself. She's attracted to me, even liked me. Yet says she couldn't.

"So, it has to be what happened with me and Lanie."

That scared me, because I was never going to be proud of that night. I'd never forgive myself for it, even though Lanie had. And now to learn of Ava's past, it all made sense.

"I wanted that to be why I hated you," she said. She reached out, her fingernail mindlessly running along the seam of my sweatpants on my calf. "I hated that you did that to her. Then I saw how Lanie was with you a couple weeks ago in the Student Center, her and Xander. I mean, they adore you. Who am I to judge you if they no longer do?"

She looked up after saying that. The impact of her words hitting me.

"There are plenty of reasons for me to not be a good choice for you, Ava."

As I said the words I didn't want her to listen to, my hand went to hers on my leg, covering it, holding it, squeezing it. Our fingers threaded together, her tiny hand in mine, as my thumb rubbed the tender skin on the back of her hand.

"But there's still one reason I haven't told you," she said. "Macie and I made a pact before you moved in. We promised each other that neither of us would fall for you or hook up with you, that it would be bad for the house."

So I was deemed off-limits by the two of them. That was interesting indeed.

But being off-limits seemed to be the only thing keeping her from wanting to be with me.

Standing, I pulled her with me. Our hands remained entwined as our gazes lingered, both of us shifting on our feet. Eventually, one hand looped behind her neck, the dark tendrils of her short hair filtering between my fingers. I watched her lips part as a soft sound emanated from her mouth.

Leaning down, my mouth against her ear, I whispered, "So, I'm your forbidden secret, is that what you're telling me?"

Her cheek rubbed against my mouth in what seemed to be her validation of our current situation. My lips rubbed along her cheek and back to her ear. I found myself nibbling on the many earrings along her lobe, then moving my lips back to whisper to her.

"Ava, is that what you want? Do you want me to be your forbidden secret?"

Pulling back, I held her face in my hands, forcing her to look at me. Her emerald eyes stared back.

"I need you to tell me, I need to hear you say it," I said.

Her face tilted in my hold, her eyes fluttering closed. But just as quickly, her lids slid open and her cheeks bobbed up and down in my hold.

"Yes, I want that," she whispered. "So much."

My forehead pressed against hers to feel the warmth of her skin. The desire to kiss her was strong, but I needed to proceed with caution. My head and heart had to be the ones thinking, not my dick. I couldn't fuck this up.

Backing away, but keeping my hands on her arms, I held my finger up.

"One sec."

I placed a bunch of the blankets and pillows on the floor, making a pallet. The candles on the table offered a glow above us. And even though my phone might die, I chose to put some soft music on in the background.

Kneeling on the blankets, I reached out a hand for Ava.

"Come here," I said.

Taking it, she knelt with me, our faces close. I kept some distance between us so I could look at her, admire her.

"You're beautiful, Ava."

I stroked her cheek with the backs of my fingers, down to her clavicle, over to the top of her chest. As I did, her nipples hardened under the tight tee she wore. That was when I noticed the piercings on both her nipples, and fuck, that was hot. It took everything in me to not grab them, pinch them, but I stayed the course.

"So freaking beautiful, skin so soft."

My finger trailed up her neck and landed on her full lips, pulling down the bottom one.

"I've dreamt of kissing these perfect cherry lips."

I pushed my thumb into her mouth, against her tongue, getting it wet. Finally able to run my finger along that damn sexy lip ring. As I rubbed the wetness along her lip, it glistened in the candlelight, begging for me to kiss it, bite it. The moan I elicited from her was deep in her throat, and my dick reacted. It swelled against my pants, and I was desperate for her to touch me.

"Then do it, Logan," she said, her words breathy. "Kiss me, please."

Our lips collided as my mouth claimed hers. Our tongues fought a battle that started weeks ago, and I had finally been granted permission to strike. My lips found that ring, pulling it into my mouth gently, giving it a tug. First with my lips, then my teeth. My tongue dipped back inside her mouth, a delicate dance between us. Her hands raked through my hair, down my back, to the hem of my shirt. She lifted it up and over my head.

Pushing away from me, she looked at me in awe. Her finger marked a hot trail across my chest as it dragged down my torso, over the band of my pants, a nail teasing to go in. Her eyes came back up to mine, those green orbs sparkling as they shimmered in the glow of the snowy light from the window.

"I've never seen someone with a body like yours, not up close," she said. "Every part of you is like it's carved of marble, like you were made from a mold of perfection."

Her compliment swirled inside me, creating a tornado of heat fighting to get out. My fingers itched to move, to touch her skin, her body, as she knelt as an offering in front of me.

"Ava." Her name came out as a tortured whisper. "May I take your shirt off? And touch you?"

Unexpectedly, she gripped my face in her hands, forcing me to look directly at her. Her look was soft, though her grip wasn't.

"Logan," she said. "We're doing this, and I want it. I love that you're asking for my consent, and here it is. For all of it. You don't need to ask again. You have my permission to do anything to me."

I nodded as best I could as she continued to hold me in her steel grip. As she released me, her lips came to mine, a soft kiss to replace the wicked hold.

She whispered against my lips. "Is that what you needed?"

I pressed my forehead to hers, suddenly holding back tears, and nodded. When we pulled away, she wiped at my eyes and then kissed the delicate skin there.

"My *tender Tank*," she said, then laughed lightly.

I didn't realize how important her consent was. Obviously, it became more important after hearing her thoughts from our first weeks together. But getting it put my mind, and my heart, at ease.

And roused my cock.

"I'd like you to get back to work, Mr. Somers," she said.

"Don't need to tell me twice."

My finger went to the edge of her shirt along her collarbone, following it to her cleavage. A spot I'd fantasized about many times. As the tips of my fingers grazed the swell of her breast, my hand flattened on her skin. The anticipation of seeing her piercing was too much. I pulled her shirt down until her peaked nipple popped out, complete with a silver bar ring. A perfect dark circle surrounded it, begging to be put in my mouth. My mouth watered at the notion.

"Ava, christ, you are so fucking hot."

My fingers were going to do some magic first. Gripping the bar and her nipple between two fingers, I gently twisted and pulled while watching her. Ava's head fell back as her mouth opened.

"Logan," she moaned.

Good, she liked it.

The other breast needed to be freed. I pulled at the material of her shirt, and it popped out. The sight of both her white, smooth breasts in front of me, waiting for me to touch them, was overwhelming.

"Ava, fuck, your tits are amazing." My hands grabbed them both, pushing them together as my thumbs flicked the bars on her nipples.

"Do you want me to take my shirt off?" she asked.

"No," I said, shaking my head. "I love what the shirt is doing, offering them up to me. They're fucking perfect, do you know that?"

Bending down, I took one plump nipple in my mouth. I couldn't wait any longer.

It was ecstasy. As I pulled it deep in my mouth, my tongue and teeth alternated having their way. She loved when my teeth grazed at the metal and skin, moaning loudly as she pulled my head tighter against her chest, clutching me, tugging at my hair.

Moving to the other breast, I did the same. My mouth worked her one nipple, while my fingers pulled and pinched at the other.

Ava writhed against me. Her hand slid down my side, across to my front, gripping my cock through my sweats. As she pumped me through the material, I sucked on her tits, back and forth, with a fury.

But then I pulled away. And she looked confused as her hand stilled.

I needed more.

My hand went to the hem of her shirt, and I started a slow lift. She raised her arms as my hands slid up the sides of her torso, pushing her shirt up as I did. Once the shirt lifted over her tits, I took each one in my mouth for a brief second, savoring the feel in my mouth.

The tiny sounds coming from her confirmed she approved.

As I pushed the shirt over her head, her hands went around my neck.

We were both shirtless.

With our bodies together, her tits pressed against my chest, their firmness felt exactly how I imagined.

Absolute perfection.

We were face to face, chest to chest.

"You're one sexy forbidden secret," I told her.

Her hands went to the band of my pants, pushing them down. I did the same to her, and her tiny sleep shorts slid over her round ass with ease. As they did, my hands came to rest on two firm, naked ass cheeks. My finger searched and found the strip of cloth riding up her ass.

A thong. *Fuuuck.*

My sweats were at my knees, as far as they could go in our position. I stood, allowing them to fall to my ankles. She rose as well and stepped out of her shorts. Her hands went to the thin straps of her thong on her hips.

"Don't." My hands landed on hers, stopping her. "Turn around."

She acquiesced and slowly spun her tiny frame around. I missed the sight of her full, round tits, but fuck if the sight of that firm ass didn't make up for it. She tilted her head slightly, her eyes looking for mine.

"Like what you see?"

The seduction in those words almost toppled me.

"You are exquisite." As I said that, my finger went to the crack of her ass, lifting the cloth. Gripping it, I pulled on it firmly, knowing it put pressure on areas of her that mattered.

"Ahh," she moaned. "Logan, what are you doing?"

"Don't worry," I said. "Does it feel good?"

All she did was nod, the words caught in a moan deep in her throat. I continued to pull on the material with one hand, as the other rubbed the skin of her ass. Moving around her hip, I found the triangle of cloth covering the front. Rubbing the mound it concealed, I searched out the hard nub near the top. I found her clit and gripped it between my thumb and forefinger, giving it a little tug. All while continuing to lift on the thong.

"Oh my god, Logan..."

Reaching further down, I felt her wetness saturating her underwear. She was soaked already.

My fingers rubbed along the length of her pussy, through the material, from top to bottom, while I pulled the thong up from behind. It tightened against her clit, allowing me to pull on it through the lace as she writhed in front of me.

"Fuck," she said, her words almost breathless. "Logan, what the fuck? I'm gonna come."

Her body convulsed in my arms, attempting to bend forward, but I wouldn't give way. My grip on both the thong and her clit strong as I held her against my chest. Alternating between pinching her clit and rubbing the length of her pussy seemed to elicit the best response from her. As I rubbed, those sweet pussy lips escaped the lace, and I got a feel of them. It tempted me to move her panties to the side and sink my fingers into her at that moment.

But that would be later.

Right then was all for her.

Her thrashing calmed as her head fell against my chest. I removed my finger from her thong, rubbing the soft skin of her bottom as I stroked her clit. She gripped my hand up front, stilling it from any further movement. Her ragged breaths were settling as her fingers threaded with mine.

"Christ, man. You work wonders with these hands."

Spinning her to face me, I gripped under her ass and lifted her from the ground. Walking us on my knees, I placed her on the couch.

"Imagine what my mouth can do," I said, a sly grin across my face.

She smiled as I admired what lay in front of me. Her short black hair framed her face as it stuck up in all directions. There were piercings on her face that sparkled in the glowing light of the room. Her heavy breasts fell a bit to the side, that gap between them beckoning my tongue. She had a toned stomach accentuated by a tiny waist.

She was so perfect for me in every way.

She lifted her ass to allow me to remove her thong. A small triangle of dark hair was revealed, trimmed and neat. I wanted to take my time, use my hands and my mouth from her feet to her thighs, but I couldn't wait. My hands immediately went to her thighs, grasping them, separating them.

A growl came from deep within me.

"You're bare."

She looked at me with hooded eyes.

"Is that OK?" she asked.

"It's more than OK, it's fucking hot."

My restraint was waning. My dick was fully engorged, and all I wanted to do was be inside her. But my desire to taste her and make her come again won.

My fingers raked up her inner thighs, forcing her legs to spread further. Her pussy was a deep pink next to her pale white legs, the lips glistening with the moisture of her climax.

I kissed her upper thigh, my tongue licking a heated trail toward her heated core. Her hands gripped my head and her thighs crushed my skull as I got closer.

My tongue dipped into her entrance, deep and penetrating. She tasted like candy as I plunged in and out, fucking her with my mouth. A finger found her clit, pulling it from its hood. As I rubbed, my mouth moved to sucking on her pussy lips. Ava's back arched from the couch, and I pushed her back down, keeping her in place with my face.

"Feels good, sweetheart?" I asked, my words a breathy against the wet skin of her pussy.

"Yeeesss."

"Well, hold on."

I moved my mouth to the swollen clit, sucking it deep into my mouth. Flicking it with my tongue, swirling it around my mouth, it danced back and forth between my lips. At the same time, my hand slid down her wetness, dipping into her entrance.

One.

Then two.

Two fingers plunged deep into her, curving up to find that spot that not many did. My fingers continued pushing deeper and deeper, in and out, until I heard that gasp from her. I knew I'd found *the spot*.

My mouth sucked on her clit, slow and steady, pulling it into my mouth and letting it go in a steady rhythm. My tongue laved circles around the tip. All while my fingers continued pounding into her, making sure to hit that spot on each return. I felt the walls of her pussy clench around me, pushing at the invasion, then letting it back in.

The muscles in her thighs tensed as she pulled at my hair, her ass lifting from the couch once again. I lifted with her, allowing her body to ride the approaching wave. My mouth and fingers never stopped their wanted assault as her labored breathing and lengthened moans increased.

"Logan," she said through gritted teeth while pulling at my hair. "I can't take this anymore."

"Let it happen," I whispered against her swollen clit and then my tongue flicked at it. She shook with the impending orgasm.

"*Fuuuck!*" she yelled.

Her body went still as it rolled through her, the walls of her pussy contracting around my hand. As it slowed, I removed my fingers and lowered my lips to her entrance. Licking the cum from inside her and spreading it over her pussy with my tongue.

"I love the taste of you."

Her arms relaxed above her head as her breathing returned to normal. She stared at the ceiling but wouldn't look at me or say anything. The nerves of what it could mean rattled my brain immediately. My insecurities settled in.

Kissing her gently on the inside of her thighs, I moved to get her thong and shorts.

"What are you doing?" she asked.

Holding the clothes in my hand, I gestured to her.

"You were so quiet, I thought maybe you wanted to be done, or were tired, or something else..."

She sat up and took the clothes from my hand, throwing them to the floor.

"Do you want to know what I was thinking?" She leaned against the arm of the couch, looking like a seductress, pulling her legs against her breasts. "I was wondering where the hell a guy your age learned to do that. Fuck, that was, just...wow. And now I'm nervous I won't be as good for you."

My heart rate settled with her words.

"I'm glad I made you feel good, and you don't need to worry. I'm nervous the second you touch me I'm not going to last long."

I laughed, and so did she.

"Well, let's get you out of those boxer briefs, then."

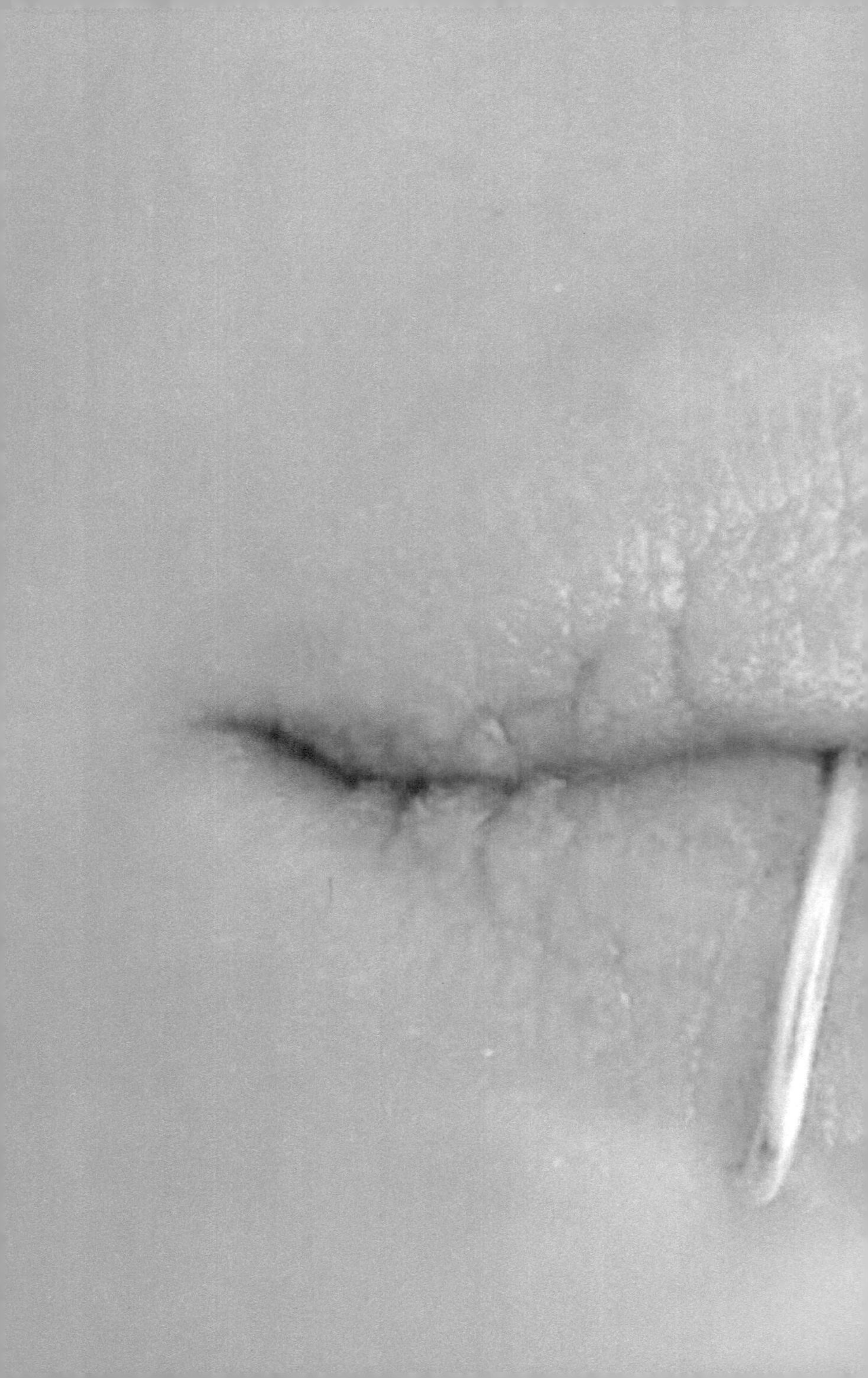

CHAPTER 16

Ava

This was not the way I'd expected the night to go when I came down to make popcorn. I thought my olive branch of a snack might give us a night of less fighting. But this was way beyond anything I would have thought.

However, not unwanted.

Not at all.

I did have this niggling notion about what we'd do after the storm, and everyone came back home. But I left that for later.

Logan stood from his crouched position in front of me, his boxer briefs at eye level from where I sat on the couch. He was still aroused; the entire length of his cock was outlined under the dark cotton. Reaching for the elastic waistband, my finger looped inside and pulled at it.

As soon as I did, we were blinded by all the lights coming back on and the TV blaring behind us.

"Christ!" I screamed. "That scared the shit out of me."

I didn't want to say the mood was ruined, but it changed. With the lights on, it seemed to remind us where we were and what the future held. At least it did for me. And I didn't want to think about that yet.

159

"Wow, look outside," Logan said. He moved to the window this all started at.

Standing next to him, we realized there was well over a foot and a half of snow outside.

"What time is it?" I asked.

Logan's phone was playing the music so he found his easily.

"It's one in the morning. Find your phone, we should charge them while we have power." He reached down and grabbed a shirt from the floor, tossing it to me.

It was his.

As I pulled it over my head, his scent filled my nose. I don't think he wore cologne, so it was his soap or deodorant. It smelled amazing. Clean, fresh, with a hint of pine.

He came to me and pulled me close, grabbing my ass.

"I like how you look in my shirt," he growled in my ear.

My heart did a little flip. Because that meant that our night may not be over. Even though the mood seemed to change, he was trying to keep it on track.

I found my phone between the couch cushions and plugged it in on the kitchen counter. Logan was getting a glass of water and searching in the fridge. What a sight it was to watch him, bent over in his briefs. He had a tight round ass, definitely the kind that benefited from his time at the gym. I may have made fun of him going to the gym so much, but I wasn't making fun of the body it gave him.

Not one bit.

"Hungry?" he asked.

I was, but not for food.

I wish I had the guts to say that to him. To be sexy like that.

He pulled grapes out of the bottom bin. Turning, he looked at me, almost as if waiting for my answer.

"Um, no, I'm good."

As I plopped back on the couch, Logan followed with his grapes in a bowl, but he didn't sit. Instead, he went to the wall, turning off the lights overhead. He also flipped off the television. The room was returned to the familiar dim glow with the flicker of the candles and the snowy light from the windows.

"I like that better, what about you?" he asked, returning to me.

Nodding, I pulled the blanket over me, suddenly chilly. He cuddled underneath with me, our feet and ankles entwining where they met in the middle of the couch. He popped a few grapes in his mouth, and I couldn't take my eyes off his lips as he chewed. His mouth was magical, and what it did to my body? No guy had ever given me an orgasm quite like he had. My thoughts returned to how he made me feel only minutes ago. I felt the heat of the blush on my cheeks and was thankful for the dim light.

Logan put the bowl on the table and grabbed my ankle under the quilt. He pulled me to him, up and on his lap in one swift move, and I was suddenly straddling him. He pulled the blanket over my shoulders to keep me warm.

I had so many questions about this man. He had the strong body of someone older than his years, yet the eyes of a boy who had dealt with more than he should have. His bright blue eyes always had a hint of storm cloud in them, waiting on the horizon to drift over and bust open.

"Can I ask you something?" When I said that, my hands went to his chest, his hands to my hips. We held one another, as if our connection on our laps wasn't enough.

"Sure, anything."

Though I wondered if he would really tell me anything I wanted to know. We were just getting to know each other.

"You're kinda young to have a dependency, no? Or am I wrong about that?"

He shifted under me, a telltale sign he was nervous about the topic. I waited, not pushing him to answer. My hands rubbed along the planes of his sculpted chest down to his ripped abs. My finger found the goody trail of golden hair that led into the waistband of his briefs, and I played with it, running my nail up and down.

"If you keep doing that, I won't be able to answer any questions you ask me, Tink."

I flinched at the name. But the seductive yet playful look on his face comforted me.

"Remember, I like that name for you, Ava." As he said that, his hand reached under the shirt I wore, rubbing circles across the skin of my belly. "And as far as me being young for an alcoholic, no, not really. I mean, statistically speaking, maybe I'm a little young. But at the center I go to for counseling, most of the people there were my age, even younger. Which, when you think about it, that's kinda sad. I think our world is getting harder for people to live in."

I contemplated his words and had to agree with him. My mother told us stories of when she grew up in the eighties and nineties and it just seemed...easier. Things were more complicated nowadays. And I would never admit it to my mom, but I agreed with her it all had to do with social media.

"Well, most people don't start drinking excessively for no reason. What was yours?" I was nervous asking him this, hoping it wasn't too invasive of a question. Considering as recently as this morning, we probably still considered each other enemies.

The circles he rubbed on my stomach continued, moving up, dangerously close to my breast. The tip of his finger grazed the underside of my boob, sending chills through my entire body.

"If you don't want to talk, I get it." And I did, he already got me twice and nothing for him.

His hands immediately moved to my hips, gripping them tightly, as if to keep them still.

"I do, I think we should get to know one another," he said. "Just a little hard with you looking the way you do while sitting on me with no panties on."

His smirk was adorable.

"Seems that's one area you and I have in common: daddy issues." He paused, his eyes failing to focus on me. "My dad never hit my mom, but he was a verbal and mental abuser, the best at what he did, which made him a menace. A true narcissist. He destroyed my mom's self-esteem, along with mine. She finally left him when I was in middle school, but he didn't leave me alone. He still felt he was my *father*." He put that last word in air quotes, his tone dripping with sarcasm. "He loved that I played football, bragged about it to all his buddies. But when he was around only me, it was one comment after another about how shitty I was, and how I'd never amount to anything in life."

Logan was getting agitated, his heart beating fast under my palm. He let out a long, deep breath before continuing.

"Eventually, I cut him off, no more visits, and I told him not to come to my games. I knew he was there, I still heard him. But at least he didn't seek me out after the games anymore. The only thing I still dealt with was the occasional annoying text either begging for us to get together, or him telling me what a shitty son I turned out to be."

I leaned against his chest, my head on his heart, and held him. His arms wrapped around me, and we lay down on the couch for a while, quiet.

"I won't say I'm sorry, because I didn't do any of that to you. But I will say that I hate him for doing that to you, and I hate that you had to endure that. My heart hurts that he was the reason for you feeling the need to turn to alcohol to escape."

His arms pulled me in tighter against him as he kissed the top of my head.

"He's not in my life anymore, so there's that, at least."

His words were so final, and I didn't completely understand them. A man like that seemed hard to keep away for good, but Logan also seemed done talking. As I lay against his heart, the beat strong and steady, the irony of our night struck me.

I'd have never thought I'd be half-naked in his arms, ever. And getting to know one another on so many levels.

About that...

I pushed against him and sat up, my knees against his hips, as my naked nether region was aligned perfectly with his not quite fully hard dick. Leaning down, I supported myself with that sculpted chest of his and shimmied back and forth along his length, feeling him grow beneath me.

"I guess we're done talking," he said with a sultry grin.

His fingers dug into my hipbones, the grip so tight it almost hurt. He stopped me from moving above him.

"If you keep doing that, our night will end before you want it to." His guttural words came from deep within as his eyes fluttered closed.

I struggled against his clutch as I bent down close to his ear. "I like that I have that effect on you."

That did something to him. He grabbed my ass as he jerked himself up to a sitting position, keeping me on his lap. The blanket fell from my shoulders, and I ripped the shirt over my head, my entire body exposed to him. His hands caressed my back, up my spine, over my shoulders, eliciting bumps on my skin along the way. When his touch hit the top of my chest, he stopped. I watched his eyes become heated as they stared at my breasts, wide with desire. He dragged his fingers across my chest, to each breast, roughly gripping each one.

"I love your tits, Ava. I've dreamt of touching them, licking them. I wasn't quite expecting the piercings."

His finger played with one as he said that. The sensation it created rippled throughout my body.

"Do you not like them?"

He responded by bending down, his tongue dipping to my left nipple, savoring and nibbling on the metal bar and sensitive skin. My hand went to my right breast instinctively, pulling at my right nipple.

"Oh, I like them," he said. "That's probably an understatement." His words were muffled against my skin as his mouth continued its work.

At the same time, the desire I felt inside, deep and low, was mounting. My lower half rocked against Logan, writhing against his hard cock, needing relief.

"Ava…I'm going to fuck you," he mumbled. "I need to be inside you."

This was not asking consent.

This was a declaration.

My hand reached between my legs, seeking his rock-hard dick. The tip was sticking out of the top of his underwear, the head smooth. Looking down, I found myself rubbing along the tight skin of the head of his cock, the glistening pre-cum leaking from him. My finger swiped it, and I brought it to my lips. Making sure Logan was watching me, I sucked the saltiness clean off, then brought my mouth to his.

"You taste good, too," I told him.

"*Fuuuck…*," he roared. "I need to get my wallet." He started to push me from his lap, but I stopped him.

"Where is it?" I asked.

He pointed to his sweatpants on the floor. I moved to them, reaching into the pocket and retrieved the condom from his wallet. When I turned back around, he was standing, completely naked.

Holy shit. What a fucking sight that was. I knew he was tall. I mean, compared to me, he was a giant. But naked, with those lines of his cut muscles, as he stared down at me, he was intimidating, almost godlike.

I found it hard to swallow my own spit.

He held his hand out for the tiny square foil, but I moved to kneel in front of him. As I did, I stared at his dick. Now, to me it was massive. However, I think it was just because he was massive. It fit his body. It wasn't out of proportion to the rest of him. I mean, christ, I think he had to be at least six feet, four inches tall. I say that because he was over a foot taller than me, and I was five foot two.

So yeah, the thing hung, big, in front of me. With huge veins running through it.

And I couldn't wait to feel it, lick it, and have it inside me.

So I did.

Leaning forward, my lips spread wide around the tip of his dick as I lowered my mouth. The smooth skin was warm inside me, stretching me to my limit. My tongue swirled across the tip, tasting the saltiness still leaking.

"Fuck, Ava," Logan groaned. "That feels amazing. I love the feel of that ring along my dick."

Slowly, my head bobbed up and down, making sure to drag the ring along the sides of him. Pushing forward, his length attempted to penetrate the depths of my throat. My one hand held him at the base, while the other gathered his balls, massaging and squeezing. And if it was possible, he grew bigger while I pumped him in my mouth.

He grabbed the back of my head, fucking me, fucking my mouth.

But then he stopped. Became completely still and held my head firmly in his hands, not letting me move.

"I don't want to come like this," he said. "I want to be inside you, but not your mouth, Ava."

Pulling him from my mouth, I looked up. I hoped he appreciated the smile I gave him as his dick slid from my mouth.

I went to work on tearing the foil pack with my teeth. I hastily rolled it over his hard length, realizing quickly it didn't cover him all the way.

He dropped to his knees in front of me. "How do you want this, sweetheart?"

I knew with his size, my favorite position would be a challenge. But I flipped over on all fours, my ass up in the air for him.

"Jesus Christ, Ava. You're gonna kill me."

I heard him spit in his hand before feeling him moisten me with his fingers. Then his mouth was on my pussy, tongue pushing inside, licking and spitting. He pulled away and hastily pushed two fingers in, prepping me. When he knelt behind me, aligning his length with my pussy, he dragged it up and down, top to bottom, then teasing my entrance with his tip.

"I'm going to start slow, sweetheart, you tell me how it feels."

He started pushing his cock inside, inch by inch. My pussy stretched around him, taking him, inviting him. He continued filling me, slowly advancing until he stopped.

"Fuck, Ava, you took me, babe. You took all of me."

His movements were slow. His one hand was on my hip while the other was pushing on my lower back. He pulled out the slightest bit, then pushed back in, testing the waters.

When he pulled out the second time, I slammed my body back against his, my open legs crashing against his.

"Aaahh!" I screamed.

He pulled himself out of me and froze, then dropped his entire body against my back, his mouth against my ear.

"Are you OK? Should we stop?"

"Fuck, Logan, no. Don't stop. You feel amazing. Fuck me harder."

A soft chuckle left his mouth as it fell against my ear in a puff of air. He kissed my ear softly before rising to his knees and regaining his hold on my hips. I could tell he was gearing up.

Gearing up for an assault I greatly wanted.

He rubbed his dick along my pussy, from clit to ass. Moving it back up to my opening, he lined himself up, and with one push, as he pulled my hips toward him, he seated himself completely inside me. The sensation as he filled me up took my breath away.

However, he didn't give me a chance to languish in that for long.

He pulled out and rammed himself back in me, repeatedly. The sound of smacking skin echoed in the room along with our cries of ecstasy. He reached under us and grabbed a hold of my swaying tits, holding them like a lifeline. With that arm, he pulled me up to my knees, my back to his front. Our slick bodies now like one as he held me tight with each punishing thrust.

Suddenly, I felt him sliding us back, pulling us up, and I was now sitting on him as he sat on the couch. He was somehow still inside me as he pushed and pulled my hips with his hands. My fingers gripped his thick thighs, trying to take hold of something, as I rode him back and forth. Both his hands found my breasts, pulling and twisting at my nipples, the sensation adding to the mounting pleasure.

The orgasm was building in my core as his cock hit parts of my pussy no man had ever touched. My movements became erratic on his lap as the waves rippled closer and closer together.

"Ava," Logan grunted. "I want to be looking at you when I come inside you."

He so easily flipped me over. As I was on my back, his blue eyes looked down at me just as his mouth landed on mine. During that kiss, he pushed his way back inside me, filling me up as I wrapped my legs around his waist. Using my heels, I pulled him deeper into me, keeping him there, grinding into him. The guttural moan he let out into my mouth, my throat, reverberated into my chest. He went back to a rhythm, and I knew he was close, bringing me back to a pinnacle on my mountain as well.

His thrusts got faster, a measured cadence to them. We were in sync as we bucked back and forth against each other, manic but deliberate.

"That's it, Logan, don't stop, I'm coming."

His frenetic movements threw me over the edge, my legs clamping down on his sides as the walls of my pussy clenched his cock in a tight hold. He grunted as he spilled himself inside me.

Our bodies stilled. His head fell against my shoulder as we lay quietly with each other, our breathing evening out. He kissed me gently on my shoulder. My nails ran along the planes of his back, his frame almost too large for my arms to span. I felt small bumps rise in the wake of my nails across his skin, and he wiggled when I got too close to his sides.

"You're ticklish," I said.

He lifted above me, that Adonis of a body still stealing my breath, and looked down at me.

"Isn't everyone?"

"No," I said.

He pulled the condom off and went to the bathroom to dispose of it. When he came back, he remained naked, only covered us with a blanket on the couch.

"Are you comfortable here? Or do you want to go back on the floor?" he asked.

He took up most of the couch due to his size, but pulled me on top of him, making him my body pillow. I cozied up into his shoulder, very sleepy.

"This is good," I said. "But your feet are hanging off the edge, you don't fit."

"I'm fine." His arm wrapped around me, and we both settled in against the pillow. "Ya know, if I wasn't so tired, I'd be putting your theory about not being ticklish to the test."

"There's always tomorrow," I said.

I think we were both asleep before I finished saying it.

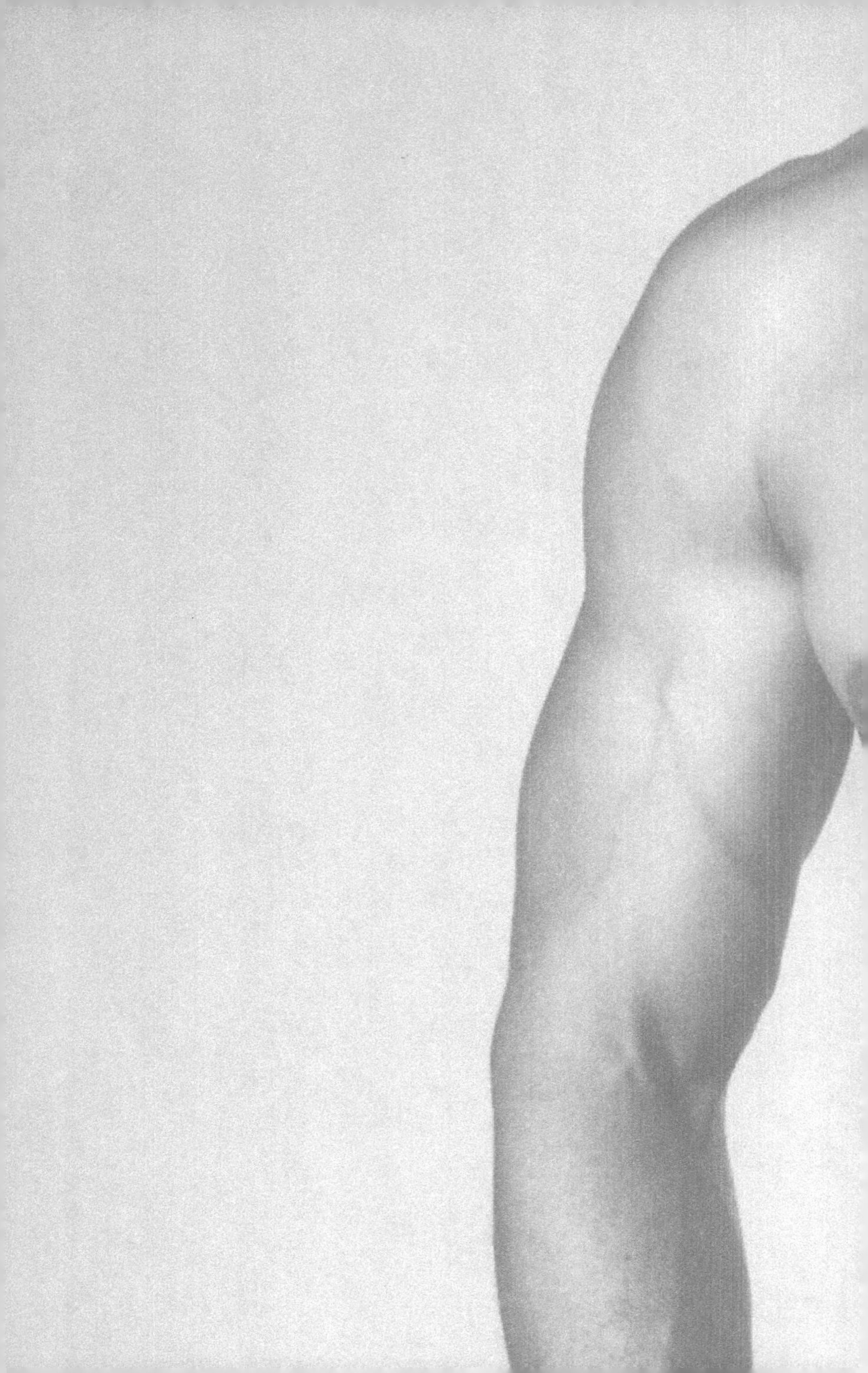

CHAPTER 17

Logan

I'd been awake for about twenty minutes already, just watching and listening to her sleep. Last night was freaking insane. First, the sheer fact that she was in my arms in the first place was literally a dream come true. She didn't hate me. Second, the sex was fucking fantastic. Like the hottest sex I'd ever had. She was a siren in bed.

Beyond that, we even shared parts of ourselves with one another. Secrets, backstory to my life I hadn't told anyone else, especially here at school.

But...

Now reality was going to hit. We needed to figure out how to move forward. How to handle "us" in this house. If there even was an us or if this was a one-time thing. I think I remember hearing that was her MO.

"Could you stop thinking so loud, it's waking me up."

She laughed against my chest before lifting her head. Her short black hair stuck up in every direction, only slightly different from how it looked last night. And in the morning light, her eyes were as bright as gemstones.

"Mornin'." My finger couldn't resist a swipe at her puffy bottom lip, pulling at it.

She moved herself up, her mouth coming to mine, giving me a soft kiss.

"Morning."

Then she was gone, away from my arms, grabbing my shirt and her thong and getting dressed.

I will say I loved that she chose my shirt instead of hers.

"I need coffee," she said as she opened a cabinet.

She moved around the kitchen as I searched the floor for my boxers and sweats.

"Wow, did you see outside?" I asked. "That's a freaking ton of snow. Everyone else is gonna have some trouble getting back here, I think." As I thought about that, I wasn't too upset about having this place to myself, with her, for another day or so.

"Do you want some?" Ava asked. She held out a mug.

"Sure."

The pot wasn't quite done, so we stood in the kitchen together, waiting and watching, in silence. It was already getting awkward.

And I didn't want that.

"Go sit down," Ava said. "I'll bring it to you. How do you like it?"

Walking back to the couch, I grabbed the remote.

"Cream and sugar, please."

I put Netflix on, thinking we could find something to watch if she didn't want to talk. Scrolling through the endless list of TV shows and movies, I couldn't decide. It would probably be best if I chose something she wanted, anyway.

Abandoning the TV idea, I picked up my phone and texted Ty.

Me: Hey, you guys get hit with feet of snow up there too

THE DOTS OF HIM RESPONDING CAME IN IMMEDIATELY.

Ty: Yep it's insane. We'll be taking Savannah out for her first time sledding today

Me: That's awesome take pics

Ty:

"WHO YA TEXTING?" AVA ASKED.

She handed me a steaming cup of coffee as she sat on the opposite end of the couch and curled her feet under her legs. I tossed her the blanket and she pulled it over herself since she was bare from the waist down and had to be cold.

"Ty," I said. "They're taking Savannah sledding today."

Her head nodded as the mug hit her lips, a slurping sound loud as she took a huge sip. The sound that left her lips envied the sounds coming from her last night, and it got a rise out of me in my pants.

"Oh, that's good coffee," she said.

I took a sip and had to agree. But I was also pretty hungry after the energy expended last night.

"Want me to make us some breakfast?" I asked her.

"I think we should talk first, don't you?"

Leaning back, I nodded. I was suddenly nervous, unsure of how this was going to go, yet I knew it needed to happen. I thought back to some words of advice Dr. Jean gave me at a session a few months ago. She told me that when I felt nervous about my circumstances to remember that it was always temporary regardless of how permanent the feelings felt. The situation was temporary.

"Yes, we should figure this out," I told her.

Ava remained quiet, sipping on her coffee. For someone who wanted to talk, she wasn't doing much of it.

"Well," she finally said. "Like I said last night, Macie really can't find out about us, or any of this. She'd be so mad at me. I'd lose her trust."

That was what she said last night. But I wasn't about to be a one-night stand while living in this house with her. Not after the night we just had.

So, I decided I was going to take the bull by the horns and really find out how she felt. "Ava, I like you. I know you want to keep this a 'forbidden secret,' and I understand why. But I'd like to make sure it's for the right reasons. I don't want to be tossed aside after this weekend. I feel like we made a connection, and I'm willing to make a go at this, whatever this is, even if we have to work at keeping it to ourselves."

She was quiet again. Then she placed her mug on the table and moved toward me, all the way to me, climbing onto my lap. She wrapped her arms around my neck and looked me square in the eyes.

"Logan, you need to understand something about me. I haven't been in a relationship since I was a junior in high school. Three years since I've had a boyfriend."

I didn't like the way this was headed.

"Him and I started dating when we were freshman, and then one day, our junior year, I found him in bed with my best friend. Needless to say, I not only lost my boyfriend but my best friend that day."

Yikes. So many reasons for her to have trust issues.

"I made a pact with myself to steer clear of relationships," she said.

Instinctively, I turned from her, not wanting to face rejection. But she gripped my cheek and turned my face back toward hers.

"Until I met you." She smiled. "Ya know, I even called my mom about you. I mean, kind of. I asked her a bunch of questions that were kind of about you. And look, here we are." She pushed against my chest with playful anger. "Don't get me wrong, I'm scared shitless, but I think I'm too far gone not to wanna give this a shot with you. I just wish we weren't roommates, it would make it so much easier with Macie."

I gripped her ass, pulling her toward me. Then my hands went under her shirt, thankful she still didn't have on a bra. I grabbed her tits, finding her nipples and those ridiculously hot piercings and playfully flicked them with my fingers.

"But think about how much fun we're gonna have sneaking around this place, fucking in every room of this house," I said.

She stood and went to my wallet again, retrieving the last foil packet I had down here. She handed it to me, pulled down her thong and pulled off my shirt she wore.

"That does sound like fun. How about for now we christen the kitchen island?"

AVA AND I PLANNED ON COMPLETING OUR SCHOOL PROJECT that afternoon since we were housebound. There was so much snow we couldn't even drive anywhere to go sledding or skating. We spent about three hours finishing up the marketing plan and creating some social media content for the company. We were both more than satisfied with how it turned out.

"I think we'll ace this thing," she said as we packed up our computers.

I couldn't disagree.

"Are you hungry?" I asked.

"Christ, man, is food all you think about? You made us huge omelets like only..." She looked at her phone for the time. "Wow, that was like four hours ago. I can't believe it's almost dinnertime already."

We slept in, talked for a bit. Then our christening of the island took us well into the afternoon. Throw in the hours we'd been working, and the day was winding down.

"And, no, food is not all I think about. Not with you dressed in only my shirt all day."

She sashayed away from me, that fine ass hidden by the long tee. I wanted to grab her, throw her over my shoulder, bring her upstairs, and do everything I'd already done to her body all over again, but in a bed.

I resisted. I didn't want to overwhelm her literally within our first twenty-four hours.

"I think I could do with dinner soon. What did you have in mind?" she asked.

"Well," I said, making my way into the kitchen. I opened the fridge, the freezer and a few cabinets taking a mental inventory. "I could whip together pasta carbonara if you'd like."

She jumped onto the island, her legs kicking over the edge with excitement.

"How could you know that's my favorite meal?" she squealed.

My arms were full of the ingredients within minutes, and I set to work on cooking her favorite dish. "Let me guess, you like the one from a very well-known chain restaurant, don't you?"

She continued sitting at the end of the island, watching my every move. It was a bit distracting having her exposed legs catching my eye. And under that shirt her bare cheeks pressed against the marble stone, that thin thong offering no cover, tempting me.

I persevered by filling pots, grating cheese, and mixing eggs. Before long, I had a full bowl of deliciousness for us to sit down to.

"Should I open a bottle of wine?" she asked as her feet thudded to the floor. As soon as she said it, she froze. Mid-step, on her way to the table. Horror filled her face and eyes when she turned to me. "Logan." My name came out a whisper. "I'm so sorry."

"Don't worry about it," I told her. But that didn't seem to quell her concerns.

She just stood there, staring at me with nervous eyes. Her hand covered her mouth as she mumbled more apologies that I couldn't hear. I took slow, measured steps in her direction, and her eyes widened as I approached. Her hand went up, waving me off, a silent request to leave her alone. I ignored her and took that hand in mine.

"Hey..." Her hand trembled against my fingers. "Ava, relax, it's OK. You said nothing wrong, sweetheart. It's all good."

My arms went around her shaking shoulders, pulling her body against mine. She nodded against my chest as I continued reassuring her.

Then a phone pinged.

"Was that my phone or yours?" she asked.

"Must be yours, I have mine in my pocket."

As she slid from my arms to search for her phone, I saw a quick swipe of her hand to her eyes. We would have to have a conversation about how to navigate this part of my life together, so that she was comfortable living hers.

"Oh shit!" Ava sprinted for the stairs. "Macie's coming home!"

I found myself running up to the second floor, standing in her doorway watching her tear through the closet for something to wear.

"How the hell is she going to get here in this snow?" I asked. Moving to her window, I looked outside and noticed that the lots were plowed, and all the cars were plowed in. But the walkways were shoveled and things were getting cleaned by the crews from the complex.

"Jace lives here, in our complex, and he has a truck, so he's bringing her here. She needs something for homework, or clothes, I don't know..."

She was racing around the room, clad in only her thong, throwing bras and pants and shirts through the air. I grabbed her by the arms and forced her to stop.

"Hey," I said. "Text her back and tell her to come eat with us. Act normal. It's OK. Get dressed, I'll go clean up the living room, and everything'll be fine."

The nod she gave wasn't very convincing, but she calmed down. I let her go and watched her move zombielike toward her dresser. She pulled out sweats and put them on. Knowing then she'd be fine, I made my way back downstairs to straighten up.

Within minutes, Ava was back downstairs. I was plating our food while she filled our glasses of water. That was when we heard the key in the door.

"He's such a great cook, you have to stay for dinner..."

Macie's words could be heard as she came into the house. Ava stiffened and her head jerked in my direction.

"Relax," I mouthed to her.

Macie and a guy, who I had to assume was Jace, bounded into the kitchen still talking to each other.

"Hi, guys," Macie said. "Hope it's OK if Jace eats with us. I told him what a great cook you are. This is Logan, and you know Ava."

The guy was tall, but didn't reach my height. He had a slimmer build than me, looked more like a baseball player.

"Hey, man, what's up?" Jace said.

He held his hand out, and I, of course shook, it. Ava ignored him.

"Sure, I made plenty."

Ava was already grabbing two more bowls and glasses as everyone else sat at the table.

"Can you believe this storm, Ava? Isn't it crazy?" Macie asked. She seemed to be working hard to include Ava in the conversation.

"Yeah, crazy."

Macie shrugged at Ava's response, or should I say, lack of one.

And suddenly I realized it would be easy to hide what had happened over the past twelve hours...because Tink was back.

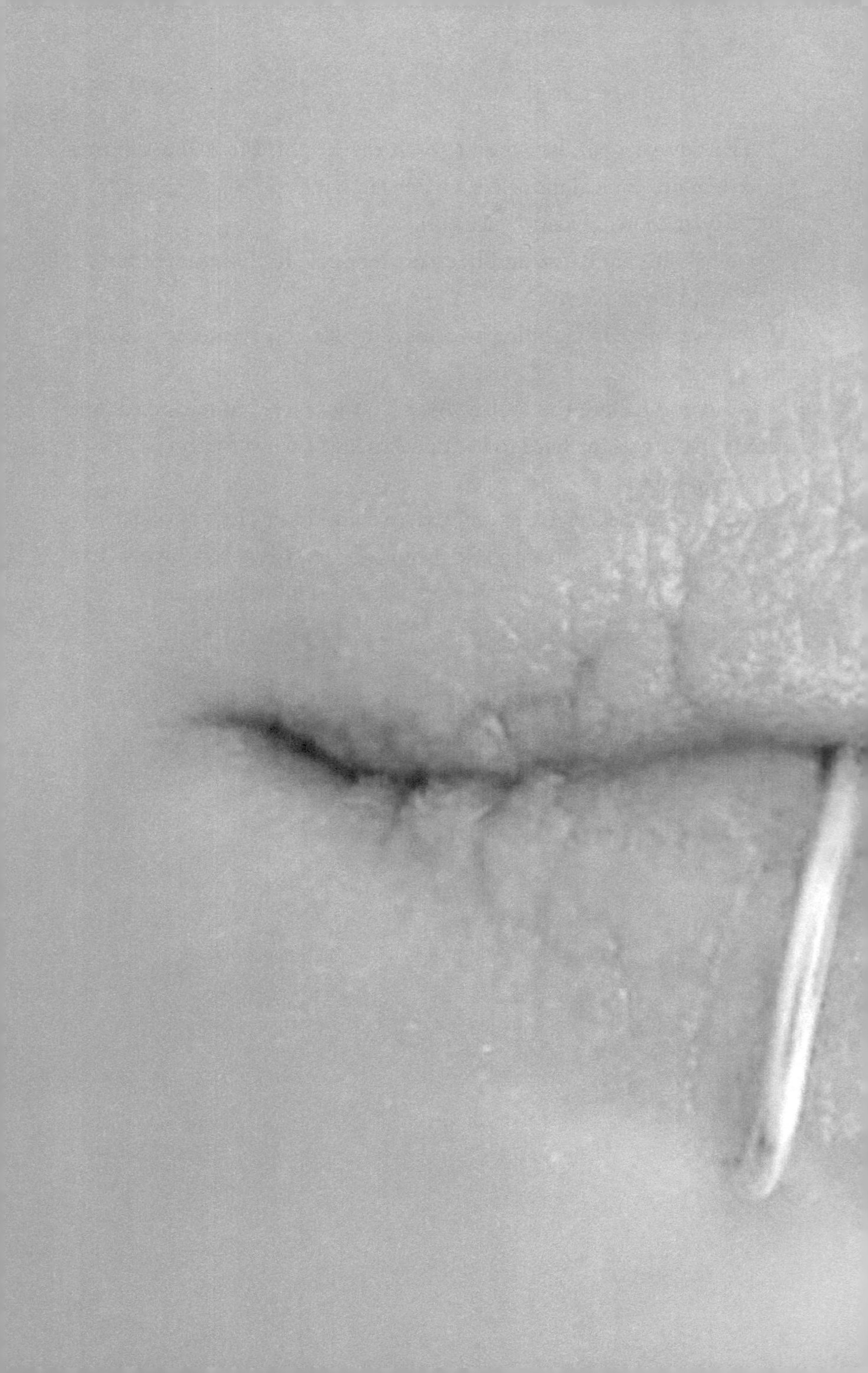

Ava

Our presentation went off without a hitch on Tuesday. Logan and I definitely aced it, would be shocked if we got anything less than an A. But between when Macie came home during the storm and when we met up in class, Logan and I hadn't really seen much of each other. And that may have been intentional on my part.

I was avoiding him, I knew that. Even though I was the one who demanded we keep our tryst a secret...I didn't know how.

When I saw him, all I wanted to do was run into his arms or run my fingers through his wavy blonde locks. Not act like we still hated each other. So it was easier to simply not see him.

As I lay on my bed, I felt like a prisoner in my own house, trying to steer clear of him.

My phone received a text. When I looked, I couldn't help but chuckle. It said it was from *My Forbidden Secret*.

Logan: Come upstairs

Me: It's the middle of the day, someone could
come home

Logan: Is it against your rules for roommates to be
in the same room talking

I STOOD OUTSIDE HIS CLOSED DOOR FOR A COUPLE MINUTES,
debating whether I should knock. Then another text came through.

Logan: Come in, I can almost hear you breathing

BUT BEFORE I COULD EVEN GRAB THE KNOB, HE THREW THE
door open. Looming in front of me was the man I hadn't been able to
stop thinking about. His jeans were tight, and I wanted him to turn
around so I could get a glimpse. He had one of those long-sleeve waffle-
knit shirts on, and it clung to his arms, the muscles thick against the
material.

"I know what you're doing," he said. He almost glared down at me,
and I could have mistaken him for being angry, but his eyes were sad.
"Why, Tink?"

Pushing past him, I sat at his desk chair. His computer was open to
something that looked like law gibberish.

"I'm not doing anything." But I refused to look at him when I
said it.

Suddenly, he grabbed the chair I was in and slid it along the floor to the side of the bed. Sitting across from me, he forced me to look him in the eye.

"Ava."

I loved when he said my real name.

"These past few days have been torture," he said. "I know you want to keep this…" He gestured between us with his hands. "A secret. And I'm OK with that to keep you happy. But we have to be able to talk, Ava. We have to be able to see each other, I mean, we live in the same fucking house. What we had before was better than this."

My shoulders slumped because I knew he was right.

I also knew that I was scared. Scared of so many things.

Logan was right. We couldn't live like this because it was even more unusual for us and would raise eyebrows with the roommates just as much.

His hands cradled my face, the warmth reaching my heart. I was unaware how much I'd missed his touch. Our lips touched ever so gently, his tongue grazing my bottom lip, searching out my lip ring. It swirled around the tiny hoop, playing with it, and it made me smile against him.

"Did you miss this as much as I did?" he whispered against my lips.

I answered him by deepening the kiss, leaving the chair and straddling his lap, both of us now on the bed. His hands held me by the waist, then my ass, pulling me close and tight as our mouths got reacquainted.

Then we heard the door open downstairs. And I panicked.

I jumped off his lap and stood frozen in the middle of his room like a deer in headlights.

Logan, however, calmly moved his chair and pointed to his bed as he took a seat at his desk. I sat on the edge of his bed, though nowhere near as calm as he was. My hands went to my mouth and face, rubbing, thinking I could erase the evidence of what we were doing. But I was probably only making my lips redder.

"Anyone home?" Becca yelled.

"We're up here," Logan responded.

She was standing in the doorway with her Stanley in one hand, a sandwich in the other, and a full backpack on her shoulder. Her coat, hat, and gloves were still covering every inch of her body.

"Christ, I need it to warm up out there so the snow can melt. I'm sick of walking through it and dealing with it. I'm sick of winter." She looked at her full hands with exasperation, as if she wanted to throw everything to the ground but knew she couldn't. "Whatcha you guys doing? Homework? Have to say, it's kinda nice seeing you two in the same room."

She started backing out of the doorway.

"I have to get this shit off me, out of my hands. I need a bath, I need to eat. I need this day to end..." Her words trailed off as she headed to her room.

Logan let out a chuckle before coming to sit next to me on his bed.

"And that's what I refer to as 'Tornado Becca.'"

Now I understood. She never took a breath or let us get a word in. Then was on her way.

"But I love her," he said.

My hand was engulfed in his before we even heard the door upstairs close, proving Becca was indeed in her room. I had no idea how to navigate this, yet he seemed cool as a cucumber.

"How is this not making you nervous?"

"That's an excellent question," he said. "I've been a ball of anxiety since getting to school. If you didn't already know, I'm still talking with my counselor on video sessions, and she helps me with my sobriety as well as my anxiety." He paused to monitor my reaction to that information. When he saw none, he continued. "Well, it's kinda weird. Since this weekend, Friday night to be specific..." He gave me an impish smile. "I haven't had a panic attack."

"Great." My eyes rolled so hard it hurt my sockets, and I hoped he was going to get my joke. "You gave me your anxiety! I've been nothing but a ball of nerves since exactly then!"

He pointed above us. I knew what he was going to say, but it wasn't going to make me feel any better. We still had Macie to worry about.

"Becca has been desperate for us to become friends. I think she'd be oblivious to anything else other than reaching her goal of that," I told him. "Macie, on the other hand, is very in tune to me. And she's the one I have the agreement with."

Pulling me by the hand, he led me from his room and down the stairs to the main living area. He brought his computer and had it open on the table but sat us on the couch. Then, he pulled up Netflix and scrolled through until he landed on the next episode of *New Girl* for me.

"Let's watch some TV together. If Macie comes home, we can look like we're doing homework or taking a break from that."

He pulled me against his side, forcing me to cuddle into his shoulder. And it felt...perfect. And I did relax. A bit.

We talked quietly about how to proceed. How to make this work.

And he was working so hard to make this work.

I thought, maybe, just maybe, it could.

By the time Macie walked in, each of us were making our own dinners. The kitchen was a chaotic mess as we danced around each other, fighting for the microwave, stove, and sink. But let's face it, all I really needed was the microwave.

I sat down to my frozen dinner, nicely heated from those microwaves. Becca and Logan joined me at the table.

"Tink, that shit is so bad for you," Logan said.

I bristled at the nickname, even though he explained what it meant to him. I'd gotten used to him using my real name, but he was keeping up the façade.

"Well, you didn't offer to cook for me, so this is it," I retorted, with my best attempt at being snarky right back. Becca sat to my right, completely oblivious to what was going on around her.

"Any food for me?" Macie asked as she walked in and foraged through the cabinets.

"It's a fend for yourself kind of night," I told her. "Chef Logan was selfish."

That earned me a gruff harumph from my other side. His fork stabbed at his grilled chicken with such force the plate slid across the wood surface. But I was following through on what we'd agreed on... back to how we were in front of the roommates.

We decided we didn't need to be quite as mean, but that it needed to be authentic.

"Well, looks like I'll be having peanut butter and jelly tonight," Macie said.

No one but Logan had been to the grocery store in a while.

"We can go shopping tomorrow," I told her.

Macie nodded as she made her pitiful sandwich and joined us at the table. It wasn't often that the four of us were at the table together. It hadn't happened since Logan and I had started our "thing."

This could be interesting.

Especially since he and I were sitting next to each other.

"Logan told me you guys kicked ass on your presentation," Becca said in my direction.

"We did. He was a pain in the ass to work with, but the meathead here has a head for business on his shoulders." My lips turned up in a slight smile, working hard to not overdo this interaction.

His snicker made me pause, hoping he understood what I was doing.

My hand landed on his thick thigh under the table, and I gave it a squeeze. I was working to be my old self, the one they expected me to be around him. I watched him put his fork down with precision before his hand came under the table and found mine. At first I thought he was going to remove it, push me from his leg. Instead, he gripped my hand in his, threading his fingers through mine, before looking my way.

"Yeah, well, Tink here is like working with a drill sergeant, and not the good kind. But I guess considering we did well, it was worth it."

He gave my hand a squeeze then let go, his attention back to his plate of food.

Our little secret moment, in front of our friends, made my heart skip a beat or two.

It was thrilling keeping this from them.

More than thrilling, invigorating even.

That shifted when I looked over at Macie. She was smiling, and my mind made me think she'd seen us, making my stomach drop and my food almost come back up. I put my fork down, my appetite now gone at the thought. As I looked back her way, she was eating her sandwich as she listened to the story Becca was telling the table, something about Ty's daughter, Savannah.

"She sounds adorable," Macie said.

She was oblivious of me.

And my worries and stress.

They all were as the three laughed at whatever Becca had said.

Then I felt his hand on my leg, his thumb rubbing small circles, as he continued listening to Becca. Like a tether, his hand anchored me to his strength, as he somehow sensed I needed it.

"Well, this was fun, but I've got work to do," Becca announced. "We should try to do this at least once a week, though. A roomies night for dinner!"

"Yes!" Macie squealed in agreement. "That would be so nice." They both cleared their dishes and kept talking about plans for a night next week as they headed up to their rooms, leaving us at the table.

We sat quietly for a moment, needing to make sure we were alone. Once we heard the footsteps overhead, Logan reached for my chair, pulling it closer, the wood pegs scraping along the vinyl floor. He took my feet and wrapped them around his waist, pulling me between his own widespread legs. As he cradled my face, he studied me with intent eyes.

"I couldn't wait for them to leave," he said. "When you put your hand on my leg, I don't know, it did something inside. The risk you took..." His lips settled on mine, gentle as air, as his tongue begged entrance into my mouth. The slow swirl of our tongues as he kissed me, as he held my face in his hands, as our bodies fought to get closer. I forgot about all the reasons doing this with him was a bad idea.

"You're coming to my room tonight," he whispered against my mouth. "Set your alarm for two a.m."

Pulling back, I shook my head at him. But he held my head still and stared me square in the eye.

"You're visiting me tonight, Tink. They're both on another floor, they won't hear us."

Of course I wanted to as well, but us *being together* while they were home, in the house with us, made my heart race. And not in a good way. But if we were going to make this work, it was going to have to be like this.

Secret.

"OK."

He kissed me on the lips one more time before moving my legs from his lap.

"I'm heading up to get some studying done," he said before grabbing his dishes from the table.

He worked at the sink while I sat, ruminating about what was to come later tonight.

"Those wheels turning in your head are about to bust out and roll across the floor, Tink." He laughed as he placed his dishes in the dishwasher. "Don't think so hard. I'm the one with anxiety issues, remember?"

As he walked back to me, I admired the way he looked in his sweatpants. The way they clung to his narrow hips and hung low enough to show the band of his boxer briefs underneath. He dipped and kissed me on the nose before spinning on his heels and heading out of the room.

"Go get some work done, Tink. Either that or get some sleep, but don't forget to set your alarm."

Two a.m.

Alarm set.

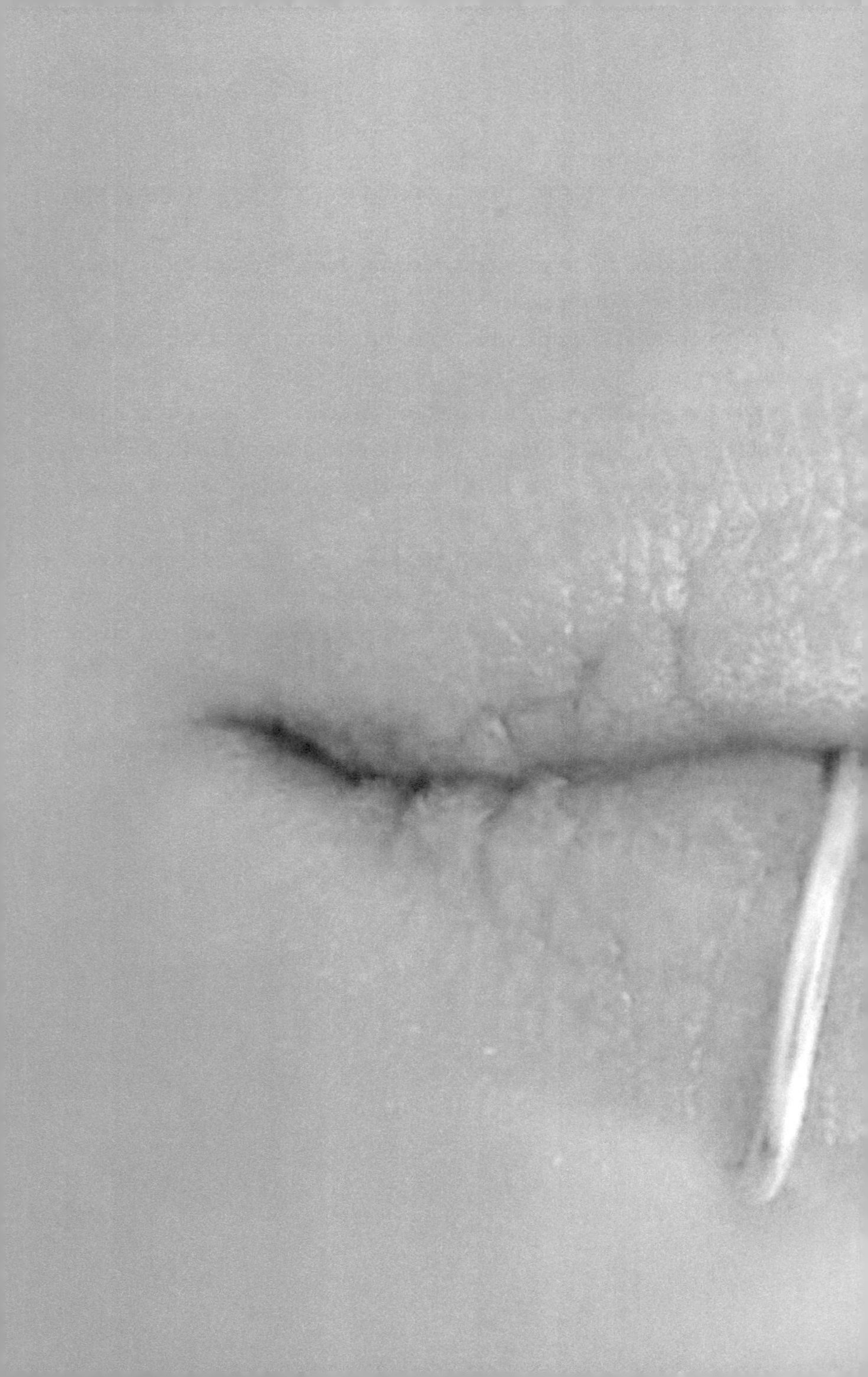

CHAPTER 19
Ava

There really wasn't a need to set my alarm, I never fell asleep. Turns out I had a lot of work to do, and by the time I finished, it was after one anyway. Besides, the way my heart was racing with anticipation, there was no way I'd have fallen asleep. So, I jumped in the shower. It didn't hurt to be clean when you knew you were having sex.

This was new for me, getting ready for a hook-up session, with a guy I lived with, would see again, and had feelings for. I kind of wanted to look nice. As I rummaged through my underwear drawer, I pulled out every piece of lingerie I owned, deciding it was time for some new ones. Instead, I settled on my prettiest black lace bra and thong set, complete with matching bows. My robe sufficiently covered my body and kept me warm as I tied the belt around my waist.

I didn't bother with makeup, but I did spray myself with perfume. Logan mentioned once he liked the way I smelled.

A few minutes before two, I opened my bedroom door and listened intently for any noise coming from above. Both Becca's and Macie's rooms were on the third floor, and it was quiet.

As I tiptoed down the hall to his door, I noticed the soft glow of his TV underneath. I put my ear against the wood and listened.

Nothing.

With one knuckle, I lightly tapped on it. Within seconds, Logan had the door open and loomed over me, his large body taking up the entire doorway.

"Hey, beautiful," he whispered as he grabbed me by the hand and whisked me into his room. He gently shut his door, careful not to make any loud noises. He spun around and held me at arm's length, looking down at me. "You look amazing, Ava."

"I'm in a robe, Logan."

"Yeah, well, you could be in a potato sack, it's never about what you're wearing."

As he spoke, his hands came to my face, stroking my cheek, down to my lips. My eyes fluttered closed at his touch, the yearning already building in my body and my mind.

Then I froze.

"Wait," I said. His fingers stilled against my lips, his eyes wide almost in horror. "Whose room is right above yours?"

"Macie's, why?"

I let out a sigh of relief.

"Good, because if she gets up, I can run back to my room, she might come to me."

His one eyebrow lifted as his mouth twitched, trying to hold back a smile.

"How often has she come to you in the middle of the night lately?" he asked.

"Well, she hasn't, but if either of them would, it would be Macie, not Becca, so it's good her room is above yours."

He laughed out loud.

Like really loud.

"Stop!" I whispered yelled while hitting his arm. My nerves were getting the better of me, I knew that, but his yelling wasn't going to help. "You'll definitely wake one of them yelling like that!"

He took my hand and walked us to his bed. As he sat, he pulled me between his legs, wrapping his arms around my middle, resting his cheek against my belly. He held my ass through the thin material of my robe.

"Try to relax, Tink, it's the dead of night. I'm pretty sure neither of them will wake up and come looking for us." His hands came back around and up to my face as I noticed the corners of his eyes turn down. "But if you're really too nervous to do this, I'm not going to pressure you."

Shit, I was nervous. Nervous about getting caught, nervous about Macie finding out and hating me for doing exactly what I told her not to do.

Yet I wanted time with him more.

As the internal battle raged inside my head, I took his hands in mine to make sure he understood I really did want to be here.

"I'm sorry," I said. "I won't let my insecurity about all of this ruin our time, I promise."

He swung his arms back around me, pulling me close.

"Are you sure? Because I don't want to do this if you're going to have your head somewhere else."

To get my point across, my hand reached down between his legs, grabbing a hold of his semi-hard dick.

"I'm sure," I said.

"Good, and enough talking," he said with a smirk. "I think it's time for me to see what you have hiding under this robe."

His hands went to the knot of the belt, slowly untying it as our eyes remained locked on each other. He pushed the material off my shoulders and watched it puddle at my feet. His attention was drawn to the lace garments that still covered my body.

"Christ, Ava, you are fucking gorgeous."

His gentle hands landed on my belly, moving toward my waist as his thumbs rubbed up against my rib cage. His thumbs worked their way to the underside of each breast as his mouth descended on mine. His tongue fought its way in, lashing at mine, as his hands worked their way behind me to my backside. My mouth swallowed his moan as he grabbed my ass, a finger lifting the strip of lace between the cheeks.

"You want to kill me, don't you, Ava?"

His kisses moved to my neck, my chest, the top of my breasts, as he pulled me closer between his legs. My hands went around his neck, then up to his head, threading through his waves. Inhaling, his scent invaded me, and it was all him. That masculine combination of soapy pine and musk.

Reaching down behind him, I pulled at his shirt, bunching it up and over his head. I needed to feel the warmth of his skin against me. My hands roved along the planes of his back, both of us holding on tight to the other.

"You feel amazing up against me like this," he said, his words vibrating against my chest.

Sitting back, his gaze lingered on me, my chest to be exact. His finger found the metal of my piercing through the lace, rubbing it gently. The pleasure it sent through my entire body made me quiver in his hold.

His hand trailed up my back, making its way to the clasp of my bra. He fumbled with it for a few seconds, realizing he needed more than one hand. Laughing at himself, he brought the other to help.

"I'm not as good at this as I thought, I guess."

Once it was undone, I stepped back to take it off.

"But this is my favorite part," he said with a smirk. "You are so fucking sexy."

He made me feel sexy with his words and how he looked at me. So I decided to make this slow for him, to tease him a bit.

Holding the cups against my breasts with an arm, I lowered the straps from my shoulders, removing each arm one by one. Then I put my hands on the sides of my breasts, pushing them together, taunting him. He reached out, desperate to touch me, but I stepped away.

"Christ, you are going to kill me, Ava," he moaned as he leaned back on the bed, enjoying the show.

"Well, I don't think that's true, but you might get blue balls while watching."

My fingers found my nipples through the lace of my bra and pulled at the bars, making them taut. Satisfied with how they now poked through the material, I moved a few steps closer to him. My one arm was under my breasts, supporting them, while my other hand lowered the lace of my bra, revealing the tops of the deep brown circles he so loved to lick.

"Want a taste?" I asked.

He leaned forward, eager to oblige. His tongue laved at the tops of my breasts exposed over the lace, down to the pigmented circle surrounding my nipple. Suddenly his lips clamped onto the hard tip and metal that stuck out through the lace, sucking deep into his mouth. His fingers found the other and twisted it between them, the glorious pain igniting a fire inside me.

"Ah, you like this." His words resonated against my breasts, the sensation heightened when his mouth returned to sucking on the other. My hands abandoned their hold on my bra, grasping his head, his hair, holding him against me.

When he pulled away, the material fluttered to the floor between us.

He inhaled deeply as he stared at me, seeming to anchor himself in the moment. His eyes stole a glance at mine, but quickly went back to my body. The back of his hand caressed the side of me, from chest, along my breast, to my torso.

"I'm not sure I deserve such beauty," he said, almost to himself.

I took his face in my hands, forcing him to look at me.

"You deserve everything life has to give you, me included."

Our mouths collided, the moment shifting. What had been pure sex was now full of emotion as well. Logan wrapped his arms around my body and stood from the bed, turning to place me down. Once above me, his arms caged my head as he lowered himself onto me.

"Wait," I said, pushing him up. "Let me take your pants off." Leaning forward, I made quick work of pushing his sweats and briefs to the ground.

"Don't take your thong off, not yet," he said as he lowered himself back into bed. "Your ass looks too good in it."

Suddenly, he flipped me over and had me on my belly. His hands were on my ass, his fingers playing with the material of my thong between my cheeks. As he massaged my ass with one hand, his other came down with a tiny slap on my butt.

It startled me.

And then I realized I liked it.

When my reaction was to lift my ass in the air toward his hand, Logan knew that and did it again. He did it a few more times, and each time, my pussy tightened.

I heard him put his fingers in his mouth, and fully expected those fingers to go inside me. But where they went startled me once again.

This time, as he smacked my ass, the other hand moved the thong aside and pushed a finger inside my tight hole. I stilled at the surprise, and so did he. Yet he continued pushing it in slowly as he massaged my ass. Then his other hand made its way around my belly and found my clit, rubbing the nub as he teased that untouched hole from behind still.

"Is this OK, Ava?"

"Yes," I moaned. Because suddenly it was more than OK.

It was euphoric.

He felt the change in me, in my body, and moved with the rhythm. My ass bucked against the invasion but opened up for it at the same time, as his finger pushed in slowly, carefully, and deeper.

"Oh my god," I mumbled into the pillow my hands were gripping tight. "Fuck..." I'd never experienced anything like this before.

"Hold on," he said as his hands left me.

The despair I felt was real as all the intense feelings were gone immediately. I heard him fumbling in the drawer next to his bed. He was murmuring curses as he obviously struggled to find a condom. As I started sitting up to help, he finally came back to the bed.

"Sorry," he said as I heard the foil wrapper rip. "Are you good to try something?"

My head snapped toward him.

"Don't worry, no dicks will go there, I promise," he said, then laughed.

My wide eyes still had his attention as I lay back on the bed.

"Were you enjoying what I was doing to you, babe?" he asked.

I nodded.

"Then trust me, what I'm going to do will only feel better. Turn over, back on your belly. Let me see that ass," he said.

Once I rolled over, he knelt behind me and ran his hands along the small of my back, over my ass, to the backs of my legs, and back up again. He hooked his fingers under the top of my thong and slowly pulled it down. His mouth was on my lower back, kissing the bottom of my spine, and making his way down. Using his knee, he forced my legs to spread wider and pulled my ass cheeks apart. His tongue was at the top of my crack, dipping below, almost at my dark opening.

The anticipation of what it would feel like when his mouth tasted me in that spot was almost too much. I wiggled my body beneath him, lifting my ass to meet his mouth. He held me still, forcing my body back to the bed as his probing tongue continued its progress.

As he made it to my ass, he licked around it a few times and skipped down to my pussy. His tongue pushed inside me, hard and deep, then retreated, licking me from bottom to top. He repeated this pattern multiple times, the in and out, then up and down, until I was in a frenzy.

His tongue slowed, and he spread my cheeks apart more. He gradually made his way up toward my ass, the butterflies in my stomach flapping hard as he did.

The tip of his tongue licked around the rim of my tight hole, and my pussy tightened. My hand instinctively went to my clit, needing to touch it, rub it, to release some built-up tension.

Then his tongue darted out and licked me fully, around my entire hole, in and out. It was exhilarating.

Then his mouth disappeared.

"On your knees, princess," he said, then smacked my ass. "And get that ass up in the air for me."

I listened, because this was all him tonight. Once on my knees, he pushed me gently down on the bed in the middle of my back, forcing my ass up higher. He grabbed me by the hips and rubbed his hard dick along the length of my pussy, starting at my clit and ending at my sensitive tight hole. I jumped a bit when he ended there because of what he said earlier.

He nudged himself at my pussy entrance, swirling the tip of his dick around to open me up for him. Then he plunged himself inside me, fully seated in one try.

"Aah!" I yelped, then dug my face into the pillow below me. We had to be quiet.

He leaned down against me, his mouth against my ear. "You like that, princess? Your pussy is so tight for me."

He went back to his knees, pulling me against him with my hips.

Over and over and over.

Then I heard the crack of his hand on my ass. I definitely heard it before I felt it, but that sting felt delicious as he kept pounding into me. He would smack me, then rub me softly afterward.

Suddenly, his hand was at my mouth.

"Open up, baby, get my thumb nice and wet for you."

He shoved his thumb in my mouth, and my tongue swirled around it. He yanked it from my mouth just as abruptly. Then, it was on the rim of my ass, circling that tight hole as he continued to fuck me. His hand rested on my lower back, his thumb pressing inside me, pushing and pushing.

The combination of his cock filling my pussy and his finger in my ass threw me over the edge. I bucked against him with such ferocity the bed shook and rocked against the wall. That was when I heard it.

And I froze.

"Did you hear that?" I asked.

He slowed his pace, but didn't stop his in and out movements completely as he listened.

We could hear the squeak of floorboards above us.

Logan slowed a bit more, but still moved inside me, dick and thumb. It was near impossible to not move; the feelings building inside me were about to burst.

"I think she's just going to the bathroom," he said.

I started rocking against him again, needing the pace to increase. As soon as I did, we heard the water of the plumbing above us and the floorboards again.

He was right. But that meant she was still awake.

But he had me so close to the edge, I honestly didn't care who heard us at this point.

I needed to come. I needed this to finish.

My hips increased the intensity of their movements, our bodies slamming against one another. And he understood. The rhythm returned. The pace increased. His thumb pushed in deeper, in and out of my ass.

I wasn't walking up that hill, I was sprinting. This was nothing like I'd ever felt before. The sensations were completely different as the room began to spin around me. My hand reached below, seeking out my clit, I needed more. It suddenly wasn't enough. Rubbing myself while he fucked me, while he pounded against me, into me, into both of my openings, had my head spinning.

"Are you touching yourself, baby?" Logan breathed out.

"Yes..."

"Fuck..." he grunted. "That's fucking hot." He stilled against me. "Shit, baby, I don't wanna come yet, you have me so turned on."

My head snapped back toward him.

"Don't stop! Please don't stop." My hand worked furiously on my clit to keep the momentum going. I didn't want to lose this impending release.

I literally could see the top.

And then Logan reared back and slammed into me.

Hard.

Oh. My. God.

I was at the point of no return.

He rammed himself against me, his erratic actions those of someone close to the edge as well. My fingers gripped the sheets, trying to keep me from crashing into the wall, our movements intense.

"Fuck, Ava, I'm gonna come, baby."

The smacking of skin against skin increased.

"Are you gonna come, baby? Come with me," he said.

I was.

The plunge was happening, right off the side of that cliff.

And it was glorious.

"Yes!" I cried out. "I'm coming!"

My neck arched back as the orgasm took hold of my body. Logan's finger left my tight hole, grabbing around my middle, pulling me up, my back against him, as he continued pumping in and out of me. His mouth went to my neck, sucking on the tender skin, muffling his moans as he started to come.

My moans were muffled when he covered my mouth with his hand, still holding me against him.

"That's it, baby," he murmured into my neck. "Come for me, all over my dick."

He stilled inside me, his body jerking a few times, as he finished his release. My body fell to the bed, and he collapsed next to me. He was still behind me, still inside me, as he held me close.

We were both quiet as we allowed our breathing to settle. Then he started shifting behind me.

"Uh, I better take care of this before it's too late," he said, pulling himself out of me. He got himself to the bathroom, then came back with a small towel. "Want to clean up at all?"

Nodding, I reached for the towel. Instead, he leaned in and wiped me clean. Throwing it across the room, I assume to a hamper, he crawled back in bed with me and pulled the quilt over us.

This was usually when I was getting dressed and hightailing it out of wherever I was. Or I was telling the guy to do the same.

But being next to Logan, after doing what we did, felt right. It would have felt completely wrong to get up and leave.

And that kinda frightened me.

"I can't stay here all night," I said.

He reached for his phone, tapped a few things on it, then put it back on his nightstand.

"All taken care of, now close your eyes. I'm not letting you go right now. The alarm will wake us at five thirty. Plenty of time before anyone will be up."

Looking at my watch that gave us almost two hours to sleep together.

It was a wonderful two hours.

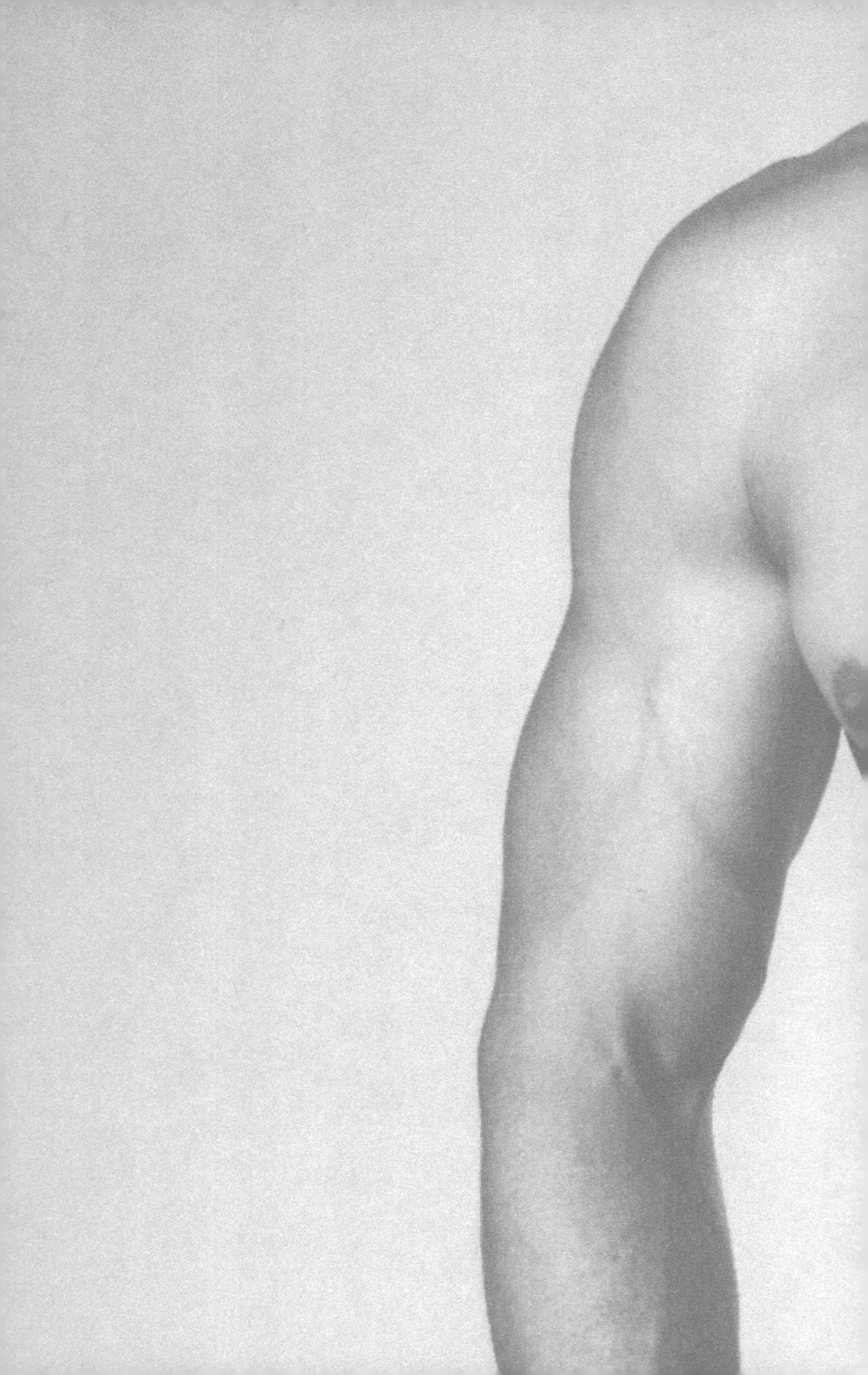

CHAPTER 20

Logan

"Hey, man, we're excited to have you," Sutton said as he slapped me on the back. He rivaled me in height and size and had also played football in high school. We talked a bit about the teams we played on and realized we probably played against one another at a point. The rugby meeting went better than expected. The guys were great and welcomed me, especially when they saw my size and heard of my experience.

"Looking forward to being here with you guys," I told him. "So, there's a gym workout tomorrow night?"

"Yeah, from five to seven. If you can make it, that'd be great."

The week had continued at home with the girls as normal, for the most part. Ava and I hadn't been to one another's room since the night we spent together in my room, but we snuck a make-out session here and there before the others got home. It wasn't quite the same, but it was something. Yet, it was a time like this, with the news of joining the rugby team, that I'd like to run home and grab her and tell her all about it.

But I couldn't. At least for now.

When I opened the door to the townhouse, I was greeted with the smell of someone cooking. And it obviously wasn't me.

It had my stomach rumbling immediately. The aromas hung in the air the way a Thanksgiving feast would, making me gravitate to the room they came from. As I entered, I saw Macie working feverishly. She was at the stove, stirring and sauteing several pans.

"Are you cooking dinner?"

She turned around at the sound of my voice, the disappointment evident on her face.

"Damn," she said. "I didn't think you'd be home from your meeting this early. I decided to make everyone dinner, since you've done it so often."

"Macie, that looks amazing," I told her while looking over her shoulder. "Is that chicken marsala?"

The brown sauce simmering in the pan with chunks of chicken and mushrooms looked pretty good as she stirred.

"It is," she said proudly. "It's one of the few meals I know how to cook, and I think I do it pretty well."

"Anything I can do?"

She looked around the kitchen, suddenly looking less confident at the sight in front of her. Bowls and spoons were scattered across the island as well as a dirty cutting board and knives.

"Well, could you work on a salad while I get some rice going?"

Smiling, I got to work pulling all the ingredients we had onto the counter. We fell into a comfortable rhythm, like dance partners between appliances. Our conversation was light as we told each other funny stories from our childhood. Her laughter was infectious, and I enjoyed having some one-on-one time with her.

"So he was about to go tattle on me, but I poured water on him to make it look like he wet himself, so he couldn't!" Macie howled at the memory of her and her younger brother.

"Oh shit, that's cruel," I said. "Sometimes I'm sad I'm an only child, but when I hear stories like that, it makes me change my mind. You were a she-devil."

She turned from the stove, a kitchen towel in her hand, with a fake scowl on her face.

"Don't call me that, or I'll towel whip you!"

Grabbing my own weapon, I twirled it to perfection. But hers was wet, so I knew I was in trouble. We bounced back and forth like jousters, looking for our best shot. She took it, and I swerved out of the way just in time.

"For a big guy, you're quick," she said as she ran to the other side of the island.

"Yeah, well, plenty of years running plays on the football field'll do that."

She knew I was about to strike, and she wasn't prepared to fight back. Her hoots and howls as I ran after her with my twisted towel made me laugh out loud as well. I was about to snap it in her direction, truly planning on missing, when we were stopped in our tracks.

"What's going on here?" Ava asked.

Although her words were soft, they conveyed so much. Her disbelief came through with an edge of anger.

When our eyes connected, I saw something that speared my heart.

She was hurt.

But why?

"Ava!" Macie yelled. "You're right on time. You can either grab a towel and help defend me in this war, or I could get back to making us dinner, your choice. Personally, it smells like my chicken might be burning."

The smoke coming from over the stove wasn't dark yet. I ran and pulled the pan from the burner, the food safe from disaster. I kept myself busy at the stove like a coward. It was easier than dealing with the version Ava who had come home.

"I decided to cook since Logan always cooks for us. I was able to get to the store." Macie continued talking cheerfully, oblivious to the silent war now taking place between Ava and me. "Do you like chicken marsala?"

I went back to finishing up the salad as I waited to hear anything come from Ava's mouth, but she remained quiet.

"Hey, Ave," Macie said. Her voice got low as she walked out of the kitchen. "You OK?"

They were on the couch, talking quietly. I chose not to listen, knowing I likely had something to do with it.

And to be honest, I didn't know how to do this anymore.

"That was delicious, Macie. Careful, you might be upgraded to chef in the house," I said.

She and I cleared the table as Ava continued to sit. She was unusually quiet, especially for her, during dinner. No snarky comments, no rebuttals to anything I said. Yet the pain came through in her eyes.

"It's so cool that you'll be playing rugby," Macie said. "We'll come see you play once the games start."

Her excitement made me eager for the season to get started, but it was still too cold. Training only for now. Training and parties. Most teams at any college were like their own fraternity. When not in season, they, of course, partied. I knew to expect it but hoped it would be less than a traditional fraternity.

At the meeting tonight, I met up with two players who also didn't drink. It didn't seem it was for any reason other than health and diet, but I was psyched to have guys to hang out with who would be sober with me.

"Yeah, I'm excited to have something else to do here at school, too. Keep my mind occupied, ya know?"

Ava's head snapped to me when I said that, obviously reading into my words.

"So, they're actually having a party this weekend, invited you guys too, if you're interested."

Macie jumped in place while clapping her hands. "That sounds so fun!"

"I thought you were with Jace now?" Ava stood from the table, glaring at Macie, then me. Her words had a nasty bite to them.

Macie's smile fell from her face. "I am. Just because I'm excited about a party doesn't mean I plan on hooking up. Jesus, Ava, what's wrong with you tonight? You're welcome for dinner, by the way."

Macie tossed her dish into the sink and stormed away.

Ava wouldn't look at me. Her eyes were trained on where Macie had just stood. I went to her side and reached for her hand.

"I'm fine," she said as she pulled her hand, and her entire body, away from me. She stormed upstairs as well.

"Sounds good, Tink."

And for the first time in a while, I felt the pangs of my anxiety hit me hard.

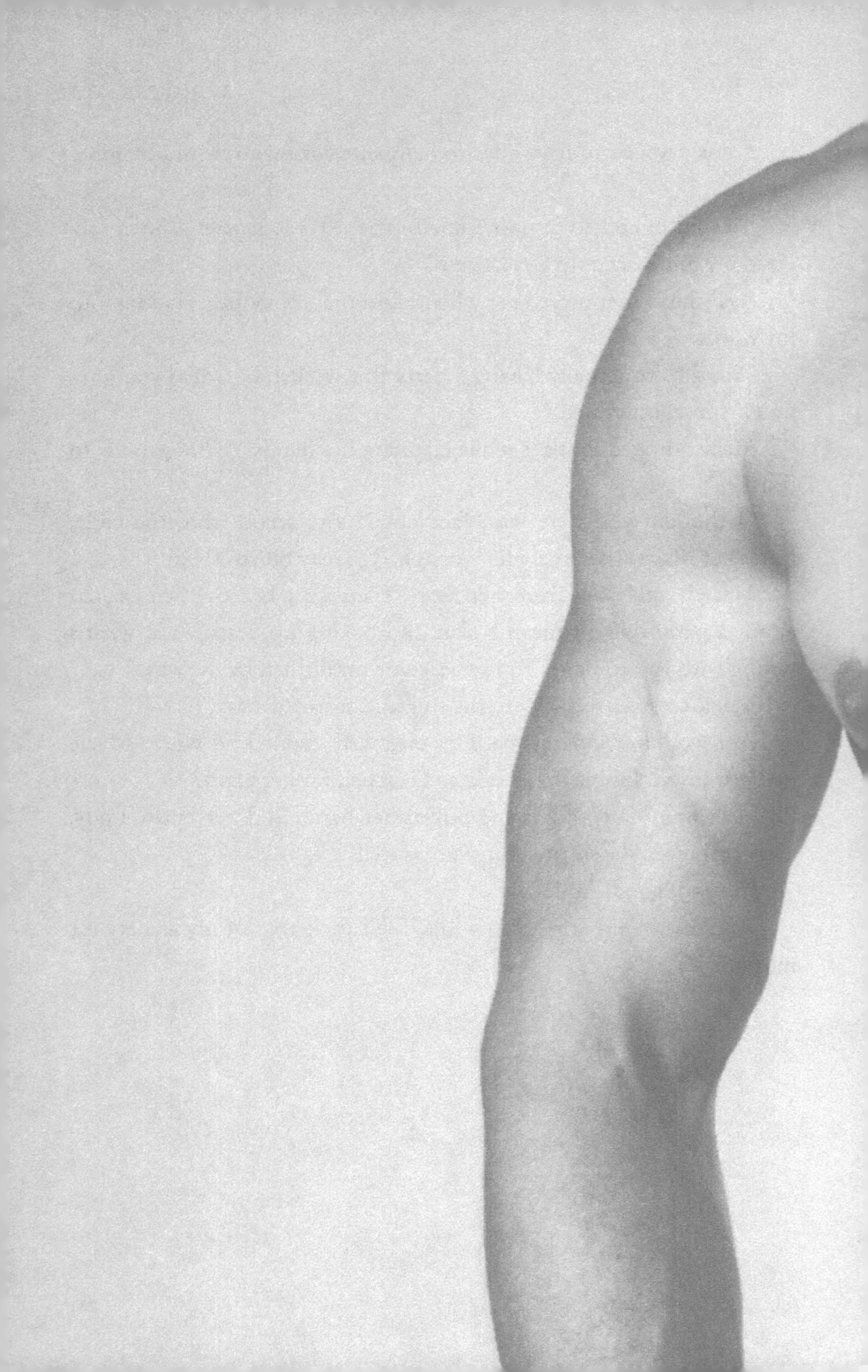

CHAPTER 21

Logan

There was no way I was letting either of us go to bed without addressing everything that had happened at dinner. She was either really upset about something or being a bratty bitch again. Either way, we needed to talk. Considering both Macie and Becca were home, it couldn't happen here.

> Me: text Macie and Becca and tell them we're
> heading to the library to work on our next project
> for marketing

There was no response right away, but I heard movement upstairs. In the meantime, I got dressed and cleaned up a bit. Then I heard my phone vibrate with a text.

> Ava: we don't have a project in marketing

. . .

Me: They don't know that

AGAIN, NO RESPONSE. BUT WHEN I HEARD FOOTSTEPS IN THE hall, I opened my door.

"Where's your backpack?" I asked. "Go get it and meet me in my truck."

She was despondent with her slumped shoulders and sullen, down-turned eyes. No spark in her at all as she turned and went back to her room.

I hustled out to my truck to warm it up and threw the bag I'd packed into the back seat. It was late already, after nine. Ice had started forming on the windshield. The light in her room went dark, and I anxiously waited for her to join me.

As she approached my truck, a slight smile formed when she saw me holding the passenger door for her. I held out one hand for her bag, the other for her hand. She obliged with both, and I helped lift her into her seat.

"Thank you," she said, with a slight eye roll.

"No problem, Tink." My smile and wink made her giggle. And my breathing calmed at the hope this would go well now that she seemed in a better mood.

There wasn't any conversation at first, only the country music on the radio. She turned it to my favorite station before I got to my side of the truck. But the silence wasn't uncomfortable. As we passed the entrance to the school, though, Ava spun in her seat.

"You missed the turn."

"No I didn't. Like you said, we don't have a project to work on. We're not going to the library."

"So then why did I need my backpack?" she asked.

"Well, in case anyone is downstairs when we get home, silly."

I drove as she intently watched our surroundings, no doubt trying to determine our destination. When I started leaving town and got on the highway, she looked even more confused.

"Don't worry, Tink, I'm not stealing you. Sit back, it's only about ten minutes from here."

When I turned off the highway onto a dusty, remote road, her eyes lit up, wondering if I'd possibly lied to her. I smiled in her direction as the truck bounced on the bumpy road, making our way up the mountain. It wasn't the biggest hill in the area, but it served its purpose.

Once I got to the outcrop I was familiar with, I pulled the truck over and turned off the lights.

"Take a look over there." I pointed out her window.

"Oh my goodness," she said in awe. "Is that campus?"

From this vantage point, the entire campus was visible. At night during winter, the view was stunning. So much more was visible without leaves on the trees. We may not be anywhere near a major city, but this was just as pretty from up here.

"It is," I told her. "Found this last year when I needed some time to myself, which was quite often." She looked back at me, her eyes soft. But she couldn't take her eyes from the flickering lights of the campus below for long. "I'd come up here and just sit, sometimes for hours. And think. While I was home, this was one of the things I missed most."

"It's beautiful, Logan. Thank you for bringing me here."

We sat, taking in the view for some time, enjoying the solitude of the night. The undisturbed area was void of any homes or people on a road that led to an abandoned workstation. I was pretty sure we wouldn't be bothered by our roommates up here.

"Ava."

She turned in her seat, pulling her eyes from the view out her window, but didn't look at me. Instead, she stared at her entwined hands in her lap. She shoved her feet onto the dash and blew out a loud breath.

"I don't know what's wrong," she said. "I'm sorry I was such a bitch tonight, and I have no idea why I was." The light of the moon caught her eyes as her head fell back against the headrest in frustration. She ran her fingers through her hair, causing it to stick up.

"Look at me, Ava."

She turned toward me, and I faced her with my arm out for her to come closer. She scooted on the bench seat and came to my side, head against my shoulder.

"When I walked in and saw you and Macie having so much fun together, I don't know, something snapped inside." Her arm went across my body, as if holding me helped her let it out. "I became so jealous that she could act like that with you, and I couldn't."

"But…" I started, but she cut me off.

She sat up, a stern look coming over her face.

"No, don't say it. There's no way we could act like that as roommates, Logan. There's no way I could do that, play around like that and… not want to fall into your arms and kiss you. It would be all over my face."

And she was right.

She was absolutely right.

"We're running out of choices, Tink."

Her face fell. That's not what tonight was supposed to be. This was supposed to fix things.

I took her face in my hands, held it, and looked into her eyes.

"We'll figure it out, I promise you. I'm not giving up on us." And then I kissed her. It had been days since we kissed. Too long.

Too long since my lips had tasted hers, since my tongue battled hers. Both her arms went around my neck as she climbed onto my lap. My hand struggled to find the button to push my seat back, our bodies tight against the steering wheel. Grabbing her by the hips, I slid us across the bench to the middle, better able to spread out.

She fumbled with my shirt, struggling to get it out from behind me. Helping her, I pulled it over my head and tossed it to the floor.

"You're next," I said.

We were frantic. This was not like our other times, there was nothing slow and measured about it. She tore her coat, then her shirt from her body. I reached behind to unhook her bra, sad I couldn't get a better view of her in it in the dark. She peeled off the dark lacy bra and dropped it, revealing her smooth white skin underneath.

My mouth was drawn to the dark pink circle in the center of her breast, and I sucked on it deeply. The feel of that metal bar and her taut nipple in my mouth made my cock hard in my sweats. I held both breasts in my hands, pushing them together. My mouth left her nipple, dipping between her breasts, lapping at her cleavage. The mounds of flesh were soft against my cheeks.

"Logan," she said, her words breathy above me. "Let me get my pants off." She pushed up on her knees the best she could in the cab, her head against the roof. I undid the button of her jeans as she wiggled them down below her hips to her knees.

"I should have told you to wear sweats," I said.

All I did was push my waistband down and pull my dick out.

She stared at it with amusement in her eyes as she struggled with her jeans still tight at her knees. I helped push them to her ankles as she kicked her shoes off. She pushed them off the rest of the way.

"We'll make it work," she said as she climbed back on my lap. "Wait, where's your wallet?"

Reaching in my pocket, I pulled out the foil square. She grabbed it and tore it with her teeth, rolling it over my length all in one smooth move. Lifting her body, she centered herself over me. But I held her over me, not allowing her to lower herself.

"Logan, please," she begged.

"Open your mouth, Ava."

My demand was gruff, but she listened as I shoved my fingers inside. They ran along the inside of her mouth, her tongue, gathering her saliva to make her pussy ready for me. My fingers reached between her legs, rubbing from top to bottom, a finger probing at her entrance.

"Ah, seems you're wet enough already."

I grabbed my dick and teased her, pushing the tip in an inch. She tried to push herself down, but I continued to hold her up by the hips. I knew as soon as she lowered herself, all bets were off. This was going to be a hard, wild ride.

One that wouldn't last long for either of us.

"Logan..."

She was desperate.

Without her realizing what I was doing, I pulled her down onto me, all the way onto my dick. Her hands went to the roof of the cab as her head fell back.

"Fuck!" she cried.

Her hips began rocking back and forth, grinding against me. Lifting herself slightly, she started bouncing up and down, her tempo erratic, her movements jerky due to the small space.

I slid to the side, my head resting against the passenger door, and pulled her closer to me. Once her arms were around my neck, my hands on her ass, I pulled and pushed her atop my body. My finger found its way between the crack of her ass, working its way down. I gauged if she wanted me to keep going, to touch her there again. When she pulled her ass apart for me, I had my answer. My finger went to her tight hole, pushing inside as we found a rhythm that felt right. Our faces were close, my eyes watching her as I brought her to the top of that hill of pleasure. I loved knowing I was making her feel good. Her eyes were closed in ecstasy, her mouth open with small moans escaping as we rocked back and forth.

She pushed up on my chest, her pace increasing as she looked down at me. The gleam in her eye before she threw her head back broke something inside me. My hand left her ass and gripped her hips, digging my fingers deeply into her skin, as I forced her to ride me hard. Eventually letting go, my hands went for her breasts as they swayed against her body. I held each in my hands, squeezing them, feeling the walls of her pussy tighten against me as I did.

I was close.

She was close.

We were both almost there, as she continued to grind herself against me.

"Keep going, Ava, don't stop," I said through gritted teeth. "Don't ever stop."

My words made her movements increase in intensity, her body sliding across mine. She took over, and I surrendered myself to her as she pounded me from above.

"Fuck, Logan." Her words were slurred with exertion. "You feel so good…"

She didn't stop, and the sweat dripped from her brow.

"I'm coming, Logan, I'm going to come!"

And so was I. I released myself inside her, my body contorting under hers, every muscle contracting as I held on for dear life. When I was completely empty, in every sense of the word, she fell on top of my chest. Her breaths were ragged as I rubbed her back, the sweat running down her spine as well.

"That was amazing," I told her.

She remained against my shoulder, pressing small kisses against my clavicle as she lay there. Our breathing eventually settled as we continued to hold one another. Although I didn't want to disturb us lying here, I did want to show her what I brought for us.

"Sit up for one sec," I told her.

Reaching to the back, I grabbed the bag I packed. As I took the contents out, I noticed she pulled up her jeans and already had her bra on.

"You don't have to put your shirt on, ya know?" I said, then chuckled. "I like how you look in that lacy thing in the moonlight."

She sat back with a shy smile, complying with my wish.

"As long as you keep your shirt off, too," she said.

I laughed and went back to my bag.

"It doesn't look like we'll need the blanket right now," I joked, considering we were both still covered in sweat. "But I brought some food and drinks."

On the bench between us, I put a spread together of cheese, grapes, salami, crackers, fig jam, and a bottle of sparkling cider. Complete with plastic flutes.

Ava's eyes went wide, and her hand covered her mouth as she looked at the spread in front of her.

"Logan, when did you put this all together?"

The other day I'd gone shopping for all of this, hoping there'd be a time we could do a "picnic" at the house. But there never seemed to be an opportunity. Once I was done with the dishes, I packed the bag, knowing tonight it would come in handy.

"A man has to be prepared."

"Well, this is amazing, thank you."

We dove into the food, feeding each other grapes and cheese. She poured the juice into the flutes, and we clinked the plastic before taking a sip. It was nice, but it would've been nicer to not have to do it in my truck.

"I'm not going to pressure you, Ava. We'll do what we need to for now to make this work." I reached across the plate of food to kiss her on the nose. "And I understand about tonight, I do. But I'm not going to stop being friends with the other girls, either."

She nodded.

"I know, I want you to be friends with them, I do. It was a gut reaction I had, and not a good one. But it was hard to see it."

We continued eating, listening to music and laughing together.

She was more relaxed than she'd been in days. Leaning against her door, she appeared thoughtful as she held a grape to her lips, her eyes lingering on mine.

"As sexy as this was, and don't get me wrong, Logan, this was sexy as fuck," she said. "I don't think we can maintain a relationship by fucking in your truck every time."

"Well, no, we can't, but we'll figure it out."

She leaned across this time, kissing me.

"We will." She cleared her throat while staring at a ring she fiddled with on her thumb.

But she had me wondering, too, if we would make this work.

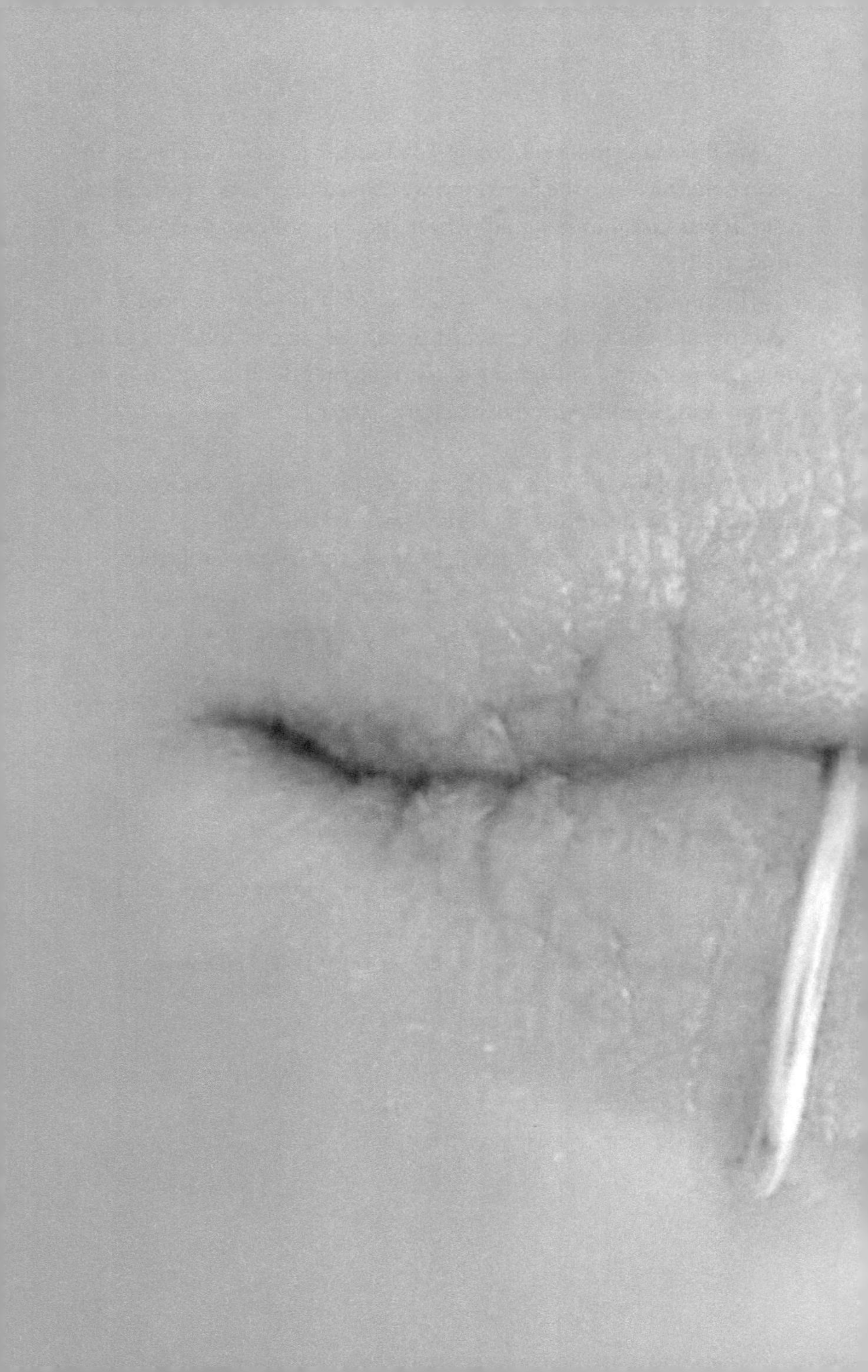

CHAPTER 22

Ava

My earbuds were hidden under my hat as I walked across campus. It was still so damn cold even though the calendar said spring was essentially here. The past couple days had been torturous in the house. Everyone was around since it was Saturday, so I left and went to the library just to get out. The music blasting in my ears soothed my nerves a bit, but the words of the song haunted me.

I tore my hat off and packed my earbuds in their case. Looking around campus, I was surrounded by fellow students rushing to their dorm, the cafeteria, or their cars. Couples huddled together as they walked to shield one another from the cold. Groups of friends talked and laughed as they met up on the paths.

I had a group of friends. A good group of friends, ones who loved me, and I loved them.

And I had a guy who seemed to like me. I mean, he put together a fucking truck picnic for me after mind-blowing sex.

God knew I more than liked him.

So why did I feel so alone?

I was having a constant battle within lately.

My heart told me to jump. Right into the arms of this guy who was proving himself to me in all the right ways.

But my brain. Well, that was showing me what could happen if I followed my heart. And everything that followed was heartache with him and a lost friendship with Macie.

I knew what my brain was doing; it was looking for his faults and highlighting them. Or even creating ones that didn't exist.

It was always forcing me to think about his past with Lanie. Or reminding me he was working on his recovery, and why would I want to get involved with someone dealing with that.

Making excuses for me.

So I could walk away and not feel guilty about it.

But the guilt was eating me up.

My phone buzzed in my pocket.

> Macie: Hey where'd u run off to? Make sure ur home in time to get ready for tonight

TONIGHT. THE RUGBY PARTY. BOTH BECCA AND MACIE convinced me to go. They were going stag, without their guys. Looking at it as a girls' night out. But there was one thing they didn't know.

My guy would be there right under their noses.

> Me: Don't worry I'll be ready

I really didn't know if I would be.

Rugby players were fucking crazy. Like really fucking nuts. More of them were naked, running around the party, than had clothes on. I knew Logan said there were a couple guys he met who also didn't drink. But I had my concerns about him being around this crew.

Macie, Becca, and I huddled together in a corner on the main floor in awe at what we witnessed. The guys were challenging one another to various bets.

Naked bets.

Run down the block, *naked*.

Do a keg stand, *naked*.

Do a funnel, *naked*.

Go kiss that girl, *naked*.

The bonus was there was not a single guy on the team who wasn't hot. Like seriously hot in every sense of the word. Their bodies were muscular and cut. They were beautiful in every sense of the word.

In that regard, Logan belonged here.

"Oh my god, this is crazy fun!" Macie yelled. She danced to the music with Becca, the two of them spinning each other like ballerinas.

We made an agreement with Logan that we were going to have a couple drinks tonight since he had guys with him who weren't drinking.

Macie and Becca took it to heart, tipsy already. The beer in my hand was nearly full since I couldn't shake an uneasy feeling that had overcome me. As I looked around, nothing seemed amiss, but it was like a prickling up my spine.

"How you guys doing?" Logan asked. He bent close to my ear, and

I smelled his familiar scent. I wanted to kiss him, mark him as mine, as I turned to look at him.

He looked hot tonight in his jeans and tight black Henley. He looked so good in black with his light hair and eyes. And the way the shirt hugged every muscle of his chest and arms, it was hard not to run my fingers up and down him.

"Good," I said back.

"We're awesome!" Macie yelled over the music, and he laughed at her.

"Great, glad you guys are having fun."

Before he walked away, I felt his finger trail along my arm, elbow to wrist. The covert action made my heart flutter as I worked hard to rein in any other reactions. Becca and Macie were oblivious as they continued dancing, branching out into the crowd.

"Have fun, Tink," he whispered so close to me I felt his lip touch my lobe. I turned to respond, but he was already walking away.

I ran up behind him and grabbed his hand, pulling him with me toward the stairs. Our roommates were still in their own world.

"Come upstairs with me," I told him when he turned around.

His startled look quickly morphed into a twinkle of mischief. He hurried me to the first floor, where it was much quieter.

"Are we doing what I think we're doing?" he asked, his voice full of hope.

All I did was pull him along, down a dark hallway. Once I knew we were far enough away from the basement, I spun around and reached up for his face. He was so damn tall it was impossible for me to reach his mouth without jumping into his arms. My legs wrapped around his waist as he held me by my ass, our lips colliding. He backed me against the wall, freeing a hand to grip my neck, tilting my head to the side. His mouth ravaged my neck, up to my ear, down my jawline.

"This is such a fucking turn-on, Ava." His mouth made its way back to mine as his teeth pulled on my lip ring, his lips sucking on it. "I want to bring you into one of these rooms, bend you over, and pull this skirt up."

His words had my pussy getting wet.

"My cock needs to be inside you, fuck..."

But then I pulled the plug. I backed off, pushing him from my neck and forcing him to look at me.

"None of that's going to happen, is it?" he asked, then chuckled.

"Well, not here."

He still held me against the wall, our bodies crushed together. I could feel his hard cock against the small piece of fabric covering me under my skirt. This would be hard to walk away from.

But we had to. I just couldn't go all night without kissing him, but it was probably cruel to have done that.

His lips were pressed into a grimace as he lowered his head to look me in the eye.

"I need a cold shower now, Tink." At least he was joking with me.

Slowly, he lowered me to the floor. I adjusted my skirt and cami as we made our way out to the main room. It was still fairly quiet, only a small group in the kitchen.

"Let's get you back to Macie and Becca," he said.

Once back in the basement, which was like a mosh pit, it took a minute to find them. His height helped, since he was able to see above most of the people there. Once we were in the vicinity of them, he leaned close to my ear.

"Maybe it's time for another two a.m. meet up."

I smiled up at him, thinking the same thing. And then he walked back into the mass of people.

As he did, a group of what had to be his new teammates grabbed hold of him, hoisting him on their shoulders. Quite a feat considering his size. The hollers coming from them caught the attention of everyone in the room.

"Hey, this here is a new recruit!" the one guy yelled.

"He needs to be initiated!" another screamed.

They put him down and huddled around him, arms interlocked in a literal huddle, with Logan stuck in the middle of it. The laughter coming from within was maniacal; I could only imagine what they were going to have him do.

Of course, I was prepared for it to include nudity. Well, let's say I expected it to. I was not prepared.

Sure enough, when the gaggle of guys pulled away, Logan was standing in the buff.

He was fucking glorious to look at.

His eyes went right to mine, but didn't linger. I saw the nerves in them, but also the excitement. He was probably regretting having his female roommates at this party, that was for sure.

In the craziness, I was pushed away from Becca and Macie. They were nowhere to be found as I frantically scanned the horde of people. I found a chair along the wall and stood on it to get a better view of the coming events and to find my roommates. As soon as I did, I immediately spotted them in the center of the room, not too far from Logan. The wide grins as they ogled him had me laughing.

Suddenly, one of the guys from the team demanded our attention. He was a big guy with muscles that rivaled Logan's. His dark hair was a bit long, hitting his shoulders, and he wore a ballcap over it. The beer in his hand spilled from its cup as his arms flung about while quieting the group.

"OK, settle down, especially the female folk. I know, he's one of the hotter ones, you're lucky girls. And one of you is going to get luckier!"

All the girls started whistling and hollering.

My stomach dropped.

The others were pushing to get closer to the dark-haired one and Logan. Logan stood stoic behind him, hands clasped and hanging low. I knew he was trying to cover himself, and he did a great job making it look casual, but his hands just didn't do the job. His manhood was still visible.

"Logan here tells me he doesn't have a girlfriend."

Louder hollers from the crowd.

Shit.

"That changes things a bit, allows us to, well, up the ante...," the guy said. "So, some guys from the team are going to walk through the crowd and pick the lucky girl who gets to spend some time with our new teammate."

A few of the guys started mulling through the crowd, flirting with the girls, encouraging their rowdy behavior. When I looked below me, Becca and Macie stared back.

"We have to make ourselves scarce," Becca yelled up at me.

She reached for my hand and the three of us went for the stairs. We knew none of us could be chosen as his "girl."

But I could, couldn't I?

As we weaved our way through the crowd, being tossed and thrown, I tried to find Logan but couldn't. Macie pushed me from behind until my foot hit a step and we headed up. The room I had just been in was now occupied with a couple on the couch close to having sex. We pushed through that room and made our way to the kitchen.

"Oh my god, this party is crazy," Macie said as she took a seat on a stool. "And christ, did you guys get a look at Logan?"

Becca whined. "I tried not to, he's like a freaking brother to me. It was kinda gross to see his ass up there, I'll be honest. But no one can deny he has a great body. He works hard for it."

"We were looking for you before," Macie said to me. "Where did you go?"

The lump in my throat was the size of an apple.

"I had to go to the bathroom."

After that, I remained quiet, letting the two of them talk as I strained to hear what was happening below us in the basement. The hollering suddenly became ear piercing but then went silent.

It had to be over.

"I think we can go back now, guys." I stood from my seat.

They filed behind me as we made our way through the next room, eyes on the floor to avoid the couple still going at it on the couch. When we made it to the door to the basement, though, it flew open.

Shooting through the doorway was a naked Logan holding hands with a pretty redhead. She was giggling as he pulled her with him, her hand reaching out for his naked ass.

He stopped dead when he saw us, our eyes connecting. His hand dropped hers as she rammed into the back of him while coming through the door.

"Hey, guys," he said, looking at the three of us. But his eyes kept returning to mine. There was an apology in them somewhere, but I couldn't accept it.

"Logan, dude, cover up that white ass," Becca chided.

"Who are these girls?" the redhead asked, slurring her words.

"Oh my god, Logan, this party is crazy!" Macie offered.

"This is fucked up, isn't it?" Logan said.

And I remained silent.

I couldn't talk. I feared if I did, I'd break down crying.

Logan turned to the redhead as he put his boxer briefs on. I hadn't noticed he brought his clothes with him. "These girls are my roommates."

"Aww, you live with girls, isn't that sweet," she said. Then she started pawing at his hand as he worked at his jeans. "Why are you getting dressed? I won you."

I won you.

Jesus fucking Christ, I was about to vomit.

His eyes shifted back and forth between the three of us, and I noticed a sheen of sweat on his brow.

"You won a kiss, sweetie. I don't need to be naked for a kiss," he told her.

I didn't know why him calling her sweetie got my ire up, but it did.

Maybe it was because less than ten minutes ago his tongue was down my throat, and now he was going to kiss this bitch.

Everyone knew about her.

But it was all my doing that no one knew about me, wasn't it?

As I pushed past him, he fell into the redheaded bimbo, and she almost fell to the ground, she was so drunk. Of course, I'd made it worse. Logan had to grab her since he wasn't about to let her fall. I didn't stick around to see what happened next.

There was no way I was going to watch him kiss her.

The footsteps behind me had to be Becca and Macie, but I also didn't wait to see that either. Once back in the basement, I got myself a fresh beer, chugged it, and grabbed another.

Turning to the dance floor, I was decidedly on the prowl.

There were plenty to choose from. All you had to do was shake your ass in the middle of the floor and they swarmed you. Within seconds, I had two new guys on me. I chose the dark-haired one over the blonde. I wanted nothing to remind me of *him.*

"Hey, beautiful," he cooed in my ear as he shimmied against my back.

His beer breath stunk, but if I closed my eyes, his firm hands on my hips helped me forget. I swayed to the beat, our bodies in sync. Putting my cup to my lips, I downed the contents in one gulp.

I was getting drunk. I needed to forget.

"Want another?" he asked.

"I'll get it." I was being stupid, but I wasn't going to be that stupid.

But wasn't I? Somewhere in the depths of my brain, I knew I was. I was being stupid and careless. With my heart. And maybe Logan's. At the moment, I didn't care.

I worked my way back through the crowd to find my dark-haired hottie waiting for me. He leaned in close, that breath nauseating me again. "You look beautiful."

I smiled. Leaning close, I asked, "Are you on the team?"

He nodded. "Yeah, third year. I played at home, too. They're a blast to be around, aren't they?"

I chugged the beer and threw the cup to the floor. There was no need for us to get to know one another. Using both hands, I pulled him against me, still wanting to forget. He obliged, grinding his body into mine.

The pulse of the music was mesmerizing as my new friend and I explored each other. His hands roved across my belly as he pushed against me from behind. My arms went around his neck, pulling his head closer. I felt his fingers inch up under my shirt, dangerously close to the bottom of my bra.

He spun me around so we were chest to chest. He was a more manageable height for me. I could see over his shoulder. As I did, I saw right into the eyes of Logan.

He was glaring at me. The anger poured from him.

We were a casualty of ourselves.

This was never going to work. How could we think it could? A secret relationship?

Ain't gonna happen. The sooner we got on with our lives, the better off we'd both be.

I stared back at him as my stranger's hands brushed against my ass. At the same time, a group of girls were fawning over Logan. They surrounded him, each fighting for his attention. That's what being on this team would be: weekend parties full of cronies looking for a hookup. If we couldn't come out as a couple, we would deal with this endlessly.

I couldn't.

It was better this way.

"Let's go upstairs," my new friend whispered.

"I don't even know your name."

"It's nice to have secrets, isn't it?" he said as he pulled me along.

My heart sank at his words.

I still went.

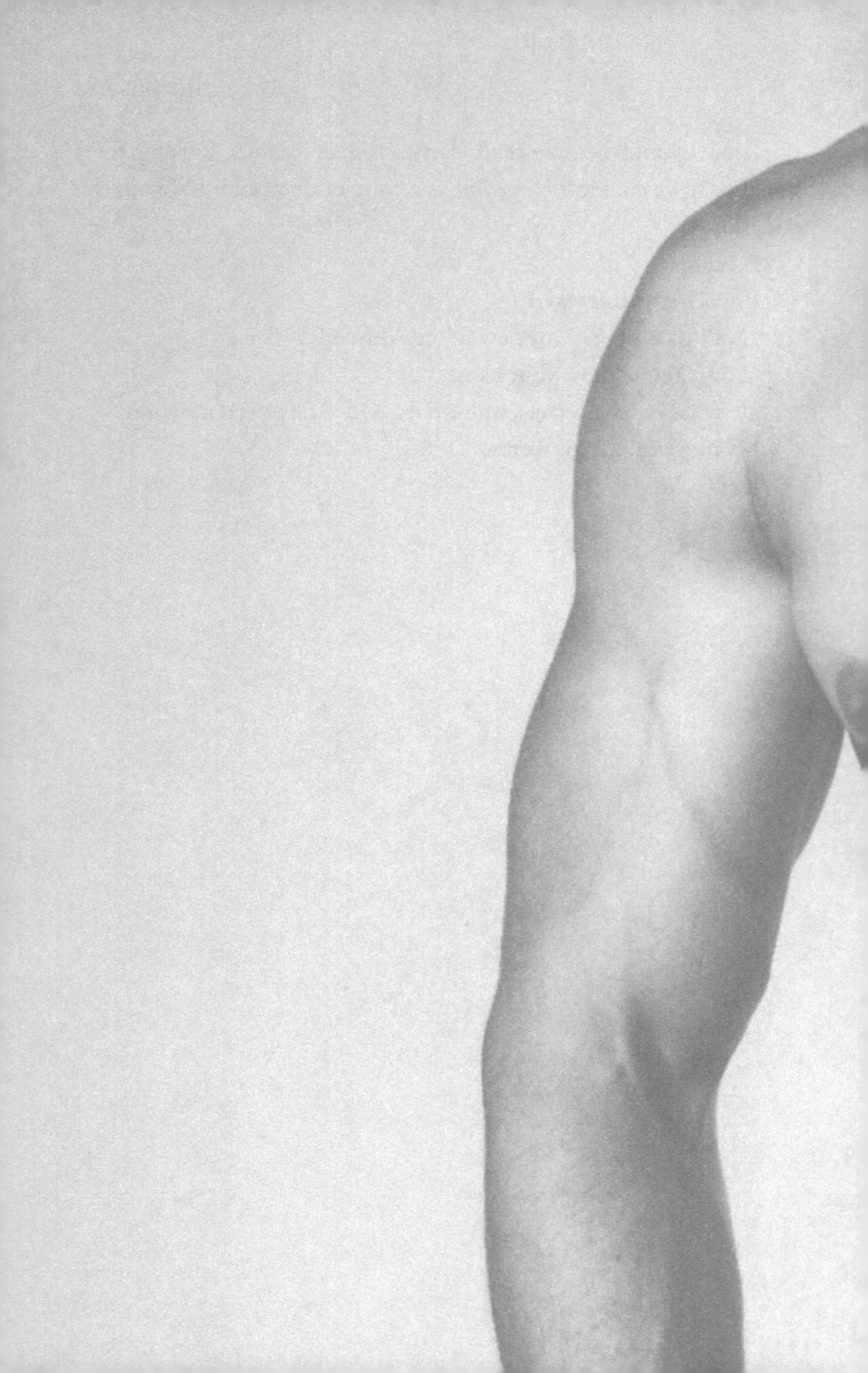

CHAPTER 23

Logan

Watching her go upstairs with that fucking asshole tore me apart. I thought bringing my roommates tonight would be fun. Enjoy a new part of my life together. Then when she took *me* upstairs, I had a renewed hope that what we had might outlive her desire to keep it a secret. The initiation was unexpected, and it had to be hard for Ava to watch. But when we all wound up together upstairs, awkward didn't even describe it.

She probably thought more happened than did, but I literally only kissed the other girl gently on the lips.

Once. That was it.

My feet couldn't get me to the basement any faster, but it wasn't fast enough. Ava was already dancing with that dickhead.

Her Tink attitude mixed with drinking was going to really fuck up this night.

"Hey, man, I'll be back," I told Sutton. He was one of the guys I was getting to know. One of the guys who also didn't drink. He'd been talking it up with a bunch of girls while I forced myself to watch the show taking place a few yards away.

"Sure, man," he said.

There was no way I was letting her do something she was, or we were, going to regret come morning. If I had to drag her out of whatever bedroom she went into, I would.

Scanning the first room, I found it empty. I stood still, listening. Nothing. No sound on this floor at all. I moved to the staircase that went to other bedrooms.

That's when I heard it. I heard her voice.

I heard the panic.

"Stop," Ava said.

Jesus Christ, that motherfucker was going to die.

I took two, maybe three, steps at a time, and made it to the top within seconds. They were at the end of the hall, a dark corner leading into a room. They stood in the doorway, he was obviously trying to get her inside. He held her firmly against the wall, her hands restrained by his above her head. She fought furiously against his hold, to no avail.

His hand was under her shirt, lifting it up.

His hand was on her breast.

His mouth was on her breast.

As she continued to struggle and say no.

The universe spun around me, the stars in my eyes blinding me from what was right in front of me. A rage started in my gut and radiated to my hands, fists at my sides.

"Get off her," I growled.

He didn't stop. Only pulled his mouth from her.

"Find your own room, dude."

"What did you say, motherfucker?"

My deathly words got his attention. He turned to look at me, his eyes wide at whatever he saw.

Ava saw me, the tears in her eyes distracting me for a moment.

She was destroyed.

Then as he backed away, I noticed her skirt was askew as well.

Fuck. Him.

In two long strides, I had him by the throat and against the wall.

"What the fuck, dude?" he pleaded.

Right as my fist landed on his face.

A satisfying crunch from his nose, blood spewing from there and his mouth.

He slumped against the wall, but I gripped him by the shirt, refusing to let him fall to the ground. He wasn't getting off that easy.

I went in for another punch but felt a small hand on my shoulder.

"Logan..."

Her voice was quiet, but it broke through the chaos in my brain. I threw him to the floor and turned to her, taking her in my arms.

"Are you OK?" I whispered against her head. All she could do was nod.

Then I heard the guy getting up at my feet.

"Ava, go find Becca and Macie now."

She took off down the stairs while I turned my attention back to the asshole who hurt her. He leaned against the wall, wiping the blood from his nose with the back of his hand, a smug look on his face.

"You're the new guy, right?"

This guy was not about to talk his way out of what he'd done. I stood, ready to throw another punch if that was the direction this went.

"What the fuck, man. Who do you think you are?" He stood tall as he suddenly felt courageous, but that still kept him a good half foot shorter than me.

"I'm the guy who stopped you from raping that girl."

He smirked, then laughed.

"You're kidding, right?" He pushed his way past me, a bit harder than I should've let him. "We were all over each other downstairs, man.

You don't know what you're talking about, she wanted it as much as I did."

My fists clenched, in and out, itching to take this guy down for good. I couldn't believe he had the nerve to defend his actions. He started walking away from me. That was when I heard tons of footsteps on the stairs.

"Are you fucking kidding me?" I asked. "She wanted it? What part of the word 'no' did you not understand? Because I clearly heard her say it to you twice in the time I witnessed what you did."

There were several other guys from the team who had joined us in the hallway by now, bearing witness to his response. They stood behind him, all staring blankly at me, waiting.

"Well?" I asked. "Why didn't you stop when she said no?"

He pushed past everyone surrounding him.

"Fuck you, dude, I don't answer to you."

One of the guys followed him downstairs while the other two stayed with me. The adrenaline brought on by it all was still surging through me as they came close.

"Guys, I'm in no mood to be told I shouldn't have laid him out." I started pushing past them, not happy the guy was now downstairs near Ava without me.

"Hey, man," the one guy said. That was when I realized it was Sutton. The other guy who stayed with me was Ashton. "Relax. We just don't want you getting in trouble, no need to do anything further. Best to steer clear of him. We have some other guys taking care of him down there, no worries."

My breathing slowed a bit, though I was still frantic on the inside. I felt the edges of a panic attack trying to make their way to the forefront. But I fought it, I needed to get the girls safely out of here.

"I need to find my roommates, get Ava home. She's probably a mess right now."

I ran down the stairs to find the first floor empty other than my three girls. Becca and Macie surrounded Ava on the couch. Ava attempted to push them away, the stoic brat that she was. But it was going to hit her, and I needed to get her out of here before it did.

"I'm getting the truck, meet me outside in five."

I grabbed my keys from the kitchen. Parking was tricky at this house, and I had to park a block away. As I pulled up to the house, tons of the guys were milling around outside, the party looking officially over.

This had been my first exposure to the team, and it hadn't gone the way I'd expected. Punching a teammate probably didn't bode well for me getting a position. My rapid heart rate and sweaty palms indicated I was not doing as good a job as I'd like at quelling my impending anxiety attack. It didn't help that as I jumped from my truck, a group of the guys walked my way.

Ashton must be the team captain, because he reached me first, the rest standing behind.

"Hey, Logan, I want to let you know we support you in what went down here tonight. We don't tolerate his type of behavior."

All the guys came to me, murmuring words of support.

The heart palpitations slowed. As I looked around, I unclenched my still fisted hands. My ragged breaths became even as my head swiveled between the guys.

"Thank you," I said. I chose to look at the ground, focusing on a tiny pebble, as I felt the moisture build up in my eyes.

Ashton walked with me as I started for the house. "No worries, man." We fell in step together as we walked toward the front door. "How the hell did you get so lucky with those roommates?" He laughed. "But seriously, go take care of the tiny one. She's going to need all of you."

And that's exactly what I planned on doing.

Becca and Macie were still upstairs with her; she didn't want me in the room with them. Which was fine, because if I were, I'd have blown our cover for sure.

I felt the panic rising.

Sitting alone in the dark, knowing she was just upstairs, drove me crazy. I wanted to see her. To make sure she was alright. Make sure that douchebag didn't hurt her. My hands rubbed along my jeans repeatedly, digging into the material, gripping at my knees. As I wiped my brow, the sweat soaked the back of my hand.

I checked my watch: almost midnight.

Definitely too late to put a call in to Dr. Jean.

The energy built inside me as I jumped from the couch and paced the room. Tearing open the refrigerator door, I stared inside but registered nothing as I looked. I wasn't hungry. After I slammed it shut, the bottles rattling in the door, I walked to the back window. The moon was hazy behind some clouds, making it much darker than normal. I checked the back slider, making sure it was locked. My mind raced.

I decided to head out front. Sitting on the stoop, I took a deep breath of the cold night air, letting it fill my lungs. Keeping it there helped me to calm down. As I let it out slowly, I peered to the side and saw my friend.

The cement statue stood guard, keeping our house safe. And he did it with a smile.

I pulled him from his sunken spot in the earth and dragged him to me. We stared at each other for a bit, and his unwavering grin seemed to be working once again.

"I think it's time you got a name, little fella," I told him.

It had to be a strong name for him to be our guardian. I pulled out my phone and searched. So many popped up, names of every culture and descent. One caught my eye because of its English and German background, like me.

Howard.

I could call him Howie.

My head snapped behind me as the door flew open.

"There you are," Becca said. "I couldn't find you." She grabbed a coat and came to sit beside me. We were both quiet, staring at Howie. She flicked a piece of dirt from his bent leg. "He *is* cute."

"Yeah, he is," I agreed. "His name is Howie."

She giggled.

"What?"

"I like it. Howie, that's a good, strong name." She leaned her head on my shoulder. "How ya doin', big guy?"

I didn't answer right away, I couldn't. Because the way I was feeling, and the reasons for it, I couldn't divulge to her. My hands rubbed at my face, trying to make sense of this entire night.

"I don't know, to be honest."

She nodded, assuming she knew how I was truly feeling.

"You did a good thing, Logan." She picked up Howie and gently placed him back in his designated spot. As she twisted and turned him into place, she looked at me. "Ava finally fell asleep. It took Macie and me a while to get her settled, but she calmed down. I think Macie's going to sleep in her room with her. I'm sure Ava'll want to see you in the morning."

My hands twisted together as so many emotions rolled through me. I couldn't decipher what I was feeling.

I didn't want to wait until morning to see her, but there was no choice now.

What I did know was I should be the one in her bed with her.

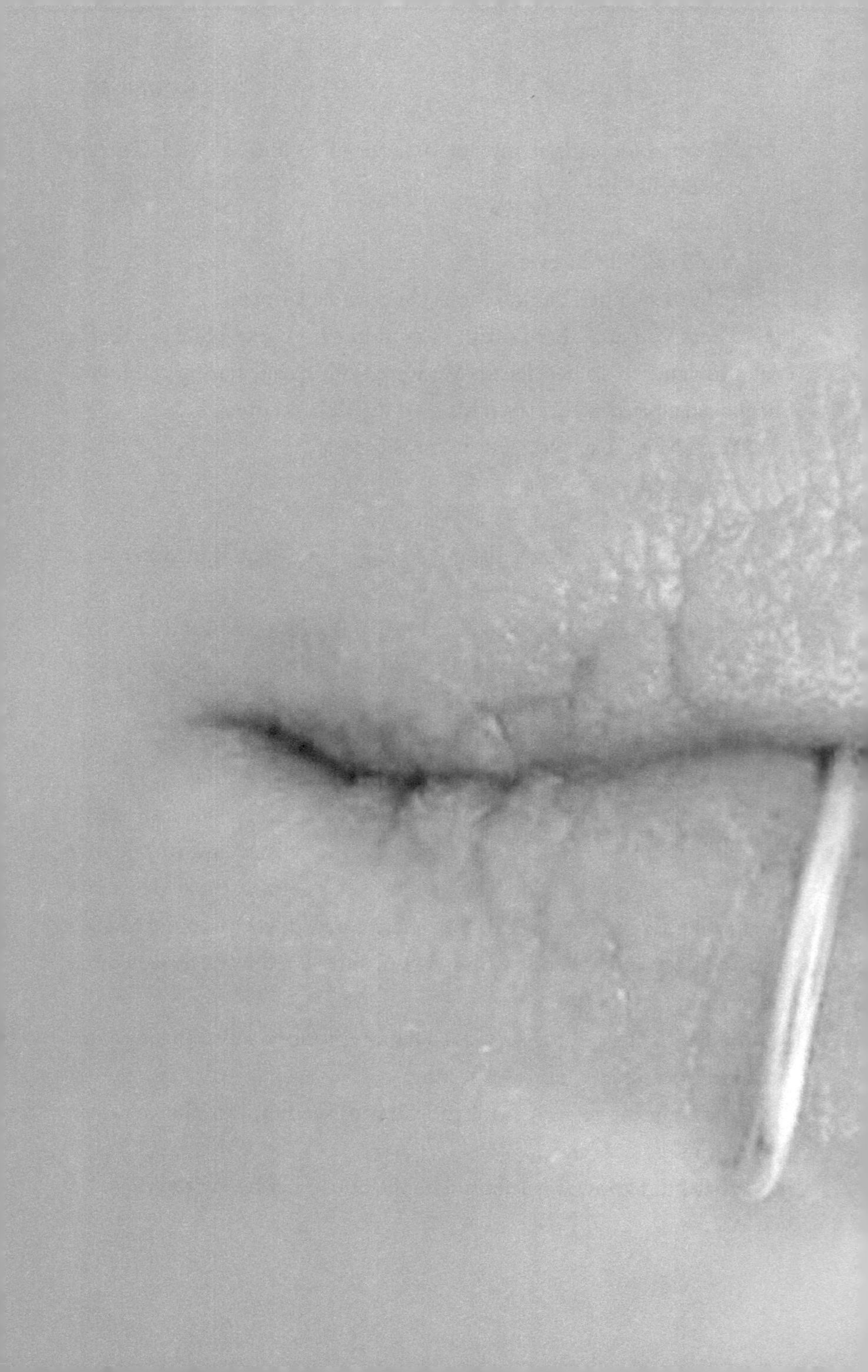

CHAPTER 24

Ava

The sunlight hurt my head as it filtered through the cheap plastic mini blinds this place provided. I guess I could have put up room-darkening shades but never felt the need. I hadn't been this hungover in a long time. As I pulled the quilt over my head, I heard the rustling of paper. Looking to my side, I saw a note.

Hey BFF - there's water and aspirin on your nightstand I ran out to get us some breakfast come down when you feel up to it
Macie

When I felt up to it.

I didn't want to see anyone.

The shame and embarrassment overwhelmed me.

Why did I allow that to happen to me last night? I shouldn't have gotten as drunk as I did, for starters. Then my anger toward Logan took over and all it did was almost get me...

I couldn't even think about what almost happened. Another guy I shouldn't have trusted. Who failed me in the worst possible way.

If Logan hadn't shown up, it likely would have been worse.

If I wasn't so mad at him in the first place, I don't think I would've put myself in that position to begin with.

Pushing the blame...I was good at that with him. But it was true. Even being in this "secret relationship" with him had taken a turn toward being problematic already. It's just not worth it, they never work out for me.

My mind strayed back to the end of my junior year of high school. I'd been with my boyfriend Cole since the beginning of freshman year. He was a year older, and when we saw each other my first day of high school, we became inseparable. In the beginning, things were good. We had a normal high school relationship. I thought I was in love, of course, and maybe I was. He was sweet, thoughtful, and always said and did the right thing. When he wanted to start including my best friend, Casey, on some of our weekends after her boyfriend broke up with her, I thought he was being even nicer.

Joke was on me.

It was almost graduation for him, and I guess he shot his shot before heading off to college.

I walked in on the two of them, hooking up in his bed. The image will forever be engrained in my mind.

Because I not only lost my boyfriend that day, but my best friend.

And from that moment I promised myself two things: I would always be a good friend, and I would protect my heart moving forward and tread very carefully in life with relationships.

Yet this *thing* with Logan was breaking both of those promises.

If Macie found out about Logan and me, I could lose her. And as far as Logan...

My heart was falling, and I had to protect it before it hit the ground and shattered.

As I rolled over, I heard the faint sounds of voices in the distance and smelled the aroma of breakfast foods. My phone told me it was almost eleven already. The rumbling in my stomach agreed.

But I wasn't in any rush to see anyone, especially Logan.

I knew I'd have to talk to him, thank him, for last night, and I would. But it would lead us to talking about other things that I didn't want to talk about. Not quite yet.

> Macie: you up? Logan actually cooked

> Me: Yep

MY PLAN WAS TO STAY PUT AND HOPE THAT BECCA OR Macie brought me some food.

Eventually, that knock came on my door.

"Yeah," I said. I started sitting up, getting excited for the food one of them was bringing me.

And the company.

Why was I surprised at who came through the door? I shouldn't have been. Of course he would take advantage of the first chance to see me.

"Hey," Logan said as he walked toward me with a plate. "Morning."

His tentative steps toward my bed were coupled with concerned eyes. He made room for the full plate of food on my night table, taking care to move things aside. He lingered with his movements, taking his time.

Avoiding me.

Then he turned to look.

"Ava."

The reverent way he said my name, with such adoration but sadness at the same time, broke me.

My tears were silent as they spilled over the lower lids of my eyes. They streamed down my cheeks, dripping from my chin. My hands couldn't wipe them away fast enough.

His eyes filled, the tears falling. He fell to his knees on the floor beside me. When his arms opened, ready to envelop me, I flung myself against him.

I had no idea he was what I needed.

My heart ripped open as he held me, and it scared me.

"Ava," he said, over and over. "Baby, I'm so sorry. I'm sorry I wasn't there to stop him before he did anything." His hands stroked my head, his fingers threading through my hair, as I squeezed him hard.

The words were in my throat, struggling over the knot to come out. My once silent tears were now quiet sobs against his chest as he worked hard to soothe me.

He brought himself up to the bed, me on his lap, and just held me.

He then understood that *this* was what needed to happen. He held me and I let it all come out.

After minutes of me crying, I pulled back to look at him. His face was blotchy as tears continued falling down his cheeks as well. He took my face in his hands, his thumbs furiously rubbing at the moisture under my eyes.

"What can I do?" he croaked out. "I have to make this right, Ava. How can I help you?"

I shook my head, attempting to shrug out of his hold. As much as I needed the strength of his presence, his arms around me, I wasn't ready for more. Not when I knew what I was planning on doing.

"Don't shut me out, please," he begged.

But I won the battle because we both knew he wasn't going to hold on to me against my will. I moved back toward my pillows, pulling the blanket up and over me. I knew as well as he did it became the wall between us in that moment.

The slump of his shoulders as he moved further down my bed showed his defeat. He had his back to me, bent over his knees, staring at the wall in front of him. The muscles in his shoulders and back tensed as he scrubbed at his face with his hands, indicative of the stress from the night before.

Further indication that our situation wasn't good for him.

Wasn't good for us.

He had so much going on in his life that he needed to consider other than me and our silly, secret fuck-buddy relationship. I wasn't going to be the reason he struggled with more anxiety, or God forbid, his sobriety. I needed to have the balls to do this.

"Ava," he said. "When I saw him touching you, my world stopped spinning. Hearing you say no, and him not stopping...I could only think about you, making sure you were safe." His head swiveled as his eyes searched for mine.

However, once they connected, I had to look away.

Suddenly, he shot up from the bed, pacing the room. His eyes went wide, his breathing ragged. He kept wiping his hands on the thighs of his sweatpants as he walked in small circles.

"Fuck," he mumbled to himself. His hands ran through his hair, then clasped above his head, his elbows banging together.

Something changed in him, but what?

He went to the window. His sudden silence was a stark contrast to the behaviors I'd just witnessed. As he stared outside, the silence that filled the room became a barrier that grew between us with each passing minute.

But for some reason, I still couldn't bring myself to say anything to him.

Not yet.

He finally turned and gestured to the plate of food on the small table.

"I made you your favorite breakfast."

Pancakes and bacon.

"You should eat it before it gets any colder." His voice was devoid of emotion.

Then he kissed me on the forehead, put his head down, and walked out of my room.

THE INTERACTION BETWEEN LOGAN AND ME WAS UTTERLY confusing. I expected the emotion and the tears from me and wasn't completely surprised he cried as well. But the change in his demeanor took me by surprise. I had no idea what happened. My only thought was he was staving off a panic attack and needed to leave, possibly to talk to his therapist.

I decided to reach out to him later. My plans to talk to him about us still needed to happen, but I could put that off until I knew he was better mentally.

Another hour passed before I felt ready to get out of bed. The first thing I did was head back into the shower. I'd taken one last night before falling asleep, but I felt the need for another.

It felt cliché, but it was so true. The need to cleanse myself was instinctive, almost hardwired into my brain. I needed every trace of that guy off me.

Feeling better, cleaner, I made my way downstairs to face people. But it was much quieter than expected; Macie was the only one sitting in the living room. I pivoted toward the coffeepot, happy to see it wasn't empty.

"Where are the others?" I asked.

"Oh my god, Ava, you snuck up on me." Within seconds, she was next to me as she pulled me into an embrace. As she held me, she spoke into the top of my head. "How are ya, girlfriend?"

I let her hold me, unsure who it was for at the moment. Her light eyes were so pretty as they looked back at me, inquisitive and full of questions.

"Logan took off," she said as she held my hands between us. "He was really upset. Becca tried talking to him, but he stormed away from her."

I stripped my hands from hers, not wanting to hear any more. As I poured the steaming coffee into my mug, I turned from Macie to prepare it. My decision to come downstairs was now thwarted by her words concerning Logan. My brain was muddled enough, I didn't want anything else to worry about.

Mainly because I was the cause of his stress and pain.

"How are *you* doing, sweetie?"

I held the cup, using its heat to warm my frigid hands, watching the swirls of steam billow above. As I brought it to my lips and gave it the obligatory blow, my eyes connected with Macie's over the top of the mug. Desperate for that first sip, I delayed answering her as I took a big gulp, knowing the warm caffeine would do nothing but help me.

"I still don't know where he went!" Becca was frantic as she came flying through the front door. She rounded the corner and stopped, seeing both Macie and me looking at her.

"Ava, I didn't know you came down, sweetie." Her tone did a one-eighty.

The unspoken conversation taking place between my two friends was unnerving. Their raised eyebrows and lifted shoulders didn't go unnoticed.

"Why did he leave?" I asked.

Becca answered quickly. "You don't need to worry about anything, we'll take care of it." She joined us at the table.

The three of us sat in an awkward silence.

Last night, they were wonderful. Theirs were the first faces I saw once I got down the stairs in that godforsaken house. They grabbed a hold of me as a group of guys ran past me to join Logan.

I don't remember much of the drive home. The three of us huddled together in the back seat as Logan raced through empty streets. Macie and Becca held me tight, the three of us holding back tears. Once the truck pulled into its usual spot, I felt Logan's strong arms lift me and pull me against his body. The girls followed closely behind until we were inside. I heard their hushed whispers as they instructed him to bring me up to my bed.

They forced Logan to leave once I was sitting on my bed, which he did reluctantly. I remember him kissing me on the forehead and hugging me before he left.

"He's like your knight in shining armor," Macie said.

She had no idea how true her words were.

They showered me, dressed me, laid with me, talked with me. At some point during the night, I woke to Macie's arm wrapped around my middle.

She was spooning me.

She didn't leave my side.

But once the light of the morning came, all I wanted to do was forget last night ever happened.

I didn't want to talk anymore.

I didn't want to remember it.

I wanted it to just fade away.

Because it shouldn't have happened to begin with. If I hadn't felt the need to "punish" Logan — to force him to see me with another guy — I wouldn't have been in the position of almost being raped.

Now Logan was hurting because of what I'd done. The position I'd put him in, put us in. And my heart hurt.

He stormed out of here because of me. I knew it in my bones, my soul. I saw something change in him right in front of me.

I couldn't be the reason he failed.

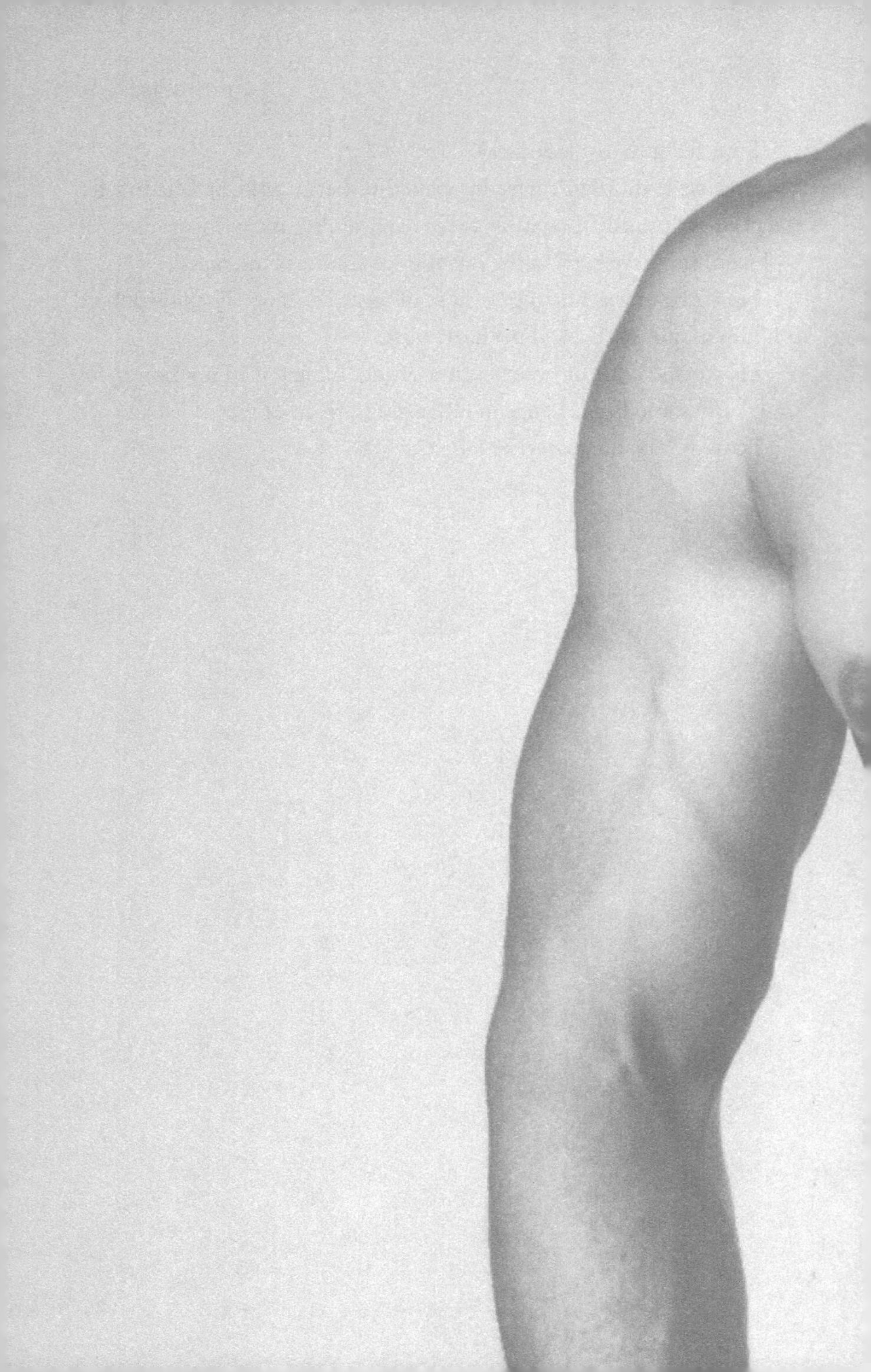

Becca tried to get me to stop and talk to her. But I ran to my truck and raced out of the parking lot, the tire marks twenty feet long on the pavement. I knew where I needed to go. Although, I was unsure if I really wanted to go there. After seeing Ava and the state she was in, I had to go.

Ava wasn't in a good place. She seemed so fragile lying in her bed, so unlike the strong, sarcastic woman she usually was. I knew the wounds were fresh, and she would need time, but it hurt too much to see her like that. Instead, I needed to do something.

So, I found myself pulling up to the rugby house. Sitting in my truck, staring at the scene of the crime from the night before, made my stomach churn. It forced me to think about what he'd done to her, to see it in my mind, all over again. I wouldn't be able to get past any of this if I didn't find out more about this guy, and what the next steps were.

Even though it was still kind of early, my knock was hard and loud on the front door. It didn't take long for someone to open it.

"Yeah," the groggy kid said. He rubbed at his eyes and bare chest as he tried to discern who I was.

"Is Ashton or Sutton around?" I asked.

He held the door open as he stepped back into the room, allowing me to follow. His eyes narrowed in on me more closely as I did.

"You the guy that had the fight last night?"

Nodding, I looked around, making sure the coast was clear. I had no idea if the guy from last night lived here with them. I didn't know much about the situation at all, to be honest.

"Man, that was fucked up. Sorry that happened to your girl, is she OK?"

My girl.

I guess to an outsider, my reaction would be that of a boyfriend. And I kind of was, or not. Our situation was so fucking confusing.

"She's still a bit of a mess this morning, but she'll be alright, I think."

He nodded, though seemed concerned still.

"Oh, hey, I'm Carter, I'm on the team, too. I hear we'll be team-mates. I didn't have a chance to meet ya last night with all the crazi-ness." He held out his hand, and we shook firmly.

"Nice to meet ya. That was kinda why I was coming by. I wanted to talk to Ashton, or some of the other guys, make sure, ya know, things are still cool. I don't like how things started with me and the team last night. I know that guy is on the team and, well..."

Carter grabbed a shirt that was on the floor, pulled it over his head, and gestured for us to head to the kitchen. For the number of people who had been at the party the night before, the place was in decent condition. Only a few stray empties that I could see.

"Want anything? Water?" he asked.

I shook my head, continuing to look around for anyone else. The place seemed desolate. Carter poured himself a huge glass of water and chugged it before talking again.

"Gotta hydrate, almost in season." He filled his glass up again. "So that dude, his name is Murphy, don't know his first name. He's off the team, so no worries. It's Somers, right?"

"Yeah, Logan Somers."

"You'll see we go by last names around here," he said with a laugh. "Anyway, he's gone. We don't put up with that shit. He knew better. There were some rumors about him, and now they were confirmed. Ashton's pissed he didn't kick him off sooner, before your girl got hurt. He'll probably want to talk to you, apologize."

Huh, so the asshole was already gone from the team. But he obviously still went to school here. I'd have to keep my eye out, make sure he didn't bother Ava on campus.

"That's good to hear, thanks for letting me know." I started heading back toward the front door. "Can you let Ashton know I came by?"

Carter nodded. "Sure, man. Will I see you at practice this week? Looks like it's warming up enough for us to get outside."

I hadn't thought that far ahead. There were so many other things to deal with in the meantime, but that would be something to look forward to.

"Yeah, that'll be great. Will there be an email?"

"Ashton sends them out the day before, look out for it."

Carter slapped me on the back before he closed the door behind me.

Once back in my truck, something Carter said didn't sit well with me. It had my heart pounding fast.

"There were some rumors about him, and now they were confirmed."

Fuck. There were easily rumors about me around this campus as well. The team could do the same to me one day if they heard about my situation with Lanie last year.

I pounded my hand against my steering wheel repeatedly, the anger at myself bubbling over.

Why the fuck did I have to be so stupid? Why couldn't I control myself last year? It only added to the self-loathing I was already feeling.

It was going to come back and haunt me forever, I knew it.

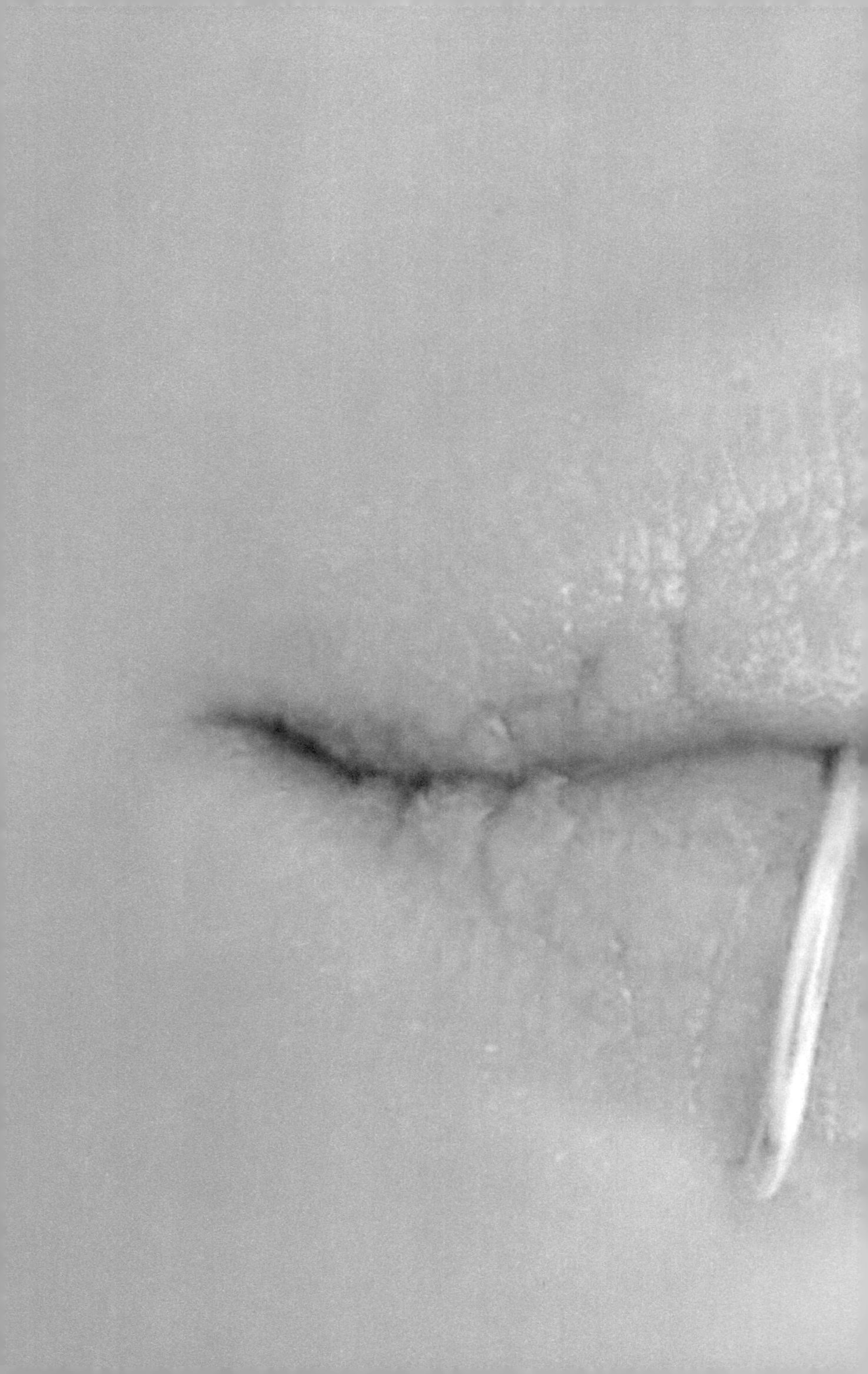

CHAPTER 26

Ava

As I stood alone at my window, watching and waiting, my anxiety rose the longer he took to get home. When he came to me earlier in the day, I refused to open up to him. I didn't want him to share in the pain I endured. He had so much to deal with in his own life. But knowing he took off, either out of anger or concern, destroyed me.

He'd been gone for hours, and I knew Becca was concerned and looking for him as well. I was about to lower the blind when I saw his truck come around the bend of the lot. He pulled into his favorite spot; it was as if everyone knew he needed to park in front of that damn frog. He turned off his truck but remained in it. He sat there for a few minutes, but eventually the driver's door opened, and his familiar large frame slowly got out. After he closed the door, he stood motionless for a minute, staring up at the sky.

As if he sensed me, his head spun and found me. His eyes connected with mine, and even from this distance, I saw the puffiness around them. His shoulders slumped as he leaned against his truck, defeat in his stance.

Finally, I heard the front door slam shut.

"Oh my god, where the hell have you been, you asshole," Becca said sternly as Logan came inside. "I was about to send out the cavalry."

It was hard to tell how serious she was from up here. Theirs was a curious relationship. As I stood at the top of the stairs, my feet froze and kept me from taking the first step.

"Where are you going?"

Becca's voice was incredulous, almost angry at him.

"I'm going upstairs, if that's alright with you?"

There was no response from her, only silence from the first floor. I hurried back to my room and closed the door so he wouldn't know I'd been eavesdropping on the interaction. His footsteps were slow on the stairs and as he walked past my room to his. I heard the quiet click of his door closing and locking, and then utter silence in the house.

Not a sound.

I could go downstairs and check in with Becca and Macie, but to be honest, I had no interest in talking to them.

The silence was welcome at the moment. Although I knew I should go to him, talk to him, tell him how I felt about our situation, it still wasn't the right time. He was still reeling from last night, almost as much as me, it seemed.

How did we get to this point?

Things were better when we supposedly hated one another. We never should have given in to our desires that snowy weekend. Our lack of discipline has led to his life crumbling before our eyes.

I climbed back into bed, ready to spend the next week there if I could. My TV was on, the volume low, but I couldn't focus enough to follow the plot of the movie playing. Turning instead to my ereader, I opened it to my most recent read. A good book was always a great escape. However, as I reread the same sentence over and over, I realized that was not working, either.

Throwing it aside, I curled up and simply decided to try to sleep.

"Ava?" A quiet knock followed the sound of my name.

I jumped from my bed and opened it to find him slumped against the wall, one hand gripping the frame of the door. Up close, his blood-shot eyes looked worse than I expected. His tight lips and white-knuckle grip further signs of what I'd done to him.

I needed to fix this. No matter the immediate damage it might incur. In the long run, it was the right thing to do.

I moved away, allowing him to enter my room. As soon as he closed the door, I turned toward him to get the upper hand on the situation.

"Logan—"

"No, Ava, please, there's something I need to say to you."

The raspiness of his voice combined with the plea of his words were heartbreaking, and it took me by surprise.

"I think you need to press charges against this guy," he said. "I went to the police station and got some information about how to do it."

I was stunned; those were not words I was expecting.

He reached into his back pocket, and the papers shook in his hand as he held them out to me. But I didn't take them from him. He shook them at me, unsure why I wouldn't take them.

"Ava." My name came out more like a command. "Please. You need to do this. What he did to you was so wrong, he shouldn't have touched you like that. He can't get away with it."

Then it clicked.

"Logan, where have you been all day?"

I took the papers, tossed them to floor and grabbed his hands, yet he still wouldn't look at me.

"Logan."

His head shifted from side to side, settling on staring up at the ceiling. Reaching up, I grabbed his face, forcing him to look me in the eye.

"Where. Did. You. Go?" Each word its own staccato sentence, my frustration peaking.

He didn't answer. Instead, he pulled out of my grasp, retreating toward the window. As I slowly walked up behind him, his shoulders tensed as he sensed my approach. My hands went to his back, but he jerked away from my touch.

He spun on his heels and faced me. Taken off guard by the sudden movement, I stepped back.

"I'm a monster, Ava." The bite in his words sliced through my heart. "You knew that from the start. You were right."

This couldn't be happening. I was too late, I'd already destroyed him. All the while, I blamed him for the words he used against me.

But it was my words that were destroying him.

He was a broken soul as he looked at me. The fog roiled around him, thick, dark, ugly, and I wasn't sure I'd be able to break through and reach him.

I stepped closer, my feet slow, concerned he might leave.

"Logan."

His hands went up in protest. Watching his eyes grow wide as I continued toward him scared me, stopping me in my tracks.

"You are not a monster, Logan. You're nothing like that guy from last night, nothing at all. You have to know that. I know you know that."

He shook his head frantically as he backed himself against the wall.

"I touched Lanie against her will, Ava. You pointed that out enough times. She says she's forgiven me, but she shouldn't have, no one should have!" He was screaming, agony in every word. "I should be in jail, she should've pressed charges against me!"

He shook from head to toe. He was like a wild animal trying to break out of a cage.

"I have to get out of here." There was chaos in his eyes as they scanned the room, unable to focus. The profuse sweat dripping from his temples and his trembling hands were further signs that he was struggling with staying grounded.

This was beyond anxiety or a panic attack. He seemed to be at a breaking point, and I didn't know what to do to help him. What I did know was restraining him was not the answer. As he moved for the door, I let him go.

Once he threw it open, there were two sets of concerned eyes waiting on the other side. Macie and Becca both looked on the verge of tears standing in the hall outside my room.

"Get the fuck out of my way!" he yelled as he barreled past them and ran down the stairs.

They slowly stepped through the door toward me, eyes wide and full of questions, as they tried to assess the situation. Becca kept looking where he once stood, no doubt wanting to go after Logan. Macie came to my side, her arms around me, consoling and comforting me.

As I looked back and forth between the two of them, it was obvious one was clear about the situation, and one was in the dark.

"What's going on, Ava?" Macie asked.

"I...uh..." How did I answer that? I knew they heard what Logan said, but what did they surmise about us? "Logan is saying ridiculous things about himself, he's distraught. Last night is bringing up his experience with Lanie."

"Did he say where he was going this time?" Becca asked as she started for my door.

I shook my head as I followed. The three of us hurried downstairs, checking to see if he was still home, but the first floor was empty. A quick peek out the front window showed an empty space where his truck had been parked.

"His truck is gone," I told them.

"I have to text Ty," Becca said. "He'll know what to do."

She pulled out her phone as she walked away. Macie turned to me.

"Let's go sit down," she said as she guided me to the couch. She turned on the TV, which I appreciated, because I didn't want to talk. As we sat huddled together, we heard Becca talking to Ty.

"Has he answered you? Is he at your place yet?" Her voice was frantic as she waited for his answers. "Ty, where could he be? He should be to your place by now. What about the rugby house? Can you call over there?"

She was pacing the floor behind the couch.

I felt numb. Macie was my best friend, and I wanted to confide in her, tell her everything, but I couldn't.

I couldn't tell her I was destroying the man I was falling in love with.

And I was going to hurt him more by walking away.

"Ty got in touch with one of the players who said that Logan was at the rugby house earlier today, but he's not there now," Becca said. She was frazzled, texting multiple people at the same time, trying to locate him.

I hated that all of this was happening because of me.

I did this.

Pulling out my phone, I started doing the same. Though our shared contacts were fewer, it couldn't hurt to try. Then I thought about the spot on the mountain, and how he would go there to think.

"I think I know where he could be!"

The three of us piled in Macie's car as I tried to remember how to get there. I knew approximately where the desolate road off the highway was, but not exactly.

"Go slower, it might be right up here," I said.

Becca was still making calls to everyone she knew in the back seat while we drove.

"Lanie's calling me back," Becca said, some excitement in her voice. "Hey..." Then her words became hushed.

"Turn here," I told Macie.

"This is a dirt road, Ava. Are you sure?" she questioned as she surveyed the dark area. "What were you two doing up here?"

"Macie, turn around," Becca said. "He's at Lanie and Xander's, he just pulled up. Ty's heading there too."

Macie slammed on the brakes and spun the car around, quickly heading back toward the lit highway. As she started the trek back toward campus, she gave me a sideways glance and a small smile. I wasn't sure if it was because she was happy we found Logan, or if she was full of questions about where we had been headed.

Regardless, I was happy about where we were headed now.

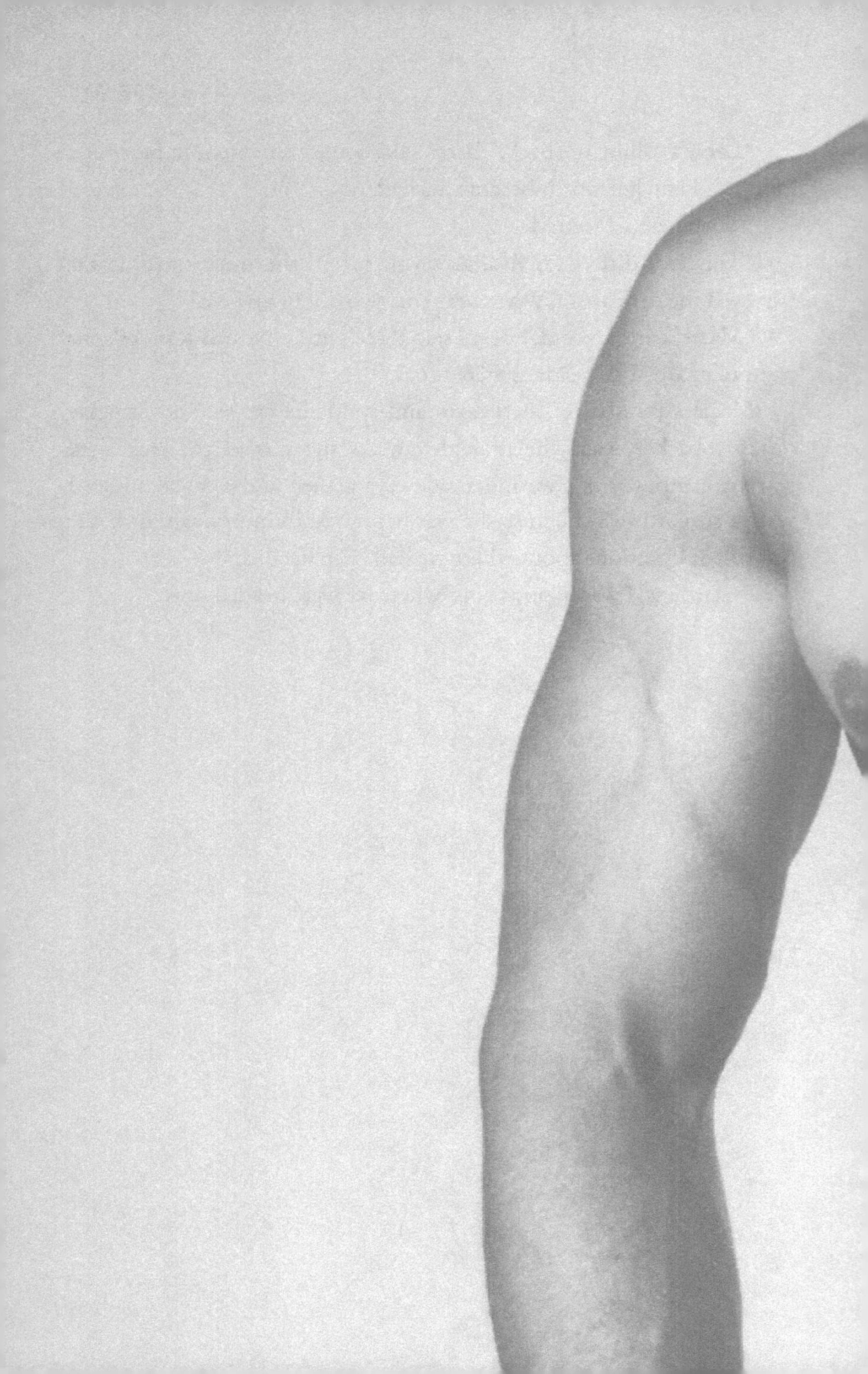

CHAPTER 27

Logan

The realization I came to about myself, and how I shouldn't be with Ava...destroyed me. She didn't deserve to be with someone who had a past like mine. A past that would continue to haunt me my entire life and wreak havoc along the way. I should have been punished for what I'd done.

Now I had to see Lanie.

I found my truck parked in front of Xander's apartment. I wasn't even sure how I found it, I'd only heard his address in passing. But his Jeep was parked nearby, so I figured it had to be the right place. My phone vibrated repeatedly in my pocket. I'd missed several calls and texts, all from Becca and Ty. Instead of answering them, I shoved the phone in my glovebox.

My finger shook as it hovered over the doorbell. But I finally pressed it.

"Hey, man." Xander answered the door. "What's up?"

I didn't know what to say to him. He opened the storm door, inviting me in. I could tell by the way he looked at me he was aware that something was going on.

"Logan," he said in a serious tone. "Are you OK? You've got a lot of people looking for you."

My hands rubbed at my head, down over my face as I stood frozen in place. I needed to do this but suddenly didn't know how. As Xander stood staring at me, his head tilting as he did, the confusion built in his look the longer I remained silent.

"I've had better days," I said.

Then Lanie was by his side. Her bright smile changed abruptly when she assessed the situation.

"Everything OK?" she asked no one in particular.

"I'm trying to figure that out myself," Xander told her. "Logan, why don't you c'mon in?" He held the door open wider. He smiled. A very welcoming smile.

As did Lanie.

I was still having trouble breathing. My hands trembled at my sides. I was struck with such intense fear to move forward with my plan. My head swiveled, looking side to side, wondering if I should just retreat and leave.

Then I felt a soft hand grasp mine. Lanie smiled as she guided me inside, Xander holding the door.

"It's OK, Logan," she said at my side. "We're here for you."

My feet allowed me to move forward as I entered the apartment. There were voices from the other side of the main floor, and I panicked.

"We're heading upstairs," Lanie said as she guided me to the steps.

She pulled me to a room at the end of a long hall, Xander already inside. He gestured for me to take a seat in a recliner he had in the corner of his room. Lanie closed the door, and they put the TV on low, I could only assume for privacy.

"I'm going to head downstairs," Xander said. "Let me know if you need me." He said this directly to Lanie.

"Stay," I said.

Xander looked at me, his eyebrows lifting.

"Please," I said.

He nodded and leaned against his desk, his arms across his chest. Lanie stayed with me, sitting on the end of the bed and leaning in close.

"I...uh..." My stuttering was due to my erratic heartbeat. The panic attack was so close. "Did you hear what happened last night? To Ava?"

Her sideways glance at Xander was my answer; they knew.

"Lanie!" I screamed. Her name came out as a plea. A howl. My head landed in my hands as I bent forward.

"Logan," she said, kneeling in front of me. "Becca told me you helped her, that you stopped the guy from doing anything else to her." She took my hands in hers, holding them close to her face, her mouth.

"You don't understand," I said, jumping up. She was startled as I stood, Xander coming to her side. "Earlier today, I went back to the rugby house, where the party was. And the guys have been great, they kicked the guy off the team."

They nodded in approval but were confused why I was still upset.

"They said he had a past, there had been rumors they didn't listen to about him. That they should have. And if they had, maybe this wouldn't have happened."

Lanie's eyes softened.

"I went to the police station, picked up some information for Ava for her to press charges against the guy." I ran out of breath and needed to draw in some air.

The two of them stood motionless, hanging on my next word.

"I'm him. I'm that asshole, Lanie." My tears were abundant now, streaming down my face. "I did this...to you."

She stood to come even closer to me, but I stopped her with my hands up, my head shaking. Xander came and held her by the shoulder.

"I'm no better than he is," I howled. Making that realization made my insides twist in disgust. "I'm no fucking better than him, Lanie! Why didn't you press charges against me?"

Lanie stepped closer, tentative with her hand as she touched my arm. "Logan," she said softly. "You're nothing like him. From what Becca said, there was actual sexual assault that took place with him and Ava. You did not do that to me."

Bending at the waist, I worked to control my breathing. The sweat beaded on my forehead and dripped down my back. I ripped my coat off, tossing it on the chair.

Looking up at the guy who once hated me, I said, "Xander, why didn't you force her to go the police about me?"

He looked between me and Lanie, seeming unsure if he wanted to step in. But when he looked back at me, he raised his shoulders and took a step my way.

"Listen, Logan. That night last year, I won't lie, it's not one of my favorite memories." His hands went in his pockets, and it made me wonder if it was to keep from hitting me like he did that fateful night. "But you and I made our peace. And more importantly, so did you and Lanie. No, you shouldn't have pushed yourself on her, but you were drunk. And you're addressing that. But there's one important aspect about that night that needs to be brought to your attention. The bigger issue with what happened between you two was Lanie's past. That's what threw her over the edge." He moved next to Lanie, his arm wrapping around her waist as she looked at him with adoration. "What this guy did to Ava is so much worse, it doesn't compare."

The guy did hurt Ava. Badly. He did things to her I never would have considered doing to Lanie without consent, even while drunk.

I knew that. I did.

So why did I still feel like a monster?

Lanie pulled me by the hand to sit in the recliner again, while Xander rolled the desk chair nearby for her to sit in.

"How about I go get us some bottles of water?" Xander said.

Lanie nodded as he left us alone. She didn't say anything as she sat across from me allowing for the quiet to be our sound. And in my current state of mind, the silence was loud enough. Eventually the muddiness in my head started to settle and clear.

"Good, your breathing is slowing," Lanie said. "You're doing well with whatever techniques your therapist is teaching you."

Looking at Lanie now, it was hard to remember her as the painfully shy girl she was last year. The first time we met, she experienced a panic attack, and my heart broke for her. I knew all too well what she was dealing with.

Her troubled past, specifically her abusive ex, led to her dealing with extreme anxiety.

"I guess you never thought we'd have that in common, huh?" I asked.

"I think I knew it on a subconscious level. You were always nice to me when I was struggling." She leaned back in her chair, comforted by my more relaxed state. "Ya know, Becca's a mess looking for you, she's been texting me nonstop. And I think they all might be here already." She was checking her phone. "Ty too."

This recent revelation that I was like the guy who did this to Ava turned my world upside down. How could she consider being with someone who had a past like mine after going through what she did? As much as I appreciated Lanie absolving me of any guilt about her, I wasn't convinced that Ava could do the same.

What came next?

"When you say 'they,' who exactly do you mean?" I asked.

"All your roommates are downstairs."

She put her arm through mine as we walked to the door, smiling at my question.

"When I came to school last year, I wasn't looking for love, Logan, but it found me." She squeezed the arm she was holding. "I think it's found you, hasn't it?"

I finally understood that my connection to Lanie last year wasn't that I was falling in love with her but that we were kindred spirits, both broken souls looking for someone to heal us. Hers was healed by Xander.

I knew my entire being was calmed by the presence of Ava. She healed me. But it was more than that. And Lanie saw that.

"Maybe," I said.

She laughed at my attempt at being coy.

"We haven't told anyone," I said.

She twisted her fingers against her lips, tightening the imaginary key. Reaching up, she pulled me into a tight hug.

"I knew that too, no worries," she whispered against my ear. "You deserve all the good things, Logan. Let them happen to you."

I wish I believed that too, but it might be too late.

"Hey," I said, stopping her from leaving the room. "What's the latest on Max?"

Her body stiffened and her eyes got distant, which concerned me.

"Logan, I don't think now's the time to bring all that up," she said.

"It's the perfect time." I brought her back for us to sit down. "I could use a distraction."

Shaking her head, I could tell she disagreed. "Probably not this type of distraction." And then she paused. "Bryce let us know that he's been leaving his house without his anklet on somehow. They're not sure how he's doing it, but they're tailing him, and they know the house arrest anklet is still in the house."

Shit. That was a real reason for concern.

There was an entire scene at BRU last year when he showed up to take Lanie with him at gunpoint. The cops, even the FBI, showed up. There was a fucking shootout behind her dorm. Her ex and one of his guys got shot. It was insane. The guy was insane; it was scary that she was involved with him in the first place. Xander stayed by her side, helping her through it.

"But they're on him, so that's good, right?" I asked.

"Yeah," she said, but her sad eyes didn't convey what I wanted to hear. "Enough about him, I made a promise to myself not to allow him to rule my life anymore. And I'm sticking to it." She popped up with renewed energy. "Besides, you have a whole bunch of people downstairs who love you and would like to make sure you're OK. Are you ready to go down, or do you need more time?"

I nodded but stopped her once more.

"Lanie, I want to thank you. I'm not sure I'm convinced I deserve your forgiveness, but I feel a lot better than when I got here."

She grabbed my arm again and kept me moving.

"Healing is like that. Last night was a trigger, so it's completely normal for you to go through this, Logan. I'd say it means you're healing well, and if it didn't affect you, that would be a problem."

"Don't you sound all professional and shit," I told her.

She laughed, and I laughed.

It felt good to laugh.

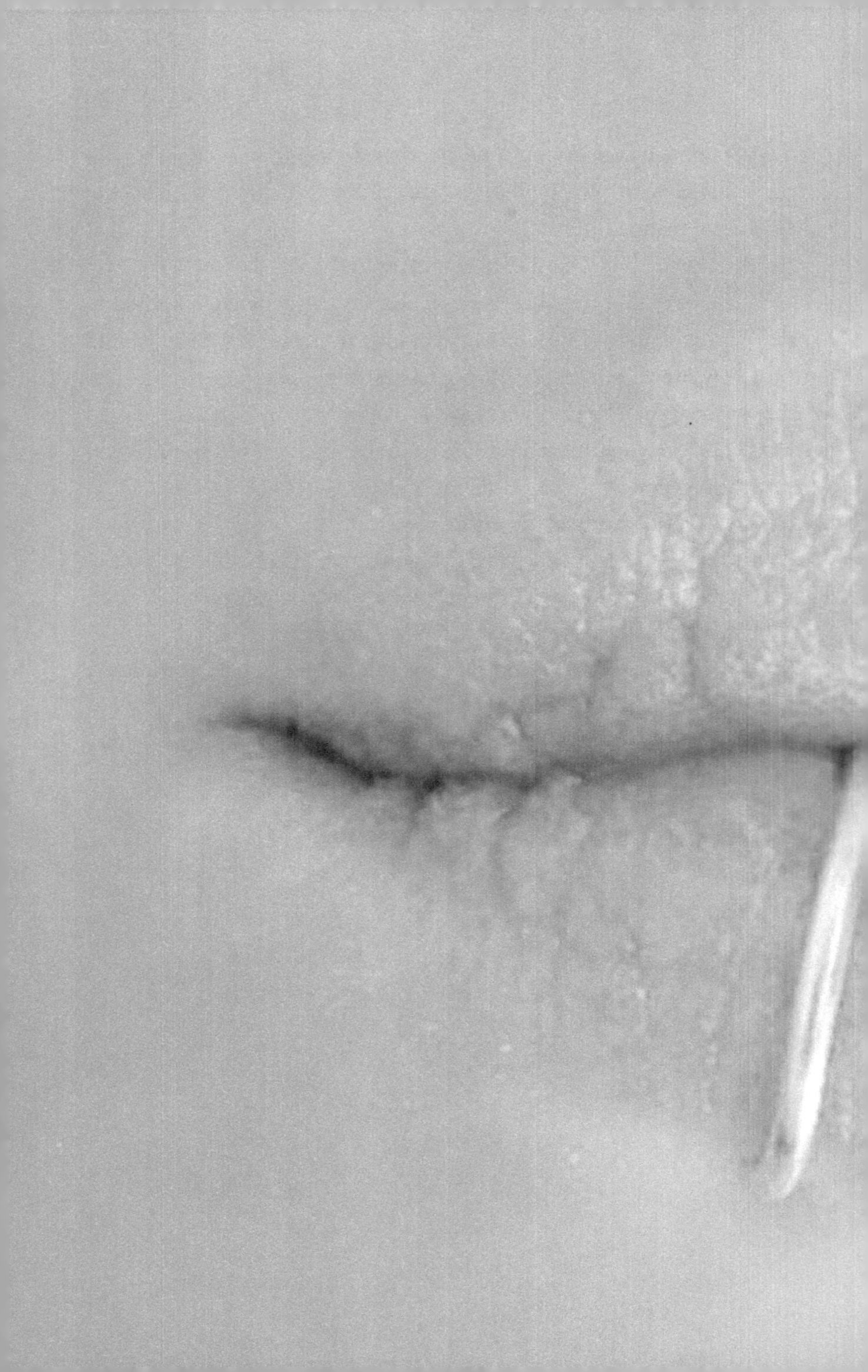

CHAPTER 28

Ava

There was so much going on once Logan came down with Lanie. We were all there: Ty, Becca, Macie, Lanie, Xander, Logan, and me. At first, everyone checked on Logan to make sure he was OK. Then they were checking on me.

And then it got awkward. We were in this party-type setting with all of us together, everyone eventually laughing and being jovial. But it didn't sit right with me.

Lanie and Becca started making plans for us to all get together again when things settled down. Ty, Xander, and Logan were talking about going to the gym. I could tell Logan was still stressed, but for fuck's sake, what the hell was going on? They were acting like life was normal, like this was normal.

What the fuck was normal about any of this?

It wouldn't do anyone any good for me to make a scene with my typical attitude, so instead I sat in a quiet corner and was...quiet. I couldn't bring myself to be a part of the bullshit conversations they were all having.

Even though I could guess why he'd come to see Lanie, there was no discussion as to what they talked about. Though Logan seemed much better than when he left the house.

Logan caught my eye from across the room as he spoke to Ty, his look lingering. There was so much that he and I needed to talk about, to say to one another.

Logan broke away from the guys and made his way to my side of the room. Sitting next to me, he nudged my knee with his.

"Are you OK?" he asked.

There was no good way to answer that at the moment, so I decided to remain silent and simply shrugged.

"I didn't mean to make all of this about me, ya know?" he said.

My head snapped toward him at his words.

"What do you mean?" I asked. But as soon as I did, the crowd around us erupted in laughter, interrupting our conversation. "I should be asking if you're OK."

Logan stood and reached his hand out for me.

"Hey guys," he said, turning to the group. "I'm gonna get Ava home. The past twenty-four hours have been a lot for her."

Immediately, all three girls came to my side saying their goodbyes and giving me well wishes. They thanked Logan for taking such good care of me. Both Ty and Xander gave me a hug.

They were all such good people.

Logan was surrounded by good people.

If Logan and I had remained friends, I could have been one of those people for him. But instead, we fucked.

Well, it was a little more than that.

We let our feelings get in the way.

And I knew that either on this ride home, or when we got there, I was probably going to shatter his heart.

I DIDN'T SHATTER HIS HEART ON THE DRIVE HOME. IT didn't happen because I didn't talk on the way home. I remained quiet, but Logan didn't push me. It was one of those comfortable quiets we often have. But as we pulled up to the townhouse, he broke the silence.

"So, I don't think it would raise any flags if I were in your room with you when they get back. I don't want to leave you alone right now."

How in the hell was I going to do this? I didn't want to. He was turning out to be exactly what my heart and head wanted and needed.

But *I* wasn't what *he* needed.

And I had to think about him.

"Yeah, sure, I think that's good," I told him.

We entered the house, the dark rooms as bleak as I was feeling. Logan didn't bother with any lights on the first floor as we made our way directly upstairs. My sluggish advance on the steps mirrored his, our mood indeed different from those we just left.

I stripped myself of my coat and shoes while I walked toward my bed, the clothing abandoned on the floor along the way. As I curled myself into a tight ball against the wall, Logan joined me and covered us with a blanket.

"I know this has been a terrible time, and I'm sure I haven't made it much easier for you," he said.

Sitting up, I hoped my pursed lips sent my message.

"What are you talking about, Logan? Without you, I...well, I can't even think about what might have happened."

He remained with his head on my pillow, those blue eyes of his darkening as if taken over by storm clouds.

"Am I right in assuming you went to Lanie asking her to press charges against you?"

He could only answer me with a small nod.

"And I'm also going to go out on a limb and assume she said no."

At that, all he did was cover his face with his hand.

"Logan, can't you see that it's me who's destroying you?" He started to sit up, but I pushed him back, keeping him on my pillow. "Last night didn't need to happen..."

"Ava, you are not responsible for what he did to you." The anger in his voice took me by surprise.

"I know." Those words came out harsher than I wanted them to. I needed to tread carefully with him. "I'm not some meek female who would think what he did is OK. I know he was wrong, nothing I did provoked him. But that's not what I mean. If I hadn't rushed away from you in my stupid rage, right into that asshole's arms, it wouldn't have happened. And if I hadn't put the parameters of keeping us a secret, none of this would have happened."

I flung my entire body against the wall behind me. The amount of anger I had for myself was mounting, and I was struggling to keep it in.

"Logan," I started. But my words got caught in my throat. "I don't want to be the one who derails you or your life. You're doing so well, you were anyway. Until I showed up, until we started whatever it is we have. I just don't know if we should keep doing this, I don't know if it's good for your recovery."

The tiny shake of his shoulders crushed me. The quiet sobs that followed had me lying next to him, holding him in my arms.

We cried together.

We cried for what we had and what we were about to lose.

We cried each other to sleep.

In the morning, I wasn't surprised to find myself alone in my bed. But I wouldn't go so far as to say it didn't suck.

Yes, it was my idea.

Yes, I felt it was the right thing to do, especially for him.

Did I have a tiny pang of disappointment, maybe even grief, that he walked away from us so easily? Without a fight? Yes.

Yet, if he had fought me on it, what good would it have done? He knew me. He knew I'd stand my ground.

I fear he knew me too well and that *Tink* would show up to that fight.

But it didn't hurt any less.

Here we were, Monday morning, and we had Marketing together.

My body moved at a snail's pace as I got ready. The sun streamed through those damn blinds again. On any other day I'd have been happy to see it, but today it didn't lift my mood. At least the forecast was for warmer weather, so no bundling up was necessary, which was a nice change.

I wasn't sure how to proceed. Would we drive to campus together like we'd been doing? No one knew we "broke up" so it would make sense to me to keep things looking normal.

But I wasn't Logan.

Sure enough, by the time I got downstairs, he had already left.

"Mace, you heading to campus anytime soon?"

She was still in her jammies, so I think I had my answer.

"Where's Logan?" she asked. "Don't you guys go together on Mondays?" She didn't stop what she was doing, her head down making her coffee.

This was not going to be the last question I'd have to field if he was going to be changing how we acted toward one another.

"I think he had something to do early on campus, maybe for rugby. That might change things with him giving me rides."

What I should have done was given myself enough time this morning if I needed to grab the bus. But that wasn't an option at this point. If Macie couldn't drive me, I wasn't making it to class.

"Let me put my coffee in my other mug, and I can drive you," she said.

The sunshine blinded us when we walked toward her car. It was kind of nice having the warmth of it hit my face. When spring actually decided to show up, those winter doldrums were easy to toss away.

But I still had a pit in my stomach.

I knew this day would be a challenge. All day long.

"You'll probably make it right on time since I can drop you right at your building," Macie said, then smiled.

Everyone was still walking on eggshells with me. There was no mention of Saturday night, no mention of what happened, no mention of anything of substance. I was surprised she didn't say something about the weather.

"Thank god the sun is out and it's warming up, right?" She put the window down and increased the volume of the radio, sufficiently cutting off all further communication. Just as well, I was in no mood to talk either.

She pulled up to my building and literally waved goodbye to me as I got out, like a mom dropping their kid off at grade school.

I couldn't be pokey like I wanted to. I worked at getting here and shouldn't be late. But my feet felt laden with cement as I trudged along the path, the entrance looming ahead.

Because a mere hundred yards away, I'd be facing him. And I had no idea what to expect.

As I pulled open the door to the lecture hall, I heard the professor just starting. I hurried down the stairs to my accustomed row.

And, alas, there was no Logan.

After sitting, I searched the room, looking for that big blonde head. But it was a large class, and the lights were already dim for the professor's slides, so I couldn't find him. Needless to say, my attention span was shit. I'd have to review the entire lesson again online.

Finally, it ended. I started packing my laptop into my bag.

"Ava Kennedy," the professor said over his mic. "Please see me."

What the fuck? I wasn't late. I hurried down to his podium and joined a short line of students waiting to talk to him. When it was my turn, he turned toward his computer.

"Hi, Ava."

"Hi, Professor Lynch."

"OK, I've been made aware that your group for the class isn't working out, which is a shame. You two did a great job on the first project. But it turns out there's another group looking to switch, so it worked." He pulled out a piece of paper and a pen. "Here's her name and email. You two get in touch."

Speechless was an understatement.

My first instinct was to rush home, barrel into his room, and annihilate him with my words.

What the hell was he thinking?

Then I realized he was thinking about himself. And that was why I did what I did last night. I knew this was going to hurt.

I wasn't prepared for how much.

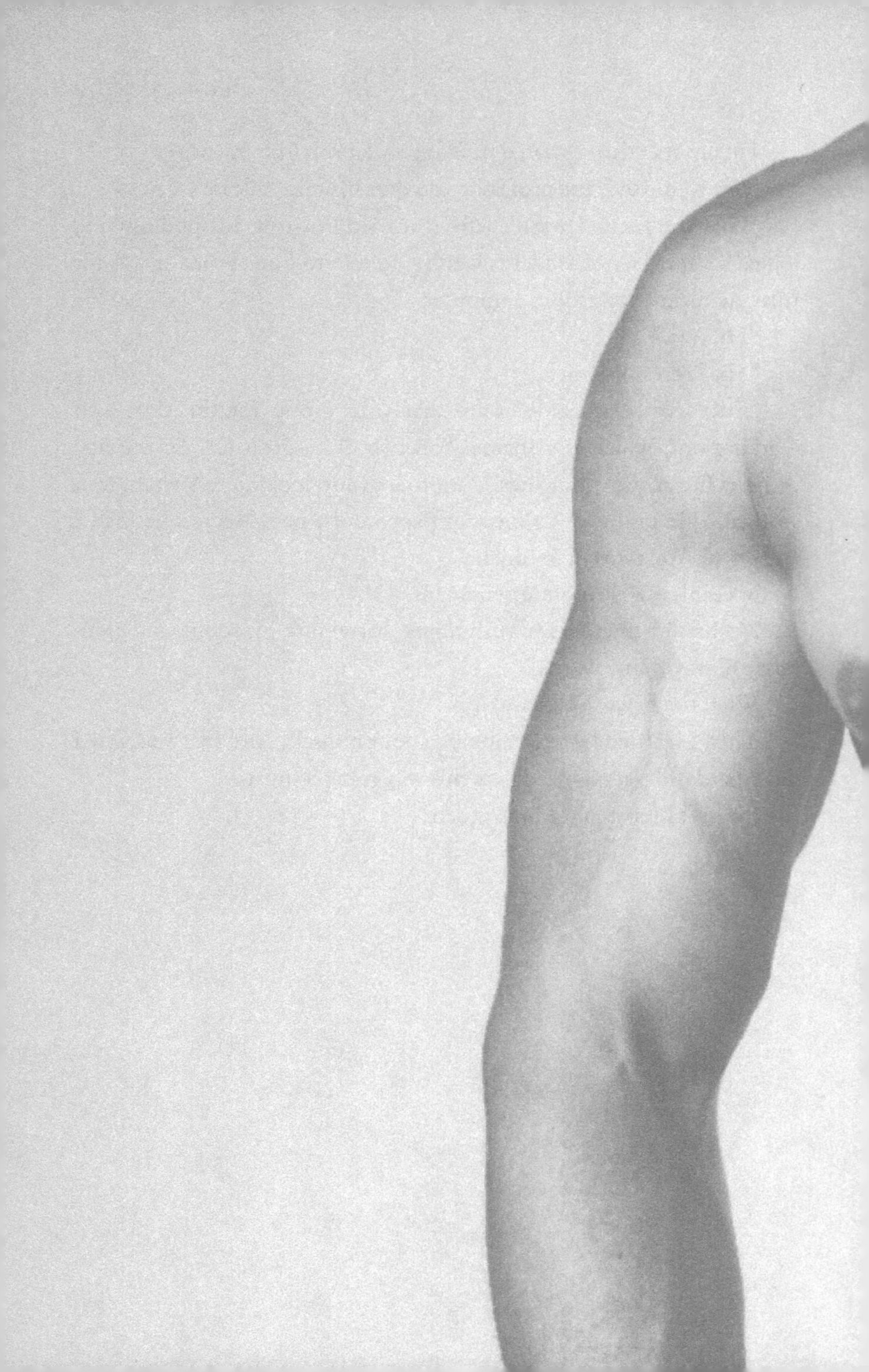

CHAPTER 29

Logan

As I sat staring at my computer screen, waiting for the meeting to start, my heart still thudded against my chest. It hadn't stopped since last night. Ava might think we slept next to each other, but that was not what happened.

I spent the entire night watching her sleep. Seeing her chest rise up and down with each breath. Watching her lips part while she was in a deep sleep and restraining myself from touching that full bottom lip. Enjoying the heat of her skin against mine. Soaking it all in.

Knowing it would be my last chance for any of it.

Because deep down, I knew her words held truth.

The anxiety of talking to the professor almost put me over the edge. I tore out of that room before Professor Lynch spoke his last words, knowing I couldn't risk seeing her.

Not today.

I needed to talk to someone, it was an emergency.

The video call was live.

"Hey, Logan," Dr. Jean said.

My desire to be home, in my bed, in my house, even in her office, pulled at me.

"Hi, Dr. Jean."

"Well, looks like we have a lot to talk about today," she said. She could read me easily, and I wasn't trying to hide my emotions, either.

I spent a lot of my night deciding if I should inform her about Ava and me. I knew she advised against what we'd done, but bottom line, it happened. And now it was having adverse consequences.

Mentally. Emotionally. Physically.

"Yeah, there's something I need to talk about before we talk about my dad, if that's OK."

AS THE DAY WENT ON, I FOUND MYSELF HOLED UP IN MY room. I left campus after my marketing class, skipping all others. My appointment with Dr. Jean took precedence. Taking care of our project group with Professor Lynch was the only reason I stepped foot on campus in the first place. I knew I wouldn't be able to work with her in the confines of this house any longer.

My appointment with Dr. Jean went better than anticipated, but I didn't have that overwhelming elated feeling I was used to after we spoke. She appreciated my honesty about Ava and even understood. She explained that it was best to focus on me, but life goes on and you can't control everything that happened around you.

There was no way I was going to force Ava to be with me if she truly didn't want to be.

My mind couldn't ignore the signs pointing to the reality of why she did what she did.

I was like him.

I was exactly like that douchebag who assaulted her.

No one would ever make me think otherwise.

And she deserved better.

But that part didn't come up in my session. And neither did my father, thank goodness. She felt with all I'd been through, we'd could table it until next week.

My phone got a text.

> Ashton: Hey, outdoor practice tonight if you can make **it, weather's cooperating**

SITTING BACK, READING THE TEXT AGAIN, I COULD ALMOST cry. This was exactly what I needed. Someone telling me to be somewhere to get my ass kicked.

> Me: I'll be there

"HEY, SOMERS," ASHTON SAID FROM ACROSS THE HUDDLE, known as a scrum in rugby, "you're going to try being a back on this play. Think football, you'll get it."

We basically scrimmaged each other as a form of practice, which was a great way for me to learn the game. As we broke from the scrum, I got into position as Sutton went to the sideline to throw the ball in play. He tossed it to the guy ahead of me, and we all started rushing forward. The ball came my way, I broke free around the corner and up the side, the goal line in sight. There were two guys coming at me, the block was going to be a hard one if I didn't weave to avoid it. At the last second, I ducked and zigzagged my way past them, sliding across the line, and scored a try. The guys ran up behind me, screaming my name.

"Somers!" Sutton yelled as I pulled myself up from the dirt. "Shit, man, you're a beast out there. This is gonna be awesome!"

He slapped me hard across my shoulder blade as we joined some others who were heading toward the bench. Practice was over.

"I've still got a lot to learn," I told him. The others we walked with laughed at my statement.

"Ya learn on the field, dude. Don't worry, after the first game, you'll be a pro," Ashton added. "Sutton's right, you're a great addition to the team. We're lucky to have ya."

Their encouraging words combined with the ass whooping of a workout practice gave me was just what the doctor ordered.

Literally.

Dr. Jean said this would be my best medicine, and she was right. The only problem was, as soon as it was over, and I was alone in my truck, the intrusive thoughts returned. Navigating how to deal with Ava living in the same house, post breakup, when no one even knew, was going to be a challenge.

Especially when I knew neither of us had stopped caring for the other.

When I pulled up to the house, I noticed Ty's car was there.

Me: Hey, I'm out front, can Becca spare you for a bit

HE DIDN'T BOTHER TEXTING BACK, THE FRONT DOOR opened within seconds.

"Hey, man," he said as he hopped in my truck. "What's going on?"

I put the truck in reverse and got out of there as quickly as I could. "Are they all home?"

"Who? The girls? Yeah, I think so, but I didn't see Ava. She was upstairs, I think."

As I continued driving, Ty didn't say much while he sat next to me. He looked out the window, occasionally glancing my way, but remained quiet.

Everyone close to me was quiet.

"Hungry? Just got done with practice and I need to eat, but I didn't want to eat at home. Thought we could grab a bite." As I said this, I pulled into the lot of a Mexican restaurant he and I ate at last year.

He tilted his head as he looked my way, his eyebrows pinched together. He opened his mouth, as if to ask a question, but chose not to. Nodding as he peered at the restaurant, he simply moved on to opening his door.

Thankfully, it was empty and we were seated quickly. Once we had glasses of water and were both reading our menus, Ty cleared his throat.

"So, are you going to tell my why you didn't want to eat in your own home?" He purposely placed his menu in front of him, his phone on top of it, giving me his undivided attention. "I mean, that is why we're here? Isn't it? You've obviously got something going on, man. What's up?"

"Hi, guys. Did you have enough time to look at the menu?"

The cute waitress next to our table definitely went to BRU. I'd seen her on campus. Her flirty voice and smile made it seem she recognized us as well. Ty kicked me under the table, no doubt to encourage me to flirt back.

"I'm ready, you?" I asked Ty.

"Yeah," he said, the disappointment clear in his response.

We ordered nachos to start, and I got chicken and steak fajitas. Ty got two beef and bean burritos with the fixings.

We'd be here for a while.

"Well, you didn't take her bait." He gestured to the waitress walking away. "And you still haven't answered my question."

"She interrupted us."

"She's gone now," he said.

As I was driving home from practice, I was torn between going straight to his place or not. So when I saw his car, it was perfect. Because I decided I was going to talk to him about Ava. But when faced with doing it, I froze.

I needed to talk about this to someone. And he was my someone.

"Yeah, well, there is something I wanted to talk about."

Another interruption.

"You guys order nachos?" some kid asked.

"Yeah," we both said and cleared a space. We dug into them, each of us piling our chips high with meat, cheese, beans, guacamole, and sour cream.

"These are as good as I remember," Ty mumbled, his mouth full of the hot cheesy goodness.

After sating my appetite momentarily, I sat back, ready to talk. Ty realized and put a hold on taking his next bite, instead cleaning his hands with his napkin.

"Everything going OK with your recovery, Logan?"

This wasn't directly related to my alcoholism, but my recovery was in jeopardy if I didn't get my emotions in check, I knew that. That was why starting on the journey of a relationship wasn't recommended.

"Not exactly, but I haven't had a drink if that's what you mean," I told him.

I saw the tension release in him as he slumped against the back of the booth. It hadn't occurred to me he and Becca may have thought that with everything going on I could have relapsed.

"I, well, so…" I was at a loss for words. "Ava and I were kind of in a relationship, a secret one, up until last night."

Ty blinked several times as he tried processing what I said.

"Wait, what?" He sat motionless at first, but then his head shook back and forth repeatedly. "No, no, that can't be, dude. You guys, like, hate each other. Don't you?"

My barking laugh startled both of us.

"Yep, we did. And then we didn't, and I think she does again," I told him. "It's confusing and messed up. Bottom line, it's messing with me because what we had while we had it was good. And to be honest, it seemed to be helping me with all my shit going on. My head was quiet when I was with her, all the chaos was calm when I spent time with her for some reason."

He sat back, staring and thinking.

"So why is it over?" he asked.

"Good question. She thinks she wasn't good for my 'recovery journey.' Mainly because of what happened this weekend at the party, and me getting into the fight because of her. She blames herself, I guess." I flung myself against the cracked leather of the bench, getting angrier as I explained it all to Ty. "Personally, I think she doesn't want to be with me because of what I did last year."

Ty's head snapped up at my words.

"Think about it, she ends what we had, which was going great, the weekend this asshole almost fucking rapes her."

Saying that out loud has my fists clenching at my sides. I shove my plate away from me as the anger surges through my body. The people at nearby tables glance our way, and I realize I need to calm the hell down.

"OK, man, maybe you just need to talk to her, talk it through," Ty suggested.

In any normal situation, that would be good advice.

But Ava and I weren't in a normal situation for several reasons.

"I think that ship has sailed, man." I went back to our nachos, and Ty seemed happy to do the same.

"I think Becca would be the better person to talk to than me, she would know the right thing to say," Ty offered. I knew he wasn't looking forward to being an advice guru.

And he was right.

"Yeah, but Ava has this thing about them not knowing, that as roommates we can't be together, so me talking to Becca is out of the question. So do me a favor and keep your mouth shut."

His hands went up in a defensive move, knowing I'd kick his ass if Becca found out.

"Here's your meals, guys." The sugary sweet voice of our waitress interrupted our conversation. She placed our platters down and both our eyes went wide.

"Hey, man, listen," Ty said. "I'm sorry I don't have some great words of wisdom for you. I'm happy you're not turning to beer, though." His smile made me feel good about myself.

I was proud of that, too.

"You still talking to your therapist?"

I nodded.

"I guess she's your best bet, then. Either that or maybe Ava will eventually want to talk about it, but I'm sorry you're going through this. Wish I could help."

"It's OK, man, I feel better just telling you. It sucked keeping it all in, ya know?"

We started picking at our meals, unsure if either of us had anything else to say on the matter.

"So, you had rugby practice today, right?"

And just like that, with the change of subject, we morphed into our old selves. Telling him about the team and the upcoming games lifted my mood.

"There's a game next week?" Ty asked.

"Yeah, the season is starting already, and I don't really think I understand the game completely. But they're convinced I'll do fine."

We continued talking about all the things we needed to catch up on while we ate.

He did exactly what he was good at. He didn't give me advice about Ava.

He helped me forget about her. A little.

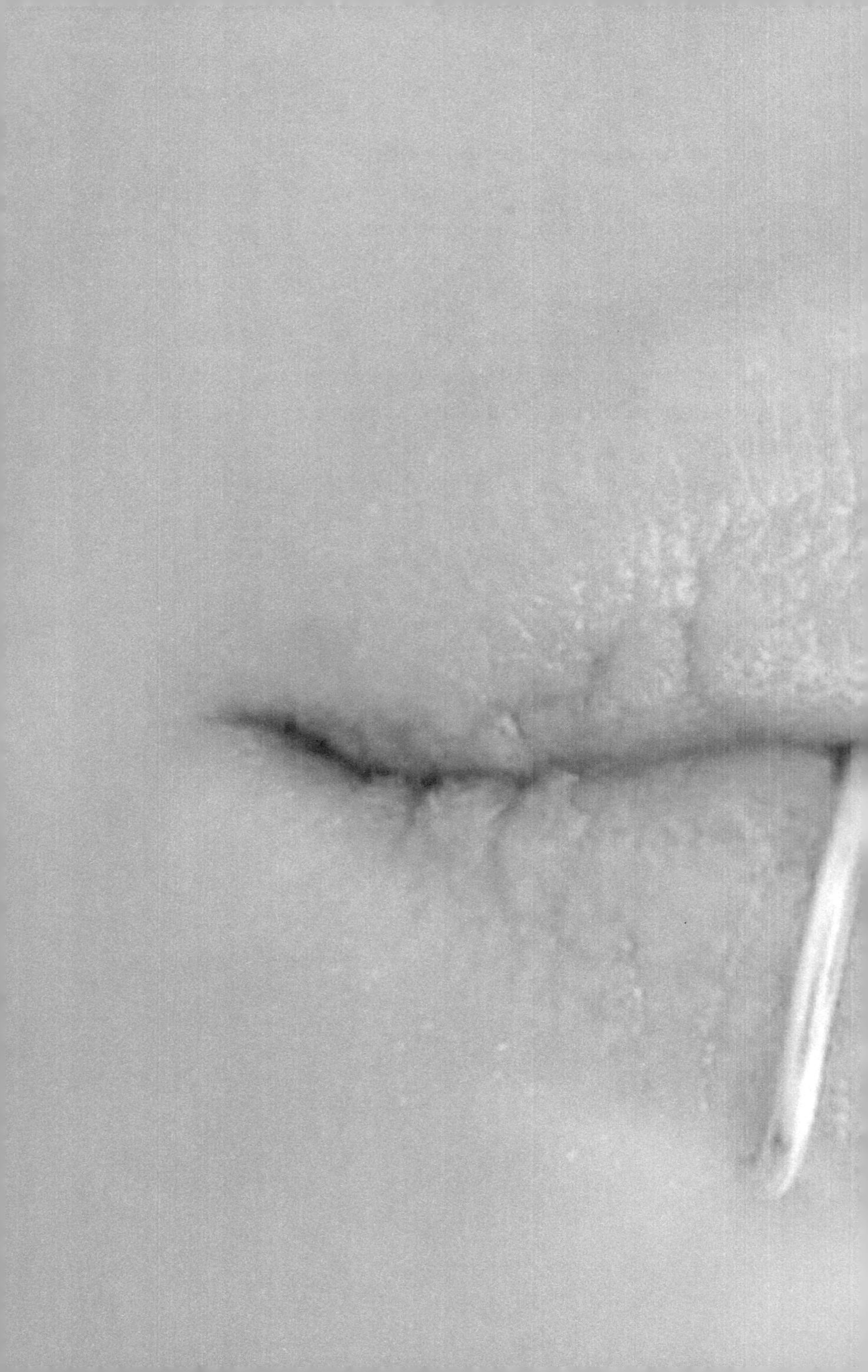

CHAPTER 30

Ava

This was possibly the most challenging week of my life. Even worse than the week after finding my best friend Casey in bed with my boyfriend Cole and having to go to school every day and see the two of them together. And much worse than the week my mother took us out of the house with my father and we went to live with our grandparents.

Being in the same room as Logan was torture.

My body longed to touch him.

My heart yearned to speak to him.

My soul ached to be near him.

But I made it through the entire week without uttering one word to him. I ate most of my meals in my room, unless I knew he wouldn't be home. The start of his rugby season helped as it kept him out of the house more often.

My new partner for Marketing was a pain in the ass, but I had to deal with it. She insisted on us solely working over Facetime, refusing to work in person. Which was fine, except most of the times we set up to meet, her boyfriend was there with her while we worked. I feared my grade would take a hit because of her, and I worked overtime on my end to ensure it wouldn't. Again, which was fine. What else was I spending my time on?

I wondered repeatedly if I was doing the right thing or not. If staying away from him was better for his mental health even though it was worse for mine. But I'd kept away from him successfully enough that I had no insight on the matter.

Tonight he had practice, so I could safely cook and eat in the kitchen.

"Hey, girl, haven't seen much of you this week. You doing OK?" Macie asked as she came up behind me. "I've been wanting to come by your room, maybe do a movie night, but I've been swamped with exams this week, I'm sorry."

"It's OK."

She turned me to face her, gripping my hands.

"No, it's not OK, and I don't think you're OK, either, are you, sweetie? This had to be so hard on you this week, dealing with every-thing. Do you need to talk about it at all?"

I tried to be nonchalant, because if I wasn't, I'd end up a puddle of tears. Shaking out of her hold, and shaking my head at the same time, I tried to convince her I was fine. It didn't work. She followed me like a puppy.

"Have you thought anymore about what Logan suggested? Are you going to file charges against that guy?" she asked.

Had I thought about it?

I hadn't stopped thinking about it, but not in the way she thought.

"I'm not sure yet," I told her. And I wasn't. The guy deserved it, I knew that, but I wasn't sure if I was prepared for the mess that went along with the process.

The kitchen was a disaster, and I decided to load the dishwasher before even thinking about what to make for dinner. But there was an ulterior motive. The job was loud, and I hoped it would discourage any further discussion.

I was never a fan of deflecting before, yet I'd become a master of it lately.

However, as I loaded the cups and plates, Macie stuck close by, leaning against the counter next to the sink. She watched my every move, as if how I held a dish would explain the mystery of my moods this past month.

I saw in my periphery that she turned toward me, her arms across her chest.

"Can I ask you something?" There was more to that question, I heard it in the tone. It held weight.

I stopped what I was doing and looked her way.

"What?" I asked. But her eyes knew, I could tell. I had to look away, going back to my task at hand.

"Ava," she said. "You've been acting out of sorts for a while, and this is hard to bring up with what happened last weekend, because, well, anyone would be out of sorts after that. But there's more going on with you, I can tell." Her tone softened. "What's go on, Ave? I don't like that you're keeping it from me."

I should have known she would assume something, eventually. My emotions were all over the place this week, so it made sense it would happen now. I couldn't look at her, so I kept working on the full sink.

"I'm not keeping anything from you."

I hated lying to her. I'd never done it before. The knot in my throat hurt as I tried to swallow.

"Ava, stop and look at me."

"What, Macie?" I snapped back at her. As I did, I threw the glass in my hand into the sink. It shattered against the stainless steel, tiny shards filtering down through the dirty dishes. The larger pieces remained on top. As I stared at them, I slumped against the lip of the sink, feeling the defeat throughout my entire body.

"Ava," Macie whispered. "I'm sorry, honey, let me help you clean this up." She started toward the closet.

"No," I said. "I'm sorry. This is my fault. I've got it. Why don't you head upstairs? I'll do this and get something started for dinner for us. Then we can talk, I promise."

The sadness in her slow nod broke my heart, but she didn't fight me as she left the room for upstairs. I turned toward the mess I'd made, unsure of where to start. The largest pieces were the most logical place, and as I lifted them out, I pulled the garbage pail closer to make it easier. There were five large chunks of glass in the pail already, and it appeared all were gone from the sink. There was no way to pick out the tiny shards, they clung to the wet, dirty dishes. So I grabbed for the silly dish gloves that Becca insisted on buying that were under the sink, and proceeded to finish loading the dishwasher, careful to rinse the glass from the dishes first.

All was fine.

Until it wasn't.

I saw it before I felt it.

The red streaks dripped into the sink, staining the water pink.

I tore the ripped gloves from my hands, pissed they offered little protection.

The cut on my wrist had to come from a large piece of glass I'd mistakenly left behind. As soon as I saw it, the burn was intense. And the blood, now gushing, covered my wrist, my hand, and the dishes below.

"Fuck!"

I didn't do well at the sight of blood, at all.

"Macie!" I screamed, but didn't know if it was loud enough.

I was already starting to lose my hearing. The fringe of darkness hit the edges of my eyesight.

And then it all went black.

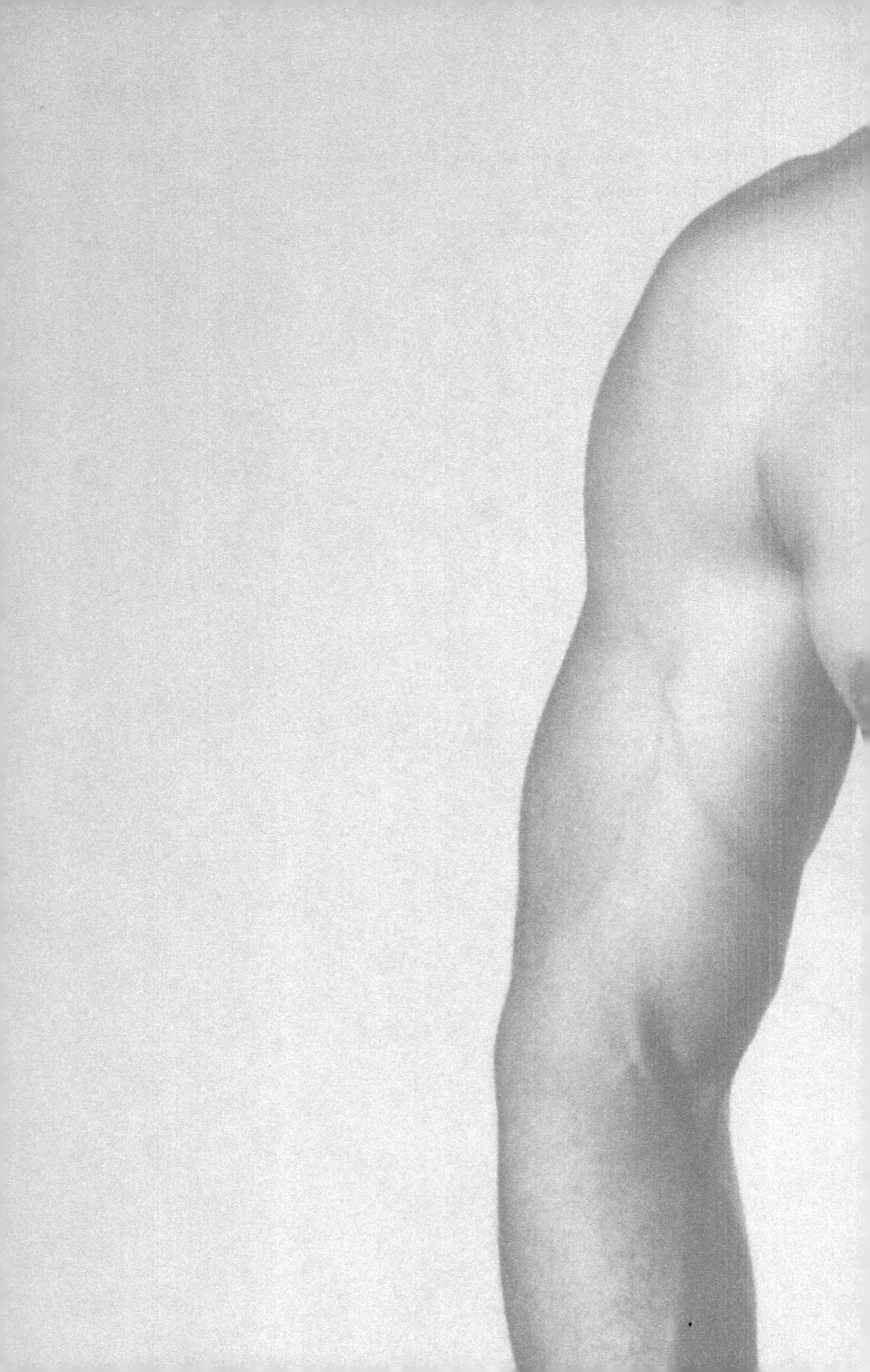

CHAPTER 31
Logan

Practice kicked my ass today. They tried me at every position from forward, to wing, to the hooker. I finished working as a back, which was my original spot, and where I make the most sense. Our first game was tomorrow, and they were working out a lot of kinks in the lineup to see what worked best.

I was smelly.

I was covered in dirt and sweat.

And I couldn't wait to shower and eat.

But as I put the key in the front door, I heard something that made my heart stop.

"Ava! What happened? Ava, wake up!"

Macie was screaming Ava's name repeatedly as I walked through the foyer from the kitchen. As I rounded the corner, the scene was horrific.

Ava was on the ground, her head in Macie's lap.

There was blood everywhere, all over Ava's body, all over Macie's legs.

"What the fuck is going on?" I raced to them both, on the ground next to Ava in seconds. "Macie, what's going on? Where is she bleeding from?" From a quick inspection, it looked like from her arm.

Then I saw it.

It was her wrist.

"No!" I yelled. "No! No, no, no..." This couldn't be happening. "Ava!"

The tears were instant and uncontrollable. As I wiped them away, I paced and thought about what to do. Ambulance or my truck? We didn't have any time to waste, she was losing too much blood.

"Macie, we have to get her in my truck, now!"

I knew where the hospital was, I would get her there faster.

I scooped her up in my arms and started running for the front door.

"Macie, go get some towels and meet me out front. Hurry!"

She ran upstairs, frantic and crying. As I approached my truck, Ava started moaning.

"Ava, wake up honey," I said as I opened the back door.

Macie came running as I laid her on the bench.

"What's going on?" Ava asked.

Macie got in next to her, wrapping the towels around her hand and arm. Ava looked down and the realization of the situation hit her.

"Logan, not your truck!"

"Do you really think I give a fuck about my truck, Tink? We need to get you to the ER, now!" My words were harsh through my tears, but I couldn't worry about that. We needed to move.

Throwing the truck in gear, I tore out of the parking lot and got us on the highway in record time. My eyes were drawn to the rearview mirror, watching her as she laid her head on Macie's lap. They were talking quietly, and I strained to hear some of what they said.

"I should have stayed and helped you," Macie said, crying softly as she rubbed Ava's cheek while holding the towels against her wrist.

"I told you to go, it's not your fault. All of this is my fault. All of it. I shouldn't have thrown the glass, then this wouldn't have happened."

Glass?

I wasn't about to ask questions, but maybe I jumped to conclusions.

Ten minutes, and I had her at the ER entrance. Jumping into action, I tore the back door open and carried her through the automatic doors of the hospital.

"We need help!" I screamed. "She's bleeding badly, most likely from an artery."

Nurses surrounded us immediately, a gurney pulled alongside for her to be placed on, but then she was whisked away.

Then Macie and I were left alone.

We moved to the waiting area together, sitting quietly amongst the other people. I knew I should ask her what happened, but I think I was scared to hear the truth.

I eventually worked up the nerve.

"How did she get cut, Macie?"

Macie put her face in her hands, distraught.

"We argued a little, and she threw a glass in the sink. It shattered everywhere, she must have cut herself cleaning it up. I wanted to stay and help, but she told me to go upstairs."

My hands pressed against my eyes, trying to relieve the pressure, or stop the tears, I wasn't sure which. The stifled cry that came from me had Macie shifting in her seat.

I turned toward her, her eyes wide at my appearance.

"So it was an accident?" I squeaked out.

The reality of my question hit her immediately.

"Yes," she said, reaching for my arm, a simple gesture of support.

And I broke. The whole week came out. Our whole past couple months. Tears fell, loud cries muffled were against her shoulder as she pulled me to her. She held me, no questions asked, which I was thankful for. Once I calmed down, she remained quiet, the two of us sitting in solitude.

An hour had passed, and that made me nervous. If it had been simple stitches, I felt as though she would have been done. My concern was she needed surgery to fix the damage.

"Friends of Ava Kennedy?" A nurse stood in the doorway of the waiting area, looking around.

We stood, our hands in the air, to get her attention.

"She's asking for you both," she said. "She'll be OK to go home, but probably not for a couple hours. They want to watch her for a bit due to the blood loss." She started walking away, so we followed her. "Does she have any family nearby, or only friends?"

"Just friends, she goes to school here," I said.

"Her family is about four hours away," Macie responded.

"I'm sure one of the other nurses contacted her parents, I was just checking," the nurse said as we continued following her through a maze of hallways and curtained off rooms. We got to a small cornered off area. "She's in here. She needed a blood transfusion, and she's on an IV. She's stitched up, but requested a sedative for the stitches, so she's a little groggy still."

The nurse pulled back the curtain, and Ava was curled up in the bed. She looked so tiny as she lay on the gurney, the blue and white gown tied at her neck. Her eyes popped open at the sound of the curtain sliding on the metal rings, but she didn't move.

Macie rushed to her side, and I let them have their time, moving out to the main area. It was busy, doctors and nurses rushing about from patient to patient. It made me want to find the nurse or doctor who worked on Ava and personally thank them.

"Logan." Macie startled me. "Can I use your truck to head back to the house? She wants some clothes to go home in, the others are kinda trashed."

"Sure."

She grabbed the keys, waved to Ava, and walked out.

That left me with Ava.

I turned toward the bed, her eyes on me, and my first instinct was to go tell Macie I would take the ride for the clothes. But as I moved closer into the tiny room, my desire to be near her won over. Seeing the bandage reminded me how fleeting it all is, and...

"Logan," Ava said, sitting up in her bed.

Her simply saying my name had me almost jumping. I moved to the chair at her bedside, helping with the IV tube as she got comfortable.

"Can I get you anything?"

She shook her head as she drew her knees to her chest, her chin resting on top.

"I'm sorry for this." Her voice was so quiet I almost didn't hear her over the noises of the ER. "For today, this week, all of it. I hated seeing you crying on the way here."

The wetness returned to my eyes. I didn't want to do this here, of all places. But there was no holding back what was coming. I dropped my head to the mattress, gripping her good hand in mine as I brought it to my mouth. The strained sob I let go against her skin had her reaching for me, her fingers raking through my hair.

"Ava," I croaked out. "When I saw you, on the floor, covered in blood, I thought...my mind thought...that you...and it was your wrist... fuck Ava, I thought I lost you."

I howled at the thought, my heart racing, but so thankful she was here next to me.

Touching me.

"Logan," she said, crawling closer to me on the small bed. "I'm so sorry I scared you like that. My god, to have thought that, to have seen me and thought that, I'm so sorry."

She didn't understand the magnitude of what it really meant.

"Ava," I started, looking up at her. "I haven't talked about my real father too much. You know that we didn't have a great relationship, and that he was a bastard to me and my mom." I stalled, reconsidering if this was a good idea. But looking at her, and the fact that we were talking again, I went with it. "Matt is like my dad for so many reasons, but one of them is because my real father is dead."

She could tell I wasn't finished by looking at me. Sitting back, she granted me the time I needed to continue.

Eventually, I found it in me to say the words.

"He committed suicide when I was a junior in high school."

Her slow blink and swallow made my tears more abundant for some reason.

"I blamed myself for a long time. I thought I caused him to do it because I refused to see him for a couple years before." As I tried to hold in my sob, it made it worse, the sound echoing in our small space. "Ava, if I'd lost you, I don't know what I would have done."

She slid over on the small bed, patting the space beside her. I squeezed next to her as she enveloped me into her arm. If it weren't for the metal bar holding her in on the other side, we would have fallen off. I gently held her around the middle as we both quietly cried for what we had, thought we lost, did lose...all of it.

The tears slowed, and I knew I should move before Macie returned, but I didn't want to, she felt so good in my arms.

"This week was hard," she said against the top of my head. "Harder than I expected."

I nodded against her, not wanting to talk. Not wanting this moment to end.

"I'm sorry about what your father did, and that you felt in any way responsible." She stroked my cheek as she spoke. "I'm sure you've since learned through therapy that you had nothing to do with it, that he wasn't well."

Again, all I did was nod.

"So, I couldn't find the leggings you wanted, but I found those really comfy sweats you love..." Macie stopped talking midsentence when she walked in on us.

I started to get up from the bed, out of her hold, but Ava held me in place. Macie looked at us, curious, then smiled.

"I'll leave the bag here."

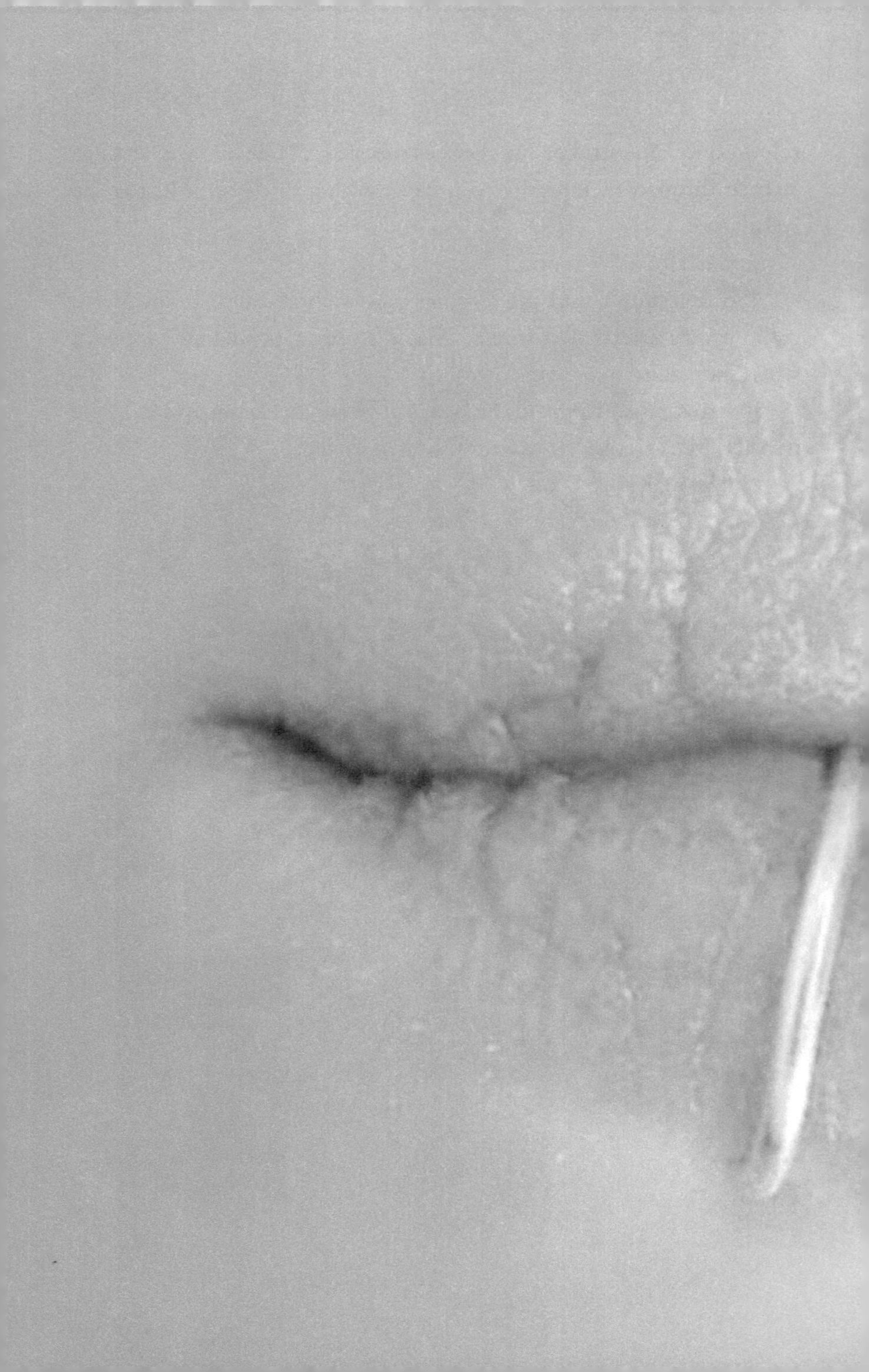

CHAPTER 32

Ava

Logan spent over an hour cleaning his truck the night we got home from the hospital. The guilt I felt when I saw the mess as we drove home was overwhelming. He should have called an ambulance, but according to Macie, there was no talking him out of his decision to drive me.

By the time he came back in, it was well after midnight and he must have assumed I was asleep. He went straight to his room.

Now, several days had passed, and not much had changed between us. For some reason, I thought our moment in the ER, his declaration of his past, was a gateway to talking again.

However, I hadn't made much of an attempt either. The hospital gave me a note to miss classes for a few days, and I took full advantage of that. Who wouldn't? But like it had been the past couple weeks, my room had become my safe haven.

My mom had been checking in on me each day. I looked forward to our long phone calls, it filled my time. She was so upset she couldn't come visit, but she was busy with Amelia's sports schedule. Plus, they were getting ready for prom and graduation, which were both coming up. Trust me, she didn't forget one detail about any of it.

The day after I got home, I heard Macie and Becca raving about how well Logan did in his first rugby game that day. We were all in the living room, and they recounted the game, almost play by play, and the scores he made, et cetera. The team had a party that night to celebrate. It took every ounce of willpower to not confront him when he got home.

Because I knew full well there were girls all over him at that party.

But I had no right.

This was my doing.

There was a knock on my bedroom door, and my heart sped up with anticipation.

"Yeah?" I put my ereader aside and sat up in my bed, running my fingers through my short locks.

"Can I come in?" Macie asked.

I knew he wouldn't be home. Why was I disappointed?

"Sure." I tried to sound enthusiastic.

As she came in, she was dressed to be heading out, a windbreaker over her arm, shoes on. She sat at the foot of my bed, a small smile to contradict the pinch of her concerned eyebrows.

"Whatcha doin'?" She looked around and saw that I was reading. "Reading anything good? And how's the cut feeling?"

Looking down at my wrist, I was reminded of how serious the injury turned out to be. The glass sliced my wrist very close to a major artery. They were able to stitch me up but were close to needing to go in to surgically repair everything. They thought it was nicked deeper than it was.

Due to the location of the slice, I had to go through a psychiatric evaluation before being released. They needed to confirm I hadn't tried to take my own life, which I understood. But it made for a really long night.

"It's getting itchy, but that means it's healing, doesn't it?"

She nodded and we both smiled.

"Me and Becca are going to Logan's game, meeting Ty there. Wanna come?"

My first instinct was to jump out of bed. I was bored, and of course I wanted to see him play. Then I thought it might send the wrong message if he saw me there.

However, over the past few days, I think I realized that the message I wanted to send him was very different now than what I originally thought.

"Can you give me a few minutes to get ready? I'd love to come."

Her smile grew wide, and she did that happy, giddy hand clap she always does.

"Yay! I'm so excited! We'll be downstairs waiting, take your time," she said.

"OK."

OK. I was doing this. Logan's game. I was going to his game. Though he would probably have no idea I was even there. We'd be up in the stands, he'd be on the field. He'd have no clue. I was simply supporting my roommate in his new venture.

Right?

"Go Mountaineers! Go Logan!" Becca screamed so loud my ears were ringing. BRU was winning, and no matter how closely I paid attention to the action on the field, I still didn't understand the game.

"It's kinda like football, they tackle like it, but the game keeps going, which is different," Ty explained.

I wasn't an expert on football either, so it made little difference. The game was a rough one, the guys got bloody. They tackled but wore no protective equipment. It was them and them only taking each other down. I enjoyed watching Logan out there, though. He seemed to be loving it, his smile bright through the mud on his face after every play.

Logan was coming off the field, someone replacing him for the current play, when Becca yelled his name. His head turned at his name, finding us. He waved, an appreciative smile widening across his face.

Then his eyes found me.

I knew because his smile faltered.

Just as quickly as it did, it rebounded, and he smiled wider yet. His hand went higher in the air as he waved to me, giving me a thumbs up.

And I waved back.

I wasn't sure why, exactly. Maybe he was thanking me for coming. Maybe I was telling him *yes, I'm here.* What I did know was him being happy to see me made my insides do a tiny flip. As I covered the smile with my hand, I looked at my roommates to see if they'd noticed.

And they were looking right at me, including Ty.

Then Logan turned around to face the field and watch his team play.

That was when I saw the back of his orange uniform shirt.

And my heart exploded.

He chose number 14.

Maybe I was manifesting things in my head, or maybe he chose it intentionally. I went with the second. The fourteenth was the date of our first kiss. And it was also the date of my birthday.

My hands went to my mouth, covering my audible gasp. Though with the sounds of the crowd, I was sure no one would have heard me.

The game continued. Logan played great, as did the entire team, bringing BRU to another victory. The guys hoisted each other onto shoulders in celebration while on the field as the fans cheered them on.

Becca grabbed me by the hand, steering me down the stadium stairs, straight toward the team bench.

"Where are we going?" I asked. But I knew. The fear of seeing him right now was very real. I didn't know why, but I felt like I needed time for what could be starting between us again to have room to breathe.

"C'mon, we saw him after his last game, too. He loved it!" Becca screeched. "He'll love that you're here this time."

The four of us weaved through the throngs of people standing about. Who would have thought this many people came to a club game? But rugby was a crazy sport to watch, so it commanded an audience.

As we approached the bench, the players were packing up their bags and still congratulating each other on their second win.

"Logan!" Becca yelled.

His blonde head turned to his name, and he came toward the entourage here to greet him.

"Hey guys, thanks for coming." As he spoke, he shook Ty's hand. Then he came and gave hugs to Becca, Macie, and me.

"Thank you for coming," he whispered in my ear. As he pulled back, he gestured to my wrist. "How are ya feeling?"

"It's healing, I'm good." I wanted the attention off me, and back to him. "This was amazing, Logan. You were amazing."

We both knew there was so much more that needed to be said between us as our eyes remained connected for that extra second longer than was necessary. But then we were reminded of our company.

"Logan!" Macie yelled. "I'm loving these games. You are so good!"

"Thanks, Macie." Turning to the whole group, he smiled, his eyes closing momentarily. "Thank you, all of you, for coming. You don't know how much it means to me." He reached down and picked up his bag. "Well, you know the drill, there's a party. And us guys go straight there, no showers or anything first. So, you're all welcome."

As he spoke with Becca and Ty, I pulled Macie aside.

"Can we run home real quick?" I asked.

She looked at me as her shoulders perked up at my request. "You want to go to the party?"

I nodded. "Yeah, but I need to do something first, and I need your help."

She agreed enthusiastically before telling Becca and Ty to get a ride with Logan. We snuck away to avoid any questions, making our way to her car.

"I'm happy you want to go out tonight. I've been worried about all the time you've been spending alone."

My head fell against the headrest as she pulled out of the parking lot. I contemplated how much I was going to say to her on the drive home.

"Yeah, I know. It's not only what happened at the party that's been bothering me, though. There's some other stuff going on, stuff I haven't been comfortable telling you." I kept my gaze out the windshield, refusing to look her way.

"Oh yeah," she said. "Well, I'm not blind, ya know. Ave, none of us are." She chuckled after saying that.

I risked a glance her way.

And the smile she had for me was warm and knowing.

CHAPTER 33
Logan

When Ava and Macie walked away at the field, I won't lie, my heart hurt a little. Becca assured me they were meeting us at the party, but I wasn't convinced.

"Shit, you stink, Logan," Becca whined.

"I know I do, I hate that we don't take showers after our games."

She slid closer to Ty on the bench seat, getting further away from me. I bet she wished she had sat in the back.

"Maybe this is why so many of the guys get naked at the parties, because the uniforms all smell like urinals," she chided.

I couldn't disagree with her. That was a good way to describe the odor. It wasn't so much the uniforms as it was the cleats and our socks. That was one thing I did change. Clean socks and my slides went on before heading inside. And I made sure to put the smelly shoes in the bed of my truck until after the party.

"Alright, let's head in," Ty said, also anxious to get out of the truck.

The three of us entered the house that had become like a second home to me lately. I'd been spending more and more time here with the guys to avoid running into Ava at the townhouse. Considering it was Friday, it was more crowded than the first after-party. The first floor was full of players crowding around the kitchen trying to get their share of pizza.

"I need food," I told Becca and Ty. "Want some?"

"No," Ty said. "We had dinner at the game. You go eat, we'll make our way downstairs."

The pangs of hunger in my stomach forced me to navigate through the people between me and the pizza more aggressively than I wanted. But when I finally put that first cheesy bite in my mouth, it was worth it.

"Here's another slice, Somers, it's going quick." Looking to my side, Sutton held a plate out for me.

"Thanks, man," I said and added it to the two I already had. "That was a great game tonight. Didn't think we were gonna pull it out, but we did."

"Yeah, right?" he said. Then a petite blonde appeared at his side, his arm going around her. "Somers, this is Amber. Amber, this is our newest beast Somers."

After wiping my hand on my shorts since I didn't have a napkin, I extended it to her. "Nice to meet you, Amber."

"Hi," she said, shaking my hand. "What's your real name?" She laughed after asking.

"I'm Logan."

"It's nice to meet you, Logan."

Sutton lost interest in me, and I didn't blame him. She was beautiful and seemed nice. As they went on their way, I turned to head to the basement to find Becca and Ty.

"Hey, it's Somers, right?" A thin brunette was right behind me once I turned around and stopped my progress. "I'm Dee, and this is my roommate Allie."

The smaller girl at her side seemed shy as she stood in the shadow of Dee.

This happened a few times at the first party. A lot of the girls come here looking to become the players' WAG, or girlfriend. It's apparently an honor to be a rugby players WAG here at BRU. I had no idea.

"Hi, girls," I said. "Did you enjoy the game?" While trying to be nice by asking a question, I was also walking away from them toward the basement door.

Dee, the more aggressive one, grabbed me by the arm, stopping me. "Where are you going?"

It was a challenge to thwart their attention but still be nice to the girls at these parties.

"I've got some friends downstairs waiting for me, maybe we'll catch up later."

As I said that, my eye caught sight of a particular fiery vixen with emerald-green eyes who had just walked in the front door. She grabbed the attention of many as she made her entrance.

She had on a short plaid skirt that showed off her powerful thighs. Her knee-high socks were paired with those ass-kicking black boots I loved so much. Her hair was smooth today, curled behind her ears, hanging low on her forehead.

Her shirt was what caught my attention the most. Mine and, I was sure, everyone else's.

I think it was one of my plain white T-shirts and she'd cut at the waist and ripped off the sleeves. Written or painted in orange on the front were the words *BRU Rugby*. In big numbers, across her chest, was the number 14.

She stood still once we saw each other. Her teeth bit at her lip ring as her fingers nervously played with the hem of her skirt. Her feet edged toward me, but something inside her kept changing her mind, keeping her where she was.

So I went to her.

As soon as I stood in front of her, my hands instinctively went to her face.

"Hi," she said quietly, covering my hands with hers.

I looked into those bright eyes as she stared back at me, hoping this was what I thought it was.

"Ava," I whispered as I bent my forehead to hers. "What is this?"

"This is me not caring anymore about anyone but us."

Pulling back, I felt the tension that had built up in my body this past week dissipate and literally fall from my shoulders.

"Are you sure, Ava?"

"She's sure, she's more than sure," Macie said as she walked by us and giggled.

It was then I realized we were still doing this out in the open, for everyone to witness. Looking around, most had gone back to their own conversations, but Ava and I needed privacy.

"I know this house doesn't bring back good memories for you," I told her as I took her by the hand. "But there's a room on this floor, in the back, we can go to for privacy. Let me just ask Carter."

I dragged her with me as I looked for him. There was no way I was letting go of her now that I had her back. I found Carter in the basement, and he gave me the key to his room once I explained.

"C'mon," I said to Ava.

She followed willingly, and for that, I was thankful. We made it to Carter's room without any interruption and once I closed the door, the chaos of the party disappeared. It was quiet and we had a private, clean space for us to...

I had no idea what we were going to do. But whatever it was, it needed to be in private.

"All of this because you like my shirt?" she quipped as she pulled it out, looking down at her chest. "Personally, I think it's rather grade school looking myself, but it was the best I could do on short notice."

I stood off to the side of the room, admiring her as she joked about it, happy to hear her sarcastic comments flowing from her mouth once again.

"Ava..." I started, but she put her hand up to stop me.

"Logan, let me talk, please. Everything I've done, almost from the start, has been wrong. I should have listened to my heart from the get-go and not worried about anything else."

She paused, her eyes getting watery.

"I choose you, Logan. I will always choose you, over everyone else." A single tear slid down her cheek. "I've made more mistakes than I can count on both hands since meeting you, but seeing you at your game today, with the number fourteen on your back. Well, it made me realize that I need to wake up. I hope you'll forgive me."

Then her eyes went wide with horror.

"Unless I'm wrong about the number...shit, were you just assigned that number?"

She started twisting her hands together and bouncing from foot to foot.

"Relax, beautiful, I chose it."

"You did?" she asked.

"I did," I confirmed.

She jumped, and I caught her, pulling her into my arms. Our hearts beat wildly in our chests as they pressed against each other. Our mouths connected as she held my face. A long overdue kiss, which started healing the cracks in my heart.

Our kiss slowed, and she motioned to get down and stand before me. We moved to sit on the bed, facing each other.

"I'm not here to take you away from your celebration, I'd like for us to go back downstairs. But I needed to tell you that I'm all in, Logan. I've been miserable this past week without us talking, not seeing each other at all. It made me realize that wasn't how I wanted my life to be. It was better with you in it." She reached out, taking my hand in hers.

Her words filled my heart. I had myself convinced that she had walked away from me for good.

I'd forever love the number fourteen.

"You've made me so happy, Ava."

"Not before almost destroying you, and us. I'm sorry for how I've been."

"Hey," I said, stroking her cheek. "There are always growing pains in a relationship worth working for. And we're working through them."

She gripped my hand and kissed that back of it.

"C'mon, let's get downstairs. You deserve to be with your team after that win today. The game was awesome, and I loved watching you out there."

We walked, hand in hand, to the door.

"You know you kinda stink, right?" she asked, then laughed.

"I more than stink, I reek. I really do love the shirt. You'll have to wear it to every game now."

She chuckled again.

"I think I can handle that."

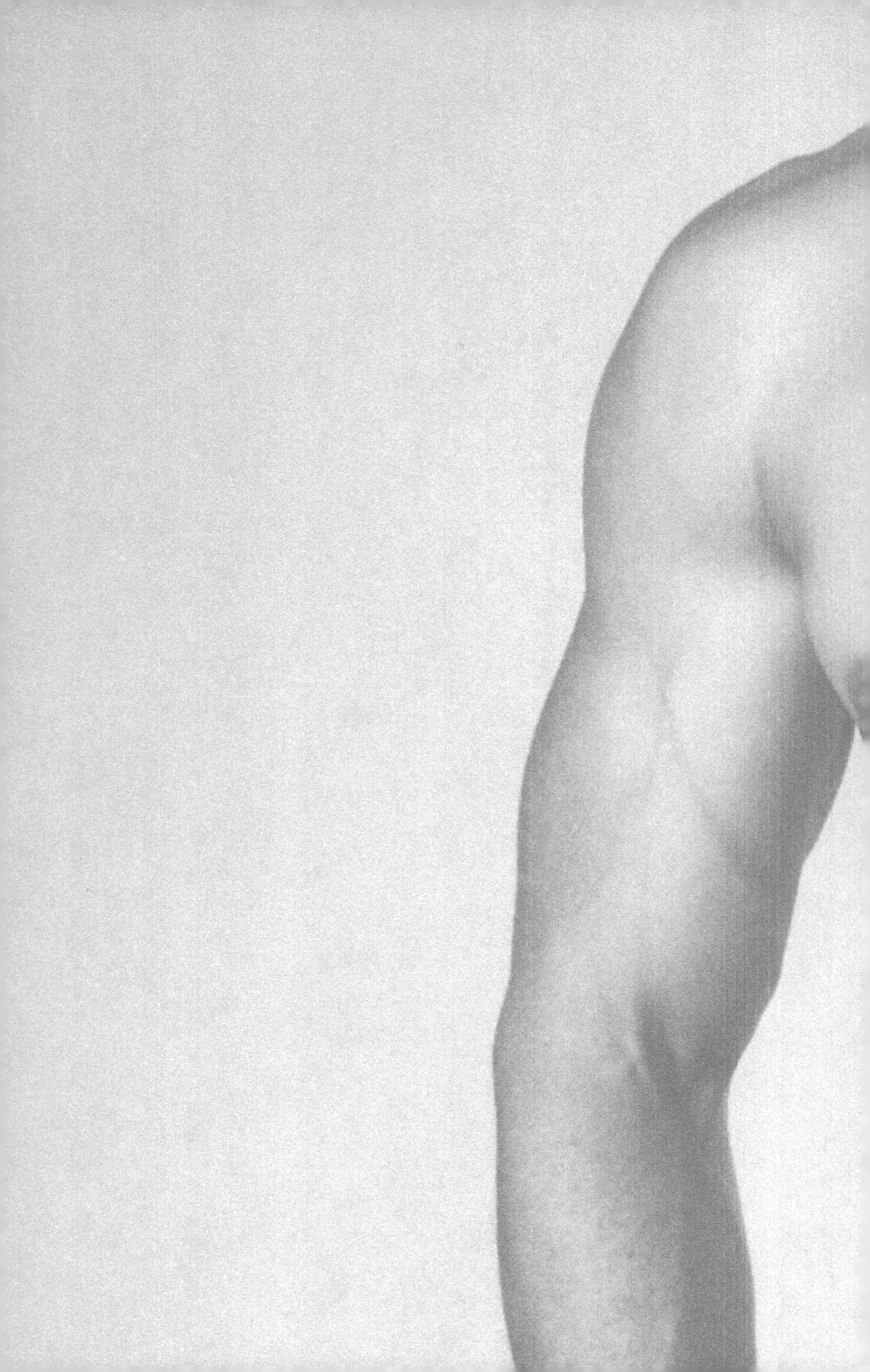

CHAPTER 34

Logan

A s I sat on the front stoop, clapping my muddy cleats together, Howie stared at me. I put my shoes down and went to pull him out from under the bushes. He'd been under there since the snow-storm when I moved him to be safe. But it was warming up with spring in full bloom, and he needed to enjoy the sunshine with the rest of us.

"Hey," Ava said. "I thought I heard you out here. Just get back from practice?"

"Yep, so I stink, really bad."

"I don't care."

She came closer, waiting for me to finish pushing the statue into the soft grass along the edge of the lawn. Once I straightened, she put her arms around my neck, kissing me deep. I'd started getting really used to coming home to this.

"Macie made her chicken marsala again," she said. "I even helped, best I could, anyway."

She gestured to her wrist, still wrapped up.

"Isn't your appointment tomorrow?" I asked.

She nodded.

"I'm taking you," I told her.

"Macie already said she could. I didn't know if you had practice."

"I'll miss it, I'm taking you. It's at 4:30, right?"

She nodded again. She was finally getting the stitches out. It had been almost two weeks since that terrible night. And we'd been through a lot since then.

We'd grown a lot in our relationship in that short time.

It was still new, we were still new. But we felt strong. It felt like we were on the right track.

"C'mon, I'm starving," I said as I grabbed her and led her inside.

Ava went right back to helping Macie with dinner. I marched upstairs to get cleaned up. I would not subject anyone to me sitting at the table in my condition.

After a quick shower and some clean clothes, I felt like a brand-new person. As I exited my room, Becca came down her stairs.

"Hey, big guy," she said. She stopped on the landing between the flights, leaning against the wall. "Got a minute?"

"For you, always. What's up?"

She gestured to my room and we walked inside.

"Just wanted to check in with you, ya know, with everything going on. Wanted to make sure you're still focusing on, well, *you* even though you're with Ava now."

I could only appreciate her concern as I leaned against my desk, contemplating how to explain it to her.

"I mean, you know I love that girl, but you come first, big guy," she continued.

"Hey, I'm good, Bec, I promise. I'm more than good." I smiled, hoping she would understand I was telling the truth. "Ava and I started our thing a while ago, before she was willing to tell anyone about us. When we started hanging out, I realized the chaos in my brain quieted, which was the opposite of what my therapist said could happen." I went to my bed and sat next to her. "And then, when Ava wanted to end what we had, yeah, I struggled. But what I learned about myself was I could deal with the stress of it all without turning to booze. I learned so much about myself through all of this. And I came out on the other side of it OK, and I was damn proud."

She reached out and gripped my forearm, giving it a squeeze.

"Logan," she said. "That's truly amazing. Like, freaking awesome. I am so fucking proud of you, dude." She threw her arms around my neck and hugged me hard.

"Thanks," I told her.

"And I am happy for the two of you, especially if you're happy. You guys are so freaking cute together."

She was already at the door, ready to head downstairs, waiting for me to join her. As we took the stairs together, she looked back at me with a sly grin.

"Not for nothin', but I called it. You can ask Lanie. I said back in January that I thought the two of you would get together."

I barked out a laugh.

"Bullshit."

"Ask Lanie," she said.

Lanie would back her up, or would she?

"Hey, Logan, can I borrow your truck?" Ava asked as she came into my room.

She looked adorable in her cut-off denim shorts and her tiny pink tank top. So adorable that I'd prefer she stay here with me instead of her going wherever she needed to go.

"I can drive you," I told her.

"No, I need to do this without you, and Macie isn't here, so I can't use her car."

I dug around in my backpack and found my keys. Without handing them over, I walked out the door and started for downstairs. She quickly followed.

"What are you doing?" she asked.

"No offense, babe, but you can barely get in my truck. I want to make sure you can drive the thing without me."

The sun blinded me as soon as I opened the door, and I was glad I had shorts on as well. Spring was turning out to be a nonexistent season around here, as it already felt like summer. When I got to the driver's door and opened it for her, I grabbed her hand, helping her up. Gave her a little boost on the ass at the same time.

"Hey," she said as she shook her ass from my grasp.

Her tiny legs were nowhere near the pedals.

"Let's get the seat adjusted for you. There's a second setting over here that you can use to save the setting, if you want." I pointed to the buttons on the side of the driver's door. As she worked on the adjustments, forward and up, I watched her from the side.

And I realized I was falling in love with her.

No. I was already in love with her. Because something as mundane as us fixing the seat settings made me giddy to be around her.

Wherever she was going in my truck without me, I didn't want her to. I wanted to go.

I didn't want to be without her if I didn't have to.

"Did you hear me?" she said.

"No, what?"

"I am a little nervous, this thing is huge."

Her tiny smile made my heart swell.

"I'd feel terrible if I did anything to your truck. If you drive me, you have to promise to not ask to see what I get, and to give me time when we get home to do something."

Using my finger, I crossed my heart as a promise. Her curt nod confirmed she reluctantly agreed, and she slid across the bench to the other side.

"Where to?" I asked.

"The nearest home center."

Well, that didn't give me any clue as to what she was up to.

When we pulled up, she got out of the truck without a word, only a kiss and a smile. I played on my phone for a bit, and she was in there for a while. So long I started getting concerned. Just when I was about to call her, I saw her tiny frame come bouncing through the double doors of the store, a couple paper bags in her arms. She opened the door to the back seat, put the bags on the floor, and hopped back in the truck.

"All done," she announced.

"OK," I said. "That's it?"

"Well, until we get home, yeah, and then I need a few minutes. You'll have to go in your room." She smiled. "You'll see, don't worry."

I did as she asked when we got home. While I waited in my room, I used the time to study. But I struggled to focus on anything other than the sounds I heard coming from out front.

Finally, I heard her footsteps. My door was open so I met her in the hall, my curiosity piqued at this point.

"Ready?" she asked.

I followed her downstairs, and instead of turning toward the living room or kitchen, she opened the front door. She gestured for me to go outside, which I did. I looked around, unsure of what I was supposed to do next. She guided me down the path a few steps, then spun me around.

That was when I saw it.

Rather, saw them.

Next to Howie was another frog statue. A female frog statue, complete with a bow on her head.

Surrounding them were tons of flowers, beautiful flowers Ava planted around them in their own little garden. There were daisies, poppies, marigolds, and a bunch I didn't recognize.

She came up next to me and wrapped her arms around my middle.

"You like it?" she asked.

I didn't want to cry, and I felt on the verge, so all I could do was nod as I squeezed her against me.

"Everyone deserves their other half, so I wanted to give Howie his," she said. "Just like you gave me mine."

Epilogue

LOGAN

As I sat in my truck, staring at the townhouse in front of me, I reflected on the past few months. The first time pulling up to this building, my anxiety roiled inside me, for so many reasons. Throughout the semester, I had my ups and downs. I now found myself in a much better place.

One of the reasons was the cute, green-eyed brunette who bounded down the front steps coming right for my side of the truck. I knew it was never good for your happiness to be dependent on another. Yet I didn't think that's what this was.

I think I just happened upon her once I was ready to be happy.

"I didn't expect you back this early," Ava said as I got out. "How did it go?"

Before answering her, I reached down, took her face in my hands, and planted a huge kiss on her luscious lips.

"Well, a girl could get used to a greeting like that." Her eyes sparkled as she stared up at me.

"You should get used to it," I told her. "And the meeting went well. Of course, it was full of locals, and no one really my age. But I think that's better, to be honest." We strolled toward the house together.

"And I found a sponsor. I figured since we're staying here for the summer, it made sense for me to have one here instead of at home."

In AA, you typically have a sponsor who helped you maintain your sobriety. Even though I was over the year mark with mine, the challenging environment I lived in led me to decide getting one was a good idea.

"That's great, babe." Ava's smile was genuine.

Once inside, I realized how quiet it was.

"Are the others home?" It was rare for us to be alone, but it would be happening more and more as the semester came to an end. Both Macie and Becca would be going home for the summer, leaving us here in the townhouse together until the lease ended in August.

"They're both upstairs studying."

We wound up in Ava's room, most likely because it was cleaner than mine, cuddling on her bed. We'd finally gotten used to showing affection toward each other with Becca and Macie home. Even with our bedroom door open when doing something as simple as lying in bed together.

It was nice.

"How was your afternoon? Did you finish studying for your last final?" I asked. Her head was on my chest, her arm draped across my body, one of my favorite positions for her to be in.

"I did…"

But her answer left me with more questions. She was keeping something from me, it was obvious. When I tried to sit us up, she pushed me down, keeping us as we were. She remained quiet for a few more minutes, her fingers finding my skin under my shirt, rubbing some random design.

Then she cleared her throat.

"I went to legal services on campus today."

I stopped breathing. Every muscle in my body froze. My fear was if

I moved or breathed, she wouldn't continue talking. Eventually, she balanced her chin on her hand, looking up at me. The sadness in her eyes combined with a fortitude I hadn't seen before.

"It was time."

Nodding in agreement, I remained quiet, hoping that was what she needed.

"They told me about the process, and that it would be a long one. But they assured me they would help me with everything, even contacting the police."

That was when the first tear fell from her eye. My hand instinctively wiped it away. My heart broke for her all over again. It was going to be hard to go through this.

"Baby, I'll be here for you, through it all, I promise. Every step of the way."

She dropped her head against my chest again, nodding once as she did. I only hoped she understood she wasn't alone and wouldn't be. My arms wrapped her tight as we nestled against each other, the breeze from the open window flowing against our skin.

"Do you have anything you have to do right now?" I asked her.

The slight shake of her head against my body encouraged me to pull her closer. I pulled a light blanket over us, hoping she got my point. And she did. I felt her relax even more against me, and sleep took us over within minutes.

THE VOICE WAS MUDDLED, AS IF UNDERWATER. IT FELT AS though I was having another dream, but it felt real at the same time.

"Hey guys…"

Then I felt the nudge against my shoulder, and my eyes slowly opened. It was Macie'e light eyes staring down at me.

"Hey," she said again. "I didn't want you both to sleep through dinner. We're ordering food in and wanted to see if you guys wanted anything."

She whispered since Ava was still asleep against my side.

"Sure, thanks, Macie." I rubbed at my face to wipe the sleepiness away. "Give me a sec, OK?"

She nodded and left us, closing the door. I looked down at the serene beauty still sound asleep against my shoulder, and my heart swelled. Each day I'd spent with her these past couple months, whether it was in secret or finally out in the open, had been a gift. My thumb rubbed against her parted lips, gently pulling on her full bottom one. She stirred against me, a sleepy moan seeping from those lips.

"Hey baby," I said quietly near her ear. "You getting hungry?"

The mention of food got her waking up. Her eyes popped open, those bright green orbs now staring at me. Her lips curved up as she became more aware of where she was.

"What are you smiling at?"

"I could get used to this," she said. "Sleeping with you is like sleeping with a built-in electric blanket. Plus a true, life-sized body pillow. But you're harder than a pillow."

She poked my pecs and biceps as she sat up. Then, those pokes changed to her rubbing along my chest.

"Don't get me wrong, I like the hardness." The playful tone in her voice started getting something else hard.

"You're distracting me," I told her. "Food. We're supposed to be figuring out what we want to eat. Text Macie and ask her where they're ordering from."

She reached for her phone and got to work on that while I peeled myself from her to use the bathroom. As I did, it made me wonder if we would share a room once it was just the two of us this summer.

"I assume you want the double cheeseburger, no onion, and fries?" she asked as I returned to the bed.

"Sounds good."

As I got back in bed, pulling her close, she put her phone on the side table.

"Thirty minutes for the food." As soon as she said that, she slid herself to sitting on my lap. "That's enough time."

I gripped her by the hips as I slid her off me, back to my side. "Oh yeah? Enough time for what?" I chided, knowing full well what she meant. But with the kind of day she had, I had something else in mind.

"What are you doing?" she complained.

"Don't worry."

My hand slid down her side, pushing at her shorts and panties. She lifted her bottom, allowing me to push them all the way off. My palm lingered on her backside, the feel of her warm, tender skin against my hand intoxicating. My fingers dug into her ass as I tilted her body more toward me, opening her thighs in the process. The other hand trailed down her belly, finding the warm spot between her legs wet for me already. One finger, then two, made their way inside the tight walls of her pussy, pushing deep inside.

"Oh, Logan," she moaned against me. "Oh my god."

My fingers plunged deeper as my thumb pushed against her hardening clit. Her moans became even louder.

"Ava, baby, you sure you're good doing this with them downstairs?"

"They hookup with their guys while we're home," she said breathlessly. "You better not stop now." Her look was stern as she stared at me.

Our chests were flush against one another as my hand continued working inside her, pushing to the depths of her pussy. Her body pushed into mine, her hands gripping my shoulders with a strength I didn't know she had. It was as if our bodies melded into one as we became entwined, the emotions so strong. Our mouths devoured each other, searching for more than we could give.

Her one hand wrapped around my neck, to my head, pulling me even closer, as I felt her muscles clench around my fingers inside her. The climax she headed toward was intense.

"Logan," she said, our mouths open, lips still touching. "Oh my god."

Her tongue lashed at mine as she took a deep breath. Her head fell back and my mouth went to that tender skin along her neck as her body trembled with her orgasm. My fingers never stopped working, making sure she reached her pinnacle, that I brought her to the top.

When her thighs clenched around my arm and her body stilled in ecstasy, I continued rubbing her clit, pushing her over the edge. The scream coming from her mouth got swallowed by my kiss, our mouths colliding again.

Her body settled in my arms as our kiss continued. As her eyes slowly opened, her hands moved from my head to my face. She caressed my cheeks as her mouth pulled away from mine.

"I will never get tired of how talented those fingers of yours are."

As soon as she said that, her hand slid to the band of my sweats, moving to pull them down. But I stopped her, pushing her hand aside. Her raised brows and wide eyes turned up at me.

"What's wrong?" she asked.

"Nothing. I'm not looking for anything in return right now, that was for you. The food'll be here soon, we have to study for finals, we have a lot going on. And you had a stressful day. I thought I'd help you relax, that's all."

"My tender Tank," she said as she stroked my cheek. "What did I do to deserve you?"

Sitting up, she followed and got out of bed to find her pants. I admired the view as she put them on.

"Food's here!" Becca screamed from downstairs.

Ava came to the side of the bed and grabbed both of my hands, making all kinds of exaggerated noises as she tried to pull me up.

"Christ, man, what does your mother feed you?" Her laughter filled the room as I let her pull me from the bed, and I fell into her arms, both of us almost falling to the floor.

"Logan!" she screeched as I caught us before we did.

Scooping her up and over my shoulder, I started for the stairs. My hand smacked her ass playfully a couple times as I carried her down the steps.

"What the hell are you doing?" she yelled.

"I'm showing you the benefits of my well put together diet, Tink. My mother and I feed me a well-designed meal plan that gives me these muscles I don't think you complain about too much when my clothes are off."

As I rounded the stairs to the hall leading to the kitchen area, I could hear the groans of disapproval from our roommates. They'd obviously heard me.

"TMI!" Becca yelled.

Macie giggled as I plopped Ava on an island stool.

"Listen, as happy as we are for the two of you," Becca said. "We don't need a play-by-play of what's going on up there."

Ava laughed out loud.

"There is no way Logan and I are anywhere near as loud as you and Ty."

That stopped Becca in her tracks. Macie and Ava froze as well. I stood on the fringe waiting to see how this played out. As the three girls all turned to look at one another, I watched as each of them started with a small smile at first. They then started howling with laughter within seconds, the tears streaming down their faces as they huddled together.

Seeing them interacting this way, effortlessly, as friends again, made my heart expand. So much of this past semester had been spent hiding emotions, which had affected the relationships in this house. Finally, being beyond that felt freeing.

Felt normal.

I knew I had a life that would never be completely normal. My challenges would be lifelong. But I was up for the challenge, and I was meeting them.

I loved it when Ava told me she *chose me*. Over all the other shit that had been going on in our lives.

Yeah, she chose me and I chose her.

But more importantly, we chose us.

Also by Krista Swanson

The Blue Ridge University (BRU) Series

All My Firsts
Book 1

Surviving Lies
Book 2

The Billionaire Brothers' Duology

Saving Us
Book 1

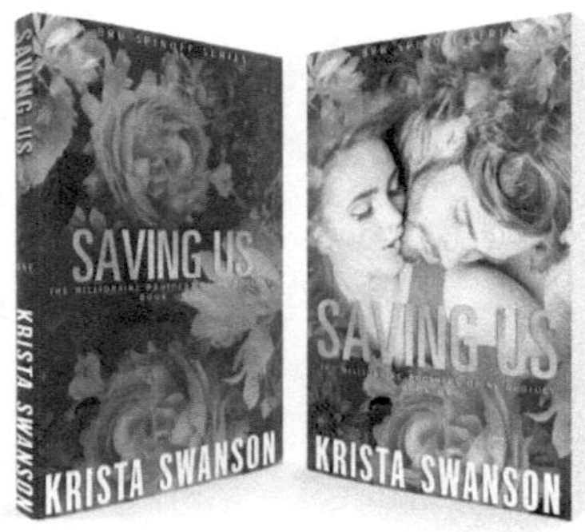

Buy My Books Here

My Website

Amazon

Acknowledgments

Logan's story was a long time coming. There were moments I thought it might never be written. Much of it came together at my mom's bedside in the hospital—which feels fitting, since she's always been my biggest cheerleader. The spicier the better, according to her. She's been eagerly waiting to read this one...

To my beta readers—Ana, Kirstie, and Taylor—your encouragement meant everything. Amid all the ups and downs with my mom, it was your love for Logan and Ava's story that kept me going. Every single comment from you reignited my motivation and helped shape this book into what it is. Thank you for your time, your support, and your belief in this story.

Emily has been with me from the very beginning of my writing journey—starting as my proofreader and, for this book, stepping into the role of editor. Handing over a book baby to be picked apart is never easy, but Emily made the process seamless. Her thoughtful, gentle feedback (like pointing out the 400+ "ands" and "buts" I didn't know I overused!) made it a no-brainer to keep working with her. Emily, thank you—I'm looking forward to a long writing relationship ahead.

This time, I also brought in a new proofreader—though she's far from new in my life. Gail has always been one of those generous souls who shows up to help in all the right ways (and yes, Vellum is easier now—thank you!). When Emily recommended her for proofreading, I jumped at the chance. Gail, thank you for everything.

To my husband—Scott—there aren't enough thank yous to thank

you. For all the nights I spun around in my chair just as you were falling asleep to say, "What do you think about this?"—thank you. I ask because your opinion always makes things better. From cover decisions to content input, your support has shaped my work in ways I'll never stop appreciating.

And finally, to my readers—

It may be cliché, but it's true: I wouldn't still be doing this without you. I hope *this* one lands exactly where it's meant to. Logan deserves this. And I think—no, I know—you're going to fall in love with him.

Newsletter Signup

Would you like to receive monthly updates?
Would you like sneak peeks of upcoming books?
How about physical copy giveaways?
For that and more, sign up for my monthly newsletter at:

https://www.kristaswansonauthor.com/

Author Bio

Krista Swanson lives in New Jersey with her husband of 30 years. They have three children but are now empty nesters (well, they seem to keep showing up though). Traveling across the US and Europe is in their plans. She loves the beach, mainly the Jersey beaches, which she feels don't get the love they deserve.

When she's not writing, she is most definitely reading. Her lifelong love of reading romances gave her all of the ideas busting to get out of her brain. While doing either, though, the mug in hand will not have coffee in it. The blasphemy—it will be tea!

She's newish at the social media thing, but working hard at it. You can find her on TikTok and Instagram at *kristareadsandwrites.* Also hop on over and join her Facebook reader's group, *Krista Swanson's Booklover's Besties.* Make sure to sign up for her monthly newsletter on any of those platforms for the most recent news, freebies and giveaways.